"This profoundly told and splendidly written story of Bud MacLeod in his growing up days of the Depression in South Georgia, is one of the most engaging novels I've read in years. Rich in character—from Bud's parents and siblings to his half-Japanese friend, Ry—*Hardscrabble Road* does what fine literature has always done: it reveals the tragedy and the tender hope of humanity. This is an effort to be celebrated."

—Terry Kay, author of *To Dance with the White Dog* and *The Book of Marie*

"Reading *Hardscrabble Road* is like discovering *To Kill a Mockingbird* when no one else knew about it. It has that kind of impact. But then this novel has such fascinating characters, such vivid descriptions of South Georgia during the Depression, and such an uplifting storyline, that one day it may also be considered a classic."

—Jackie K Cooper, author of *Memory's Mist*, and critic for The Huffington Post

"George Weinstein's authentic voice brings Bud MacLeod to life, a vivid character drawing me into his tough and tender Southern world. Bud fights to save his own soul with determination and heart. *Hardscrabble Road* is a bittersweet and gripping story that will steal your heart."

—Patti Callahan Henry, *New York Times* bestselling author

"Wow! What a great read. Pitch-perfect characters and evocative details make *Hardscrabble Road* a ride you won't want to end. I was on board from the first gritty page. Excellent storytelling, George Weinstein!"

—Lynn Cullen, author of *Twain's End*

"It could be worse for Bud MacLeod—at least he has four limbs and a spleen. The great thing about the narrator of George Weinstein's novel *Hardscrabble Road* is that Bud possesses plenty of heart, perhaps to make up for his stutter and birthmark. In the tradition of Erskine Caldwell and Harry Crews, Weinstein has written a novel filled with rage, violence, Sisyphusian efforts, and—deep-down—tenderness and wonder."

—George Singleton, author of *Calloustown*

"When a writer sits down to write a blurb for another writer's work, there's an aching urge to craft a sentence or two that shows off his own prowess at the game of words. Same with me. Instead, for George Weinstein, for his *Hardscrabble Road*, I have six words: this is a damn good book."

—Sonny Brewer, author of *The Poet of Tolstoy Park*

"Unflinching in its portrayal of abject poverty and life in a deeply dysfunctional family—beautiful in its depiction of a boy who, somehow, survives it all."

—Augusta Trobaugh, author of *Sophie and the Rising Sun*

"In *Hardscrabble Road*, George Weinstein has compiled a haunting tale that will stay with you long after you've turned the last page. Because circumstances beyond young Bud MacLeod's control have left him at the very edge of life's abyss, I found myself cheering so strongly for him that I realized it had been more than a half-century since I'd been so affected by such emotional circumstances—that being Salinger's Holden Caulfield."

—Jedwin Smith, author of *Our Brother's Keeper* and *Fatal Treasure*

"George Weinstein's *Hardscrabble Road* cinematically brings the Deep South of the 1930s and 1940s to life. You'll never forget Roger 'Bud' MacLeod."

—Jessica Handler, author of *Invisible Sisters: A Memoir*

"George Weinstein has written a magnificent novel, stark, funny, heartwarming—and with a sense of time and place worthy of Eudora Welty. Weinstein did his work so well that I was startled anew, each time I looked up from reading it, to find myself still in the here and now."

—Diane Thomas, author of *The Year the Music Changed: The Letters of Achsa McEachern-Isaacs and Elvis Presley*

"*Hardscrabble Road* is an unflinching and engrossing novel about growing up poor and close to the land in Depression-era South Georgia. A must-read for fans of Harry Crews. I was swept away by this beautiful, gritty story!"

—Julie L. Cannon, author of *Twang*

# Hardscrabble Road

# Hardscrabble Road

A Novel

George Weinstein

Atlanta, Georgia

Published by
Southern Fried Karma, LLC
Atlanta, GA
www.sfkpress.com

Books are available in quantity for promotional or premium use. For information, email pr@sfkmultimedia.com.

ISBN: 978-0-9979518-2-0
eISBN: 978-0-9979518-3-7



Library of Congress Control Number: 2018932240

*For Kate*

*Ever lighting my way and building me up,*
*knowing me better than I know myself.*

# PROLOGUE

Chet's tenth punch knocked me down for good. I spun and toppled face-first into a ditch. As usual, his fists brought my world into sharp focus: the army ants toiling beside my nose, furrowed snake tracks, straw-colored weeds like human hair. Stubborn grains of sand clung to my lips when I tried to spit out the South Georgia dirt.

Any fool would've known not to mess with my brother Chet. At fifteen, he seemed to be held together by coiled springs vibrating with tension. Papa used to slap the fire out of me, getting in as many licks as he could, but Chet always struck like he meant each blow to end the fight. Still, I'd shake my head, listening to the loose parts rattle like coins in a Prince Albert tobacco can, and come back for more. I never beat Chet, but I never quit.

I scrambled out of the trench alongside Hardscrabble Road, appreciating that he didn't offer his hand. Chet never tried to humiliate me; being a year older, he only whipped me to confirm the proper order of things. He even said, "Sorry I landed one on your birthmark."

A port-wine stain colored the upper-left quarter of my face, like a clock shaded crimson from nine to noon. Proof of the Injun in my blood, a rawboned bully once joked, a heartbeat before Chet cleaned his plow. He and my oldest brother, Jay, would defend me against the whole world with bloody knuckles and bared teeth.

Frigid wind blew icy needles of dust at my eyes as Chet and I resumed trudging along the dirt road, pulling sleds of firewood. He tugged the heavier one, its frayed rope taut over his shoulder. Though it was my turn to drag the larger share, Chet's fists had just settled that argument. I hoped we'd collected enough to keep Mama's rented house warm during the late-winter freeze.

Ahead of us the sky and land looked equally pale, one heavy body mashing down the other, both drained of life. A car took shape down the road. Dust rose high behind it like a cock's plume as the '42 Chrysler Royal Sedan, painted in lurid oxblood, tore up the ground heading our way. Chet seized the pitted hatchet from his sled. He raised his arm, weapon poised.

As if in response, the driver waved to us and tooted a melody with his car horn. He flashed past in a blur of chrome highlights and white walls. Behind the glass, fur-trimmed coat sleeves and hands swaddled in calfskin gloves were all I noticed.

Chet lowered the hatchet as cold dust settled over us: South Georgia snow. I shivered in my light wool jacket and overalls as he chucked the small axe atop his load of twigs and gnarled tree limbs. He leveled his narrow-eyed stare at the receding sedan the way he sighted down our single-shot rifle. "You know who that was, Bud?"

I would've accepted a ride from Hitler or Tojo—any chance to get out of that place. I brushed away dirt with hands chapped red from our fistfight and the cold, saying, "I reckon I don't."

Chet spit between our bare feet. He muttered, "Papa's back."

# BOOK ONE

# CHAPTER 1

NOT YET OLD ENOUGH TO WORK IN THE COTTON FIELD, I SAT AT the edge of our front yard, where my brothers had swept the coarse white sand in wavy rows like pomaded hair. The summer sun baked the ground, the fields, and me. I cupped a handful of warm sand and carefully stuffed my mouth full of grit. When I couldn't fit one more grain, I sat on my haunches and held all of it in until my cheeks ached. Like the egg-timer in Mama's kitchen, I let the sand drain out. Then I took a fresh fistful and reloaded, my face pooching out as I aimed to beat my personal best.

Dirt was the lowest common denominator for me and my family growing up in South Georgia during the Depression—though "lowest" and "common" told on us too. Dirt covered everything. Most roads consisted of rippling earth scraped once a year by the county. Dirt was embedded in the soles of our bare feet and was ground into our pores. We were rich in dirt, and dirt poor.

The front door slammed. Papa bounded down the steps, and without breaking stride, slapped the back of my head. "Goddammit," he said as sand exploded from my mouth, "don't mess up the yard." He strode toward the field where my brothers, Jay and Chet, had taken a breather. Papa cussed at them, removing his belt. He flicked the three feet of worn brown leather away from him the way you'd play out a bullwhip, before commencing to lash.

PAPA HAD ME WORKING PART-TIME alongside my brothers by my sixth birthday, in 1936. During the following summer, I labored all day under the sun with them. Before supper, I'd wash my hands and face in the basin on the back porch and, as the light faded, slump onto a bench at the kitchen table. My muscles ached and torn blisters smarted along my fingers while I looked over the same meal as the night before: leftovers from identical noontime dinners.

A kerosene lamp spilled dim yellow light over butter beans cooked in fatback, tomato slices, cucumber rounds splashed with vinegar, wedges of raw onion, tiny Irish potatoes, and triangles of cornbread. Mama hadn't reheated anything; she wouldn't fire up the stove on a hot summer night. The food sat at Papa's end of the table. He waved away the flies, took heaping amounts from each bowl and plate, and began to eat. We didn't say grace.

His large head tilted down as he shoveled the food in. Narrow grooves creased his thatch of brown hair, still obeying the commands of his comb that morning. The tops of his pink ears were bent over as if he'd worn his white J.B. Stetson at the table along with the snub-nosed Colt he forever kept snug in his waistband.

Mama always spoke first. She sat at the opposite end of the kitchen table, farthest from Papa. The features of her pale, oval face were hard to make out in the flickering light, except for her eyes. As ever, they glinted as dark and hard as marbles. She blew a stray ash-blond wisp from her eyes and said to me, "Bud, thank you for the beans."

I sat on Papa's right, near all the food. He wouldn't let me sit on his left because he couldn't abide looking at my birthmark. I lifted the bowl of beans and greasy, sloshing pot likker with care, aware that Papa would seize my wrist if he wanted more before it got passed around. He seemed content with the portion he bolted. I handed the bowl to eight-year-old Chet beside me, and he set the bowl beside Mama's empty plate.

Darlene, across from me on Papa's left, said, "Thank you for them 'maters." My sister, then going on twelve, was the oldest by two years. Mama had styled Darlene's blond waves as she'd done her own, with curling irons heated in the oven. The kitchen oftentimes stank bitterly of singed hair.

Flies jerked away and lit on the bread as I passed the tomato slices. The bright red flesh had creamy starburst patches like marbled fat. Mama next claimed the cornbread. Jay, age ten, asked for the "cukes," and Chet wanted the onions. My brothers wore their brown hair like Papa and had the makings of his wiry frame. Soon, all the food lay out of my reach and became scarce in the dishes.

I asked for the cornbread first, since only two thin wedges remained among the crumbs and flyspecks. Papa smirked, his eyes flint-gray like the arrowheads in the creek. "M-m-mama, th-th-thank you fer the c-c-c-cornbread," he stuttered in a whiny voice. His imitation of me was dead-on.

Mama snickered and asked me, "Y-y-you sh-sh-sure?"

"Yes, ma'am," I said, looking at my empty plate. Neither my brothers nor Darlene made fun of my newfound stammer. They kept their faces blank and passed what I could manage to ask for. I assembled a puny meal, leaving some of everything for Papa.

A tabby cat I'd adopted and named Fred rubbed against my leg. While my siblings had all taken kittens from the same litter, Fred was a stray. I pushed aside the few slivers of fatback I'd found among the beans, saving a treat for him.

After Papa scraped the remaining leftovers onto his plate, I made a mistake. Already jittery, I reached for my jelly glass and knocked it over. Cold well-water poured through gaping table slats and splashed onto Papa's trousers and the rough planks of heart-pine flooring.

He backhanded me like he was socking a fastball down the line. I tumbled off the long bench and my head bounced on the wood floor. Numb, I lay there without making a sound.

Mama didn't stop eating. Water pattered onto the boards like a drunkard relieving himself while Papa stared at my siblings to make sure nobody else got out of line. They looked at their food, knowing better than to glance my way. When Papa said, "Something wrong with your forks?" they began to eat again.

My mouth and chin began to throb in tempo with my heartbeats while I blinked at the shadowy ceiling beams. Spiders had woven thick webs above the kitchen table. A good many flies that joined our mealtimes ended their lives up there. When we ate, the spiders ate too.

"Roger—" Whenever Papa used my given name, it always meant trouble "—get your ass up here if you know what's good for you." I staggered upright and scuffed back to the table, the calluses on my bare feet proof against the splinters. Fred and the other cats had run out the back door. Chet frowned at me, clearly afraid that I'd bring down Papa's wrath on everybody. Even with the ringing in my head and the flies gathering on my cold food, I reached for my fork.

Papa backhanded me once more with a blow like dynamite against my jaw.

Sprawled on the floor again, I tasted blood on my split lip and had to choke down the vomit brought on by my woozy head. I wiggled loose molars with my tongue, producing more blood inside my mouth.

Mama gave a tired sigh and said, "Mance, you could hurt that boy."

"It'll toughen him up."

"He ain't quite seven."

Papa jabbed the sharp tines of his fork into the table and said, "Goddammit, he's old enough to make his hands work right."

"You didn't need to crack him twice."

"Not another word outta you, Reva." Papa drew the ugly revolver from his waistband. He slammed down the snub-nosed Colt near Darlene, making her flinch. My brothers straddled their benches across the table from one another, ready to run.

Mama crossed her arms and leaned back in her chair. "Aye God, will you look at that! You really gonna kill us this time, sweetie?"

"I'm gonna start with you if you don't shut your hole." He grabbed his fork and speared the food on his plate. With a smirk, he pointed three skewered butter beans at her and said, "Not that it ever stays closed. Neither one."

"You sonofabitch," Mama said. "Put that thing away—or finally use it!"

"Your cooking might kill me first." He snorted and chewed the beans. With his elbow he nudged Darlene and said, "That's a good one, huh?"

"Oh, Daddy." Darlene started to cry. She ran to her room, her long skirt flapping.

"You bastard," Mama shouted, "now look what you done."

"Goddammit…" Papa's hand dropped over his gun.

As our parents pushed out of their chairs and continued to cuss each other, Chet yanked me upright. Following my brothers, I hurtled through the open kitchen door and down the porch steps, tensed for a bullet in the back.

I dashed across the backyard, much slower than Jay and Chet. Like in a nightmare, I seemed to be running in place. Mama yelled louder. I imagined a gunshot cutting her down and then a second bullet firing at me. Jay and Chet disappeared around the barn. I hoped this time we'd run all the way out of Miller County and keep going. A hand almost jerked me off my feet.

Jay pulled me into the shadows where they hid. Our parents' fracas continued, but I couldn't make out their words as I fought for breath. I only heard the explosions of their voices.

Chet nudged me and whispered, "Take a look."

"Unh-uh." Blood pounding in my head made the bruised places hurt more.

"Go on, scaredy."

The shouting stopped after Mama got in the last word. A loud bang made us jump.

Jay said, "Easy now. Somebody slammed a door is all."

We crept to the edge of the barn. Chet shoved me playfully and then stepped into the open himself. Jay followed him while I peered around the corner. The sunset had draped our back porch in gloom. Lightning bugs drifted across the darkening barn lot. Crickets had begun their familiar chatter while cicadas droned. I'd begun to relax when Papa emerged from the kitchen doorway and pointed at us.

Chet scrambled over the hog-wire fence that ran around our rented property like a net. He disappeared into the woods. Jay stayed beside me as we fled, keeping hold of my hand until we were deep in the forest of pines, oaks, and cedars.

The crunch of leaves underfoot echoed all around, making me believe that Papa was running after us. As I turned to look one way and then another, I kept tripping over roots that humped out of the cool ground. Overgrown shrubs and looming trees blocked the last of our daylight, and Chet became just another shadow up ahead. If Jay ran as fast as he could, I'd soon be all alone. He remained at my side though—he knew I was afraid of the dark.

I wanted to keep going, but my brothers halted in a clearing. Spring Creek flowed beside us, wide and deep as a river. Spanish moss dangled from almost every tree limb that arced over the water; the long, twisted fingers showed greenish-silver in the twilight. On calmer nights we fished from those banks. Now we just gasped, hands on knees, staring at the muddy ground as skeeters whined in our ears. A painful stitch in my side kept my breathing so shallow I thought I'd pass out.

Jay straightened first. "Bud, you all right? 'Cept for your lip, you're as white as a fish belly. Even doughier than ol Chet-here."

I stuffed my hands in my overall pockets so my brothers couldn't see them shake. Raising my bruised chin, I said, "I'm f-f-fine."

"You're gonna get us all killed," Chet said, knocking my shoulder with a gentle punch that staggered me. "I was for-sure he'd let 'er rip this time."

"Naw," Jay said, "I think he just pointed his finger at us. Bud, we need to get'chu some grabby gloves." He described a plan where he'd trace my hands on flypaper with his pocketknife and, using Mama's darning needle and thread, sew me a pair of sticky mitts.

Chet said, "Just don't forget to take 'em off before smoothing down your cowlicks. Papa won't have nothing to grab onto if you wind up bald." He tugged a little at my short, unruly blond hair and made a tearing sound.

I took a swipe at him but he dodged away. While I patted my hair, always trying to press more of it down over my birthmark, I asked Jay why Mama kept goading our father.

"He got her back up is all—she wouldn't take no more from him."

Chet picked up a handful of stones. He hurled them at the creek as he said, "Ain't...gonna...take...NO...more...from... NEITHER...one—"

"Whoa there!" A deep voice boomed from the woods, giving us a scare. Footsteps stirred the leaves and pine needles on the opposite end of the clearing as a tall Negro with thick shoulders emerged from the trees. Nat Blanchard carried a cane pole and bucket in his long-fingered hands. "You gonna scare away my catfish," he said. "I didn't come out here to haul up water." Nat was one of two Negroes who sharecropped in the cotton field Papa rented. Dressed like us, in overalls and a pale blue work shirt with the long sleeves rolled up, he also wore his favorite hat, a dun-colored fedora. It perched way back, revealing his high forehead and thinning hair. He said, "You fixing to use poles or stone 'em dead?"

Chet ground together the remaining rocks in his hand. Jay looked away from Nat and said, "Reckon we forgot our gear."

"Ain't like y'all to be forgetting a thing like that." With a deep bend, he set down his pole and bucket and continued descending into a baseball catcher's squat. Now at eye-level with me, he touched my split lip and murmured, "Your papa going after y'all?"

I shook my head. "S-s-squaring off with Mama."

Chet threw a rock into the woods and said, "He was gonna shoot everybody."

"Never," Nat said. "He only needs to blow off steam. I heard him tear out in his pickup so all the squabbling's over." When we didn't budge, he said, "How 'bout if I take y'all back?"

He left his fishing gear and followed us through the woods.

Jay, leading the way, said, "Nat, we'll get our stuff and fish with you."

"Y'all gotta be ready at daylight for chores. You need to be dreaming now, not fishing." He patted my shoulder and said, "Think your papa was a bear tonight, wait'll he catches you napping in the fields. Bless your heart, he'll tear you up."

I tasted the dried blood on my lip and said, "He's trying to m-make a m-man outta m-me."

"Ain't no rush, boy. You'll get there soon enough."

We crossed through a small glade open to the starlight. Chet pointed at a channel sloping into the earth. "You can drop Bud off here," he said. A land turtle called a gopher had dug its burrow there. A year ago, Papa had started to devil me at supper that I wasn't related: two years separated all my siblings, but I was only a year younger than Chet; besides, no one else in the family had my port-wine birthmark. The truth was that he'd found me in a gopher hole. Everyone at the table had put on a face serious enough to wear to church and swore that they remembered the time when Papa brought me home from a hunting trip. I used to think they were humoring him, but now I wasn't so sure.

Nat snorted. "Y'all quit hacking Bud about that."

Jay said, "But I remember it. I was teaching Chet-here how to shoot marbles when Papa brought Bud home in a tow sack. He said, 'Lookee here at the possum I treed,' and dumped baby Bud on the ground."

I said, "L-last time you told it, Papa said he'd g-got a orphan polecat."

Chet said, "Yeah, and we was making stick men, not shooting marbles."

"Fellas, I remember it clear as day. Nat does too." Jay's broad smile was in his voice even if I couldn't see it.

When my brothers had repeated Papa's story to Nat, he'd sworn up and down that it was so. Now he said to me, "I'm right sorry I went along with it. That's a powerful-bad thing I done to you." He sounded sincere, but maybe he was coddling me because of my bloody lip.

We climbed our fence and crossed the pitch-black barn lot. The kerosene lamp was unlit in the kitchen; our rented house stood dark and silent, as if waiting for something to happen. My brothers said goodnight to Nat. On the porch, they washed their feet in the ceramic basin and toweled off, murmuring to each other. They padded inside without hesitation.

I took Nat's hand, dry and tough and as big as a skillet, and looked at the black rectangle where my brothers had vanished. I stuttered, "Why ain't I l-l-like Jay and Chet?"

His fingers folded overtop of my knuckles and gave me a quick squeeze. "Someday you won't never give a thought to being in the dark. Not long past, your brothers was just like you."

"M-maybe we really ain't kin."

"This is your home," he said very gently. "You's a part of this family and loved the same as everybody else." Then he took me up the porch stairs. I kept washing my feet over and over in the basin full of dirty water until he tapped me with the towel my brothers had used. The kitchen doorway gaped like the mouth of a cave. With a pat on my britches, he nudged me inside.

I held my breath while I scuffed through the room and entered the hall. Nat had gone when I glanced back. I slid my hand along the wood-plank wall, touched my parents' closed bedroom door and Darlene's on the opposite side, and stopped at the threshold of the parlor, where Jay and Chet breathed deeply in the single bed we all had to share. As usual, they sounded confident of their place in the world. Meanwhile, Nat's careful words ran in a loop through my mind, which distorted their emphasis and shadings until they confirmed my worst fear.

I was an orphan.

# CHAPTER 2

Papa sang out as he stalked down the hallway:

> *"Hamestrang crackin*
> *Collar cryin*
> *Let's git goin*
> *If we're gwine!"*

My eyes snapped open at "crackin." I slept with my head at the foot of the bed; Jay and Chet's toes twitched against my arms. They scrabbled off their ends of the stifling feather mattress and we all hit the floor before Papa reached "gwine" in his mule-plowing song. Not to do so would've meant a belt-lashing or worse. Papa wouldn't hesitate to grab a fistful of our hair and yank each of us from bed, so we made sure we'd climbed into our dusty overalls before he loomed in the entryway. His belt pressed the snub-nosed Colt against his shirtfront.

"Jay," he said, "I'll only say this once..." He rattled off a list of chores and fieldwork we had to finish by supper. "And you'll do it right if you know what's good for you." His orders to ten-year-old Jay always began and ended the same way. When Papa left our room, Jay repeated the chores to the letter, giving me and Chet our duties. Only six-going-on-seven, I got the lightest work but would try to help my brothers too. Jay always kept the hardest labor for himself.

As the sun cleared the treetops, the summer heat throbbed like an oncoming brushfire. The kitchen floor warmed my feet where sunlight baked the heart-pine. With yawns and grumbles, we shuffled to our places at the table and dropped onto the benches. Darlene's bedroom door remained shut. Since school wouldn't start again until September, she slept in most mornings. She usually did her only chores—sweeping the front porch and helping Mama shell peas and corn—in the late afternoon, unless she'd gone to stay with girlfriends or hosted their visits, in which case I got her duties too.

Fred greeted me with a rub of his flat orange crown against my ankle while my siblings' gray-striped cats sat at attention, alert for scraps. Our hunting dogs, Sport and Dixie, had to stay on the front porch; they lay in the open doorway and stared down the hall at us with yellow eyes.

Mama turned from the stove with a skillet that held fried eggs sizzling in red-eye gravy. The yolks were as orange as the bacon drippings in which they swam. She slid an egg onto each of our plates and returned with a pot of grits. She and Papa hadn't crossed words since the night he'd pulled his gun, so she held her mouth a bit looser and almost looked us in the eye as she served breakfast.

Lonnie Nugent perched at the cook's table—the end of the kitchen counter—eating the same food. A rangy Negro in his mid-twenties, Lonnie was Nat's partner in sharecropping and lived alone in a shack on the other side of our rented cotton field. He ate the first two meals of each day in our kitchen. He always dressed the same as us: a long-sleeved work shirt and overalls. The sun had darkened his skin to the color of the flies darting around his food. He snatched one with his left hand, shook his fist hard, and discarded the pest on the floor while eating a syrup-drenched biscuit with his right. He wiped his mouth on a faded kerchief and said, "The general got my orders?"

Jay nodded and swallowed his mouthful of grits. Lonnie sometimes went with us to the Saturday picture-show, where he'd sit way up in the colored balcony while we grabbed seats down front. He'd taken a liking to the Westerns and cavalry stories. Jay had set his rank as sergeant; Nat received a commission to lieutenant. Chet and I were privates but at least our general had given us pretend horses to ride. Jay said, "Sergeant, you're to hoe out the cotton with me and Lt. Nat, same as yesterday. The commandant wants us done by supper."

The back porch creaked as Papa went through his morning routine. He stood in the shade, knees bent and shoulders sloped, the way I imagined he'd gotten set to field a grounder during his old barnstorming baseball days. I watched him through the kitchen doorway as he kicked out his right foot and held that leg even with the porch floor. Then he crouched on his left leg until his seat almost touched the wood planks. His arms drifted outward for balance, but he never tipped or even wobbled from the effort. Whenever I tried to imitate him, I'd fall right over. He rose and practiced the strength exercise on his right leg with equal ease. Neither my brothers nor I could ever match him.

With a flick of each wrist, Papa shot his heavily starched cuffs and strolled around the side of the house. He always waited to eat his breakfast after us, "in peace and quiet," he'd say.

Just as we soaked up the last of the red-eye gravy with our biscuits, Mama took away our plates. She plopped the dishes and forks into a galvanized basin full of greasy water, rubbed off anything that stuck, and set them in a drain rack to dry. Lonnie waited until Mama had finished her cleanup and then washed off his own plate and fork and set them on a separate rack. "Thank you, Miz Reva," he said. "That was mighty fine."

She mopped the counter with a graying washrag that she'd cut from the same bolt of gingham as the homemade apron she always wore. In her tight voice, she replied, "You're high near family, Lonnie. Family don't need to say thanks." They had the same brief conversation almost every day.

He headed out the back door, hauling the basin to water her garden, and we filed out after him to begin our chores. While leaning over a hog-wire fence and sloshing rinse water at the base of Mama's tomato vines, he called to me, "Hey, Private. Your buddy's done chewed some lettuce clear down to the dirt."

Our dogs kept away every critter except a small honey-brown rabbit that I'd seen once at sunup in Mama's garden. It had a creamy blaze between its long eyes and a shocking pink scar on its back where something big must've taken a bite. Fur hadn't grown over the damaged skin. Either the rabbit didn't understand that it was in even more danger in Mama's garden or it didn't care. It had sat beside a row of carrots and worked its little mouth as it watched me.

The rabbit had moved over to the onions by the time I'd run inside, got down Papa's single-shot .22 rifle from the kitchen wall, and took aim from the back porch. We always kept the rifle loaded. I could've awakened Sport and Dixie and sent them after the rabbit, but I wanted to show everyone what a good shot I'd become.

The rabbit's narrow face regarded me, mouth twitching as if in mockery of my nervous stutter. Its ears bent sideways and I could see the broad pink scar on its back, a clear target as I sighted along the barrel. The action was so stiff I barely managed to cock the hammer. As soon as I pulled the trigger, I knew I'd missed.

The rifle boomed and dirt behind the rabbit kicked up. I'd killed some Irish potatoes. Chickens in the henhouse squawked as the gunshot echoed. Our dogs gave chase too late; the rabbit had crawled under the wire fence and bounded away.

Papa ran out bare-chested, hitching up his trousers and shouting, "Goddammit, that ain't a toy." He snatched the rifle from my hands and nearly knocked my head off with its walnut stock. As I lay on the porch, holding the lump growing behind my ear and crying loud enough to match our rooster, I could see the rabbit in my mind, the pink scar flaring on its back, taunting me as it escaped.

Now, I looked at the mushy green base of lettuce the rabbit had chewed level with the ground, and cursed it with the only swear-words a six year old was allowed, "D-d-dadgum, blasted thing. M-maybe we can learn Dixie t-t-to sleep out back."

"Better a dog gets cracked upside its head than you." Lonnie filled the basin from the hand-pump and went back inside to deliver the fresh water to Mama.

Already late with my chores, I trotted toward the chicken coop. Our rooster changed its patrol route across the barn lot to cut me off. Papa had named all our animals; he called this little lord That

Goddamn Rooster. I tossed aside some leftover biscuit and dashed into the darkened henhouse as the rooster collected his daily toll.

Hens and young chicks clucked and cheeped and fluffed their feathers to scare me, a rusty rainbow of colors in the gloom. My knuckles grazed coarse feathers as I reached into the warm, humid pit beneath a few hens to gather eggs in a wire basket. The previous week, the mail-rider had delivered our order of twenty-five new biddies in a long box. As usual, a few were dead. I'd removed three plush, cool balls of greenish-yellow fluff and put them over the fence into the woods. They had disappeared when I checked later that day, most likely eaten by our razorback hogs. In my daydreams, though, they'd only played possum when we opened the lid, and a whole kingdom of wily chickens lived deep in the forest.

After leaving the eggs in the kitchen, I helped Chet set out more hay in the mule pen for Mike, Blue, and Della. Both of us breathed through our mouths because of the stink of manure and unwashed animals, shifting our jaws back and forth to blow the ever-present gnats away from one eye and then the other. Every breath had a dual purpose; we never wasted anything on the farm.

Chet slung his arms around Mike and Blue's necks to bring them closer together. He whispered into their long, trowel-shaped ears and laughed when they snorted.

"What'chu s-s-saying to 'em today?"

"I asked who'd win a fight between Hopalong Cassidy and The Lone Ranger."

"They'd never fight," I stuttered. "Both of 'em are good guys."

"You and me fight all the time."

"Well th-they ain't brothers."

Chet didn't take my bait. "The Lone Ranger's a mystery man," he said. "Who knows who he really is?"

We recited in unison, "The Shadow knows." Chet handed me a massive bale of hay and ordered me to the barn. The top of the straw pile poked at my eyes.

I tipped my head back so I could talk without getting a mouthful. "Can a private give orders?"

"I'm an older private than you, so sure."

My arms trembled under the weight, but I still had a question. "Who c-can I order around?"

"Nobody. You don't rank."

I staggered into the barn. With a grunt I dropped the load into the stall of Papa's black warhorse, Dan, then climbed over the gate to stand before him. With the rest of my biscuit, I made a peace offering to the huge stallion. He seized it in one alarming bite that grazed my palm like a steel trap slamming shut. As I scooped out the dung he'd left overnight, Dan stamped his hooves within a gnat's eyebrow of my bare feet. I called out to Chet, "So who'd Mike and Blue s-say would win?"

"Not telling." He shoveled mule hockies into a wheelbarrow, and I added Dan's heavy manure. Later, we'd put in chicken droppings swept up from the barn lot and work it all into Mama's garden.

While my brothers and I kneeled beside our three rawboned cows, each filling up a bucket with warm, frothy milk, I asked Jay who'd win the fight between our two favorite heroes. He pumped on a teat until he got milk to squirt out roughly in the rhythm of The Lone Ranger's theme. I cheered and Chet shouted, "No—Hopalong," but Jay said, "Actually, fellas, Tonto could whip both their backsides. He does all the heavy lifting out West." Jay hauled two of the buckets himself onto the back porch so Mama could skim off the cream for churning and make buttermilk with the rest.

We prodded the cows into the woods to scavenge, and then I hand-pumped water into a dented hubcap. As I set it in the shade for the chickens, That Goddamn Rooster sprang at me with a wild cry and spurred my leg. Talons ripped my clothes and skin while he beat my knees with his strong wings. I kicked him away and limped to the back porch. "I'm gonna sh-shoot that doggone—that damn—"

"A mouthful of lye soap don't taste any better after breakfast," Mama called from the kitchen.

With a broom handle, I swirled a thatch of spider webs from under the porch roof. Jay got a handful of kerosene in his cupped palm and made a dirty gray poultice flecked with cocooned bugs. We pressed it on the cuts and tied the curative in place with strips of worn-out rags. Sweat slicked my back and armpits. The morning had just begun.

"Can I use your hoe this time?" I gripped my rusty straight-neck grubbing hoe, but pointed at the gooseneck tool that Chet had gotten for Christmas six months before. Everybody, even Nat and Lonnie, had received a newfangled hoe but me.

"Not my fault Papa figured you was too little to need one." On Christmas Day, Jay and Chet's hoes were propped against the chairs they'd set in front of the fireplace the night before. A scaly orange and a bag of marbles perched on all three of our seats, while Darlene found fruit, new shoes, and a store-bought dress on her chair. I asked where my hoe was and Papa sent me to the barn to look for it. By the time I'd come back empty-handed, my presents were missing. Papa had said I'd get them next year if I didn't mouth off again.

I pointed at Chet's hoe and said, "For a little while, j-just until the train whistles for dinner."

"That's all morning."

"Pretty please?" I laced my fingers together around my cracked hoe handle and stared at Chet.

"Aw, shoot, take it. Use it all dadgum day for all I care." He threw the hoe at me, but easy enough for me to dodge.

"That's OK, I'll keep mine." I walked toward the cotton field dragging my heavy hoe, making a wide trough in the sand.

"Well, hellfire, Bud, why'd you put me through all that?" He grabbed his gooseneck grubber and caught up at a run.

"Not telling." I failed to keep the smile off my face.

He bumped me with a sharp elbow, muttering, "Idiot."

So my brothers and Nat and Lonnie weeded around the cotton plants with their gooseneck hoes, mostly using their wrists and arms to dig out the grass, sandspurs, and dandelions. I chopped with my old straight hoe, my back and shoulders aching. Sweat ran down my legs, making the cuts from That Goddamn Rooster sting, while sunlight blazed through a flimsy straw hat to brand my neck and head.

Weevils had ruined the cotton. Tiny, wriggling larvae nestled in almost every boll, eating up the thin white strands that should've been growing into fluffy clouds by now. I asked Nat why we bothered with grubbing that crop, since Papa planned to replace the cotton with peanuts. Nat's hoe blade chopped, snick-snick, while sweat dripped from his chin and nose. A salt ring whitened his hatband. He said, "Me and Lonnie gotta make some money off this cotton. We got no moonshine to be selling like your daddy does, nuthin to fall back on."

Lonnie said, "I'll sift through a whole field to make one good bale." He was our champion cotton-picker. Before the weevils, he'd pick six hundred pounds a day, crawling on his knees as he plucked two rows clean at a time. All for five cents a pound.

Mama came out to work in the adjacent cornfield for a few hours before she had to make dinner. We didn't see Papa until he rode out on Dan to inspect our progress around noontime. He sat upright in the saddle, one hand holding the reins and the other resting on his belt, between the silver buckle and the grip of his Colt. The white, wide-brimmed Stetson hid most of his face in deep shade. Musk from Dan's warm flanks filled my nose as hooves crushed the sand in the next row. I sensed Papa leaning over to watch me.

I jabbed at a single blade of grass sprouting beside a scraggly cotton plant. The hoe edge dug out a handful of sandy dirt but I'd missed my target. Huffing, Dan pounded the earth. The saddle creaked as Papa towered above me. I choked up on the neck of my hoe and dragged the blade once more. The grass almost pulled free of the soil. I struck over and over until I'd chopped the sprout into bits of green.

Papa hocked and spit a gob onto my dirty bare foot. "Goddammit, you're gonna take all day to get one row—"

A high-pitched horn blew from the direction of the crossroads, a mile away. Chet flung down his hoe, but Lonnie murmured,

"Mm-mmmm," his voice lifting upward in warning. My brother had been too eager to hear the train whistle that we used to signal our dinner-break. He stooped to grab his tool as the car horn sounded a second time.

Papa vaulted from the saddle, his belt-hand already drawing the leather from around his waist. "You think it's quitting time?" He yanked the belt free and flicked it at Chet's head. The pointed tip reddened my brother's ear. "You got better things to do?" He spun Chet around and lashed his back. Papa struck with fluid ease, the belt a dark blur as he snapped his wrist over and over. Chet hunkered, arms protecting his head, but made no sound. He held still and took it.

Nat and Lonnie watched their feet while Papa cussed and walloped Chet. Jay mirrored the sharecroppers. His suntanned knuckles turned white as he strangled his hoe. Papa stalked over to him and whipped the belt across Jay's fingers, shouting, "Turn around, Goddamn you." Jay was responsible for the three of us; the general always got punished when his troops did, so Papa beat him almost daily. He cried out as the leather snapped against his back and seat. Each of his sobs was interrupted by a screech as the belt bit into him again.

I trembled so much that I almost dropped my hoe. Dan watched me with a cool brown eye the size of my palm. His head twitched up and he looked toward the crossroads a moment before I heard the Seaboard Railroad engineer blow his whistle.

Papa drew the belt back again and stopped. The band of worn leather and broken stitches dangled against his arm. His wrist rotated like he was flipping a baseball to a teammate; he flicked the belt around front and pushed it through his trouser loops. Cheeks flushed, he blew out a breath and said, "Y'all get cleaned up for dinner." His eyes were small and glassy; I wondered how the world looked to him at that moment—I wondered how I looked. With a creak of the saddle, he mounted Dan. The horse stared at me again, first with one huge eye and then the other as Papa turned him around to canter back to the barn, a distance of only thirty yards.

Nat and Lonnie dashed over to Jay. They patted his arms and rubbed his head and said everything would be all right. Jay's sniffles and ragged breath finally calmed. He tried to smile at the men. He once told me that he'd gladly trade Papa for either one of them.

Chet drew himself up. He exchanged a nod with Lonnie. The cords tightened in his neck as he lifted his chin high and walked stiff-legged to the outhouse at the end of one row. As I trotted toward the back porch, I tried not to hear the crying that escaped across the field.

# CHAPTER 3

LATE THAT AFTERNOON, WHILE WE FINISHED HOEING AROUND THE cotton, Papa rode Dan out to oversee us again. Sweat had dried on my clothes in ragged white streaks; the dust I'd raised with my hoe stuck to my wet skin and left a noose of dirt around my neck.

Papa passed Jay and Chet's rows and called out to me, "Bud, you're going to West Florida tonight, so wash them granny beads off your neck. Lonnie, you come too." After he turned Dan around, I felt my brothers' stares on my neck more than the sunburn. Papa always took one of us because revenue agents wouldn't ambush his truck with a child aboard. I tried not to get a big head, but...he picked me!

Lonnie sat on the back porch steps in a washed and pressed shirt and overalls while we ate. His legs jiggled and he couldn't keep his hands still. I pocketed the last cat-head for his supper; the flared edges of Mama's hand-shaped biscuit broke off in my pocket and mingled with my knife and six pennies like tiny brown teeth.

I gave him the bread while we waited side-by-side in our Model B Ford truck. Papa came out in a fresh shirt, always looking his best to do business with the whiskey-makers. His tongue scoured food morsels from his teeth, pushing out his face with a fat bulge that moved counterclockwise around his wide mouth. When he sat behind the wheel, the walnut grip of his revolver touched my arm. It felt as cold and smooth as a bone.

He drove us down the narrow dirt road, past my Uncle Stan and Aunt Arzula's rented place and Nat's two-room shack. Hardscrabble Road, a wider dirt track, took us to the highway. Papa turned south on US 27 near Colquitt, then returned to dirt roads that led us southwest into Seminole County where he'd grown up. The sun dropped out of sight.

After we made our way into Florida, Papa halted at a crossroad and switched off the engine and headlights. We waited in silence.

Crickets chirped and skeeters whined near my ears, but I couldn't hear anything else. I craned my neck to look around. Papa had never stopped on the way to the Ashers' place the other times he'd taken me along. Lonnie slid down beside the passenger door. Negroes weren't allowed in West Florida after dark.

A car approached from the opposite direction. Papa turned his lights on and off twice and received three flashes in reply. He gouged my ribs with his elbow and said, "Keep that face of yours in the shadows. And you better talk right if you know what's good for you." The car rolled across the intersection and stopped beside us. A red dome-light perched on the black-painted roof and a gold six-pointed star gleamed dully on the driver door.

The driver emerged from the car. A badge clung to his shirt, identical to the one on his door. He was in his mid-thirties like Papa, but a lot fatter. Lonnie slid down farther, his head dipping below my shoulder. The lawman hitched his trousers, which were weighted down by a huge holstered gun, and put his hand through Papa's open window. "Hey, Mance." He shook with Papa and said in a surprisingly pleasant tenor, "What's this treat you promised me?"

"Wanted you to meet the boy I named for you." Papa dropped his hand over my thigh. His fingers went almost clear around my leg. "Roger, this here's High Sheriff Timberlake. He's a Roger too."

The High Sheriff squinted through the thick folds of his eyelids and over his rounded cheeks. I pressed my head against the seat, trying to keep the port-wine stain hidden. My jaw moved a few moments before any sound came. Papa squeezed my leg hard enough for me to gasp. The words tumbled out with my breath: "Pleased to know you, sir."

"How old are you, son?"

"Six, sir. S-seven in October."

"They call you Roger—that right?"

"An-an-and Bud, sir."

Papa's tightening grip left me numb from the knee on down. A fire blazed where he crushed my thigh and the pain spread upward into my hip. He explained, "Reva calls him 'Bud' whenever he's bad, so he hears it lots of times."

Timberlake laughed. "That so? I was a bad little feller myself. You know that me and your daddy been business partners longer'n you been alive?"

"N-no, sir."

He looked past me and said, "Nigger, ain't no use sliding down like some shadow trying to slip under a door. You're okay, boy, long as you're riding with Roger's daddy. Roger gets big enough to drive, you can ride with him too in my county."

Lonnie straightened beside me. Sweat glistened on his face as he murmured, "Yes, sir. Thank you, sir."

Timberlake slapped Papa's arm and said, "You named a fine-looking boy after me, Mance. I thank you. He's much too handsome to be yours." He laughed again and then dropped into his car with a grunt.

Papa waited until the High Sheriff had driven away before releasing me. He started the engine and drove another hour in silence. Feeling in my leg returned like a swarm of needle pricks. I let the pain ebb on its own; I knew better than to soothe those aches with him beside me.

Graded dirt roads became wagon trails and then cow paths as a swamp closed around us. Tall grasses scraped beneath the truck. Papa and Lonnie raised their windows as twisted branches whacked both fenders and raked the glass and roof with crooked fingers.

We braked hard. Lonnie threw his arm across me to keep my head from cracking against the metal dashboard. Papa jerked the truck forward and stopped once more, playing his usual game with the lurking Asher boy called Seth. As we started forward again, a wildcat yowled above us and then the pickup shook. Papa cussed but kept going; Seth had dropped into the truck bed. He grinned at Lonnie and me through the back window and lowered the sawed-off shotgun in his eight-year-old hands. A dozen raccoon tails dangled from a strip of rawhide that circled his bare, scrawny waist. He never wore anything but that.

Up ahead, a campfire smoldered where the swamp gave way to a large clearing. Orange and yellow light flickered across the Ashers' low-slung house and lichen-covered barn, piercing the gloom that swallowed the surrounding trees. Half-a-dozen men slouched in chairs around the smudgy fire and cast jagged shadows across the dirt yard. They dressed the same as me and Lonnie, but wore felt hats crushed low over dark eyes. Some had hair shot through with gray that turned rusty in the firelight. Others' beards were so black that they almost disappeared, like the dark side of the moon. A quart jug of homemade whiskey sat on each man's lap, alongside a drawn revolver.

Seth leaped from the truck bed and scampered across the clearing. The oldest man stuck out his leg, but Seth hopped over it and ducked under another's arm. His shadow sprang ahead of him as he passed the campfire, raccoon tails bouncing off his bare rump. As we climbed from the pickup, Seth ran indoors and pulled Nadine onto the porch. Nadine was my age. I never saw any of the Asher women, only this little girl. She dressed in a dirty shift but someone had braided her copper hair in smart twists and graceful loops that rested on her head like a crown.

"Lookee here, Nadine," said her father, Ray, the one who'd tried to trip Seth. "Your sweetheart done come all the way from Georgia to see you."

As all the Ashers laughed except her, Ray's oldest son pushed out of his chair and marched toward me. By the careful way Angus set each foot down, I guessed that he was stone drunk. Ray called, "Now, Bud, you owe Nadine a kissing. You plumb chickened out last time and made her feel bad. She took to her bed for days." Some of the men laughed again as Angus seized my arm and pulled me across the yard.

Papa and Lonnie hauled five-gallon wood barrels of bootleg whiskey from the barn to the truck bed as Angus dragged me onto the rotting porch. Papa never looked at me, but Lonnie held my panicked gaze every time I glanced his way. Chilly sweat drizzled down my ribs while hot blood pounded behind my face and made my head ache. Angus pushed my shoulders and Seth prodded Nadine closer. Her eyes were clamped shut, and she pressed her arms tight against her sides. She breathed as fast as a trapped animal.

When my feet refused to budge anymore, Angus leaned me against Nadine's bony, heaving chest. Her skin smelled of spoiled buttermilk and wood smoke. I pushed out my lips as far as they'd go and made a birdlike peck against her cold, tear-streaked jaw. The Asher men cheered, and Seth gave Nadine a little shake. She dashed inside without looking at me. I felt ashamed, like it'd been my idea. Like she knew I'd often dreamed of rescuing her and hiding her in our barn, and that she always rewarded me with a kiss.

When Angus released me, I hopped off the porch and ran for the truck. It seemed like a mile away, across fire-lit ground with armed drunks everywhere. I tumbled over the leg that Ray thrust out again, which prompted another cheer from the Ashers.

I limped to the passenger door, panting and trying not to cry. Lonnie finished loading the moonshine and stood beside me. He patted the middle of my back with a comforting hand.

Papa presented an inch-thick fold of cash to Angus, but Ray called, "Wait a damn minute." He raised his revolver and fired once into the air. Lonnie's hand trembled against me as the swamp pines around us swallowed the gunshot echo. Ray gestured at Papa with his gun barrel as if pointing a long finger. "You been buying my liquor for high near fifteen years, Mance, but I ain't never seen you take a drink of it."

"I ain't feeling too good, Ray. Got me some epizootic that's giving me the trots."

"Well, this'll kick it in the ass, blast it right out."

With his whiskey jug, Angus knocked aside Papa's outstretched hand and said, "Unless you're too good for our 'shine." The other Ashers stood, grumbling and cussing. Some of them swayed and had to plant their feet wide for balance. All of them had shifted their revolvers into their shooting hands except for Angus, who pushed the jug against my father's chest.

I'd never seen Papa take a drink. Chet once said that if our father had been a drinking man, he would've killed us all long ago during one of his rages. Papa's gaze flicked from Angus to Ray and the other armed men. His free hand rested on his hip beside the snub-nosed Colt.

Two of the Ashers lurched toward me and Lonnie. Their shadows reached our bare feet and crawled up our bodies as they drew closer. Others, including Seth, began cussing Papa for being so high and mighty.

"Aw, hell, gimme that." Papa cupped the underside of the jug with his large hand and lifted it from Angus' grip. His head tilted back as he took a long swig. The only sound came from the pop of damp kindling in the campfire until Papa handed the jug back to Angus and said, "That's damn fine whiskey."

The Ashers flashed yellow teeth as they grinned and returned to their chairs. They echoed Papa's comment and spiced it up with more cussing about exactly how powerful-good their liquor was. Angus took Papa's money and drank after him without wiping the smooth ceramic lip or showing any other sign of disrespect. He offered his jug for Papa to finish on the trip home. Without hesitating, Papa thanked him and took the whiskey, curling his index finger through the small circular handle.

Papa told Ray he'd be back for more on the next moonless night, and got into the truck. I tucked in between Lonnie and him. My father put the jug on the floorboard at his feet, started the engine, and wheeled around to head back down the path. The truck sagged from the weight of the barrels of whiskey. The wheel wells scraped hard against the rear tires when Seth jumped onto the bumper and held the tailgate with one hand. He clambered over the wood lids and got onto the roof. The nearly naked boy knocked once above our heads with his shotgun and caught the next low branch, disappearing into the trees.

* * *

We followed the same route back into Georgia, but then Papa took a zigzag path of dirt roads as he stopped at farms and behind shops and houses in the small towns. He sold the whiskey to retailers, who'd empty the large barrels into fruit jars for resale. Those were the folks most likely to be caught in a revenuer raid.

Lonnie helped Papa unload five, ten, or sometimes twenty gallons of whiskey at each stop. Every bootlegger would taste the latest batch in a cup or slurp from a gourd ladle and offer Papa some along with a fistful of money. He took the cash but nothing more. Each time we returned to the road again, Lonnie would wipe the sweat from his face with a kerchief and say, "Mr. Mance, I sure could use me a drop of that 'shine at your feet. I'm fixing to fall out from thirst." Finally, Papa passed the whiskey jug, his hand shaking.

My father kept rubbing his eyes and yawning. More than once he had to jerk the wheel to keep the truck on the road. He stuck his head out the window into the rush of air and nearly put us in a ditch. I'd never seen him have such trouble before.

I reckoned that he needed to talk to stay awake, because he slurred, "Round about '30, I promised Timberlake I'd name my next boy after 'im. Your mama took to calling you Bud soon as you was—" He gave me a cockeyed smile and said, "Soon as I found you in that gopher hole. I go along with her just to keep the peace, but you're always 'Roger' to me, yessir."

He clenched his jaw to stifle another yawn, but a moaning sound escaped through the down-turned corners of his mouth. He took a few deep breaths and said, "You know as how y'all visit your mama's mama every other Sunday? Ever wonder why you never, not once, ever go and visit mine?"

I hesitated, afraid to make him angry by saying the wrong thing. While I worked on my answer, he muttered, "My daddy was bad to drink, like his brother. They got into a...into a brawl once, both of 'em tight as ticks, and started wrestling over Daddy's shotgun in the front room. My mama stood in the corner yelling at 'em to quit, and crying up a storm, just a-bawling. I was your age—ran and hid out by the woodpile." He wiped the sweat from his face and dragged his damp hand over his trouser leg. "The gun went off, both barrels, and like to have broke my daddy and uncle's arms. They picked theirselves off the floor, deaf as posts, and found Mama. The buckshot had cut her in two.

"They buried her out back with no trouble from the law or her folks, who had nuthin to do with her anyway after she took up with Daddy. Neither him or my uncle drew another sober breath." He paused and then his voice came out in a rush: "And all them liquored-up sonsabitches can go to hell with 'em." He pounded the steering wheel, jerking the truck, and shouted, "Goddammit!"

Lonnie swiped the last of the whiskey off his mouth and hid the jug between his feet. Aiming the truck with care, Papa took us up another dirt track that led to a barn. We waited for the bootlegger to appear as I held my breath. I'd never heard Papa say so much or sound so pitiful. Probably, this was when he'd turn the Colt on me—not in a rage but the one time he was drunk.

Papa clenched his jaw and moaned again. His eyes looked wet in the moonlight. "Goddamn 'em," he said. "Goddamn everybody."

# CHAPTER 4

I FELL IN LOVE TWICE IN ONE MORNING ON MY FIRST DAY OF SCHOOL. It took a year longer than it should have to start first grade. Mama held me back until 1938, hoping my stuttering would pass, but it had worsened instead. Now I'd be a year older than everyone, seven-going-on-eight, and I had my birthmark to shame me too.

On the first Monday in September, Papa didn't wake us with a song about plowing with mules. Instead, he shouted from the hallway, "Get to your chores. If y'all miss the bus, you're walking." Goose bumps raced over my skin as I realized that his usual school-term warning finally applied to me as well.

Jay and Chet unfolded clothes that Mama had pressed—overalls and a long-sleeved shirt, same as our field duds—and began to dress. I stayed in bed, suddenly afraid of schooling, being away from home, and having strangers make fun of everything wrong with me.

Chet punched my ribs through the sheet. "Come on, Bud, get up. You'll make us late. You think Papa won't give us a striping before we have to walk?"

We finger-combed our hair Mama had cropped the day before, taking turns with her hand mirror as we raked dirty fingernails through the uneven thatches. My yellow cowlicks stuck up worse than usual. I didn't have a prayer of covering up the birthmark.

I took my Blue Cloud cigar box from under the bed. The pasteboard cover showed an Indian chief wearing a full feathered headdress, with a red kerchief tied around his neck like a railroad engineer. Inside I kept some flint arrowheads, a few marbles given to me by Jay and Chet, my whittling knife, and a train-flattened nickel—not worth one cent, let alone five—that Papa once paid me for washing his feet. I filled my pockets, hoping something there would bring good luck.

My brothers propelled me down the hallway and into the kitchen, where Mama had set out a breakfast of fried side meat, biscuits, and cane syrup. Gray-blue smoke poured from the oven as coffee beans roasted. The bittersweet haze stung my eyes while we ate.

On the table, she'd lined up four brown paper sacks holding our school dinners. Darlene sat at her place wearing a new dress bought for her in Bainbridge. Her blond hair was curled and styled with ribbons; she and Mama had worked on it for hours the night before.

Jay said, "Grab another biscuit, fellas, and let's get to our chores." In the garden, my rabbit box lay on its side. Something had sprung the trap during the night, but the critter must have pushed over the wooden box and fled with the turnips I'd left as bait.

Chet rapped my shoulder. "Better call that rabbit your pet, as much as you're feeding it."

"Could've been a fox or c-coyote or something."

"Naw, look at them pellets it left behind, to let you know it was there. Like Zorro's Z."

After we got done with our morning chores, Jay washed his face and neck in the basin on our back porch. I waited for Chet to finish and had to wring out the drying-towel so it wouldn't make me even wetter. This towel had seen a week of use, and Mama would clean it that day along with the rest of the laundry. Monday was washday for as far back as anyone could recall. My shirt collar collected what water the towel could not.

I'd hoped that Mama would send me off with a kind word, but she focused on the tabletop butter churn: milk burbled in the glass box as she spun a pair of beaters with a side-mounted crank. The coffee grinder sat near her elbow with tobacco-like flecks of milled beans scattered around it.

"I'm g-gonna miss being here with you, Mama," I said. The soles of my bare feet itched from the grit they'd collected in the barn lot. I scraped each one over the top of the other foot, bobbing from side to side, waiting for her reply.

"I ain't gonna miss the noise," she said over the clash of beaters within the churning cream. Then she looked at me, really looked. I leaned closer, making sure I'd hear any nice thing she might say. She glanced down at the churn and murmured, "Reckon my hand'll fall off afore this turns to butter."

I grabbed my sack and joined my siblings on the front porch.

A mile-long hike over fields and down Hardscrabble Road brought us to the bus stop. Our hunting dogs followed us all the way. I worried about Sport and Dixie's safe return home since stray dogs often got poisoned or shot. I used to be there for them when Darlene and my brothers would leave for school. Who would look after them now?

Darlene stood apart from me and my brothers as we kicked up dirt with our wrestling. The bus pulled up in a swirl of dust that even she couldn't avoid. "Morning, kids," Mr. Clemmons said as we stepped up through the open door.

I took a last look at our dogs; they sat upright in the grass and stared back with their yellow eyes. "Go on home," I told them. "Git!" Sport gave me a small wag before the door closed.

The bus had wooden benches that ran along both sides and a double-wide bench down the center. Pegs held open worn canvas shades above the window frames. Dirt outlined every plank in the wood floor, but the surface was as smooth as a frozen pond.

The girls sat on one side of the bus and the boys on the other. Darlene joined her girlfriends, who were all beribboned and decked out in new-looking dresses too. Jay and Chet moved to where our six-year-old buddy Fleming sat with some older boys I didn't know. I kept my head turned to the right while listening to them, to hide my port-wine stain against the window frame.

Across the aisle, Darlene told her friends, "Mama says I can sit up with boys this December, when I'm thirteen." She glanced at the ones near Jay and rolled her eyes. "Maybe they'll start looking better by then." She and her pretty girlfriends giggled, leaned in close, and commenced to whisper.

Everybody had one hand clasped over the edge of their bench. I wondered why just before the bus lurched forward and I slid into

Chet. He put me back in my place with a swift, pointy elbow to my ribs and grunted, "Don't start, Bud."

As we rode to the next stop, Fleming told us about visiting kin in Columbus, a hundred miles north. "Everything's electrified. They got streetcars and a bunch of picture shows. I saw the same *Flash Gordon* chapter at two different thee-aters." He had a crush on Dale Arden, but then again, he had a crush on every girl. It was disgusting.

The warm wind ruffled my hair while the bus bounced on its springs. Sunlight on my head made me sleepy. I drifted into a daydream of running to the other side of the bus and kissing all of Darlene's friends. Unlike Nadine Asher, their skin would be warm and smell like talcum powder. They'd smile and kiss me back and leave overlapping red circles on my cheeks.

The bus stopped and I shot halfway up the bench, which had been polished to a fare-thee-well by thousands of cotton-covered behinds. While everyone laughed and teased at me—"Check your drawers, Bud, they done growed wheels!"—I slid back to my brothers and wondered what other surprises awaited me. Why would I slide one way when the bus started and the other way when it stopped? I studied on this so hard that I didn't notice when Cecilia Turner got on board.

Cecilia was only nine but already starting to blossom into a real knee-weakener. She'd grown some over the summer and had just begun to pad her frame with curves that looked as soft as biddies. Her homemade clothes were now a half-size too small. The boys stopped talking as she paused at the front of the bus. I noticed the silence first and then followed their stares.

Mr. Clemmons pushed his porkpie hat back with one finger and said, "Boy-hidee, Cecilia, you look purty as a speckled pup."

She thanked him with a smile and a little curtsy: pale fingers grasped the sides of her flower-print calico dress and gave a tug upward, exposing pale calves. Jay swallowed hard. She flicked an auburn wave behind her shoulder and crinkled her pea-green eyes at us. Fleming forgot to breathe until Chet punched his gut. Cecilia chose our side instead of the girls' and walked down the aisle toward me. "Hey, Bud," she said in her throaty voice, flashing teeth that must've been white-washed. She sat just a foot away, on my left side. I wouldn't have to hide much of my face from her.

I gazed at her and felt ashamed that I'd been kissing other girls in my daydream. I pledged once again to be true to Cecilia forever. Maybe she'd run away with me when I got a little taller. I wanted to ask for her promise to wait for me, but instead I said, "H-hey, Cecilia. You're sure g-growing up all over."

Chet whacked my shoulder, hissing, "You gotta head full of stump water," but Cecilia laughed and said, "This your first day of school?"

"Yeah, b-but I'm not scared."

She seemed to be looking at me alone as she smiled again. Other kids had boarded and sat, and the bus moved forward. I bumped Chet again; this time he shoved me with both hands. I slid into Cecilia and my head settled against one of her new curves before she eased me away. For the rest of the trip, I was between a rock and a soft place.

THE ELEMENTARY SCHOOL HOUSED SEVEN grades in a long brick building at the edge of Colquitt, across the street from the high school. Kids came from forty-leven directions, pouring off buses and wandering over from the nearby neighborhoods. As Cecilia fell in with her girlfriends and disappeared into a crowd, I began to get nervous all over again. Something in my bowels loosened. Jay took hold of Fleming, who was starting the first grade too, and told him to watch out for me. Fleming stopped looking scared as he focused on my well-being, and I felt better because someone would be on my side. I said, "Thanks, General." Fleming and I went inside.

I lost sight of my brothers in the crush of people. The flow of children swept us along in a blur of overalls, shirts, and dresses. All the girls—even the ones from the country—glowed in shades of white and pink, like the inside of the big conch shell Papa had hung from a nail in the barn. The town dudes' skin looked rosy too, but every country boy had nut-brown hands and was toasted from the neck up and ankles down. We shuffled along aimlessly under the bright electric lights until a burly man in a dark suit and wide maroon tie shouted, "First-graders to the far end of the school."

Chet leaned against the doorway of his third-grade classroom, his wiry arms crossed and the usual scowl darkening his face. He called to us, "Don't let anybody bully y'all. You let me know if somebody tries to crawl your frame."

When we entered our room, the first-grade teacher greeted us and introduced herself as Miss Wingate. She was in her early twenties with wavy shoulder-length blond hair. Her store-bought dress flattered a figure that had no apparent straight lines.

She smelled like a field of gardenia and jasmine, and Fleming and I had no problem taking in all the air we could. We just didn't want to give any of it back. Finally, he said his name and I had a bit more time to inhale greedily. She looked me in the eye and seemed to pay no attention to my birthmark, which temporarily made me forget about it too. I almost forgot my name as well, but managed to stammer it.

"Welcome to your first day of school," she said. "Take a seat on the rightmost row, beside the wall." At a desk in front of Fleming's, I put my paper sack under the chair, sat down, and stared at her. The girls in the class smiled in her direction and whispered to each other about her clothes, shoes, and perfume. The boys kept to themselves but flat-out gaped.

I recognized her name. Valerie Wingate's father owned dry-goods stores and groceries in Colquitt, Bainbridge, and Eldorendo. With all that money in her family, she didn't have to work. I fantasized that she took the teaching job in hopes of finding the perfect boy to mold and one day marry. A quick look around the room took in all my rivals as they sat there slack-jawed and watching every move she made. I vowed to become perfect for her.

Miss Wingate led us through our first morning, explaining the rules of the school and her class, and the penalties for disobedience.

She told us when we would go outside for dinner and when the buses would take us home. I half-listened as I envisioned running up to her and—

"I'll call the roll," she said. "As you hear your name, stand and tell everyone about yourself." Neither of my brothers had warned me that I'd have to talk in front of more than two dozen strangers. Cold sweat scraped down my ribs like a hag's fingernails.

As Miss Wingate began to announce the first name, my legs twitched, almost sending me to my feet. Ronald Abercorn stood and gave a nervous account of his life. The next child, Mabel Atkins, followed his shaky lead.

I couldn't figure out the order of the roll call since I didn't know my letters. Every time a child stopped jawing I thought it was going to be my turn. My hands pressed flat on the desk and my elbows stuck outward. As I remained in a constant state of being about to spring to my feet, I couldn't focus on what I'd say. Instead, it occurred to me that Miss Wingate had me sit against the wall to hide my birthmark; it horrified her. She thought I was a monster.

She said, "Fleming Harrison," and he rattled off his age and where in the county he lived—"used to be near the Bradleys and now we live by Old Man Slaughter's place"—his parents and brothers' names, his three hunting dogs, two barn cats, and favorite picture show: *Flash Gordon*.

About halfway through the roster, she called out, "Roger MacLeod." Then she said it again. In my nervousness I didn't recognize my own name.

I almost pushed my desk over as I shot upright. "Everyone calls me 'Bud,'" I got out with some stammering. The other children seemed poised to break up with laughter. They probably thought I'd flunked first grade in '37. I faced forward to hide the port-wine stain as much as possible. A few girls snickered behind their hands.

Miss Wingate prompted me from her desk, "Please tell us about your family, Bud."

Nothing came to mind. Who was I? Oh yeah, I was an orphan with a birthmark and a stutter. The furthest thing from her perfect boy.

I decided to tell the truth. "I don't know m-my real family, ma'am," I said. "My papa brung me home af-af-after he found me in a g-gopher hole." The dam burst and laughter echoed throughout the school and probably across Miller County. Maybe Nat and Lonnie heard it while they tended the cotton. Maybe they shook their heads and said a quick prayer for me.

The husky man who'd directed us to class appeared at the doorway and hushed everyone with a hard stare. I remained standing, knees locked. He said, "Miss Wingate, does that boy need the paddle?"

"There's just a misunderstanding, Mr. Gladney. Everything's going to be all right." I recalled Nat and Lonnie promising the same thing and wondered when that day would come.

Mr. Gladney looked at her for a few moments. When his expression softened into a smile, a pink flush crept up from beneath the collar of her dress and, like a thermometer rising, bathed her throat and face before she glanced away. He said, "I want you in my office—with that boy—if there's any more trouble out of him." His hard-soled footsteps echoed down the hallway.

Our teacher patted her upper lip with a lace kerchief. She told me I could sit. Fleming pushed the chair behind my knees so that when I collapsed, I landed in my seat. Had I fallen to the floor, I would've died of mortification.

As my ears rang and a chill raised goose bumps over me, another boy stood and babbled. Miss Wingate kept glancing at me with kind eyes and a gentle smile. I wondered if she had me sit beside the wall to protect me from teasing about my birthmark, to spare me the embarrassment I just brought down on myself.

THE OTHER HALF OF THE class recited their stories without a problem. Miss Wingate laced her fingers together upon her clean desk and said, "Do any of you know why I called you in the order I did?" We stared back at her; a few children gave exaggerated shakes of their heads. "It has to do," she continued, "with what we call the alphabet." She stood, brushed her skirt against her legs, and began to write on the chalkboard.

When it was time for the class to go outside for dinner and playtime, she asked me to stay a moment and sit with her. She patted a straight-back chair beside her desk, as close to her as I'd been to Cecilia on the bus.

My classmates took their brown bags, syrup buckets, or burlap sacks outdoors, just beyond the classroom wall. A few windows overlooked the sandlot where a waist-high fence of hog-wire kept the boys and girls separated. Miss Wingate and I were left alone. Together.

With a V-like frown, she asked who told me about being found in a gopher hole. "Everybody I know," I replied, which rearranged her expression. A dimple in her cheek like the letter C appeared as she tried to hold back a grin. My bloodhound of a nose sucked in a sweet ribbon of air. I forgot to turn my head so she couldn't see the awful birthmark.

"Bud, I know that you were not found in a gopher hole. You're the fourth child of Mance and Reva MacLeod, and don't let anyone tell you differently." Why was I so ready to believe the worst story but not the best news? I must've looked doubtful, because she held my hands and said, "It's a fact."

"Really, ma'am?" I wanted to stretch out that wonderful moment of acceptance, and the feel of her soft, gentle fingers, so unlike Mama's.

"I promise you, that's the truth."

Eight boys from various classes watched us through the windows. No doubt they had a crush on her and hoped to see me get scolded or, even better, paddled. I enjoyed an unfamiliar sense of triumph as they scowled at me.

A middle-aged Negro woman appeared in the doorway holding a cloth-covered tray. Miss Wingate said, "Please come in, Lucy." She introduced me and reported, "He's going to be my star pupil this year." I almost fainted with pride.

Lucy congratulated me as she set the tray down in front of my teacher and removed the cover. I was surprised to see just a ham sandwich and a banana. I'd imagined that Lucy had a feast to deliver. The maid excused herself and withdrew.

Miss Wingate apologized for the big show. "Father insists on sending his driver over with Lucy. I'm embarrassed enough without them bringing me a banquet too." I couldn't begin to imagine my teacher's life, but I would've bet that she had a clean washrag and towel on her back porch every day of the week.

I got up to let her eat in peace but she asked me to stay. She shouted toward the boys at the window, "Don't miss your dinner and playtime. Class starts again soon."

A boiled egg and half of a baked sweet potato stained the bottom of my sack. I rolled the egg in my hand and peeled the brittle shell from the eyeball-slick egg white. While Miss Wingate nibbled her sandwich, I gulped down my dinner.

She waved the banana like a dowsing rod, her red-painted fingernails gleaming despite the chalk dust. "Did you ever hear the one about the two country brothers taking their first train ride?"

"No, ma'am."

"They get on board, find their seats, and open the sacks their mama packed for them. Each has a surprise: a bright yellow banana, something they'd never tasted before. Well, the train starts off and is chugging across the countryside. One of the boys decides to try his banana. He peels off the skin and just as he's taking his first bite, the train shoots into a tunnel and everything goes dark. He cries out, 'Hey, Jim Ed, don't eat that nanner! You'll go stone blind!'"

I laughed hard, my love for her complete. Miss Wingate flushed a bit as I mooned over her. She said, "Go out and play. Make some friends."

Outside, as Fleming described to me the Cadillac Phaeton that had brought Lucy, a teacher announced the end of dinnertime. We formed up to go inside, and somebody jabbed the back of my head. I spun around, shouting, "What was that for?"

A thickset boy sneered down at me. "You better leave Miss Wingate alone, peewee. She ain't interested in no red-faced shrimp."

The line began to move, and Fleming whispered, "That's Buck Bradley. How'd you set him off?"

Buck socked me a few more times before I could escape to my classroom. My head throbbed for the rest of the afternoon, making it hard to focus on Miss Wingate's lessons. I'd figured that school was the one place I'd go where no one would hit me.

When Miss Wingate released us for the day, she murmured personal farewells as we filed past her. To me, she said, "Goodbye, Bud. You tell me a joke tomorrow." Her smooth fingertips grazed the back of my neck, taking away some of the hurt where Buck had pummeled me.

In the hallway, children streamed from the classrooms. Bare feet and shoes trod on one another as we neared the bottleneck of the front door. I got jostled along with everyone else, but some big hands kept pushing me. When we burst through the doorway, Buck shoved me while Fleming, small and lanky, tried to hold him back. A ring of children soon surrounded the three of us. Boys and girls from every grade all shouted for a fight.

Buck pried off Fleming's fingers and slapped him away. Then he charged me, knocking me onto the dirt. I struggled to my feet and he pushed me down again as Mr. Gladney began making a path through the children. The buses drove up at that moment; the circle collapsed around us as everyone surged forward. The crowd carried us along like leaves on Spring Creek. When Fleming grabbed my arm, I almost swung a fist at him. He pulled me in the direction of our bus and got me on board.

Mr. Clemmons looked me up and down. "Boy-hidee, Bud. Someone use you to sweep the yard?"

We sat down and I lay my head back. It went past the canvas shade and out the open window. My skull bonked against the side of the bus, and the shade flapped closed against my neck.

I heard Jay shout, "Who chopped off Bud's head?"

"What happened to your duds?" Chet added. "Mama's gonna tear you up when she sees them." He did try to help by pulling me inside, which scraped my head against the sill and my face against the shade.

I bawled in huge gasps, not caring who saw me. One good thing about a hearty cry, though, was that my whole face turned crimson and my birthmark about disappeared. In great sorrow I looked almost normal.

Across the two aisles, Darlene and Cecilia and the other girls stared at me, all of them looking as fresh as they had that morning. I stopped crying, straightened my spine, and tried to appear brave. Jay rubbed circles on my back and Chet cracked his knuckles while Fleming gave them a story about my day that was too sunny to explain my blues and didn't mention his heroics at all. He said, "Buck went crazy. I can't feature what got into him."

I knew the reason, but how could I tell them that Buck and I were in love with the same woman?

Chet said to Jay, "He's in your grade?"

"Nope, still in the fourth. We was in class together up 'til this year. He got held back."

"He's a big'un."

"Mm-hm." Jay glanced at me and said, "Don't worry. He messes with one of us, he's gotta deal with all of us." He and Chet discussed how many brothers Buck Bradley had, their ages, and sizes. They made the bus feel like a Western saloon; the Earps were strapping on their six-guns to avenge their little brother.

On the walk home, a white coupe with a rumble-seat approached us at a good clip. Chet said it was a DeSoto, but Jay had decided on a Plymouth. Darlene didn't offer an opinion, while I tried instead to recognize the man behind the wheel. The stranger didn't glance our way as he drove past, bathing us in dust.

Papa's Ford pickup was not beside the house. We waved at Nat and Lonnie in the cotton field and climbed onto the porch where we fended off our dogs. Sport and Dixie wiggled their whole bodies for us and barked hello. Tails lashed my legs with frantic wags.

In the side yard, drying laundry stirred on a clothesline. Large galvanized washtubs were tipped over in the dirt to drain. A rubbing board leaned against the battling-block on which Mama had pounded water from the garments. My dirty clothes had to last me until next Monday.

Looking through the open front door and down the hallway, I saw Mama in the kitchen. She faced away from me, dropping an apron over her shoulders. Her work-reddened fingers tied the two long apron strings behind her. They moved as fast and sure as Darlene forming a cat's cradle with a skein of yarn. Seizing the two loops she'd made, she yanked the bow taut.

The dogs kept yipping at us. Mama turned then and glared at me. Before I could step out of sight, she shouted, "What is it? Don't you give me that fisheye. Get over here!"

She stood with hands balled against her slender hips while I shuffled to the kitchen. Once I would've sworn that my mother was the most beautiful woman ever, but now I recalled how Miss Wingate had treated me with such kindness and how sweet Cecilia had been.

I needed to distract Mama's attention from my clothes, so I asked if someone had come to see Papa.

"No, why?"

"A str-str-strange man drove past us on th-the road." As I drew closer to Mama, I smelled a musky odor I didn't recognize and took in so much air that it hissed up my nose.

Her face colored: not a gradual pinking like Miss Wingate's delicate skin, but the violent red of hog butchering. I wondered if she knew: had she looked inside me and seen my disloyalty?

She grabbed a wooden spoon from the counter and spun me around. The first lick against my dusty backside broke the spoon in half. The pieces bounced on the floor as Mama reached behind her for another weapon. She gripped my shoulder so hard that her fingertips pressed against my bones while her empty hand slapped the countertop. She had to settle for spanking me as fiercely as she could.

At last I was propelled in tears toward the open back door with the words, "Get to your chores. And don't you ever sniff me again!"

Somehow I'd succeeded in distracting her—she didn't even notice my clothes.

# CHAPTER 5

Papa missed supper and hadn't come home by Tuesday morning, but Jay got us up when That Goddamn Rooster crowed. A brief downpour during the night had left the air thick enough to stir. As we did our chores, taking a deep breath felt like trying to suck water through a burlap sack.

Beneath the low clouds, nothing moved. Even the flies lay sprawled on the dung they ate instead of flitting away whenever we hustled past. Only the rain bird sang; its tune sounded backward from other birdsongs, jarring instead of musical.

At school, we practiced our letters, but the paper was spongy and tore beneath the blunt-tipped pencils. Small tree frogs that only croaked when a storm was due joined the rain birds' song. Miss Wingate had to shout to be heard over the warnings that came from every oak and cedar around the building.

An hour before our noontime break, a secretary from the front office came by to announce an assembly in the schoolyard. Hundreds of children and a couple dozen adults gathered on the sodden field. We formed a half-circle around Mr. Gladney, who glanced down at the sand caking his black wingtips and stepped onto a tree stump. He kept his hands behind him, a posture which thrust out his stout middle and strained the button holding his suit jacket closed. From my place in the second row, I couldn't tell what he hid from us.

"Now all of you listen up," he started, loud enough to drown out the rain birds and tree frogs. "Yesterday was the worst start to any school term I can remember. I had to settle down a class in one of the lower grades in the morning. In the afternoon, I had to break up a fight. Maybe some of you older students forgot about discipline and self-control over the summer. Maybe some of you younger children haven't learned these qualities yet. Well, for those that need reminding or require a good first lesson, I'm going to show you something."

I braced again, just like the morning before, waiting to hear my name called. My knees locked and I swayed in place.

Stains darkened the armpits of Mr. Gladney's jacket and his white shirt collar wilted as it drank his sweat. He brought his left hand around front to display a foot-long paddle that had three one-inch-wide holes drilled diagonally through it, like a giant domino. He swung it as he scanned our faces. The paddle cut through the air with a shrill whistle. We all shrank back a few steps, crushing each other's feet.

Mr. Gladney lowered the paddle and raised his right hand. He clutched two well-used boxing gloves by their graying laces. The rounded leather fists had faded to the color of his knuckles. "I work too hard to have time to beat each and every one of you that deserves it. So, if you want to fight, I will keep two pairs of these in my office. If you spar without the leather though—" he swung the paddle again "—you'll get a licking from the wood."

After he dismissed us and we moved back inside the schoolhouse, Miss Wingate cut me out of the crowd. She stopped the front-office secretary as well and asked her to watch over the first-graders for a few minutes.

My teacher led me down the hall, saying, "There's nothing to be afraid of." Whispers and finger-pointing dogged me as I followed her to Mr. Gladney's office.

She put me in a straight-back chair in front of his desk, pressed the long skirt against the backs of her legs, and sat beside me. Interlaced fingers rested on her lap; she composed her face with a gentle smile of curving red-painted lips. I remembered Mama beating me after I'd smelled her, but I couldn't help inhaling Miss Wingate's perfume. That sweetness almost calmed me, but my fear and the humid air oozing through the open window made my head feel like the dough that Mama would knead and punch.

Mr. Gladney marched past us. He tossed the paddle and gloves on his desk with a jarring clatter and dropped into his leather chair. He said, "Please excuse me, Miss Wingate," and mopped his face with a monogrammed linen handkerchief. I made out the stylized WCG, proud that I knew my letters already. He darted his gaze in my direction and said, "Boy, are you staring at me?"

"N-n-n-o, sir. Your hanky." I pointed at the monogram and stuttered, "Miss Wingate is learning us the alphabet."

"Maybe she can *teach* you not to point." He unfolded the kerchief and held it up in both hands; it looked like a checkerboard of creases except that nearly every square was shaded with sweat. He said, "All right, tell me what you've learned."

"I r-reckon that says W-C-G, sir."

He nodded and refolded and tucked the linen into his back pocket. "You're very lucky, Roger. For two reasons. You have the finest teacher in the school." He smiled at Miss Wingate. "No, in this state. She taught you the alphabet just that fast."

Miss Wingate lowered her face as she flushed. Her left leg bobbed up and down and sent tremors through her body. The rapid heel taps on the floor raced against my heartbeat and almost won.

Mr. Gladney continued, "Secondly, Miss Wingate interceded on your behalf after yesterday's brawl. No one could say for sure who the other two boys were, but you were accurately described by twenty-three children. Don't grow up wanting to be another Dillinger, son—your birthmark is a dead giveaway."

I covered the port-wine stain as if he'd hit me. Miss Wingate stopped tapping her heel, which brought my focus back to her. I wondered why she bothered to save my skin and how she'd done it.

"Look at me, boy. I got my bad-eye on you, so watch out. If you want to fight, use the gloves. I normally don't give someone a warning, but since your guardian angel asked me—" he smiled at her and held his hands up "—how could I say 'no' to an angel? Now go on. Have a pleasant afternoon, Miss Wingate."

She thanked him and led me out by the hand. As we walked down the empty hallway, my bare feet slapping the linoleum in counterpoint to her heel-taps, I shortened my stride so we'd take a long time getting to class. Voices of teachers, chalk clicking, and recitations by students echoed around us. I said, "Mr. Gladney sure th-thinks you hung the moon, ma'am."

"You think so?" Her fingers tightened around mine, but then she let go altogether. "All I did was ask him to give you another chance. Don't mind all that angel foolishness."

My hand had dropped to my side, but I imagined that I could still feel her smooth, warm grip. Her closeness made me feel bold. "You probly hear that angel talk from a p-passel of fellers."

"My father keeps them away—nobody's good enough to suit him."

I stammered, "Maybe you can sneak in somebody real short like me."

She laughed, quick and pretty like a whippoorwill song. "You did owe me a joke," she said. Classroom doors opened on both sides of us; children streamed into the hallway with their dinners, heading toward the backdoors. Miss Wingate said, "I better not keep you inside with me again—I don't want anyone to pick on you for being the teacher's pet."

The secretary had just released our class to go outside for dinner. All my classmates stopped and stared at me as I walked to my seat. Hopalong Cassidy riding his horse into the room would've gotten less attention. As I retrieved the paper sack under my chair, Fleming clapped me on the back. I was thankful for his friendship, but I envied him too. Nobody had remembered him, but no one could mistake me.

OUTSIDE, BOYS CLUSTERED IN SMALL groups to shoot marbles where the ground was firm. Jay and Chet hunkered shoulder-to-shoulder playing Box, trying to knock opponents' marbles out of a square traced in the dirt. I didn't want to risk the few I had. Fleming took Jay's place when my brother trotted over to me. He said, "I talked to Ernie Bradley from the seventh grade. He doesn't know what set

Buck off." He clicked some marbles together in his palm. "Maybe he just needed to blow off some steam, like Nat says about Papa."

"Wha-what if he keeps steaming at m-me?"

"Then we'll talk to 'im; I mean really preach good and loud. Don't worry, ol Buck had first-day-back jitters is all."

On the other side of the hog-wire fence, most of the girls talked in clusters while they ate or danced across hopscotch squares drawn in the dirt. Some of them had brought skipping ropes made from clotheslines; girls on both ends sang while they counter-spun two ropes and a dozen girls were bunched in between, timing their jumps. "Bluebells, cockle shells, eevie, ivy, over..." The humidity seemed to press down their hair and skirts as they hopped in place. All around us, the tree frogs kept up their mournful croaking and the rain birds cried.

Some boys not shooting marbles played Bullpen, which looked like the jump-rope games except a boy stood on each end and chucked a rubber ball at a dozen leaping classmates. Other boys wrestled: one would try to pin the other on the ground until the loser shouted, "I give, I give!" or "Uncle!" and the winner would immediately hop off and help him up. When Buck Bradley hoisted a wan-looking third-grader to his feet and looked for another victim, I retreated to the schoolhouse wall and ate my buttered biscuit.

Beside me, a faucet provided water for drinking. As I straightened up, dragging my sleeve across my wet mouth and chin, someone slapped the back of my head. Buck muttered, "We ain't done, shrimp."

I rounded on him, stuttering, "I ain't gonna fight you and get a licking from Mr. Gladney too."

"I dare you to take a swing at me, mush-mouth."

"Uh-uh. I ain't gonna." Behind Buck, I saw a number of boys ambling our way. They smiled at each other and shadowboxed.

Buck craned his neck like a turtle, sticking out his cleft chin. He stood almost a foot taller than me; his jaw looked like a boulder above my head. He said, "I double-dare you."

The tree frogs and rain birds seemed to take up the same taunt as the heavy air pressed me from all sides. "You can d-dare me all you—"

"I double-*dog*-dare you." He tipped his face down at me and grinned with yellow, crooked teeth. Two were missing.

A dozen boys murmured around us. They'd never let me live it down if I refused a double-dog-dare. My shoulders slumped. "I'll g-g-get the gloves."

"No gloves—they're for sissies. Take the first punch." He backed against the wall, lowered his hands, and said, "See, I got nowhere to run."

As the boys began to cheer for the fight, I pulled my fist back and thought about where to hit Buck. I decided on jabbing his stomach since I'd have to come off my feet to punch his face and if he dodged, I'd smack the brick wall. Sand slid under my foot as I stepped in close—

And then I was lying on my side, pushed away by Chet. He bounced Buck's head off the bricks with two fast punches. Buck hit Chet square on the breastbone, right over his heart, a lick that would've broken my ribs. Chet just kept swinging. The boys around us yelled for both sides since they wanted to see a long brawl. Buck snapped Chet's head back with a punch that split open his eyebrow, but my brother didn't even flinch. His fists landed again and again on Buck's chest and face, leaving red blossoms that quickly darkened.

A growl came from Chet's throat that I'd heard when he fought boys other than me. Blood ran into his right eye and dripped from his jaw. His feet shuffled to keep Buck in front of him and his fists flew. Only Buck calling it quits or a point-blank gunshot would make him stop.

Mr. Gladney shot him. At least the paddle sounded like that when it landed against Chet's head. The principal shouted, "Stop this," but Chet had already fallen at my feet.

The crowd began to break up. Buck held his ribs and leaned against the wall. Blinking his untouched eye, Chet smiled up at me.

Swollen lips slurred his voice. He said, "Papa's gonna lay me out when he sees my face."

"Maybe he w-w-won't come home again."

"Naw, we ain't that lucky."

Jay knelt beside Chet and said, "Shoulda gotten the gloves, big man."

"No time, General. Had to save Bud-here."

Mr. Gladney nudged Chet's ankle with his shoe. "In my office." He pulled Buck away from the wall by the bib of his overalls and yanked him toward the door, leaving a trail of red spots from Buck's bleeding face. Chet slapped away the hand Fleming offered and pushed himself to his feet. He staggered a few steps, squared his shoulders, and followed Buck and the principal.

ON THE BUS RIDE HOME, Chet shifted from one haunch to the other. He'd told me and Jay that the paddle didn't hurt any worse than one of Papa's stripings with a gallberry branch. Half of his face looked like a run-over eggplant. Four stitches strained atop the purple and green swelling above his right eye, and blood stained his shirt collar and overall bib. Buck had looked worse when I saw him waiting for his bus, held up by two of his brothers.

If anything, the air had grown heavier since noontime. Even Cecilia, Darlene, and her friends had gone from looking dewy to damp. When I closed my eyes I could imagine that Mr. Clemmons had driven us into Spring Creek and now we breathed water.

Tempers rose with the humidity, and fights broke out. A boy named Billy, sitting across the aisle from Chet, jumped up and shouted, "I can take you, Mac, don't think I can't!" Chet jackknifed off the bench and punched Billy in the throat. He drew back his bruised fist again but saw that the fight had already left his challenger. After a longer brawl commenced between other boys, Mr. Clemmons stopped the bus and put those two out on the side of the road, far from home. He drove off, leaving them in a swirl of dust. They shoved each other once and pointed fingers, but then trudged down the dirt lane together.

Jay tapped Chet's leg and said, "Good thing Billy didn't punch back."

"Yeah," Chet said, and Jay joined him with: "Good thing for Billy." They laughed a little and even Billy joined in, though he was still coughing.

We dragged home and stumbled through our afternoon chores. Chet and I collided on several occasions as we tried to get our work done. After I clipped his knee with a pail, Chet hit me with a blow identical to the one he'd delivered on the bus. I fell on my seat just like Billy, except that I got up. The humidity crumpled my head into a tighter and tighter ball. I sprang at Chet and he clobbered me again. We repeated this dance all over the yard. Finally, Jay yelled, "Knock it off! Let's get through with the chores, fellas."

When I bent over to catch my breath and take stock of the tender patches where Chet had punched me—just about everywhere from the waist up—That Goddamn Rooster spurred the back of my knee. I shouted, "He's a goner," as I hobbled toward the house to get Papa's .22 rifle. "I'll blow 'im to bits."

Papa stood in the kitchen fussing at Mama. "Goddammit, I got a right to do whatever I want."

"You ain't here for a night and a day and make like nuthin's the matter." She pulled the tablecloth edges away from the leftover food in the center and slapped down dishes and forks, saying, "You can just go to hell."

"I'm already there! God knows why I came back."

"'Cause you got bored with—" She eyed me as I mounted the steps still yelling for the rifle. "Bud," she shouted, "you shoot that bird and I'll cook both of you together in my fryer. Now you settle down and call your brothers inside."

She lit the kerosene lamp to brighten the gloomy kitchen while I limped to my spot. Papa took his place beside me, muttering and pulling up his waistband. Each time he yanked the top of his trousers, the butt of his Colt nodded at me.

Darlene sat on his other side, holding her elbows outward as if to cool her armpits. Lamplight turned her blond hair as yellow as a candle flame. Jay brought in a bucket of fresh well-water and filled the glasses, while Chet took his seat and kept his bruised face turned from Papa much the same way that I hid my birthmark.

My father heaped his plate with food, and I passed the bowls around until everyone had helped themselves but me. Papa gulped some water and said, "It's not cold enough, Reva. Go get me some ice."

Mama was staring at Chet's wounded face. She muttered, "Ice man comes tomorrow, in case you stick around."

"Goddammit, get me what's left."

"There ain't no more!" Mama pushed out of her chair and stomped onto the back porch. She returned with the burlap bag in which she wrapped a fresh ice block every week. Water drizzled across the floor as she stalked over to him. "Aye God, you need some cooling off too." She threw the sopping Croker sack onto his lap.

Papa leaped up and side-armed the bag at her. The wad of wet burlap hit Mama full in the face. Droplets spattered over all of us at the table. She wrenched it away and ran for the rifle on the wall.

A flash illuminated everything in the room as bright as midday; a peal of thunder shook the house and made my eardrums pop. Sharp, bitter ozone raced through the kitchen as rain and hail poured down like millions of marbles dropping onto the tin roof.

Mama was deathly afraid of storms—she left the rifle suspended on its nails and hurried down the hall. The next thunderclap drowned out the slamming of the bedroom door. She gasped and wailed, "Oh, Jesus, oh, God, protect me. Sweet Jesus…" The only time I heard her pray was during thunderstorms. I imagined her edging her heels in a small circle so she could look at each wall and the ceiling and wonder which one would fail her first.

When Papa slapped the table, the forks and plates jumped. Cussing, he charged down the hall and kicked open the door.

Mama screamed, "Don't you—" and his Colt fired once, sounding like thunder. Papa reappeared in the doorway, slinging on his yellow slicker and Stetson. In a minute, his truck skidded over the wet sand of our drive, and he was gone.

I ran to their bedroom, afraid to look but needing to see what Papa had done. His story about his own mother getting shot in half played in my head. Meeting me at the doorway was the stink of gunpowder.

Mama turned in her small circle and looked up as the storm continued to boom. Overhead, the exposed tin rattled like an angry knocking from God. The air seemed to be filled with snow, but then I saw the torn feather pillow that Papa's bullet had blown off her side of the bed. A clean hole gaped in the wall: wide enough, I imagined, to stick my finger through and feel the rain.

Thunder blasted the air overhead. Mama put her fingers over her mouth and glanced at me.

I could hardly look into her eyes during a cloudburst. I'd seen the same fright in animals just before a slaughter. Keeping my voice low, unsure of whether she could hear me, I said, "He didn't hur-hur-hurt you, Mama, did he?"

Her voice escaped through the slits between her fingers: "He can't." She returned to her slow spin, and I eased her door closed.

The thunderstorm settled into a steady rain that my brothers and I watched from the front porch after cleaning the dishes. I scratched Dixie's side until she started to paw at my hand with a bicycling rear leg. She turned onto her back and showed her belly for rubbing. I plucked a tick off her and flicked it into the yard where the sand drank up the rain without any puddles forming. I stuttered, "You reckon that he aimed to kill her?"

Jay shook his head. "If he was going to, she'd be deader'n a hammer." He was smoothing the hair on Sport's face and head. Every time he stopped, Sport opened his yellow hound dog eyes and stared at Jay until he began again.

"B-but why shoot her pillow?"

Chet hopped up and paced the length of the porch. "Why's he do anything? Let's get our cane poles."

Jay said, "Nuthin's gonna bite tonight on the creek. You got ants in your pants."

"Runs in the family. Both sides." Chet dropped onto the porch swing. The rusty chains creaked like old tree limbs in a high wind.

I sat beside him. "What's that mean?"

"You're too little."

Sport and Dixie leaped to their feet, ears up, faces pointed toward the dirt road that our driveway joined. They didn't growl, but their noses took in a lot of air and they stared hard into the rainy night.

"Papa's back?" I asked.

Jay leaned forward at the front edge of the porch until the tip of his nose got wet. "I think it's the Woman."

"Where?" I left the protection of the overhanging roof and stood on the top porch step. Warm rain thudded against my scalp and shoulders and ran inside my shirt. With the edge of my hand, I shielded my eyes. Dixie whined behind me. I focused hard and made out the streaks of rain coming straight down. Then I spotted a pale shape on the dirt road, walking away from us.

The Woman always dressed the same way, in a white flour-sack dress that blended with her porcelain arms and face. Regardless of the weather or time of day, she wore a lily-white bonnet and walked with her empty hands at her sides. She had on white high-button shoes that never got dirty or left a mark in the sand. The Woman was a haint.

No one could say for sure who she'd been in life, how she'd died, or why she wandered the countryside. I stared into the darkness for a long time until I'd lost sight of her. I'd stopped being aware of the rain soaking me. I couldn't get any wetter.

Jay looped a finger over the back of my overalls, giving me a start. He tugged, and I stepped under the porch roof. "A-a-anyone ever hear her talk?"

"Naw, she just walks," Jay said. "A kid at school said he saw her point once, but when I asked him to show me, he stuck out a finger and put it up my nose."

Chet said from the swing, "That's all this sitting around is good for, picking your nose."

I sat beside him and peered at his profile of swellings and stitches. "Thanks for jumping in against B-B-Buck. He would've stomped me flat."

"I hit him all wrong. 'Stead of punching him straight on, I shoulda uppercut more."

"Anyway, you sure showed 'im." I jabbed the air a few times and practiced an uppercut.

"You tell me if he picks on you anymore. He owes me now."

"Why's that?"

"The principal asked right off how you was 'involved.' I said it was my fight: I picked it and I won it." He shrugged. "Buck went along with my story, so he only got popped once."

Jay said, "How many times did Mr. Gladney pop you?"

Chet shrugged again. "More'n once." He pushed off the swing, setting me rocking. "I'm gonna get my pole."

I said, "What about s-school?"

"I'm suspended for a day. Woulda been three, but I thanked Ol Man Gladney for letting me go fishing the rest of the week, and he told me to get back to school on Thursday."

I pointed to the dirt road and stuttered, "But what about the Woman?"

"Everybody knows she only goes after folks who're gonna do bad things. She won't go after me for fishing." He walked into the rain. I leaned over the railing as he strolled along the side of the house. I watched Chet until the night swallowed him up.

# CHAPTER 6

Papa's truck was parked beside the house when Jay, Darlene, and I returned from school, and his laugh, as rare as a blue moon, echoed down the hallway from the kitchen. Mama's voice drifted out to us as well, saying, "I declare, Mance. Ain't you the one."

I said to Jay, "Today's a good'un."

"Too bad ol Chet's missing it."

Chet popped up from the truck bed, his slingshot drawn back. He nailed my hip with a dirt clod that exploded across my overalls. I felt surprise rather than pain, but Darlene waggled her finger at him and said, "Your face is gonna look even worse if you shoot me."

"I'd never shoot a silly ol girl," he said and clambered to the ground. His face held more colors than a crazy quilt. "Anybody miss me today?"

"Buck stayed home too," Jay said. "His brothers told me his eyes wouldn't open this morning."

"Probly he just wanted his beauty sleep." Chet guided a punch in slow motion at my nose and said, "But don't you go starting more fights than we can finish."

After we did our afternoon chores and washed up on the back porch, Papa called from the kitchen, "Hey, boys, lookee here at what I got y'all." On the table sat a machine of black-iron that Papa had bought to separate corn from the cob. When we did that by hand every week, rubbing a dry, spiny cob against the hard kernels, bloody blisters always plagued our fingers.

Mama demonstrated the machine to us, feeding husked corn into the top. A hand-crank spun the cob and cut off the kernels, which fell from a chute at one end. Silk and the bare cob slid out the other side. "Yessir," Papa said, "science is gone as far as it'll go." He handed a shaved cob to me. "It'll be smoother going yonder in the outhouse too." Mama giggled at his joke, as if she'd forgiven him already for the gunshot. Maybe she really believed he couldn't hurt her.

All of us but Papa took a number of turns with the machine. In my outstretched arms, I carried a couple dozen sleek cobs to our two-holer beside the dying cotton field and dumped them in a burlap sack with older, rougher cobs. We'd used more than three-quarters of the Sears and Roebuck catalog lying beside the sack. I squinted in the twilight at drawings of women's clothes and shoes while I breathed through my mouth. On account of the flies, I barely parted my lips. The air in the outhouse had a bitter tang, but the stink was worth avoiding.

Coarse paper turned under my fingers as I sat over one of the holes and looked for examples of all twenty-six letters; I didn't know how to sound out the words they made. Pretty soon though, I figured that Miss Wingate would teach me enough so that I could read any remaining pages. Maybe someday I'd know enough words to figure out my parents.

Fairly soon, the light dimmed so much I couldn't see the catalog any longer. I confirmed that the new cobs were indeed smoother, then pulled up my overalls and stepped outside. The moon hadn't shown itself yet; only a few stars glimmered in the blue-black sky. The weevil-infested cotton stirred in the breeze: hundreds of crouching, twisted shapes appeared to edge a bit closer to me. Beyond them the harvested corn stalks rattled. I imagined them as dry, eyeless creatures, rooted, trapped: dreading the knife-like blades of the cutter we'd roll out in late September to chop them near to the ground. At the north end of the field, Lonnie's shack was dark. He often went out at night to the Negro diner in Colquitt or the juke-joints on the highway. I couldn't imagine walking all that way after dark, with the Woman out there and who-knew-what other haints and boogers.

I'd given myself a good scare with these thoughts and dashed for our house with its pale kerosene light in the kitchen window.

I focused on that dim glow, ignoring the rustling all around me. Suddenly the lamp disappeared. The house was another dark shape with the woods looming behind it. Trees seemed to block out half the sky.

As I tried to run faster, weeds snatched at my toes. The mules snuffled and brayed restlessly in their pen, as if they knew something was out there with me. The closer I got to the house, the less I could recognize. Everything was hidden from me.

A girl screamed—no, it was Darlene's crazy, high-pitched cackle. She laughed again: "Eeeeeeee-heeeeee-heeeee!" Hands clapped, and someone produced the kerosene lamp on the front porch. I pumped my arms as I cut to the right and ran toward the joyful sounds and the shadows cast across the dirt driveway.

Papa leaned against the railing with his back to me. My brothers sat cross-legged on the floor with our dogs, and Darlene was on the top step. They all watched Mama, who perched on the porch swing with her hands covering her mouth. She commenced to play "Barbara Allen" on the harmonica she carried in her apron pocket. Jay and Chet whistled along with her. Darlene hummed, since we all knew that whistling women and crowing hens always came to bad ends. Papa even made a few musical sounds in his throat.

It was worth braving the nighttime to see everyone getting along. I only recalled a handful of other times when Papa and Mama had agreed to such a truce. My siblings craned their necks every so often and looked out at the front yard, but no one asked about me. A tire on Papa's truck provided me with a backrest as I sat in the dark, watching my family act the way I always imagined that other families behaved. I was afraid to join them and risk breaking the happy spell.

Darlene kept the peace at home a while longer by bringing two of her girlfriends to supper on Thursday afternoon. Though Mama would refuse to fire up the stove in her broiling kitchen to cook a fresh evening meal for family, she'd never serve leftovers to company. "It's good to see y'all again, girls," she said, wiping swollen hands on her apron. "You're welcome to stay as long as you'd like." She told me and my brothers to build a fire in a sand pit out back. While we filled a huge pot with water for boiling, she strode across the barn lot to kill our supper.

One squawk from the henhouse started the other birds screaming. Mama soon emerged with her hand clamped under the head of a plump, ash-colored Dominecker. The hen flapped a few times and then gave up, dangling limp just before Mama whipped her arm around like she was throwing a windmilling uppercut and wrung its neck.

The bird's dirty yellow legs jerked and the wings fluttered again as the body twitched in Mama's grasp. Above her fist, its head was still, its scaly beak parted and fiery red wattles and crest fading faster than a cut flower. She handed the still-warm hen to me and said, "Scald it good before you start plucking." I felt the fleshy parts I hoped to eat. Having company always meant fried chicken.

Our guests stayed until Saturday morning, which meant that my parents remained on their best behavior. At mealtimes, they were quiet except to ask a few polite questions about school. The girls, one a redhead and the other a brunette, sat on either side of Darlene at supper. Jay interrupted their chatter with little comments that made them giggle, while Chet tried to hide his battered face from them. For my part, I mooned at our guests openly from across the table until I recalled my pledge to be faithful to my two true loves, Cecilia and Miss Wingate. The redheaded girl reminded me of Cecilia—I looked long enough to make sure of that.

Darlene walked her friends back home after Saturday breakfast. Jay and I gave the departing girls some long, final glances and then took up our grubbing hoes. When Papa rode out to the cotton field before noon, I worked harder than ever to root out sandspurs, pale-green clusters of sticker balls that kept coming up around the ruined cotton.

Papa's saddle creaked as he shifted his weight in the stirrups, and Dan snorted and scuffed the dirt with a hoof as big as my head. Papa said, "I'm fixing to take the family to the picture show in Bainbridge after dinner."

My brothers and I cheered. "Thank you kindly, Papa," Jay said, while Chet and I whooped. In his big white Stetson, Papa looked like one of the cowboy heroes on the screen. He turned Dan around with just a tweak of the reins and cantered back to the stable. I admired the ease with which he controlled the huge horse and how confident he looked up there. Gleaming sunlight made a halo of his hat brim. Just like that, I'd forgiven him for everything.

Nat and Lonnie continued to dig up the sandspurs a few rows away from me. Jay called, "Y'all are coming, ain't that right?"

Nat kept grubbing as he said, "Mr. Mance said 'family.'"

Lonnie straightened his back, lifted his straw hat, and swiped a sleeve across his sweat-slick face. "Lots to do here. Be sure y'all tell me how our cavalry boys make out 'gainst them Injuns."

Chet said, "We'll act it out for you." He pointed his hoe like a rifle and pretended to shoot.

"It ain't right," I said, "that y'all don't g-got a rest coming to you."

Lonnie shrugged. Sticker balls had spurred his overalls in a thicket of sharp points from his waist down to his ankle-cuffs. They looked to be eating him alive. He said, "Come day, go day—God, send Sunday."

Bainbridge was the nearest large town, down US 27 from Colquitt; we always wore shoes when we went there. I washed and dried my feet and pushed them into hand-me-down loafers that each of my brothers had worn in years past. The coarse, torn lining would rub the hide off my ankles and pinch my toes.

I dipped a rag into the drippings bowl Mama kept on the stove and rubbed grease over the scuffed leather. This brought out a gleam like Miss Wingate's chalkboard after I would sponge it for her. Jay and Chet shined their ratty loafers too. Our hunting dogs took a sudden interest in our feet; we raced to the truck bed so they wouldn't eat our shoes.

Mama came through the doorway, forcing stray hairs into place. Two more bobby pins stayed clamped between her lips as she made her way to the truck. She wore a store-bought dress of blue and green stripes. When she lowered her arms, the muslin relaxed against her body and revealed a neckline she'd cropped much too low.

Darlene followed behind her wearing the same dress, but with the original collar. She touched Mama's back and said, "Can you fix these?" In her blond tresses, sky-blue bows sat perfectly placed. Still, Mama tweaked the satin butterflies before patting her own hairdo some more.

Papa emerged sporting a brown corduroy suit jacket, matching trousers, new chocolate-and-cream-colored wingtips, and a starched white dress shirt that shone like the Stetson he'd scrunched down over his ears. He marched past Mama and Darlene and opened the driver door. The dogs retreated to the porch as he called, "Come on, Reva, get in the damn truck. Your hair ain't what folks'll be looking at."

The bobby pins wavered in Mama's mouth as she muttered what sounded like, "Didn't think you noticed these no more."

Darlene sat up front with the grownups. After Papa started the noisy engine, I nudged Jay and said, "N-noticed what?"

"You're too little," Chet told me.

We jostled each other as the truck bounced over ruts in the dirt road. Dust boiled out behind the rear tires and hung for a moment in the air. As the dirt resettled, specks of mica glinted in the sunlight. On the path to the highway, we passed the rented shotgun shack where Uncle Stan and crazy Aunt Arzula lived. He lifted a forefinger off his plow handle to hello us as he followed his mule across the field he sharecropped. The leather straps that looped over his shoulders pressed his sweaty shirt and overalls tight against his back.

Heading south on US 27, I was lulled by the sudden smoothness of the paved road and the high-voice singing of the tires upon it. Yankees sped around us on their way to Florida. Children sat in the backseats of many of the cars, and we'd make eye contact sometimes as they sailed past. Their parents' cars always looked new to me and every child seemed to dress in nice clothes. They'd often laugh and point at us.

Jay shouted, "New York," naming the state stamped into the license plate of a passing car, and Chet yelled, "That's number 417." They'd been playing that game for as long as I could remember. At any time, Chet could recite the scores for each of the thirty-seven states Jay had spotted.

Jay said, "DeSoto Airflow."

"Unh-uh, Lincoln LeBaron. The fourth one."

"No, sir."

While they argued, I stuck my head around the truck cab and squinted into the wind at the receding red car. I tasted its bitter exhaust as I murmured, "Going on a vacation most likely." I wondered what that would be like, driving to the Florida beaches instead of crashing through the swamps to pick up another whiskey load from the Ashers.

Mule-drawn wagons and Hoover carts—automobiles converted into wagons for lack of gas money—crowded the south end of the Bainbridge courthouse square. A few trucks and autos were parked in front of the shops bordering the square. The air smelled of manure, cut grass, and burned oil.

Papa parked diagonally to the curb in front of a drugstore, a block from the movie house. As we clambered out, a Negro man shouted from the sidewalk, "Hey, boss, set me up!" It was Vernon Harris, who'd grown up in our part of Miller County forty years before. He tipped his sweat-stained hat to us, a shy smile twitching his gray mustache. He was the eighth child of ten, all with a first name starting with V. Everybody, including his parents, called him V8.

Papa pushed back his Stetson and smiled, teeth and all. It was a sight so unusual that I liked V8 more than ever. Papa said, "Sure, I'll do that." He walked inside the drug store and strode up to the soda fountain. A minute later he came out with a paper-wrapped Moon Pie and an RC that dripped beads of water down its twin-pyramid label. He handed over the goods to V8 with a casual nod.

"Thank you, Mr. Mance. Y'all looks like you put on the dog and is doing the town. Gonna eat over at the Cottontail Café again? I see your truck there lots of times."

The smile on Papa's face died a quick death. "No, we're just gonna catch the picture show. See you around."

V8 thanked him again and lifted his hat to Mama and Darlene with the hand clutching his Moon Pie. Metal taps on his shoes clicked as he set off down the sidewalk.

We followed Papa to the Roxie Theater, where he gave Mama fifty cents.

She said, "You told me you'd come in this time." Her fist squeezed the two quarters.

"I don't feel like it now."

"You promised." She had to step aside as other customers paid their ten cents at the ticket window and entered the two-story building.

"I've got some Florida business to do."

Mama looked him over and said, "I thought you got dressed up for me."

"Just forget about the whole Goddamn thing. We're going home." Papa grabbed her hand that clutched the money, but she wrenched free of his grip.

The young woman in the ticket booth stared at us. When her gaze met mine, she mouthed, "Trash."

Mama said, "Go on and get outta here then. Do your 'business.'" She turned her back on him and shoved the quarters at the ticket-seller. "Just five."

Papa stared at her for a moment, working his jaw, but then stalked up the sidewalk. With muttered curses, Mama led Darlene inside. While they went to claim their seats, I lingered in the lobby with my brothers, inhaling the smells of hot, buttered popcorn and fizzing colas. We looked at the electric lamps in the ceiling and light bulbs surrounding every movie poster on the walls like picture frames.

"Two bulbs burned out around ol Gene." Jay pointed to the Western ad showing Gene Autry strumming his guitar, punching a black-clad bad guy, and snuggling with a dark-haired lady.

"Same two is always burned out." Chet indicated the feature that played on weeknights and the Saturday late-show and said, "Got a new flickerer beside *The Prisoner of Zenda.*"

I cupped my hand just above a light bulb to feel its steady warmth as I took in the illustration of a mustachioed man sword-fighting a black-clad bad guy and snuggling up to a blonde. Not every hero got to play a guitar. "Just think," I said, "c-coming here during the week to catch a show or s-seeing the midnighter."

Jay said, "Yeah, and imagine Papa setting us up to a RC and Moon Pie." He waved his arm, signaling us to follow him into the dark theater cooled by squeaky ceiling fans.

We found Mama and Darlene centermost in the front row, sitting erect in the wooden pull-down seats. My brothers and I slouched on Mama's other side in birth order, with me at the end. Sometimes I had nightmares about the booger-man reaching for me in a pitch-black theater. I had plenty of elbow room on my right, but I'd rather have been surrounded.

I focused on the huge rectangular screen in front of us instead of the gloom. My legs bounced as I anticipated the sudden brightness the projector would cast. Jay once told me what an oasis was, and the picture show had become that for me: something I could see shimmering even from a ways off, a place of peace and happiness where I could lose myself for a little while. I loved to sit right down front, pretending I could see the images before anyone else. They all got the hand-me-downs, not me.

Twice, Mama leaned forward and said, "Aye God, Bud, you're shaking the whole row. You keep fidgeting and I'll make your drawers itch for real." Even with her threats, I could barely sit still in the near-dark. Cigarette smoke drifted over us, invisible and sharp-smelling as ammonia. Behind me, a couple whispered and crunched popcorn from a rattling bag. Someone else slurped a cola and burped.

Everybody stopped talking and, for a moment, put a halt to their eating and drinking as the cartoon began to play. From *Silly Symphony* to the final coming attraction that would follow the Western, I always wanted to stop time and make it last forever. Instead, the Movietone newsreel came on before I'd finished laughing at the jigging cows and pigs. A chapter of *Zorro's Fighting Legion* also went past in a blur, almost as fast as the masked hero could carve a Z. Thanks to Miss Wingate, I finally understood that he was writing the first letter of his name.

Even the hour-long Western was what Jay had called a mirage; before I could understand what was happening, the scene changed, over and over. The songs slowed time down, as did the parts where Gene swapped slobbers with the girl—but then I wanted it to go fast and get to another barroom brawl or gunfight. By the time the last image faded and the white screen was blank, I panted like I'd run for ninety minutes, trying to catch up.

Once again, we'd sped through the oasis. Time to trudge across the desert again. Cotton-headed, I stared at the screen. Mama walked past me, and I staggered upright to join the others as we followed her into the blinding sunlight.

# CHAPTER 7

My parents must've found it too hot to argue on the trip back home. Darlene and Mama retreated to the house, each one fanning her face with both hands. Papa slammed the driver door and said, "Boys, get my pole and we'll do some fishing." Jay and Chet traded looks. Fishing was the only thing Papa didn't do well; we would spend most of our time climbing trees along the shore to untangle a line he cast into the branches. Worse, he'd stand there cussing us as we tried to rescue his hook. Jay said, "How 'bout swimming?" He wiped his sleeve across his forehead. "It'd sure feel good in this heat."

Papa stared at us a moment, sweat staining his shirtfront. He pointed to me. "Can you swim yet?"

"No, sir," I stammered.

"Then go fetch your Uncle Stan. We're gonna learn you if'n we have to drown you."

"F-f-fishing sounded m-mighty good to me."

Papa started around the back of the truck. "What are you s-s-s-skeered of, boy?"

I took a few steps backward, trampling the swept yard. "Nuthin, sir."

"Then fetch your uncle and meet us at Foster's Drain."

I left my shoes on the porch and trotted along the driveway until Papa had gone inside the house. My brothers waved at me. I'd hoped that one of them would tag along, but neither one was much for Uncle Stan and Mama's sister, Aunt Arzula, who was clearly touched in the head.

Slow, shuffling steps on the warm dirt finally delivered me to the field where Uncle Stan trudged behind his old mule, Viola, breaking new ground for fall planting. The plowshare between them hissed as it cut through the sandy soil. Lather covered Viola's flanks, and sweat darkened every stitch of my uncle's shirt and much of his overalls. They plowed to the end of the row where I stood. Touching Viola's nose reminded me of our feather mattress after Mama would sun it all day in the yard.

Uncle Stan rolled his shoulders, making the leather harness rise and fall. He stood a few inches under six feet tall, lean and wiry, but looked tired all the time. His lower jaw, usually stubbly by noon, hung slack; his reddened nose drooped; and the skin under his eyes bagged, as if his face was melting. A battered straw hat drooped low on his head. His work shirt and overalls gapped at the neck and hung loose in the legs; his body seemed better suited to the nice clothes Papa wore. As ever, he squinted when he looked at me, his eyes the blue of worn-out dungarees, and I wondered again whether I'd once given him a bad scare or somehow made him permanently angry at me.

"Hey," he said in his soft voice.

"Hey. P-p-papa's taking us swimming at Foster's Drain. He, um, s-sent me to fetch you."

"Why?"

Viola nuzzled my hands and pockets, her snorts like steam from an overheated radiator. "It'll be crowded there, with white folks downstream, so Lonnie and N-Nat ain't allowed to."

"Ain't allowed to what?"

"Learn me to swim."

His eyes closed completely. I waved flies off Viola's head while he stood still and melted some more. One eye opened a little. "Your mama gonna be there?"

"No, sir."

His eye shut again and he squeezed the leather grips of the plow, which had turned almost black from years of use. With a sigh, he said, "OK." He raised the plowshare out of its furrow. In a louder, more confident voice than he used with people, he called, "Viola, haw." She turned left, and they tromped along the edge of the row to a small barn. "Gee, gee," he ordered, turning the old mule to the right to get her through the barn doorway.

A high-pitched voice screeched, "Bud, you get over here." Aunt Arzula stood on their porch, looking swollen under her clothes. As I approached her, I counted three dresses she'd put on, each of the collars scooped differently, the sleeves of various lengths. Tiny red poppies on one homemade outfit contrasted with the green diamonds of another and huge sunflowers from the third calico pattern. I saw an old pair of men's brogans on her small feet; she had to scuff to keep the work shoes from sliding off while she walked to the porch steps. She held out a fruit jar brimming with water.

I thanked her and eyed the glinting surface for wiggle-tails. My aunt had a bad habit of not skimming off mosquito larvae after she drew up a pail from the well. Sure enough, a dozen flicking, tadpole-like swimmers crisscrossed the water with more ease than I could ever muster. I tipped the jar toward me as I raised it to my mouth, spilling the top few inches onto the steps and my hot feet.

She put her hands on her hips, stretching the seams on the outermost sleeves. "In all my born days, you're the spillingest boy I ever seen. You ain't never drunk right even once in my house."

"Yes'm," I murmured. Four wiggle-tails had stayed in the glass. I slurped water, crossing my eyes to keep track of the swimmers as they headed for my mouth. Only three remained when I looked into the jar again. I wiped a hand across my lips and moved my tongue around the insides of my cheeks, but knew I'd swallowed the bug.

A crow cried and Aunt Arzula turned around twice clockwise and then once the other way, muttering something to herself and rubbing a bald spot on the side of her head where she'd worried away all the hair. She focused on me again. "Wha'd you tell Stan that run him off like that?"

I told her of Papa's idea for a swimming lesson.

"So he's gonna touch the river bottom?"

"Yes'm, I reckon he will."

She made a drawn-out O sound. "I'll have to make the house safe for baby." She shuffled inside and began setting flat things on the plank floor: smoothed out rags, a serving tray, dented baking sheets. Her heavy shoes kicked some of them askew, forcing her to reset the makeshift walkway.

I put her fruit jar on the porch and slipped down the stairs. In the shade along the side of their home, I waited for Uncle Stan. Near the stacked-stone foundation pillars that made a breezeway under the house, a small cemetery plot lay. A pile of rocks marked where they had buried their baby daughter ten years ago. Mama once said that her always-strange sister had gone downhill soon after the infant suddenly took sick and died. As Uncle Stan walked toward me across his half-plowed field, I wondered how he managed not to go crazy living with Aunt Arzula. Maybe he was hoping to melt away.

He had removed his work boots and now stood before me barefoot, the skin below his denim cuffs as white as a maggot. "Don't y'all still swim at Fan's Wash-Hole?"

"The drain flows a lot faster." In fact, the tumbling current had nearly drowned me several times.

With a sigh, he said, "Let's get this over with." We headed into the woods and took a path leading to one of the largest streams that drained into Spring Creek. Uncle Stan walked ahead of me, yanking off a leaf or two from the occasional saplings we passed. He kept the young green leaves balled in his fists.

The trail curved among fifty-foot cedars, massive oaks, and slender pines. Reddish-brown needles and leaves carpeted the forest floor. The air held moisture from the mile-wide creek to our left and the fast-moving brook ahead of us. The old Foster place, an abandoned homestead, perched on the near bank of the "drain." Long ago someone had made a ten-foot ladder from sturdy branches and bailing wire and set it against the shallow-pitched roof. Naked and dripping, Jay and Chet and other boys hollered as they jumped from the roof of the ramshackle house and plunged into the water. They climbed out downstream before the current took them into Spring Creek. Then they raced back to the ladder, clambered up, and dove off again.

Papa stood on the bank, dressed in an old work shirt and overalls, the outfit he used to wear during baseball practices. "What the hell took you so long, Stan? You take Bud out for a snort first?"

The leaves that Uncle Stan had squeezed into green pulp fell from his hands. He said, "Hey, Mance. What're you fixing to do with him?" His thumb jabbed toward me.

"You go downstream and we'll have a catch." Papa hopped down to the shore, disappearing from view.

I followed Uncle Stan to the eroded embankment with its six-foot drop. The back of the Foster shack sat on the cliff edge. Three more boys splashed into the current below. My uncle jumped to the shore and sunk calf-deep in the mud before slogging into the water beside Papa. As I searched for a safer way to go, Papa said, "Goddammit, you shoulda throwed 'im down here."

I draped my shirt and overalls on a sweet-shrub and eased over the edge. Tree roots protruded from the cliff. Like a possum, my toes curled over slender wood and I started down, naked body pressed against the slimy wall.

Papa called, "Birds got nests along there. Don't let 'em think your muddy tallywhacker's a worm. Heh, heh, heh."

Terrified, I jumped backward and sat down hard in black mud. Wading a little ways into the brook, I tried to wipe muck from the crannies where it had lodged. My brothers gave Tarzan yells as they sailed off the roof. Like cannonballs, they slammed into the stream, dousing me with spray.

Uncle Stan flung his straw hat onto shore. He tromped past me and plunged into deeper water. With a few arching strokes and a couple of kicks, he was carried twenty yards downstream by the steady flow. He stood chest deep and leaned into the force of the current. Water streamed down his skin and drained from his clothes.

While I watched my uncle, Papa grabbed me around my waist. He said, "Can't learn if you're daydreaming, boy." He rocked me back, dragging my face through the water, and heaved me into the air. I soared, stretching my limbs as I sailed over the deep, clear brook. Then I fell like a gunshot quail.

I landed in the water face-first, making a huge splash. The current tumbled me with a thousand forceful hands. I tried to open my eyes, but the water stung them too much. A pressure like two giant fingers against my eardrums kept me from hearing anything as I sank. My arms and legs flailed, and I bit my tongue to keep from trying to breathe. Blind and deaf and out of air, I twisted in the river. I expected to hit the bottom, but instead I surfaced, coughing out water and snot.

Papa yelled, "Swim, Bud, swim."

As I gulped air, I pictured how my brothers and Uncle Stan had swum. I raised my right hand, arched it over my head, and slapped the water in front of me while I tried to get my legs kicking from behind. My feet sank as if someone clung to them. Writhing, I went under again and bubbles burst from my mouth and nose. My toes scraped the muddy bottom. Pushing upward sent me wheeling as the current spun me. This time I was going to die for sure.

I hit a tree trunk. Some branches closed around me before my head and chest were jerked above the surface. My legs kicked against the stump as I sputtered.

Uncle Stan said, "Breathe," in the same command-voice he'd used for Viola.

I sucked in air through my mouth since my nose still felt waterlogged. He held me until I'd stopped choking, and then he faced me upstream. I hadn't drifted very far from Papa, maybe fifty feet. Still close enough to see—even through squinted, burning eyes—the disgust on his face.

"Goddammit," Papa spat, "I said swim, didn't I?"

"Yes, sir." I hacked and gasped some more, making my throat even more raw.

"Well if I have my druthers, I hope to see you drowned before I see you quit."

"I won't quit."

Uncle Stan held my chest in one arm and raised my feet with the other. "I'll keep you from sinking. Kick your legs while paddling your arms." He guided me against the current and coached me. As I focused hard on keeping my limbs moving, he said, "You know, when you was drowning, that birthmark about disappeared. Your whole face was as red as a Radio Flyer."

"Thanks for catching me."

"Hell, Viola could do this job better'n me. Wanna know another thing?" He jiggled me in the water. "You don't stutter when you're choking." When I laughed, he said, "Stick with your papa and he'll make you just like everybody else. Ain't that what you want?"

"More'n anything."

He gave me a push, and I swam a dozen confident strokes before I started thinking too much. The current began to spin me and I splashed in panic.

As I went under again, Papa grabbed my shoulders. "How 'bout you actually try this time." He tossed me back downstream.

I swam until my feet sank—then I tumbled and choked. Uncle Stan rescued me and gave me more tips while guiding me upstream. For the first time I could recall, he didn't look hangdog. I thought he would've been eager to return home, but he stayed and taught me.

After an hour of this, Papa called for a race. He lined me up alongside Jay and Chet. I had to hop from one foot to the other to keep from going under as my brothers stood in place, chest deep. Uncle Stan returned downstream and posted himself at the finish line. Papa shouted, "Go!" and we dove, spraying water in every direction. My muscles felt weak from all the exercise I'd gotten already, but I focused on Uncle Stan and swam toward him. Jay surged far ahead, but Chet caught up; they raced side by side while I struggled.

A high-pitched squeal echoed behind me. I wondered if some boy had broken a bone jumping from the rooftop, but couldn't pay any more attention. Jay and Chet had long since passed Uncle Stan and kept racing. I foundered, gasping and kicking, eyes swollen into slits from the water. My uncle had to be nearby. I knew he'd grab me at any moment—I was counting on him.

My feet hit the muddy bottom before I realized that I'd drifted toward the far bank and could stand up. Behind me, the screeching now included laughter and splashes. I rubbed my eyes and blinked at Uncle Stan. He stood transfixed, as did Papa farther upstream. They watched two pretty teenage girls who swam and slapped water at each other. On the Foster rooftop, the oldest and loveliest of the young ladies posed in a homemade one-piece swimsuit of royal blue. Whistles, hooting, and shouts rose up from boys who'd put on their overalls before returning to the water. The girl swung her arms forward, hopped from her perch, and sliced into the stream, prompting the other kids to cheer.

Another girl, younger but already stunning, appeared on the roof: Cecilia Turner. Her red-check swimsuit almost matched her auburn hair. She held up my shirt and overalls and shouted, "Somebody missing these?"

Half-a-dozen boys crowed, "Bud!" and I hunkered down so far that wavelets tickled my nose. I couldn't sink any lower without drowning.

Cecilia shaded her eyes and peered up and down the brook. She called, "Where's he at?"

"Here!" Jay clamped his hand in one of my armpits while Chet grabbed the other and they yanked me out of the water almost to my shriveled groin. I kicked them and beat at their heads until they dropped me with a splash. Cecilia covered her face with my balled-up clothes as she bent over laughing. Everyone else roared with her. My brothers quickly fetched their duds, while Papa and Uncle Stan called it quits and headed home, separately.

Cecilia sang out, "Bud, come and get them." She disappeared from the rooftop, but screamed from the woods a minute later. "Bless God," she cried to someone I couldn't see. "You scared me half to death!" Shrubs rattled as she pushed through them on her way to the embankment, leaving my clothes behind. Reddening scrapes from the branches striped her fair arms and legs. She glanced back at the undergrowth and dove into the water. When she surfaced, she swam to where her girlfriends played, forgetting all about me.

Through the same shrubs came an odd-looking boy. Limbs and leaves made no sound when he passed through; they seemed to part for him. The stranger was about my size and just as thin, with the browned face and arms of a country boy. He wore patched overalls and a too-big shirt with the sleeves rolled up past knobby elbows. A straw hat covered all his hair except for uneven tar-black bangs. Something was wrong with the boy's face. His narrow eyes looked lidless and the bridge of his nose was so slight that it almost disappeared when he looked upriver. My overalls and shirt dangled from his outstretched hands.

I lurched across the brook, flailing more than swimming. On account of the girls, I stayed in waist-deep water and whispered up to where the boy stood on the bank. "Hey! Them's mine."

He peered down at me. In a loud, high-pitched voice, he said, "Are you coming up here to get them?"

The kid hadn't called the others' attention to me as I'd feared, but I still kept my voice low. "I c-can't get out with them girls yonder."

"Do you want me to come down there?"

"Well I reckon so."

The girls squealed, drawing the kid's attention upriver. They splashed back at the boys who'd slapped water at them. The stranger said, "Could I throw them down to you instead?"

"You always ask this m-many questions?"

"My daddy says I have a questing mind."

"Do what?" A breeze had dried the water on my skin, leaving me chilled. I crossed my arms over the gooseflesh on my chest as I shivered. Narrowing my eyes in imitation of the boy, I stuttered, "You afraid of water? Ain't you learned to swim yet?"

"My daddy taught me never to be afraid of anything." He pouted his lips. "You ask a lot of questions too, you know."

"Your mama ever do anything?"

"She died when I was born." He said it in the same way as everything else, another fact stored in his head.

I apologized for my rudeness. To make up for that, I said, "Meet me downstream." I felt the boy looking at me, so I tried to swim with grace, but my paddling became more frantic as my chin dipped below the water. A portion of the embankment jutted out enough to shield my climb, so I scrambled up tree roots and then used the bushes as a screen. The boy hadn't met me with my outfit, so I shouted, "Hey, kid, where you at?"

"Same place."

"You fixing to come here?"

He said, "You know where I am, but I can't see where you went. It's logical for you to come to me."

"What's lo-lo-logiwhatsis mean?"

"It stands to reason. It makes sense. You sure don't know many words for someone who asks more questions than I do."

Blood rose in my face and I stammered, "It's just that you talk so funny." I dodged between trees, making my way toward the boy. He watched me the whole time, studying me the way I peered at box turtles and bugs. I covered my groin with my hand as I walked and said, "What'chu l-looking at?"

"Just looking. For a little boy you have a lot of muscles."

I put a large rhododendron between us, feeling unusually awkward about being naked. "Who you calling little, shrimp? You're teenier than me."

"Do you work on a farm?"

"'Course I do. Don't you?" The boy said no, so I asked, "Then how'd you g-get so much sunning?"

"I study things outside all day. My daddy says I'll be a botanist or entomologist or some other scientist."

"Now what're you yammering about?"

"I'm explaining to you why I'm suntanned, since you asked. Here—" He handed me my clothes. I used the shrub as a screen while I dressed. When I stepped into the path again, he said, "My name's Ry Shepherd."

I introduced myself, telling him to call me Bud. Clothed but still feeling uneasy, I snapped, "What happened to your face?"

"I just told you about my suntan."

"No, I mean your eyes and all."

He probed his skin from the black hairline to his small chin. His brow creased as he frowned at me. "Nothing happened to my face. What about yours?" Ry pointed at my port-wine stain.

I punched him. That is, my fist shot forward, aimed at his nose—except that he wasn't there anymore. The boy had side-stepped and I nearly fell over. "That's dumb," he said. "What'd you do that for?"

Now with my pride doubly hurt, I swung at him again. This time, he snatched my arm as it sailed past him, grabbed the back of my shirt, and used my follow-through to tumble me into an elderberry bush. Leafy canes snapped all around me. As I rolled onto my hands and knees, Ry said, "You don't make sense. Are you mad at me?"

"Heck, yes, I am." I staggered a little, still dizzy from the somersault. "You m-made fun of my b-birthmark."

"Oh, that's what it is. I have some moles on my skin, but nothing like that. Does it hurt your face?"

"Shut up about it!" I relaxed my fists and said, "How'd you throw me?"

"It's called judo. My daddy taught me. He learned it in Japan."

I sighed, exhausted by all the strange words. "What's a Japan?"

"A country of islands on the other side of the world. That's where he met my mother."

"Did she have s-s-slitty eyes and a tiny beak too?"

"You shouldn't be mean, you know."

I liked that I'd found a way to hurt him, so I made my voice squeaky like his. "Does it hurt your face?"

"Why are you like this?"

I stammered, "You ain't even from Miller County."

"My daddy was born here." Ry tapped his lips with an index finger and asked, "Does your birthmark make you stutter like that?"

After I missed him with another punch and he threw me again, I looked up at swirling treetops. I closed my eyes and said, "No. Th-th-they ain't related." I peeked at him as the spinning eased. "If your d-daddy's from here, where you been hiding away?"

"We live in San Antonio where Daddy teaches at the University of Texas."

"I heard of Texas." I sat up and nearly puked. After swallowing hard, I said, "Why're you here instead of Texas?"

"Daddy's traveling. I'm eight, old enough to go by bus to stay with Granny and Grandpa until he gets back. I memorized the bus schedules, transfers, and stops between San Antonio and Columbus, Georgia."

"I know where C-C-Columbus is, doggone it."

"Well, there's also a Columbus, Ohio, and one in North Carolina and—"

I held my head. "Shut up a minute, OK? Why do you t-talk so much?"

"Can I touch your birthmark?"

"I'll clobber you if—" I stopped as cool fingertips stroked my right temple and eyebrow. My throbbing headache disappeared, as if drawn out by his hand. Though I was furious that he touched the port-wine stain, the soothing in my head had stilled me. I waited until he finished before I yelled, "I swannee, Ry, I'll s-s-sock you if you do that again."

"I'm going to collect some more specimens. See you, Bud." He lifted a burlap sack and walked away.

I muttered at the receding figure, "I hope not."

# CHAPTER 8

Every other Sunday, we went to the old home place where Grandma lived. My mother's sisters and their families joined us there. Only two men stayed away: Uncle Stan and Papa. For reasons no one would tell me, Grandma had banned my uncle from the property. Papa stayed away just to be contrary.

To get there, we hiked cross-country to a sandy trail that took us through miles of untamed fields bordered with pines and oaks. Mama led the way, swinging a basket packed with fried rounds of crackling-bread, fresh-churned butter, and strawberry jam she'd made in the spring. She didn't trust me or my brothers, so she had Darlene carry the pasteboard box that held a fresh-baked blueberry pie.

I brought along a pull-toy Jay had made for me. He'd fashioned it from a lidded syrup bucket that rolled on its side and was filled with clicking pebbles and sliding sand that he said made sounds like the ocean surf. Bailing wire ran through the flat ends of the bucket and joined up to form the handle. As I pulled it behind me, I searched the fields for the pink-scarred rabbit that was still gnawing Mama's vegetables.

Where two trails intersected, a rubbish heap sprawled. Lying amongst the trash mounds were mattresses burned up after TB victims had died upon them, busted wagon wheels and axles beyond repair, shattered crockery, maggot-infested waste, and blown-out car tires. My brothers each chose a rubber wheel to roll beside him.

I ambled well in back of Darlene and Mama, listening to the sluice of sand and pebbles and daydreaming about what an ocean beach would look like. "Heads up," Chet shouted. His tire rammed the back of my leg, knocking me flat. Cheering, he ran to pick up his wheel while I brushed sand from my overalls. As he bent over, Jay's tire butted him like a goat.

Mama looked over her shoulder. "You trip up me or your sister and you'll wish to God you hadn't." She walked faster, putting Darlene behind her, and said, "Mind you don't drop that dessert."

Darlene sighed. "Mama, why didn't you have just girls?"

"Honey-lamb, I shoulda stopped with you."

"But if I had a little sister, she could carry this-here pie."

THE OLD HOME PLACE RESTED in a broad hollow. Smoke rose from the stovepipe in the detached kitchen. A tin-roofed barn and smokehouse sat on either side of the kitchen building behind the house. Within the hog-wire that fenced the front yard, our boy cousins raced around and played ball on the sand-lot, while the girls jumped rope or talked in huddled groups. Sunlight flashed green off a nearby pond filled with overlapping lily pads and surrounded by a thicket of river oaks and buttonwood bushes.

I left my toy inside the fence and caught up with Mama. "C-can I help out in the kitchen?"

"You mean 'C-c-can I steal as m-much food as I c-c-can?' Well, OK—carry this." She thrust the basket against my chest, almost knocking me over. "You drop it, though, and you've had it."

I followed her and Darlene up the porch stairs, along the dog-trot hallway, and into the backyard. Smells of fried chicken and fresh biscuits drifted from the kitchen. Mama was right about my motives, of course. Since children had to wait for second-table, helping out before dinner meant snatching mouthfuls of food before it all got cold or, worse, disappeared.

Nailed above the doorway to the kitchen, a horseshoe had slipped around and pointed downward. The luck was running out, but I couldn't stretch far enough to put it right. There were so many reasons to grow up faster. Reaching things up high. Marrying Miss Wingate or Cecilia or both. Running away from home.

Mama and four of her sisters, who were all older and far less pretty, bustled within the large, sweltering room where grease spotted the plank floors and walls and smoke had blackened the rafters. Sunlight poured in through open windows and added to the heat. The women talked over one another and puffed cigarettes as they took bubbling pots off the two-burner woodstove, pulled iron pans from the oven, and chopped, diced, and sliced at the countertop. Within minutes, Mama's dress stuck to her back in damp patches; darkened ringlets of blond hair clung to her neck.

Aunt Lizzie, a frowsy platinum blonde with a huge bosom and the manners of a woodsman, piled biscuits on a plate. Her lower lip puffed out with snuff while she screamed, "Hellfire and damnation, I'm trying to talk to y'all, you sorry bitches." Flecks of tobacco sprayed from her mouth and peppered the bread. In the momentary silence, she said, "Like I was saying, I asked that man of mine where'n the hell he was off to, what with his crops growing up in grass, and he says 'Fishing.' So I tell him he can start right in with fishing for his damn peanuts 'cause there ain't no telling where they are in his field." She pushed the biscuit plate into my arms and spun me toward the door. With a slap on my behind, she said, "I better hear you whistling the whole way up and back here."

I walked outside and competed with the birds as I carried the cat-heads toward the house. Aunt Lizzie's rant about her husband Roscoe followed me: "I swannee, if he wasn't such a good-looking man, I'd part his hair with a axe. That no-count is so lazy, he wouldn't take a job in a pie factory. He wouldn't pick up a stick to hit a damn snake."

Before returning to the kitchen, I pocketed a snuff-stained biscuit and a fistful of fried okra so fresh that the grease blistered my hand. On the next trip, I managed to sneak a chicken leg. I pressed my back against the house, out of sight of the kitchen and below the open dining room windows. The breading crunched and the smoky dark meat left my lips smeared with juice as I stripped the leg clean. With a snap, I broke the leg-bone and sucked out the marrow. I tossed the leftovers to Grandma's old mutt Penny and gobbled up the biscuit and okra.

With a satisfied burp, I continued my journey around the house to where the other children played and awaited the call to second-table. Penny followed close at my heels, like she usually did when we visited. I nodded and traded a "Hey" with Jake, my favorite uncle, who sat in a rocker on the front porch, swapping stories with two other uncles—Roscoe was still fishing down at the pond—while the Elrod sisters they'd married made final preparations for dinner.

In the bright sunshine of the sandlot, girls stood in groups chattering while a ragged circle of boys tried to break long black horsehair across their noses. Blood stained almost every face, but no one could be called "sissy."

My brothers leaned against the fence with another boy-cousin, rubbing kitchen matches on the inside of their bare arms, tracing simple designs over and over. The sulfur in the match would leave a temporary scar better than any horsehair because pictures could be made with it. I thought I might trace "VW," imagining a secret beneath my shirtsleeve that I could touch while I watched my teacher, but my uncles' conversation made me pause. I drew a wavy "VW" in the sand with my toes while I listened to the men gossip.

Uncle Doyle said in his low growl, "Yeah, some are wearing 'em shorter, but it still ain't like ten years past." He licked his rubbery lips. "Sudden breeze came down the street back then and you got a show, let me tell you."

Aunt Lizzie opened the front door and stuck out her head. Her white-blond hair lay pasted against her forehead and frizzed into a cloud everywhere else. "Any of y'all seen Reva?"

Uncle Davy said, "Unh-uh."

"Well, damnation, she said she'd fetch my Roscoe in to dinner, but I ain't seen hide nor hair of either of 'em yet. Sonofabitch—" She slammed the door shut as she cussed, shaking dust from the porch roof.

Davy said, "Uh-oh."

Doyle snorted. "Funny how she cusses him but always says 'My Roscoe.' Like she's putting everybody on notice."

"She's got no call to worry," Davy said. "Roscoe'd rather fish than eat. Than anything, I reckon."

"I dunno. He's been known to cast his rod—"

Uncle Jake rocked forward and stamped his foot, hushing his two brothers-in-law. "Gents, Lizzie just summoned us, indirectly like, to the table. I say we tuck in before it gets cold." After the other men had gone inside, Jake walked over to me, tall and gangly, and asked, "What's your favorite part of a bird?"

I jerked my head up, pretending to be awakened from a daydream. It was just dawning on me what my uncles were talking around, what adults had been saying in a sideways fashion for a long time. I felt grown up but sad and scared for all that. "I-I-I usually get backs and f-feet and such."

"I'll give you a surprise—" he looked at my zigzagging VW and said "—lightning boy." He disappeared through the doorway in a few long strides.

I went around to the back porch so I could keep tabs on what food would be left. Mama strode across the field between the pond and the house, heading toward me. I liked the way the shadows on her skirt changed shape as her legs scissored—right, left, right, left—through the knee-high grass. The summer heat seemed to have put a rosy color on her face and she smiled to herself, a rare and wonderful thing to see. However, when our gazes met, she shook her head in frustration. The smile melted into a hard line. She said, "You seen your Uncle Roscoe?"

"No'm."

"Maybe he's gone and drowned hisself."

Aunt Ruby came out and stood behind me on the back porch. Stern and rail-thin, she always wore a disapproving look on her face. I glanced up and saw that her scowl had deepened. When Mama asked if she'd seen Roscoe, Ruby answered, "We sure haven't."

Mama wiped a line of sweat from her upper lip. She said, "I looked all around the pond for that man —behind every tree. Got myself overheated for nuthin." She fanned her face with both hands and blinked at her sister.

My aunt studied Mama as closely as Ry had peered at me in the woods. Then Ruby glanced past Mama's shoulder and said, "Reckon you didn't look everywhere."

Uncle Roscoe now sauntered across the meadow toward us, looking as fresh as always in a starched white shirt beneath deep-blue overalls. He wore a carefully knotted maroon tie tucked behind the bib: his traditional Sunday fishing outfit that he never seemed to get dirty. Mama often remarked on how, though he was forty years old, his features had stopped aging ten years before. His handsome face had a constant smile and remained unlined. He also never sweated, and every hair stayed neatly combed back and shiny with pomade.

Aunt Ruby pursed her lips and hissed at Mama, "Be sure to wash your hands before coming inside." She walked through the doorway, her heels making a racket on the floor.

Mama said to me, "Don't that beat all. Where was he hiding?" I shrugged in reply, careful not to sniff, but she'd already turned to the washstand at the end of the porch and began to rub her hands with lye soap and filmy water.

By the time she'd gone indoors, Uncle Roscoe climbed the porch steps. He wore leather work boots into which he'd tucked his overalls, but even they looked clean. "Howdy, Mr. Bud," he said. He bent over with his hand out and I thought he was going to tousle my hair, but instead he whisked off a few tiny blades of grass from a boot tip.

"They b-b-biting OK?" I grinned up at him, trying to appear cute and bright: the kind of boy a perfect-looking man might want to raise up.

His smile broadened. "The best fishing in Georgia's right here, yessir." He washed his hands and, instead of using the soggy, graying towel draped over the porch rail, he shook his hands like they were on fire. Taking a square of ironed kerchief from his back pocket, he finished drying his fingers and then cleaned his nails.

Aunt Lizzie shouted from the dining table, "Roscoe, get in here this minute. Hellfire and damnation, you've held up more folks than Jesse James."

Grandma said, "Language, child—I'm about to say grace."

"Coming, love," Roscoe sang back and patted his perfect hair before he went inside.

If I didn't act too obvious, I could look in on the grownups at the dinner table without getting scolded. Of them all, Uncle Roscoe had the oddest eating habits, even stranger than Aunt Arzula, who chucked balled-up bread under the table. After Roscoe loaded his plate, he pushed all the food together in a heap and said, "Thank you for the syrup." Uncle Doyle passed him the pitcher and he poured cane syrup over everything. Maybe the sugar kept him preserved.

After the uncles smoked their after-dinner cigarettes and everyone finally pushed back from the table, the women took away the used dishes and utensils and the men returned to the porch, except for Roscoe and Jake. Roscoe went back to the pond without one look at Mama; of course, he didn't look at his wife Lizzie either. Jake made a show of smoking another cigarette on the back porch until everyone had cleared out. Then he sat down beside me on the stoop.

"Best I could do," he said, taking a plump chicken thigh from the napkin he'd palmed. It had cooled, but I could taste the spices in the breading and the juicy meat better because it didn't burn my tongue. He watched as I stripped the bone clean, sucked out the marrow, and gave the remnants to Penny, who ran off with them.

"Th-th-thank you for that." I smiled up at him, wishing not for the first time that we lived closer to him.

"I wanted to get you a breast, but your Aunt Lizzie took the biggest and your mama got the best—" His face flushed and he wiped his mouth. "The chicken, you know." He blew out a breath, rubbed damp palms against his trouser legs, and started over again. "Look, Bud. You can't listen to what other folks say."

Uncle Jake had never scolded me before; I could feel the fried chicken coming back up my gullet. I stuttered hard, trying to reply. "I wasn't listening to nobody, sir. I—"

He raised a finger, silencing me. "You play like you got your head in the clouds, but I know you got your ears open. I ain't saying it's bad to hear what folks talk about. I mean that you don't wanna take it to heart."

Lizzie and Maxine came out of the kitchen balancing stacks of plates still dripping with water, and they headed toward us. With a finger-wag under my nose, he murmured, "Don't pay gossips no mind, lightning boy." My uncle grunted as he pushed to his feet, a giant standing above me. He walked through the house, taking long strides, and I heard the creak of his rocker out front.

Aunt Lizzie said, "Wash up, Bud, and give us a hand. Time you did some work around here."

As I helped to set the dining table, I surveyed the remnants of food and tried to imagine how far it would stretch among fifteen kids. Grandma only had ten chairs, so the youngest ones—including me—had to sit on the porch steps while we ate. Being the smallest, we'd also get the least portions. To avoid fighting over who took too much, my aunts would prepare fifteen plates of food, with a spoonful of this and a dollop of that, a chicken foot on one plate and a grizzled neck on another. Narrow cornbread wedges would be subdivided. Aunt Lizzie thrust two glass sweet-tea pitchers into my hands and sent me to the well.

Behind the kitchen, I drew up a bucketful of cold water and skimmed off the wiggle-tails. Loose flakes of tea and undiluted sugar had made a tan sludge in the bottom of the pitchers, so I sloshed a little well-water into both and gave them a shake. I tipped back one pitcher and then the other, savoring the sweet, coppery dregs. Then I filled them with more water for second-table. All the while, I tried to imagine Mama taking up with Uncle Roscoe and having him as my new father. He was never mean to me like Papa, but not really nice either like Uncle Jake. As handsome as he was, he wouldn't want folks to think that I was his son. He'd welcome my brothers, but I'd be left behind for sure. Would Papa keep me? Could Nat or Lonnie raise—

"Hey!" Mama shouted. "Everyone's waiting on you. What're you doing just standing there?"

Heat rose in my cheeks as I tried to think of something to say. So she wouldn't know I was thinking about her and Uncle Roscoe, I asked, "W-w-what's Papa do when we c-c-come here?"

"Oh my stars, the sun'll cook that pea-brain of yours before it can puzzle that one out."

"So w-what's he do?"

"Same as me." She took the pitchers from beside the well and stalked away, muttering, "Wondering what's gonna become of you."

While fourteen kids shifted in their chairs or on the back steps and stared at their dinners, Mama filled a hodgepodge of jelly glasses and jars with well-water. Aunt Lizzie gave me the last plate of food—a crispy chicken foot and other portions almost too small to name—and sent me to the porch. When I sat on the sun-heated bottom stair and surveyed the paltry leftovers, Penny emerged from the breezeway and lay at my feet. Indoors, Grandma stood behind Jay's chair and said grace, her voice so faint that the five of us outside only knew she'd finished when the ten oldest kids started to eat. Almost no one talked during second-table: our focus was on food.

Dinner ended soon after it began, and Mama shooed us into the yard. I stood with my brothers and cousins, trying to come up with something to do.

"Y'all wanna play dodgeball?"

"Too hot for that."

Chet slung his arm around my neck. "Wrestle?"

"Naw," I said, "I might p-puke up dinner."

One boy whispered, "The train."

"Yeah!" Chet released me and flicked his finger against my arm. "Or is you as much of a chicken as that foot you ate?"

I raised my chin and said, "I done the tr-train before."

We hiked a mile to the railroad track. I put my already-mashed nickel down on the rail, hoping to stretch it further. In my mind, I pictured a hair-thin silver disk the width of my hand.

Everyone had some doodad that he placed atop the rusty iron. We all toed the track and looked east, each hoping to be the first to spot the Seaboard engine.

"There!" several teenage boys cried out.

Jay said, "No, fellas, just a cow crossing the tracks." Even cousins older than him deferred to his judgments.

We bent forward and back to see around each other. One cousin dropped down and put his ear to the track like Indians did in the Western pictures. In the excitement, I nearly stopped thinking about Mama and Uncle Roscoe and what would become of me.

"Smoke!" someone yelled.

"Dust devil," Jay said.

Finally, the steam engine appeared on the horizon with everyone shouting, "Train!" For a few moments, the boy playing Indian was held down by his brother, who pinned him screaming to the track. It would mean death—though a manly one—to stand at the rail when the locomotive roared past, so we all began to ease backward by very small steps.

"Hey, sissy," Chet shouted at me, "you're halfway to Grandma's."

I stopped and pointed at his toes, farther from the track than mine. "Am not. You're b-b-backpedaling so fast you done burned up the grass."

Whenever someone challenged our courage, we'd ease closer to the rail and the onrushing train. Then we'd edge backward again to safety, the line of us as wiggly as a snake. No one wanted to look too eager to escape a sudden, bone-crushing death.

The train whistle bellowed angrily as the huge locomotive rushed past. The engineer opened a valve and steam shot out the side. It hit us with hellish hot breath.

Some of us screamed but Chet just laughed, hands on hips, as the jet of white mist washed over him. Jay held me up by my overall strap to keep me from staggering. A few of the other boys fell back with hands covering their faces but quickly rejoined our line as we cheered and waved. All of us wanted to grow up to be train engineers.

The railroad cars sailed past in an endless clatter. Ladder rungs alongside boxcars, sliding doors left open—so many invitations to jump on and have an adventure, to escape our parents and everything they did and didn't do. I reached out and imagined gripping an iron handhold and swinging aboard the way Hopalong Cassidy mounted his galloping horse.

After the caboose went by, we scrambled onto the tracks to see how the crushing wheels had improved our offerings. Chet shouted, "Neat—it crushed my arrowhead into dust."

Jay had set down a few pieces saved from a game of jacks. "Stars!" he said. "Squashed and six-pointed."

I burned my fingers picking up the flattened nickel, but to wait for it to cool off or toss it from hand to hand was sissified. The silvery oval seemed larger and thinner. The pictures on the coin were now as blurry as dreams.

# CHAPTER 9

SCHOOL CLOSED FOR A FEW DAYS FOR PEANUT HARVESTING, SO Papa hired us out to nearby farms. My brothers and I spent the daylight hours feeding peanut plants into mechanical pickers and then baling hay made from the stripped peanut vines. We'd stagger home after nightfall, filthy from the mix of sweat and dust, and put our wages into Papa's open palm. On Saturday, he gave each of us a dime from the combined five dollars we'd earned so we could see the latest Western picture show.

During the weekdays that followed, no matter the mood of my parents or the hardship of my chores, I always looked forward to the bus rides with Cecilia and to classroom time. Miss Wingate emphasized rules and discipline, getting us to sit up straight and correcting our English at every turn. "You may talk however you wish, outside of school. When you're in class though, you will pronounce words as your teachers do. You will learn to form sentences that are proper and precise, that explain what you mean."

She wrote on the board and recited, "'I OBEY THE RULES.' This is a sentence you will learn. Four words that say a lot. Reading and writing might be scary to some of you. But all that's needed is to know your letters, children, the letters you're learning already."

I didn't care much for all the copying Miss Wingate made us do, but I liked to watch her write at the board. The chalk clacked and swished and squeaked as her fingers and wrist danced left to right, creating bold tracks for us to follow. As we scrawled her assignments, she'd pace the aisles, high-heels click-clicking, and give encouragement and gentle corrections. Initially, I made lots of mistakes so she would lean close and bathe me in her attention and perfume, but she caught on to that. Soon, she'd merely say, "Pay attention, Bud," and keep walking. I found that making no mistakes earned glowing praise and fond glances, and tried to make up my own sentences.

One time, she pointed at an addition I made and said, "This is fine work, Bud, and it's good that you want to learn faster. Do you have anything to read at home?" When I told her we had a few pages left from the Sears and Roebuck catalog, she grimaced and said, "I'll ask Mr. Gladney about letting you go door-to-door at dinnertime to collect newspapers." Miss Wingate already brought in copies of *Life*, *Collier's*, picture-show magazines, and old newspapers from her own home so the whole class could practice reading the easy words she'd underlined.

The next day, the principal denied her request. He said I was too young to leave the grounds. I thought that learning to read might offer an escape—like daydreaming—but his denial mostly upset me because I hated dinnertime at school.

I'd decided not to hide behind my brothers. Jay and Chet might not have minded me shadowing them, but I wanted to show how I was growing up. After the beating Buck had received, he seemed to avoid me, but almost everybody else shunned me too. Because Chet had fought my battle, I'd become the sissy of the sandlot. Fleming used to eat with me, but I'd sent him back to the marble games when bullies began to pick on him too. No one tried to fight me, but, from a distance, boys whispered, "B-b-b-b-ud." With my back turned, someone would say, "Hey, Bud Rogers-s-s, did Ming do that to your face?" They called any dark bruise to the face a "MacLeod" as in, "That's some MacLeod under your eye, a genuine thunderhead."

Miss Wingate kept after Mr. Gladney until he relented to a degree: he'd allow Darlene or Jay to collect newspapers door-to-door. On a day when Jay went off-grounds to scrounge some reading material, and Chet was home serving another one-day suspension for fighting a townie classmate who'd mocked him, the bullies got closer to me than usual.

Some seventh-graders gathered at the spigot in the schoolhouse wall, only twenty feet from me. Two of them stood close together, blocking my view of the others. They all giggled as water sprayed out of the faucet. In a minute, the flow of water stopped with a squeak. The boys acting as shields sauntered my way. One of them pointed at a wrestling match and muttered something and the other nodded. They seemed to be ignoring me on purpose. I jacked myself upright, so wary of those two that I didn't notice the boys behind them.

One boy said, "B-b-b-b-ud," and stepped in front of me. A sky-blue globe the size of a cannonball was cupped beside his ear; I'd never seen a water balloon before. He hurled it at my groin, too fast for me to do anything but twist and raise one knee. The balloon burst against my fly and soaked me down to my shins. "He wet hisself," he yelled. "He peed his drawers!"

A second balloon, tossed by another kid, exploded against the top of my head. Burst rubber slithered under my collar, following the streams of water. I was afraid to look up, afraid to get a third one in the face. "Hurry up, Buck," a bully shouted. "He's primed for you."

Buck said, "The sissy wet his britches and cried all over his shirt." I squinted at him through rivulets of water. He held a third balloon, round and pink. Water leaked from one end where he'd pinched it closed instead of tying it off. The opposite tip was rose-colored and Buck tweaked it. "Remind you of something, peewee? Wasn't too long ago you was sucking on your mama's." He plucked the tip again. "Or do ya still?" With a single long step, he was right in front of me. Pushing the nipple-like end against my mouth, he said, "Go on, suck it."

I moved my head back, whacking the brick wall. Cold, wet rubber enveloped my face as Buck said, "No one here to s-s-s-s-save you. Taste that titty." He lifted the balloon away and spun it around. His pinched fingers hit my lips and sprung apart, opening the balloon. Water jetted into my nose and mouth. As I choked, Buck tucked the limp balloon inside my sopping shirt. He said, "What'chu gonna do about it?"

Coughing wracked me as the boys whined, "B-b-b-b-ud." I wiped my eyes and glimpsed Jay strolling across the road, coming toward the school with armfuls of newspapers. When he noticed me, he dropped everything and sprinted my way. Before he could arrive, I heard myself say to Buck, "G-g-go get the gloves."

The growing crowd parted for Buck so he could fetch the boxing mitts. He whistled as he sauntered away.

Jay arrived, gasping, and said, "Who did this?" He faced the other boys and shouted, "Who did this?"

I tried to clear my throat. "Don't m-matter. It's gonna get settled."

A couple of the bullies crowed, "That's right," and "You bet it is."

"Whoa, Private. What're you fixing to do?"

The sliver of bravery I felt a moment ago had shredded like balloon rubber. I said, "Get beat up."

The bullies smirked at me and joked, "Betcha that B-bud Rogers gets knocked into space."

"Leastwise his whole face'll match."

"Reckon he'll lose his stutter with his teeth?"

Jay turned his back on them and said, "Don't fight Buck. I'll take him on, and the rest."

Water dripped from my soggy overalls onto my feet. Even my back had gotten soaked. The wetness hid my nervous sweat as I began to imagine Buck clobbering me. I said, "Just t-tell me how you'd do it."

Buck returned with a set of gloves dangling from each hand. Mr. Gladney trailed him. Jay said, "He drags his feet a lot. I'd make 'im chase me."

A ring of boys closed in, nudging us toward the sandy lot where even more kids crowded around. I hoped that Cecilia and Miss Wingate couldn't see within the wall of boys. Buck threw a pair of the globe-fisted mitts to me. They struck my face and I bobbled them. Jay laced the heavy, worn leathers onto my hands, tying big double-knotted bows. With the boxing gloves on, I couldn't close my fingers into tight fists. It felt like weights had been strapped over my open hands.

While the seventh-graders helped Buck with his gloves, Mr. Gladney said, "You sure you boys want to do this?"

I lifted my gloves and knocked them together, trying to look like a boxer, trying to look like Chet. Immediately, the heavy leather and padding made my arms droop. A number of boys laughed around me. I said, "Yes, sir. I-I told Buck to get the gloves."

"He splashed you with a little water, right? Now you're asking him to punch you?"

"Yes, sir."

The principal shrugged and gave me a smirk. "Well, it's your funeral. You get in too much trouble for even the best guardian angel." He called, "Let's have some room here. Spread out, make the circle bigger. OK, a couple of rules: no hitting below the waist and when I say you're done, Buck, that's it. Don't kill the boy. Now go." He clapped his hands together.

With a sneer on his lips, Buck charged across the hard-packed dirt, right glove poised beside his ear. I backpedaled and put my arms together, holding them in front of my face and chest, elbows pointed down. Buck punched my exposed shoulder. It felt like getting hit with a pillow-wrapped anvil. He slammed his left glove against my arm, sending shock waves deep into my ribs.

Buck pounded me with both hands, right-left, right-left. I didn't counterpunch, but just kept moving clockwise around the ring of screaming boys while I protected my face and chest. He dogged me. His boxing gloves whumped and hissed as he landed blow after blow, each one almost knocking me off balance.

My arms trembled from the punches they absorbed and the weight of my gloves. Buck's sweat rained on me as he closed in again and hit me hard. My head jerked with every strike, but I continued to move in an unsteady retreat around the circle of noise. Jay shouted, "That's it, Bud. Make the monster move!"

Fleming yelled, "Mr. Gladney! Stop the fight!"

Another combination of punches staggered me. I fell on my backside and crab-walked into a thicket of denim-clad legs. "Get up," the boys shouted. "Look at the baby learn to crawl!" To save my dwindling strength, I let them hoist me to my feet, but they pushed me at Buck. He swung a mighty right fist that barely missed my nose. His momentum turned him around, so I backpedaled again, my arms shielding me once more.

I peeked enough to see his next charge. His blows had slowed down, but he still hit hard enough to numb my muscles. He snuck a roundhouse punch around my glove and tagged my ear. Instantly, the skin grew hot and sore. Pains shot through my neck as it tried to keep my head from snapping loose. I fell back into the crowd. Some boys pulled me up and shouted, "Try, you sissy!"

Buck grunted as his right glove glanced off mine. I thought he'd try to box my other ear, but his left fist came in very low, just above my groin. The shock of it nearly made me pee as I backpedaled again, doubled over.

Mr. Gladney shouted, "Keep your punches up, Buck. Let's finish this."

Buck towered above me, hollering, "Put up a fight."

I remained bent in half, frustrated and furious. My body ached like Papa had beaten me. The principal—who could've helped me—acted as callous as Mama. I wanted to tear Buck to pieces, but I had only enough strength to throw one punch.

From my throat came Chet's low growl. My right arm dropped in a long arc as if my shoulder had suddenly broken. The weight of the glove carried my fist down to my ankles and then it turned and sailed upward, yanking me off my feet. Like hitting a baseball right on the sweet spot of the bat, I barely felt the impact as my knuckles connected with Buck's jaw. My uppercut caught him beneath his cleft chin and lifted him three inches off the ground.

Buck's arms hung limp as he pitched backward onto the dirt. He landed hard, with the thump of a fifty-pound flour sack tossed off a roof. His head bounced twice at the end of his thick neck, his gloves rolled palms-up, and then he was still. Unseeing eyes gazed at the sky from behind their drooping lids.

The crowd roared. Some cheering boys slapped my back and shoulders until they knocked me to my knees while others imitated my uppercut. I couldn't lift my arms; they were as wobbly as Mama's tomato aspic.

A few kids gathered around Buck. "Dayum," one said and then glanced at the principal nearby. In a quieter voice, he said, "Buck-here is as dead as a door nail."

Another said, "He just got cold-cocked."

"Nope, he's graveyard dead."

"Dead to the world, bless his heart."

Mr. Gladney gave me a grudging smile and shook his head. He edged up the knees of his suit trousers and crouched beside Buck. As soon as Buck blinked and moved his jaw in a small circle, the boys around him walked away. "Dayum," the first one murmured again. "I sure thought he was deader'n a hammer."

Fleming pushed through some kids reenacting the fight and screamed to me in wordless excitement. Jay hoisted me to my feet and then lifted me into the air, yelling all the while.

I was now tall enough to see over the shouting, cheering kids. Miss Wingate stood at the edge of the crowd with a few other teachers. She clutched a lace handkerchief over her mouth and looked at me with reddened eyes. I smiled at her but my victory didn't seem to make her any happier.

Cecilia leaned on the wire fence that kept the girls on their side of the playground. She and Darlene and my sister's pretty friends all waved at me. For a moment, I felt ten feet tall.

Jay jiggled me and kept yelling. He finally set me on the ground but had to keep hold as pain rushed through my body. I managed to lift my gloves-covered fists and say, "Thanks, General. C-could you help me off with these things?"

# BOOK TWO

# CHAPTER 10

Buck shied away from me permanently after his licking, and the teasing ended. Some boys even invited me to play marbles and throw the ball in Bullpen. Every once in a while, a kid would point me out and murmur to a friend, "That's the one that whupped Buck."

As if to balance this, I'd gotten—and stayed—on Papa's bad side. Twice he caught me burning kerosene as I peered at hand-me-down newspapers late at night, running my print-blackened index finger below the words while sounding them out. "Goddammit," he said, waking Jay and Chet, "you're wasting fuel." Both times, he sent me outside in the dark to pick a whip-like gallberry branch from the piles he kept in the smokehouse. I had to lift up my nightshirt in front of my brothers, who pretended to sleep, and try not to cry out as the whipping stung my legs and backside. On Friday night, I'd chosen a switch that was too slender for his liking, so he wore out that one against me and then sent me back to the smokehouse in tears to get two more.

When Jay prodded me awake on Saturday, my first thought was that I'd slept through Papa's mule-plowing song and Jay was trying to save me from another beating. With a gasp, I rolled out of bed, threw off my grimy nightshirt, and started to pull on my field clothes. My overalls scraped the raw wounds and made me clench my teeth.

"Whoa, Bud!"

I peeked over my shirt collar. Jay stood beside the bed, and Chet—not Papa—leaned against the doorjamb. Gray daylight leaked through the open window and a steady drip of rain plopped on the sill. I rolled up my sleeves as I stammered, "Everything OK?"

Chet said, "It's too wet to do much. Papa's gonna take Mama for a drive."

I heard Mama in their bedroom saying, "—to Columbus in a while. At least let's go as far as Albany." She pronounced it "Albennie." Papa grunted a noncommittal reply.

For breakfast, we grabbed some biscuits from the pie safe and a handful of cracklings from the canister beside the stove. Mama used so much lard in her dough that the week-old bread flaked like it was fresh-baked. The pork skins smelled rancid-sweet but still tasted like chewy bacon; they'd have to do until the December hog-killing.

Lonnie called out to us from the back porch, where he sat drinking coffee from a chipped mug. Rain pattered on the tin roof and dripped off the edges in a curtain of water. When we came outside, he said, "Mr. Mance asked me and Nat to look after y'all. So let's get the work outta the way and have us a big time."

The rabbit had returned, digging under the fence we'd replanted extra-deep. It had left my trap alone. Instead, it gobbled up one of Mama's carrots and left pellets like orange- and green-tinted jelly beans.

We scampered through the soggy chores, and our parents left without a word to us. When we told late-sleeping Darlene that they had gone, she put on her yellow slicker with its matching rain hat and boots and took Mama's flimsy umbrella of wicker and cloth. She said, "If Mama asks, I'm going to visit with the Turners."

I said, "Say hey to Cecilia," and then had to endure my brothers' ribbing about my "girlfriend." With a quick wave, Darlene set off down the sandy drive. In the downpour, the yellow rubber encasing her gleamed like egg yolk.

Nat came over a while later, rainwater running off the brim of his dun-colored fedora, his clothes as soaked-through as our own. Lonnie brewed more coffee and warmed some buttermilk for me and my brothers as we dripped dry on the back porch. The men sat in ladder-back chairs sipping from steaming mugs. Lonnie had put our heated milk in bowls, and we slurped from the rims as we sprawled on the floorboards. I lay on my side; the lash-marks still smarted. Lonnie said, "Reminds me of Birmingham weather. Seems like it rained most every weekend when I was a youngun."

Chet set down his emptied bowl. "Your folks still there?"

"Mama is anyway. Daddy's doing a hard twenty on some road gang."

"W-w-what for?" I sucked my lips to pull any lingering milk into my mouth.

"He was bad to drink and fight. Got liquored up in a juke joint there in '29 and stabbed a man slap dead."

Nat rested his elbows on his knees. "You gotta get you a wife, Lonnie. You's the spitting image of your daddy. Having a family might settle you down some."

"Can't find a good woman like you done, Nat. Leona—she's the last one. Too bad she don't got a sister. We could be brother-in-laws."

"Plenty of good women out there still, Lonnie. You gotta look for 'em at church instead of them joints in Colquitt and Eldorendo. Come on with us tomorrow, you'll see."

Lonnie drained his mug and said, "I can't tell how a woman shakes it at church. Yonder in Eldorendo, I know straight-away."

"More to life than, uh, dancing and drinking, Lonnie."

"A heap more to it than working and praying, Nat."

Nat shifted in his chair but couldn't get settled. He appeared to be blushing as he looked away from us. With an elbow-nudge at Lonnie, he murmured, "Me and Leona still dance plenty. You gotta find somebody to dance with on Saturday and pray with on Sunday." Lonnie grunted and Nat continued, "Even our boy Ennis has got him a wife and two younguns. He just turned twenty, five years shy of you."

"If I recall rightly, Ennis met his lady at Kazzy's outside of Boykin. Folk don't worship God in that-there house." Lonnie stood and slapped down his mug on the chair seat. He announced, "The rain's taking a break. Who wants to take a slide?"

We jumped to our feet, crossed the sopping back yard, and lined up beside the barn in birth-order. Lonnie hefted Jay onto the steep tin roof where my oldest brother used an old rope we'd nailed up there to climb to the peak. Nat helped Chet and then me atop the barn. The rain had left the metal slick in patches, but there was enough rust for good footholds as I stood and, pulling myself hand-over-hand with the frayed rope, walked up the incline. At last, I sat with my brothers on the roof peak. I couldn't see over the surrounding trees, but at least I perched higher than some birds, including That Goddamn Rooster.

"Go!" Lonnie said, and Jay pushed off. He lay back, arms crossed over his chest, as he slid down. His clothes scraped against the metal, sending forth crackling noises. With a whoop, he sailed off the roof. Lonnie caught him, dipping Jay low as his thick arms swung with my brother's momentum. Their laughter floated up to us.

Chet and I slid down side by side. Muscles in my neck strained to keep my head just above the metal surface as I watched the quilt of dark clouds above me. The thrill of sliding blocked out most of the pain from Papa's lash. Rusty tin clawed at my overalls and the wet, smooth patches hissed beneath me as the wind tickled the soles of my feet and whistled up my denims. In the next instant, my body took flight. I fell without a sound, forgetting my war-cry. Chet shouted, "Woo-hoo!" but I couldn't see him or anything but the lumbering clouds. I seemed to fall for a long time and flinched as I thought I'd hit the ground, but it was Nat—he'd snatched me out of the air. I lay across his arms like I was his child and he was rocking me to sleep.

Nat helped me onto the roof again. When he ran around to the back of the barn, the real game began as we tried to trick Nat and Lonnie about which side we'd slide down and how many of us would go at once. No matter how hard we made it for them, we trusted that they'd catch us every time.

Jay waved to Lonnie and then tipped backward to slide headfirst down Nat's side while Chet and I dove forward with our bellies on the wet, rusty metal, our arms held straight ahead. We headed for Lonnie, who set himself to catch us, widening his stance and bending his knees. I seemed to sail much faster than before—Lonnie and the barnyard rushed up at me. Chet and I cried, "Yeeeeee!" as we rocketed into space. Lonnie managed to grab one of us under each arm and fell back into the muck of wet sand. My brother and I landed face-first as Lonnie collapsed on top of us. We lay there in a pile, laughing hard, and then wiped the grit from our faces and got up to do it again.

THE SUN BROKE THROUGH WHILE we scrounged some dinner. We planned a lazy afternoon on Spring Creek, so Nat and Lonnie went off to get their fishing poles. As we gathered our own gear from the barn, Papa's truck pulled up.

Mama slammed the passenger door and stomped toward the house, clutching her handbag and nothing more. "You think I'm made of money?" Papa shouted after her.

We retreated inside the barn again to stow the poles and buckets and hide ourselves until he went inside. Dan huffed and stomped in his pen as we shushed each other. When the horse grew very still, I knew without looking that Papa had come into the barn.

"Hey, what're you boys up to?"

Jay said, "We thought we'd go for a swim."

"No," Papa said, "I feel like working out some kinks from driving your mother to hell and gone. Grab the bat and balls and meet me on the road." He went to the house to put on his practice clothes.

Lonnie greeted him and looked in on us, pole in hand. "Your daddy going fishing too?"

While he and Nat followed the trail to Spring Creek, my brothers and I got set to chase Papa's home runs. Jay had learned to pitch hard and straight; Papa would smack line-drives at him if he didn't spot the ball perfectly. We didn't need a catcher because Papa crushed everything thrown his way. He made me and Chet play in short so his towering shots would seem to go even farther.

Papa stood where our drive intersected the dirt lane, bat cocked over his shoulder. A long-billed cap embroidered with a stylized B shaded his eyes. "Bud," he yelled, "come in a few more steps. What're you, afraid?"

Jay had a burlap sack full of old baseballs at his feet. He wound up like Papa taught him and pitched a fastball that Papa corked well over my head with a tremendous crack. As Jay threw, Papa nailed baseballs down the dirt road and out of sight, each one booming like a rifle shot. I wondered if some of them might roll to the highway.

"Papa," Jay called, using the line that always made our father happy, "you sure branded some rawhide." He shook the bag upside down to show that he was empty.

"Make sure all of 'em come back to the corral," Papa replied. He whipped his bat around a few times, and we grabbed our bags and went on what Chet called "the Easter egg hunt."

I found two almost side-by-side near Uncle Stan's place. He knelt low to repair a length of fencing when I approached. Since the swimming lesson, I wasn't so afraid of him and he looked at me with more ease. I stuttered, "Sir, did you see any baseballs?"

"Baseballs? From those sounds I heard, I thought Mance was taking target practice."

"B-B-Batting practice, sir."

"Yeah, I heard a few stars fall over yonder, Roger." He pointed farther down the road. I must've cocked my head at the sound of my real name because he said, "You don't mind me calling you Roger, do you?"

"No, sir."

"It's a good name. Lotsa folks are called Bud, but there's only one Roger I know of." I apologized about Papa batting in his direction, and he said, "Maybe I got it coming." He glanced back at the house where Aunt Arzula had begun singing to herself with the musicality of a catfight. "Be nice to have a rest. Tell your daddy to aim better."

My brothers wandered in the fields along either side of the road, stooping every so often to bag a baseball. Jay mostly used his left arm, nursing the right so he could manage more pitches. He shouted, "Count off! I got five."

Chet yelled from the woods, "Seven here, after I fetch one out of this tree."

"I got four so far." There were twenty in all so I set off in search of the ones Uncle Stan had pointed out. The road followed gentle rises and dips as I searched, coming up with two more. I walked halfway to Nat's house, going past the distance record Papa had set previously. Surely the others couldn't have flown so far. I checked the high weeds but found nothing.

Chet waved his sack and shouted to me. I shrugged, lifting my hands in the air, and plodded onward. Over the next slope, I stopped and backpedaled a few steps when I saw the dead body.

A boy lay near a ditch along the side of the road, arms akimbo, legs splayed. A straw hat lay crushed behind his head. He was dressed in overalls and a shirt with rolled sleeves. I guessed that the baseball beside him had broken his head. Morbid curiosity was stronger than my urge to scream for help. I staggered closer and saw that Papa's record homer had killed the boy I met in the woods. The one who'd called himself Ry Shepherd. I shuffled forward as I recalled my encounter with him, his odd way of speaking and a face as memorable as my own.

Ry's expression looked just as I'd remembered him: a slight frown of concentration. His narrow eyes stared at the sky. What had he been studying on when the ball pounded him? I had no doubt he died looking at something of interest or "collecting some specimens," whatever that meant. My throat tightened and eyes burned, surprising me. I hadn't realized that I'd liked the boy.

I thought that the ball would've smashed in his forehead or left some kind of bloody bruise. Maybe it hit square on the crown of his hat. Did he scream or wasn't there time? He stared unblinking at the sky. Maybe he saw the ball streak toward him like a shooting star and died of fright.

As I drew close, Ry sat upright. "You know," he said in that annoying, squeaky voice, "that could've hurt somebody."

I sank to my knees as my heart throttled down and my weight seemed to triple. I said, "I-I-I oughta kill you."

"Twice in one day?" He resettled the straw hat on his head.

"I didn't h-hit that ball. My papa did."

"He must be very strong."

I rubbed my backside and said, "He is."

"Granny wouldn't tell me how to find your house, so I had to ask around. She told me not to go near your father." He flipped the baseball to me. "Now I know why."

"She might frown on b-b-bootlegging."

"He's a bootlegger? Can he show me how to make a still?"

"Bud," Chet yelled, trotting down the road with Jay, their burlap bags swinging, "can't you hear Papa cussing? We're taking too long."

"Get up, Ry." I stood and used my body to shield him from my brothers' view. I worried that they would remark on his odd-looking face as I had. From the corner of my mouth, I murmured, "Keep quiet. I'll talk to 'em f-first."

"Why?"

"Shut up." I called out to my brothers, "Hey, I got somebody for you t-to meet."

Jay stopped a few feet away from me and said, "Who's that peeking around your arm?"

I jabbed my elbow behind me, but met only air as Ry dodged. I stammered, "I wanna tell y'all about him first. Now, he can't help how he looks, just like me. He's half-Janaplease."

"Japanese," Ry said.

"Shut up." I poked at him but missed again.

Chet frowned and tried to look past me. "Bud, how'd you come to be half-Janaplease?"

"Japanese."

"Shut up." Another jab missed. I said to Chet, "I ain't half-anything. I'm saying not to make fun of him."

Chet snatched the sack from my hand and peered inside, counting. He told Jay that my additions made twenty.

Jay grinned at me and said, "Well if you don't never let us see him, we won't know to make fun of him or not."

"You're not allowed. That's what I'm saying."

"OK, OK, we won't." Jay put up his hands, surrendering. "I swear on the red fannies we're all gonna get from Papa any time now, I won't make fun. And ol Chet-here won't neither."

After Chet gave me a few exaggerated nods, I said, "All right. Here he is." I stepped aside and watched my brothers look him over.

Jay said, "You got a name?"

I said, "He's called Ry."

Chet feinted at me with the bulging bag. "You gonna do all his talking?"

Ry introduced himself and said, "Can I see your father's still?"

"We gotta get back right quick," Jay said, "or Papa'll have us all seeing stars. Come on with us, Ry. Papa don't have a still but I'm building one piece-by-piece in the woods." Jay led us toward home.

On the way, Chet said, "Ry, Bud told us about your fighting moves."

"Judo? My daddy taught me. Do you want to learn?"

"Yeah, that'd be neat." He telegraphed a punch at Ry's shoulder, but the boy twisted away in time. Chet said, "Funny, Bud ain't learned to dodge that yet."

"I couldn't teach Bud anything. I kept throwing him but he wouldn't learn."

I stuffed my hands in my pockets and said, "Hey, I learned a little." They weren't paying attention. I kept trying to interrupt, but Jay was going on about some other inventions and Chet wanted to know more about judo. I was glad they liked Ry, but I wished they would share.

We approached Uncle Stan's, where Mama leaned against a porch post in the shade, sipping from a jelly-jar of water. She still wore her favorite going-to-town dress and talked while Uncle Stan listened. He kept his hands buried in his pockets and rocked from heel to toe. Aunt Arzula scuffed onto the porch in her too-big shoes and handed him a full glass before returning indoors. He skimmed off the surface with a quick flick of his finger that must've sprayed Mama. She licked the back of her hand.

Uncle Stan took a big drink and kept on swallowing, tipping his head way back. He appeared to have drained the glass but kept it against his mouth, the glass and his big, curving hand blocking his face. Maybe he hoped that she would go away by the time he lowered his shield.

She murmured something that tilted his head forward in a laugh that quickly became a cough. He glanced our way and pointed us out to Mama. When she faced us, Uncle Stan dragged a sleeve across his mouth and then his sweating forehead. Mama said, "Where in hell have you three—" She cleared her throat and said, "Who's your friend?"

I said, "He's c-called Ry Shepherd."

"Pleased to know you, Ry. You in Bud's class?"

"No," I said, "he's vi-visiting from Texas. Ry's half-Jap-an-ese." I made sure I got it right. "From Japan, on his mother's side." Ry frowned at me, his mouth closing.

"Oh my stars. I make a Japanese fruitcake every December; it takes a pound of coconut. Maybe you can tell me your mother's secrets."

"His mother's d-dead," I said, proud that I'd remembered so much about him.

"Bud, we say 'passed on.' I'm so sorry, Ry. Bless your heart—"

Papa shouted, "Goddamn lollygaggers." He dragged his bat behind him like a plowshare, the only plowing he ever did. "I mighta known y'all couldn't stay on task. Reva, I sent you to fetch these boys and now I gotta round up every one of you—" He pointed the bat toward my uncle. "What'chu drinking there, Stan?"

Uncle Stan's mouth barely moved. "It's water, Mance."

"Don't spoil your thirst now. Save it up for tonight."

Uncle Stan looked at his boots. Mama set her glass on the porch rail and clapped her hands. "All right, you boys, come on back to the house. Ry, you best go home."

Ry said, "Yes, ma'am," and backed away from me and my brothers. After Jay whispered, "Come back later," Ry nodded and set off down the road.

Papa flipped the bat around, catching the barrel, offered it up to my uncle. He asked, "Wanna take a swing, Stan?"

"No thanks."

Mama stepped off the porch. "I was just saying how you and Stan oughta do more together. He and Arzula's right down the road and you both like to—"

"We're busy men, no time to pal around. Anyway, Stan's got plans come a Saturday night, don't you?" My uncle continued to look down. Papa said, "Now y'all get your asses back home before I put this bat to good use."

"You talking about my ass too, dear?" Mama laced her fingers behind her.

"Especially yours. Come on, game's over." He marched back up the dirt road.

Mama strode after him. Her backside seemed to waggle a little more than usual. I glanced over at Uncle Stan, but he was no longer there. The man had slipped inside his dark house and disappeared.

# CHAPTER 11

OUR PARENTS' USUAL SHOUTING MATCH AT SUPPER BECAME A food fight. Then Papa overturned the kitchen table before any of us had a chance to eat. Before driving off, he shouted at Mama, "I've had enough of you." She slammed their bedroom door even louder than Darlene had banged her own.

My brothers slouched on the porch, stomachs growling, while I lit the now-dented kerosene lamp and, sitting in the parlor, practiced reading aloud with a crumpled newspaper. Darlene's door creaked open. In a voice strained by her latest crying jag, she said, "Mama, I need you."

"What is it, honey?" Mama crossed into Darlene's room and closed the door. Their voices slipped through the ill-fitting wall planks that I sat against. I rested my head on the rough-cut boards and tried to follow their conversation while reciting from the paper, so they wouldn't know I was snooping.

As I quietly droned, substituting "something-something-something" for all the words I couldn't read, Darlene said, "What sort of boys did you sit up with when you were young?"

"Oh my stars, when did I get old?"

"You know what I mean."

Mama said, "Well, I liked the ones that made me feel good: told me how pretty I was and all that sweet talk. I liked the good-looking boys a lot; I was a real somebody when we'd stroll through town. Folks would point us out and watch us go by."

"So how'd you wind up with Papa?"

"He did some of that, told me once I was a princess straight out of a storybook. He wasn't Clark Gable or Ronald Colman but he had his charms. You shoulda seen him on a ball field." Darlene's bed creaked as Mama eased onto it. "He's got scars all up and down his legs from getting spiked at second base." I envisioned her touching spots on Darlene's shins and knees to show her where the baseball cleats had torn into Papa as she said, "Here and here and even higher." She giggled. "But he gave as good as he got. And after some games, I'd wait for him in the bleachers while, right under my feet, he beat the dogshi—the stuffing—outta them roughnecks and learned 'em a lesson."

"You weren't afraid of him?"

"Maybe a little, but it made being with him a thrill. You never knew what was gonna happen."

"Like now."

"Oh we fought a lot, but we made up faster. We even threw food at each other, but he didn't storm off back then. We always felt closer after a tussle."

"So, what happened?"

I forgot to keep reciting, so I read aloud, "And the something-something man held up th-three banks and four ar-mor-ed cars."

Mama was answering Darlene, ending with, "...will come around—things always do. Why the questions?"

"No reason."

"You worried about sitting up with boys?"

"No'm."

"You need some more rags? I don't want you spotting that new dress of yours."

"Maybe twice what you gave me before." She sniffed a few times. "A townie said I smelled like the butcher and some other boys laughed—I hate 'em!"

"They're not all bad, honey. You got nuthin to be skeered of; just pick out boys that'll make you feel good."

Darlene cleared her throat and said, "How do you know which one?"

"Why only one?"

"I thought—"

Mama lowered her voice, as if someone might overhear. I had to turn my ear to the wall, still murmuring nonsense, as she said, "No, sweetheart, it ain't that way."

"You had to choose sometime, right? You had to pick Papa."

"Eventually, once I saw that he'd make something of himself with the bootleg business. It wasn't until after we jumped the broom that he started hoarding his money." When Darlene began to speak again, Mama cut her off. "A girl's gotta look after her own self. If your papa got hit by a train tonight, then where'd I be? No husband, no money coming in. Hell, he won't tell me where he keeps the money he's got. Where would that leave me?"

"And me. And Jay and—"

"Right, right. So you gotta keep your eyes open. You find somebody that'll make you feel like a princess and has good prospects, but always know where the next one is. Just in case." The bed frame creaked again as Mama stood up. She said, "Don't you worry 'bout courting. It's as easy as falling out of a boat."

"Into the water?" Darlene sounded mortified.

"As easy as that. You get used to it real fast and, if you pick like I told you, you'll like it so much you won't wanna stop. Me, I never minded getting wet."

"QUIT IT," CHET SAID, AND nudged me with his toe every time my stomach rumbled. After Mama returned to her room, I'd practiced a little more but couldn't focus on the words, so I joined my brothers on the porch. I wanted to tell them about what I'd overheard, but had to wait until we were far from the house. We slouched in silence as the bone-white moon rose higher.

Sport and Dixie came alert at the same moment. They stood and hurried to the porch steps, peering out into the night with their ears up. Instead of growling, they displayed the same keen interest as when the Woman had appeared on the lane that bordered our yard.

In a few minutes, Ry came up the dirt road, whistling in the dark. I knew it had to be Ry because even the tune he chose, a complex melody with dozens of notes, was far different from anything I'd ever heard. Jay and Chet did their whippoorwill impressions and I cooed like a mourning dove. Ry whistled his tune louder and we responded until Mama screamed, "Aye God, I'll fry the next bird I hear."

Even Ry stopped his music-making. He climbed the hog-wire fence, walked across the sand that I'd raked earlier, and greeted us all by name in a squeaky whisper. Just like Nat, he wore his hat at night, the brim down low over his black hair. Crouching so the dogs could smell him all over and lick his face, he asked, "Where's the still?"

Jay said, "I've got some parts buried in the woods."

"Y'all look at that," Chet said, "and I'm gonna catch some supper. I'm starved."

I said, "Ry, do you fish?"

"Yes, I do. My daddy—"

"Yeah, I f-figured he did."

Jay and Chet retrieved our gear from the barn. Along with two buckets for collecting our catches, Jay had slung a couple of gill nets across his shoulders; rusty railroad spikes dangled and clanked from the bottom of the linen mesh, nearly scraping the tops of his feet. Chet brought a pitted hatchet and a burlap Croker sack that bulged at the bottom; its contents clicked like wooden beads.

I took the tin buckets and gestured at Chet's hatchet, joking, "We can bring Sport and go p-possum hunting too."

Ry asked what I meant. Jay explained that you hunt possum by treeing one with a dog, chopping down the tree, and capturing the critter in a sack. "Then you gotta pen the fella in a chicken coop and spend a week feeding it corn to clean out its insides. They'll gobble up the nastiest stuff in the woods; you don't wanna eat one straight outta the tree."

Chet added, "Sport's a great possum dog. Papa fed 'im gunpowder when Sport was a pup, so he ain't a-feared of nuthin."

Sometimes I wished that Papa had given me the same gunpowder-laced biscuits.

Along the way to a slough near Spring Creek, Ry tried guessing what Chet had in his sack: wooden buttons, chinaberries, pecans. Jay and I walked behind them. I sidled close to Jay along the narrow path bordered by trees and huge shrubs. Racket from crickets and cicadas seemed to press down, completing the sensation that we walked within a low-ceilinged tunnel. The only light seemed to come from a swirl of lightning bugs. I stuttered to Jay, "What would we do if Papa got killed?"

"Chet says he's too mean to die." The swaying railroad spikes clinked together as he walked, with the steadiness of a blacksmith hammering horseshoes.

"But what if a train h-h-hit him tonight or something?"

Jay said, "Why're you saying this stuff?"

"I just wondered." A leafy branch that Chet pushed away snapped back and swiped across my face. My hands were full with the bucket handles, so I was defenseless. In the darkness, the surprise of being hit shocked me more than the actual slap.

Jay made "hmm" sounds for a minute. "I reckon we'd all go live at the old home place with Grandma."

"And then Mama would marry again? And we'd l-live with her and Uncle Roscoe?"

"Uncle Roscoe? He's married to Aunt Lizzie. She couldn't marry him too."

I thought that she still might try, but I said, "With somebody else then."

"Probly, if she gets lonesome."

When Ry asked who we were talking about, Chet said, "Nobody. Now you got one more guess coming to you about what's in this-here sack."

"Then what?"

"Then you'll shut up. You're bringing my head to a point and I'm gonna have to slug you."

Ry eased a few steps away from him, walking sideways in the tight space with his back against a row of shrubs and trees as constant as a picket fence. He asked Jay, "Why do all of you want to hit me?"

"I don't wanna hit you," Jay said.

Ry slowed his steps until he walked alongside my oldest brother, which forced me to the back of the line. I said, "I don't w-wanna hit you no more," but he wouldn't walk with me. For the rest of the journey, I brought up the rear.

The dirt underfoot turned to bog, too watery to be called land and too dirty to cup a fistful of pure water. Overalls rolled to my knees, I squished my toes in the gritty bottom of the swamp, more like wet cinders than mud. The slough where Chet led us felt cool and calm when I dipped my hand in. It was almost as still as the big galvanized tub of well-water in which each of us bathed on Sunday mornings in the kitchen. The slough was certainly cleaner than the bathwater left to me after the five others washed themselves.

Chet and Jay stripped naked and waded in, each with a gill net, traipsing through chest-deep water about fifty feet apart. They secured their nets to cypress knees and tree stumps along both banks and pushed the railroad spikes into the sandy bottom to hold the net firm. The topmost thread of linen flashed white in the moonlight as it ran level across the water surface.

Jay called, "Bud, mash up them walnuts."

On a sandbar, I took the blunt end of the hatchet and began walloping the closed burlap poke. The un-ripened nuts softened in their cracked shells and then turned to pulp with successive blows. Ry crouched beside me and said, "Walnuts?"

"You was close, g-guessing pecans." I thudded the bag a few more times as Jay and Chet laughed and slapped water at each other. "These-here are green walnuts."

"How do they help you catch fish?"

I stammered, "There's something about mashing 'em up. You slosh the sack around in the water between them nets and every fish gets poisoned. They come up for air and you scoop 'em out. Some try to escape and get caught in the nets."

"That's not nice."

"Why not?"

"Are you going to eat 'every fish'? The minnows too? What about the fish downstream?"

I whacked the bag a couple more times and carried it to the embankment, saying, "That's why we d-do this in still water." Ry tossed some pine straw into the slough; I could barely make out the coppery stems as they slowly floated toward Jay's net. I said, "They was splashing. No t-telling how that's stirred up the slough."

My brothers had stopped playing and now stared at us, the water level a few inches higher across Chet's bare chest than Jay's. Ry tossed in more pine straw and we all watched it spin and float toward Jay's net. Ry said, "Where does this water go?"

Jay said, "Spring Creek."

"The big one?" When Chet said, "Yeah, so?" Ry continued, "So-o-o…how many fish did you plan to eat?" The straw hat shadowed his face, but I could see his small chin thrust out.

Chet stamped through the water, splashing the surface with both arms. "Now lookee here, kid. I plan to eat every durn fish that y'all don't. Gimme that." He mounted the sandbar, ripped the Croker sack from my grip, and jumped back into the slough.

Ry ran along the shore, past where Jay had secured his net, and hopped in the water fully clothed. He waded out until only his head and hat were visible. "If you dunk that bag of poison," he called, "I'm going to drink and drink. What'll happen to me?" He opened his mouth wide, like a gator, as if he planned to take a bite out of the slough, and sunk until his chin rested on the surface.

Chet shouted, "You'll get a goozle full of water, that's all. There's no current, doggone it."

When Chet began to lower the bag, I quickly stripped and joined Ry downstream, shivering in the cold water. Like him, I opened wide. I didn't know if I'd really drink, since that seemed close to drowning, but I thought he was right; he needed somebody on his side. It was the first time I'd ever gone against my brothers. I hoped it would be the last.

Jay waded over and put his hands on Chet's shoulders, murmuring. Their foreheads almost touched.

"Fine!" Chet said. He stepped back from Jay and hurled the poke onto the shore.

Jay splashed his hands on the surface while he approached his gill net, trying to herd fish that way. Chet made a bigger ruckus marching to the net he'd strung up. He submerged and then surfaced a minute later with a large bream, twice the size of his hand. While small fish could maneuver through the linen mesh, large fish would get their heads caught and, when they tried to back out, they would ensnare their gills in the fine threads.

I hurried to shore and met Chet with a bucket. "Some buddy you got yourself," he said and dropped the flopping fish into the tin pail. When it tried to jump out, Chet punched the bream and it lay still in the bottom. He looked at his fist and then at me.

Before Chet could clobber me, I ran to Jay's side with the other bucket. He emerged with a three-pound bass. After depositing it, Jay waved at Ry. "Come on out, fish-lover. We caught a little supper after all."

Ry came ashore. Water drained from his clothes as he walked stiff-legged in his sopping overalls to where Jay and I got dressed. Ry looked into the bucket and said to my brother, "I hope you're not mad at me."

"'Course not." Jay pushed some water from his body and climbed into his clothes. "You're right—we shoulda picked a slough that wasn't running a bit. I'm glad Bud stuck up for you."

After Chet dressed, he tramped toward us. "Well I hope you're happy, Mr. Japan. We got only two fish to divide."

Ry put up his hands and stepped away. "I ate supper already. That's more for you."

Chet slammed down his bucket. It turned over and the fish slid out but was either stunned or dead. "You're durn right that's all ours. We could've ate real good if you hadn't butted in."

"Why didn't you poison the water, Chet?"

"Shut up!" He ran at the boy, his fist drawn back.

Ry dropped to one knee. The punch sailed over his shoulder and he seized my brother's overall bib and fly and flipped Chet onto his back. It looked so predictable when I watched it happening to someone else.

Chet lay as still as his bream and stared just as wide-eyed. "Bud," he said, "this what happened to you?" When I said yes, he worked his jaw back and forth and stared at the bright moon. Finally, he said, "Ry Shepherd, if you show me how to do that, I swear I'll never try to hit you again."

Chet ate his bream and Jay split his bass with me. Ry sat by the fire, his clothes steaming, and told us about San Antonio: crisscrossing railroad lines and broad highways, old tile-roofed stucco buildings and what he called the first "skyscraper" in Texas, which towered hundreds of feet above everything else. He told us about the university where his father taught, but he might as well have been describing a city on the moon. Even Jay was distracted, staring off into the swamp.

Chet finally said, "Don't y'all have woods and criks and haints and stuff?"

"Away from the city. There's no such thing as ghosts though. They're not scientific."

Jay said, "What's science got to do with a haint? Haints don't give a flip about science. There're regular folks around here that would stymie science to bafflement."

I almost offered up Papa and Mama as examples. Instead, I said, "Like this wi-witch we got, Wanda Washburn. That Wanda has magic powers. She can heal wounds and ca-cast a double-whammy. All the Negroes are scared of her." Ry sighed loudly as I continued to stammer quietly in the firelight: "There's this colored man called Robert Bryson. He has a fine Packard car—"

"It's a Pierce-Arrow," Jay said. "I've seen it."

"A Pierce-Arrow then. He's right proud of it. Won't let hardly nobody ride in it. 'Bout ten years ago, he's zipping along on a f-f-fiery hot day, and he ups and passes Wanda Washburn, leaving her in the dust. Well, she sends word that Robert wouldn't be able to swallow another drink, not water, not nuthin." I shivered to add drama. "Soon enough, he's on the lift—"

Ry said, "What's that?"

"That means he takes to his b-bed. He's wasting away. Every time he tries to sip something, it won't go down—"

"Just lays in his mouth," Chet said, "like blood."

I flashed some anger at being interrupted again. "Anyway—with his life near over, he sends word to Miz Wanda that he's sorry for passing her b-by, that he'll never do it again."

"I'll bet she lifted the spell." Ry sounded bored.

"Well, yeah, right…anyway, she sends our friend Nat's boy to tell Robert that he could swallow again. Now he stops by her p-place every day in case she wants a ride."

"Golly, that's really scary," Ry said, suddenly sucking in his cheeks like he was shriveling up.

Jay had continued to stare into the dark. Now he pointed his stick at the swamp. "OK, how 'bout a haint? There's one for you. Tell about what's so and what's not to the Dutchman."

I shivered for real as I peered deep into the gloom. A faint yellow glow the size of an orange drifted in our direction, weaving among the twisted oaks and giant cedars. Jay whispered, "They say that back fifty years ago, this old Dutch fella named Jan Kleinsomething-or-other got hisself killed nearby and was dumped into a well. His spirit haunts these-here woods—he glows like a big ball of light."

Ry murmured, "Is this a joke?" He edged closer to the swamp, standing beneath thick arms of Spanish moss.

"No joke," Jay said. "If he touches you, you'll die."

The ball of light emerged in a distant clearing, now looking more teardrop-shaped. It faintly illuminated the face of an old Negro woman. Chet said, "Speak of the devil; it's Wanda." He looked at Jay with a silent plea, his bare feet twitching like an impatient horse's hooves.

Jay grinned. "Private MacLeod, if you catch ol Wanda unawares, give 'er a mighty good scare." He returned a salute, and

Chet dashed into the swamp with barely a splash. He was soon out of sight. Jay said, "Ry, let's see if we can give Chet another tumble. Maybe get Wanda in the bargain."

"Aren't you afraid of sneaking up on a witch?"

"She'd never put a spell on white folks. That wouldn't do." He led us into the marshland. As Jay took us in a wide circle around Wanda—and probably Chet—the swamp water ebbed and soon we walked on solid ground. Spanish moss reached down from every limb. He whispered, "Sneaking up on anybody, even a old colored lady, is kinda fun, right?"

"I guess," Ry said. "I wish it was the Dutchman, though."

I'd done well to creep quietly until, like a fish in our gill net, my face pressed against a huge spider web. Silken strands raked my cheeks and forehead, and darting legs scrambled down my neck. I spit and did a little jig as I brushed my face and knocked the spider off my back.

Far to our left, Wanda yelled, "What's that, a three-legged mule on a tin floor? Don't even think 'bout scaring me. Just step out and account for yourself."

Jay said in my ear, "She must've heard Chet. Maybe we can get somebody yet." Jay led us closer to the glow from Wanda's torch, which she called her "flambeau." She appeared to be standing in place; the light didn't move anymore.

As we approached the clearing, my steps got shorter and lighter. I didn't breathe. We crept behind a six-foot-thick cedar trunk. I peered out, ready to duck back as soon as I saw her, but she wasn't there. Her flambeau, made from a long shaft of heart-pine, was wedged in an oak knothole. The noiseless flame curled and flickered in the air. I didn't see Wanda or Chet. When I looked at the woods around me, I couldn't see any details—the torch had ruined my night-vision.

Jay said, "I got a bad feeling about this. Let's run for the clearing."

Ry and I scurried after him. Ten feet from the open space, as we passed another huge cedar, a brown claw ripped across Jay's face and the creature snarled. Jay screamed, covering his head.

While I hollered, Ry snatched the claw and the sleeve-covered arm attached to it and hurled Chet into the clearing. Jay crawled on all fours, now laughing as he collapsed beside Chet, who lay on his back looking dazed again.

"Hey," Wanda said beside my ear. Screaming, I scampered under the torch, the only bright spot. Heat from the burning pine oil above my head soothed me as I shook. Even Ry looked jittery as he shuffled into view alongside Wanda. The old woman had a cotton satchel slung across her chest that she once said her mother had worn as a slave in Louisiana. Wanda would fill the bag with roots, herbs, and even the droppings of certain critters.

She reached into the satchel and pulled out a buckeye nut, the very best good-luck charm. My brothers and I had spent many a day looking for buckeye trees. A pocketful of buckeyes would make everyone on the playground treat a boy like a millionaire. In the firelight, the nut looked like a large chocolate-brown gumdrop with an egg-shape on one side lighter than the rest of the shell. Within the oval was another dark patch surrounding a cream-colored center; this "eye" stared at me as Wanda displayed it between her fingertips.

"Nice to see Chet get his comeuppance," Wanda said and gave Ry the nut. "Why are you sneaking around with the MacLeod boys?"

"They're my friends." He examined the buckeye, saying, "Does this poison fish too?"

"Mercy no. That buckeye's like a rabbit's foot."

Ry thanked her and dropped the buckeye into the pocket of his overalls. Which would bring better luck, I wondered, a buckeye or the foot of the rabbit that kept snacking on Mama's garden? I decided that I'd like to have both.

Jay and Chet brushed off their bottoms, and Wanda said, "Let's get'chu home. Your father's gonna need y'all tonight." Overruling all objections, she took us back the way we'd come, her flambeau lighting our way. The torch burned like an oil lamp, steady and soundless. Tree trunks shone yellow in the firelight and the forest floor became a carpet of orange.

I asked Ry to show me the buckeye. He handed it over, whispering, "You can keep it."

"Don't you w-want it?" It was slick from his still-damp overalls and felt as light as a wish. On the underside was a depression that just fit the pad of my thumb.

"I don't believe in charms or luck."

I rolled the nut between my palms as if rounding a mud ball and put it deep into my pocket before he could ask for it back. As we gathered our gear at the slough and threw sand on the smoldering fire, Jay said, "Does Papa really need us?"

"Give him a shout," Wanda said. "Later, you might have to twist his arm. Be sure to stop by your Uncle Stan's place."

# CHAPTER 12

MY BROTHERS TOLD RY GOODNIGHT AND HEADED FOR THE BARN to put up our gear. I hesitated, not sure whether to follow them or heed Wanda's advice immediately.

Ry asked, "Do you believe what Wanda said about your father needing you?"

"Why not?" I made up my mind and led him across the yard.

"Telling the future is like ghosts and charms. Those things aren't real."

"But I've seen a haint c-called the Woman and—"

"You thought you did."

"You think you're so smart, Ry."

"No, I really don't know much—yet."

We climbed the hog-wire fence bordering the road. I quick-stepped ahead of him and blocked his way. With his hat pulled down, I couldn't see his expression; I didn't know if he was merely egging me on. I raised my voice, saying, "Then why do you keep t-telling me what's so and what's not?"

"Are you going to try to punch me again?"

"I swannee, you're the m-most—" I snatched the buckeye from my pocket and hit him in the chest with it. He didn't even flinch when the nut bounced off his overall bib. "You keep it—I hate you!"

"I still like you. You're crazy, but I like you." He picked up the buckeye lying at his feet, drew his arm back and heaved it. Ry threw like a girl, but still hurled the nut so far that I couldn't hear where it landed in the dark. I must've gasped at losing my treasure because he said, "Don't worry, it's not gone." He opened his hand. The buckeye nestled in the middle of his palm. He said, "Take it. You know you want it."

"Stick it." I spun around and stomped down the road. Ry walked behind me. As we approached Uncle Stan's ramshackle house, headlights slanted toward us from Hardscrabble Road. My urge to follow Wanda's advice vanished; I imagined how Papa would laugh in my face and then beat me when I said I was there to help him. I scrambled into a ditch filled with tall grass and brittle Queen Anne's lace.

Ry climbed down beside me. He whispered, "Who are we hiding from?"

"My papa—that's his truck h-heading our way. You're right about Wanda. Let's let 'im be." I peeked over the berm and ducked down as his tires chewed up the rippling ground and headlights sliced over me.

With a squeal of brakes, he stopped his truck a few yards from our hiding place. The hinges on the driver door creaked open and his boots hit the ground. "Stan!" His shout made me flinch. "Get your ass out here and tell me something."

Uncle Stan's voice slurred from inside the house. I had to strain to hear him over the truck engine. "Clear off, Mance. Sumbitch bastard comin in my yard…I'll shoot you. Don't think I won't." I heard sobbing from Aunt Arzula.

"You're too drunk to piss straight, let alone shoot," Papa hollered. "Your shotgun probably looks as wavy to you as your pecker right now." The truck door slammed, and he continued, "What were you and Reva talking about?"

"I don't talk to her."

Papa's voice became playful. "Gee, why don't you, Stan? She's a fast, good-looking woman. Ready for anything. Why don't you like my wife, Stan?"

"Hey, Mance, I do like…I mean, shit, I—"

"So, Goddammit, what were y'all talking about?"

I eased out of the ditch and crept behind the rear tire. From there, I rose up on my toes and peered over the side of the truck bed as Ry joined me. The engine chugged, and cool, dusty metal vibrated against my fingers. Papa took a few steps toward the front porch and looked at the black rectangle of the doorway, hands on hips.

Uncle Stan's voice echoed a little, like he was deep within his house, hiding in the dark. "Your boys," he said. "She was lookin for your boys."

"What else was she looking for, Stan?"

"That's all. I swear it. Now get gone!"

"Tell me about my boys, Stan. What'd Reva say about 'em?"

"Leave me alone, damn you." His voice cracked. "I don't talk to her."

"Since when, Stan?"

"A long time. Go'way!"

Papa folded his arms and relaxed his stance, settling in like he could taunt my drunken uncle all night. He called, "Since your baby died?"

"Shut your mouth about her."

"I never seen Eliza Jean. Liza, Liza, Liza. Was she a pretty little peach?"

"Stop!" Both my uncle and my aunt were crying now. Uncle Stan wept and mumbled what sounded like, "'Eliza Jean, poor baby." He sobbed a little longer and then shouted out, "Seven, eight years back. I quit dealin with Arzula's whole damn family then. All them Elrods."

"Reva too?"

"She's the one told me." His voice screeched like he was pulling a long knife from his gut. "Told me I had to stay away. From the Elrod place and everybody."

Papa unfolded his arms and his right elbow jabbed outward like he was scratching his stomach. I realized that he was drawing his Colt revolver. He aimed the gun at the doorway; moonlight slid like oil across the blue-black metal. Papa thumbed back the hammer and said, "Stan, I think you're trying to put something besides words into Reva's pretty mouth."

"You sumbitch—" Uncle Stan ran toward the doorway, his white shirt like the blazing target on a buck. His shotgun drifted downward as he stumbled on a pan Aunt Arzula had left on the floor. Both barrels fired, blowing a giant hole in the porch. His next step landed in that gap, and his leg disappeared beneath the floorboards. Uncle Stan pitched forward onto his face while his shotgun clattered down the steps. Black suspenders crossed his back in a big X. He lay still, as if Papa had shot him dead.

Aunt Arzula shrieked my uncle's name and then hollered, "Mance, don't!" Papa mounted the stairs, pointing his Colt. He knelt beside the dazed man. His face was in shadows, but I could imagine what I'd seen too often: his cold expression and small, glassy eyes. He poked the barrel of the revolver behind Uncle Stan's ear.

A full, body-shaking cry took hold of me. I banged on the truck panel and screamed, "Papa, no!"

He sprang to his feet and aimed toward me but then lowered his gun. "Bud? Goddammit, what the hell are you doing there?"

I pawed away the tears and moaned, "Don't, Papa. D-don't do it. Please."

"He tried to shoot me. You want your papa's head blowed off? You want me dead?"

"I don't want anybody dead."

"What's he to you, boy? Just another Goddamn drunk. Another sonofabitch taking up with your mama."

"He wasn't. They was j-j-just talking." I pictured the pistol firing and the smoke licking the barrel and Uncle Stan's head splitting like a melon.

"Really, Mr. MacLeod," Ry shouted. "That's all they were doing." He crossed in front of the truck where the yellow-white glare of the headlights splashed him. The boy looked tiny compared to Papa, who stood and gestured down at him with his gun.

"Who the hell are you?"

"Ry Shepherd, sir. We met this afternoon. I'm Bud's friend. And Jay's and Chet's."

"What're you doing here?"

"Bud was walking me home, sir."

Uncle Stan groaned and Papa kicked the side of his head. Aunt Arzula cried out, "Don't kill him, Mance."

"Who's gonna miss 'im," Papa shouted back. "Or a stone-crazy twat. Or even two little boys?" He still had the hammer cocked as he pointed the Colt at each of us in turn. "Who's gonna miss any of y'all?"

Ry said, "Would you shoot a girl, Mr. MacLeod? A little girl?"

"Ain't no girls here, you—"

My friend curled his fingers over the front brim of his hat and drew it away. His other hand undid bobby pins and eased a long, coiled braid of black hair off the top of his head and over a shoulder. Ry glanced at me, face lit up by the headlamps, all delicate cheekbones and slender brows and liquid eyes. Now so clearly a girl. She said in that high, squeaky voice that suddenly sounded feminine to my ears, "My real name is Rienzi, Mr. MacLeod. If you still don't believe me, I'll prove I'm not a boy." She hooked her thumb under one of the straps that held up her overalls.

"Quit it. That's enough." Papa stared at her, blinking hard as if waking from a dream. Whatever rage had overtaken him seemed to retreat as he took a deep breath. His thumb eased down the hammer of his Colt, and a smirk thawed his tone of voice. "Bud's kinda young to have a girlfriend."

"We're just friends, sir. But I'd like to know him and his family better."

"Sure, sure. Stop by anytime." He tucked the gun into his waistband and peered at Rienzi. "You ain't from around here."

Sidling around the rumbling truck, I said, "He's—she's—half-Japanese."

"Like the fruitcake, huh?" He glanced inside the house and yelled, "Quit blubbering, Arzula. Stan's not worth wasting a bullet on." He gave my uncle a half-hearted kick and said to Rienzi, "Well, climb aboard, sweetie. We'll take you home."

* * *

Rienzi sat between us as Papa turned the truck around and drove us toward the highway. She told him where her grandparents lived, about five miles away, and we rode in silence. The truck continued to send vibrations through my body, and the poorly maintained roads jostled us quite a bit, but I blamed my shaking on Rienzi. Sparse, downy hairs on my skin stood out like feelers. Whenever she leaned my way, they quivered a warning.

I'd chafed against her opinions when I thought she was a boy; recalling her bossiness now mortified me. Further, I hated that I'd been tossed around by a girl. Worst, she'd seen me naked. Twice.

The Shepherd place looked much nicer than ours: a white-painted farmhouse and picket fence that seemed to glow in the moonlight, and outbuildings that looked brick-red in the sweep of the truck headlights. Papa pulled up behind a shiny Lincoln Zephyr parked near the house. He said, "What you saw tonight is our secret, OK, little lady? I'll keep your secret if you keep mine."

She said, "Yes, sir. Thank you for the ride home."

"Hey, Bud, scoot out so she can go. Be sure to walk your sweetheart to her door." He laughed as we exited.

Shuffling beside her along a swept brick path, I felt Papa's stare on the back of my neck. Rienzi carried her hat; her long braid swung between her shoulder blades. She said, "You'll keep my secret too?"

"I-I-I reckon. Why'd you pretend anyway?" I opened the white fence gate and walked through before remembering my manners around girls. I started to apologize, but she didn't seem to notice my mistake.

She latched the gate behind her and said, "Everyone talks to boys. Boys get to do what they want; girls get left out. Whenever I dress like I want to, Granny says I'm not ladylike."

"Are you go-going to pretend to be a boy f-forever?"

"Absolutely. If you tell my secret, I won't talk to you again. I'll find new friends." I rubbed my birthmark and she must've read my mind. "I know I look different. Someone else will be my friend, though. Somewhere."

I stuttered, "I won't tell, but you gotta promise not to tell anybody that you beat me up."

"You beat up yourself—"

"Promise!"

"I swear I won't tell anybody."

"Doggone, Ry-Rienzi, you ain't supposed to swear: it's a sin. You swannee instead." She sighed and I went on, "And double-promise n-not to tell anybody that you saw me naked. Twice."

"I double-promise, one for each time." She glanced behind us and asked, "Are you scared of your father?"

"Yeah. Well, sometimes." I tried to walk taller. "Not a lot, I mean, not really. No." As she and I approached the porch, I said, "Can I touch your hair?"

The front door opened. An older, bespectacled woman in a quilted housedress and felt slippers stood at the threshold holding a hurricane lamp. She said, "I declare, Rienzi, we was about to telephone the High Sheriff."

"Sorry, Granny. This is Bud MacLeod. His father drove me home." She waved at the truck and Papa tooted the horn twice.

The woman pursed her lips and her glance cut from the truck to me. "Nice to meet you, Bud. Your father's a famous man."

"Is tha-tha-that a fact, ma'am?"

"Oh yes. Everybody knows him." She stepped aside, making room in the doorway for Rienzi, and said to me, "Have a good night now."

Rienzi lifted my hand and I thought she was going to touch it to her braid, but she put something curved and smooth into it: her buckeye. She whispered, "Good luck."

I thanked her and she went inside. After the door closed, I squeezed the nut in my fist. Starting back to the truck, I wondered what her hair felt like; I imagined hemp and then corn silk. Before other textures came to mind, her final words struck me. Maybe she thought it was a good thing that I believed in luck. I stared at Papa's truck as he raced the engine, making it roar.

When I clambered inside the truck, I'd expected him to beat me for surprising him at Uncle Stan's, but he sat there tapping his thumbs against the steering wheel, his face in shadows. Happy with my good fortune, I held the buckeye with fingertips only, like Wanda had, not wanting to use up its powers.

Papa leaned an elbow out his window as he spun the wheel with his other hand, turning the truck in a tight half-circle. As we rolled down the driveway, he said, "Tell me about this girlfriend of yours."

I stammered, "I didn't know she was a girl. She fooled me good."

"You do know girls from boys, don't you?"

"Yes, sir. Darlene's a-a-a girl. And Mama. And—"

He snorted. "Your mama stopped being girlish a ways back." The truck shook as he drove along a washboard dirt lane, making a racket. He turned onto a smoother path bordered by harvested peanut fields, just ruts and barren rows. "It's a strange girl that plays in boy's duds. It's right peculiar. She probably whistles too."

"Her gra-grandma knew of you, Papa. Do you know the Shepherds, sir?"

"All I know about them is that no Shepherd's ever bought a drop offa me." From his flat tone, I couldn't tell if he hated or respected them for that. Or both.

While we drove home, a swirl of questions from Papa's rousting of Uncle Stan addled me. Again I imagined the bang and the gun smoke and— To try to clear my thoughts, I leaned out the passenger window. The wind stroked me, ruffling my hair. The roaring air forced tears from my eyes while I lost myself in the sluice of a thousand fingers grazing my scalp and stripping my face clean.

After a minute, Papa whacked my shoulder. "Goddammit, Bud, I'm talking to you!"

I sat up straight, hands in my lap like he'd taught me. Polite and defenseless.

"I said you also owe me a promise."

"I-I won't tell a soul, sir. I double-promise."

We bumped up onto the highway where the tires keened against the smooth pavement. Driving fast now, Papa held the wheel steady with his left hand and said, "Hey," to get my attention. I couldn't see his face, but I felt his gray stare. With a short, fast jab, he punched my mouth.

My head snapped back from his fist and rebounded off the doorframe. As I whimpered, covering my bloody lips with cupped hands, he said, "It'll be a whole lot worse if you tell. I'll teach you a powerful lesson, boy." He faced the road and rolled his shoulders. From the way he kneaded the steering wheel, I knew he wanted to hit me again.

I tried to cry myself to sleep, but my body stayed tense, awaiting another blow. Hunched against the door, I gripped the handle and thought about opening it up. I wondered how much I'd feel as I bounced and skidded on the concrete. How quick would I die? Face-first, I told myself, that'd be the way. Right on the birthmark.

In the country, lots of men killed themselves and some boys did too. I'd once heard that suicide was a sin, but didn't know for sure. We never went to church, except when the Primitive Baptists had the free dinner-on-the-ground every June, so I never read the Bible. Would I go straight to hell? Before I summoned the courage and anger to push the door open, Papa slowed the truck and turned onto the dirt of Hardscrabble Road.

I wiggled two baby teeth with my tongue. They'd started to loosen over the past weeks, but now I could swing both of my upper front teeth like a dog-door Jay once hung in the barn. Thin, salty blood trickled from my gums and the deep gashes inside my swollen lips.

Papa turned the truck onto the narrow road leading home. Passing Nat's place, I wondered if he and his wife would let me hide there for a while. There was Lonnie's tiny shack too; he'd be out all night at the juke joints. I wouldn't feel safe at home until Papa's anger gusted in another direction.

He sped up as we neared Uncle Stan's, zipping along so fast I couldn't spot the hole in the porch. When I faced forward again,

I screamed. He hollered too, and we plunged through a woman suddenly standing in the road, pointing at us.

The truck fishtailed as Papa braked hard and wrestled the steering wheel. The front end hadn't smashed against her body; somehow we'd missed the woman. The Woman. I looked out the back window and saw a dim shape all in white facing us again in a cloud of dust, arm still raised, and then I couldn't see her anymore as the truck slid on the hard-packed dirt.

Papa jerked the wheel to keep us out of the ditch where I'd hid with Rienzi. The truck stalled and we rolled to a stop. "Was that Arzula?" he shouted. "Goddamn, what happened to her?" His hand shook as he wiped sweat from his lip.

"It was the W-W-Woman, Papa."

"Horseshit. You trying to scare me?" He shoved me back against my door. "Huh? We're just seeing things is all, a bird or something flashed in the lights."

The Woman was gone when I glanced out the back window. I whispered, "She p-pointed."

"Goddamn you, quit that. Stuttering, sonofabitch bastard! Red-faced—" He leaned over and began slapping me quick and hard. I tried to cover up like I'd done with Buck Bradley, arms protecting my face and chest, but Papa knocked them aside with ease. I screamed until my face grew numb from repeated blows.

I turned away, giving him my spine and ribs to pound. The metal door felt as hard as a shovel when I wedged my head against it. I wished I'd jumped before. The shock of his blows stole my breath until I didn't make a sound. Not even a grunt as Papa walloped me.

"Mance." It was the tone Uncle Stan used to command his mule. Click—he thumbed back a hammer on his shotgun.

Papa panted and gulped. "Careful there, Stan. You might hurt the boy."

"You got a head-start." Though firm, his voice sounded a little thick and nasally.

I stayed down as Papa eased away from me. "Naw, Stan, I'm just—"

"You say my name the way you say 'shit.'"

Papa oomphed as if the shotgun barrels had shoved against a tender spot. He spoke fast. "It's a good name. I just like to say it is all."

"You like to say Roger's name?"

"Sure. Sure I do."

"Say it." Stan's voice softened. "Tell him you love him."

Papa didn't hesitate. "I love you, Roger."

Uncle Stan said, "Roger, do you believe him? It's OK, you can sit up. Do you believe him?"

When I eased upright, sharp pains stabbed my back. I wanted to cry out but I couldn't make a sound. My mouth opened and closed like a fish.

Stan repeated his question. My left eye had swollen shut, so I had to face them full-on to see. I couldn't make out much of my uncle's face as he peered through the driver window. The shotgun rested on the doorframe, twin barrels angled up against Papa's neck.

Papa looked at me steadily, confident that I'd answer in his favor. He said, "Go on, boy. Tell him."

I wanted to lie rather than see him murdered. But no voice came out when I moved my bruised, bloody lips.

Stan said, "Guess that's a no, huh, Mance?" Click went the other hammer on his shotgun.

"Goddammit, Roger! Come on, tell the man."

"Maybe he didn't hear you earlier. Say it again. Say how much."

Words exploded from Papa's mouth. "Roger, I love you. A little whipping don't mean nuthin; you shouldn't have egged me on is all. Uh, I love you more than, well hell, more'n anybody else in the family. You know that, right?"

I'd never heard him sound weak and pitiful before. His naked pleading broke my heart. I nodded but kept my movements small so I wouldn't hurt my stiffening neck.

Stan said, "That look like a nod, Mance, or a head-shake?"

"He's nodding yes! Yessir, he's nodding away. That's a good boy."

"Roger, do me a favor and take his gun. Everybody'll sleep better that way."

I eyed the walnut grip poking from Papa's waistband. Uncle Stan encouraged me until I closed my fingers around it. Papa narrowed his eyes like he was about to hit me again. Instead, he sucked in his hard-muscled stomach so I could lift the heavy Colt away. I cupped the revolver on my lap; the weight of it kept my hands from shaking.

Uncle Stan took a step from the driver door. "You done good, Roger. Now climb on out. You're staying here tonight."

It took all my strength to force my aching body to move. I could barely stand on the dirt road and had to wedge the Colt into my pocket so I wouldn't drop it. When I pushed the truck door closed, it swung slowly and didn't latch.

Uncle Stan said, "Go home, Mance. Never stop at my place again—got it?"

"Yeah, I got it." After a couple of tries and some muttered cussing, Papa started the engine and drove toward home. Until then I'd forgotten about the buckeye I dropped in his truck; Rienzi's gift had brought me good luck after all.

"Looks like you're about to topple over." Uncle Stan lowered the triggers on the shotgun and used the same gentleness to ease his arm around my shoulders. "Jesus, I got a helluva headache. How 'bout you? Oh, still not talking?"

I shrugged, sending an explosion up through my neck and down my spine and legs. Moaning silently, I leaned into my uncle and let him drag-step me onto his gunshot porch.

"Watch that hole now. The first step's a killer." He led me inside the dark parlor and sat me in a chair. After some clattering, he struck a long wooden match. Leaning forward, his hand glowing orange, he lit a kerosene lamp atop the weather-beaten table I slumped beside.

I flinched at the sight of him. His blood-caked nose looked wavy along the bridge, likely reset by his own hands without using a mirror. Bruises under his eyes looked almost black in the lamplight, as did a goose-egg on his forehead and a knot on his chin.

"Yeah, well you should see yourself." He sat across from me and smiled, revealing chipped teeth. "You and me, we're quite a pair. You gonna say anything?" He narrowed his gaze at me and his old scowl crept over his wounded features. "A little thanks maybe for saving your life?"

I mouthed, "Thank you," but couldn't make a sound.

"He sure busted you up good, but probably I was a little hard on him. Not like he was trying to kill you. Not like he did this to me neither—Arzula said I fell after I killed our porch. Guess I had a bit too much to drink." He touched his nose with his fingertips and winced.

After a time, he said, "I gotta take you back there, you know. Your brothers and sister'll miss you. Your mama too. Even Mance." My uncle brought his fist down hard on the table. "Jesus, Reva sure picks the winners, don't she?"

# CHAPTER 13

I FELL ASLEEP IN THE CHAIR AS UNCLE STAN MURMURED TO HIMSELF. He must've carried me to a pallet in the corner of the room because that's where I awoke before dawn. Besides the throbbing in my face and across my back and neck, a tender patch had formed on my thigh from sleeping atop the Colt in my pocket. The sky had lightened to a bruised grayish-purple.

My lips moved as I tried to whisper my brothers' names, but no sound came out. I lay there trying not to remember Papa whaling on me. I focused on working my front teeth forward and back with my tongue. They'd loosened even more and seemed to be held to my gums with skinny threads. I sat up and pulled my scabbed upper lip into a sneer. The pain of reopening those wounds would hopefully mask the hurt when I yanked out my teeth.

With thumb and forefinger I grasped the slick teeth and pulled down. The roots holding them in place seemed to run alongside my nose to my eyes. Tears and snot coursed down my face and salty blood seeped from my gums long after the threads snapped. In the dim light, I made out two little red-tinged rectangles. They were so light and thin I couldn't believe they could cut through paper let alone corncobs and raw sugarcane.

Once, when I'd lost a baby tooth, I showed it to Jay and asked, "What's it made of?"

"Bone, just like your head." He explained how my skin and all hung on my bones like clothes. "If you dig up a old body, you'll see them bones, nuthin more." Mama took away the teeth I'd lost before, but she hadn't known about this one. Under the house, I made a little hole beside the grave I'd dug for a broken stick-man, and I buried that tooth. Since then, I always buried my teeth under our house, little pieces of me in my very own cemetery.

Now I had two more castoffs from my body to put in the ground. I couldn't just bury them anywhere, though I considered sticking them in the dirt beside Eliza Jean's grave. Maybe like a peace offering from my family to hers. When I pushed to my feet, I left bloody fingerprints on the thirsty wood.

I hobbled home in the predawn, fighting dizziness, my thumb and forefinger pinched tight around the two slim bones. My tongue wouldn't stay out of the barn-door-sized hole in my mouth. Both of my exposed gums had scooped-out places and if I shoved hard with the tip of my tongue, I could feel the tops of new teeth cutting through the tender pink craters.

Sport and Dixie yawned on the porch and wagged their tails but didn't get up when I came through the fence gate. That Goddamn Rooster hadn't crowed yet; with my left eye still swollen, I saw a blurry image of him fluffing out his wings and preening the way Papa had rolled his shoulders after punching me.

Under the house, I leaned over my graveyard. Half-buried pine bark was the tombstone for Jack the Stick-Man, snapped in half during rough play with Chet before my brother outgrew stick-men wars. Beside the tombstone were a half-dozen flint chips, broken arrowheads the Indians had thrown away, that marked the pieces of me I'd buried. I plunged a finger into the sand, planted one tooth, and then made a second grave. Sand shifted to cover my bones as soon as I'd buried them. I traced two little circles to mark their resting place so I could return with more flint grave markers.

I backed out from under the house as the rooster crowed. As sore as I was, there was no point in trying to race back to Uncle Stan's; anyway, I didn't want my brothers to have to do my chores. The rooster so enjoyed his singing to the dawn, head thrown back, red-feathered neck stretched out, that he didn't bother me while I crept around to the back porch.

In Mama's garden, the scarred rabbit gnawed a radish between its paws. Its long eyes cut from the wailing rooster to me as its prominent buckteeth shaved the bitter white flesh of the vegetable. I hated radishes, so I didn't mind if the rabbit ate every one of them, but it seemed to taunt me with its huge, strong front teeth.

The Colt sat heavily in my pocket. I tongued the twin gaps in my mouth and recalled the last time I'd tried to shoot the rabbit: Papa had walloped me with the rifle butt. I didn't need another lump on my head. With my left eye only half-open, I was no judge of distance anyway, and since I still didn't have my voice, I couldn't call for our dogs either.

"Hamestrang crackin, collar cryin…" Papa opened the bedroom door and strode toward the parlor to wake my brothers for Sunday chores before we went to Grandma's. The rabbit dropped the half-eaten radish, scurried under the fence, and bounded across the field. Its back looked as pink as a fresh gash.

Papa marched through the kitchen and stepped onto the porch, stopping short when he saw me. His usual starched white shirt gleamed except for a dark patch on the right side above his waistband: gun oil.

My hand covered the pocket where his Colt pressed against my thigh. He worked his jaw and said, "You got permission from Stan to be here? Huh?" I moved my lips and tapped them with my fingers and gave a little shrug. He said, "I meant what I said about our secret. Don't you say a word."

I shook my head and almost reeled from the pain in my neck. Thinking a peace offering would calm him, I tugged the Colt from my pocket and handed it over.

The smooth walnut grip burned my palm when he wrenched the gun away. "Goddammit, you don't point a gun when you're giving it up. Don't you know a thing? You handle the barrel. Otherwise—" he pointed his forefinger at me and dropped his thumb like a hammer "—the other fella might think you're gonna shoot 'im." With a flick of his wrist, he snapped open the action to examine the six loaded chambers. He slammed it closed again and slid the Colt into his waistband, covering the stain on his shirt.

Patting the faint bulge near his hip, he said, "Felt like I was naked as a skint rabbit." Over the sounds of my brothers coming into the kitchen, he murmured, "I told 'em you stayed with that odd little buddy of yours last night. We all got secrets; you ever get to talking again, mind you remember that."

I nodded a little as Jay poked his head through the doorway. "That bed was so comfy without…Hey, what happened to your face?"

Papa said, "Got into a brawl with that kid. Lost his voice too."

"No kidding. Man, I didn't know Ry would do that. He tossed ol Chet around, but—"

"Get to your breakfast. Chores are waiting."

Papa turned from me and began his strength exercises, lowering on his right leg with the left kicked out ahead of him. I wandered inside.

"Oh my stars," Mama said, slopping grits onto my plate. "Ain't you gonna be a sight at the old home place. Chet, I told you not to knock Bud around before our Sunday visits."

Chet held up his hands. "I didn't touch 'im. Go on, tell Mama."

I flapped my lips and shook my head a little.

Mama banged the pot on Chet's head. "I swannee, you kicked out his voice and two teeth to boot."

"Honest, I didn't." Chet rubbed the top of his head.

Jay dug his spoon into the puddle of grits before him. "Papa said that Ry whupped up on Bud. That's the boy that you met yesterday, Mama."

"Them Japanese got some nerve." She returned to the sink, muttering, "Now I'm gonna have to explain to Ma and everybody."

Lonnie dragged himself onto the back porch, saying to Papa, "Morning, boss." Deep in the throes of a hangover, he gripped both sides of the door jamb to pull himself through.

Mama said, "Got a brace of woodpeckers noodlin your noggin?"

"Yes'm." He eased onto his stool at the cook's table where his breakfast steamed. When he noticed me, he set down his spoon. "Hey now, Chet, what'd you do to Bud?"

My voice didn't return that day. At Grandma's, Uncles Jake and Davy tried tickling me, but stopped when all I did was cry in pain and frustration. Some of my cousins said that leaning me into the path of the Seaboard locomotive would help, but my brothers talked them out of it. Still, Jay and Chet agreed, a really good scare might bring my voice back. When we sat down to Sunday night supper, they talked to Papa about letting us play the tombstone-shaped Philco radio after we ate; he liked to hoard the power in the heavy batteries for his favorite hillbilly show *Lum and Abner*.

Jay said, "You know how scaredy Bud gets during *Lights Out*; a good scream'll get him talking again. Besides, tomorrow's his birthday. He needs to have his voice for that."

"That right?" Papa said, stiff-arming my shoulder. "You gonna be eight?"

I nodded. My neck had loosened and my eye opened late in the afternoon. I'd given up on ever trying to talk again, though. Even the buckeye I'd retrieved from Papa's truck hadn't helped. Maybe being mute was better than being a "stuttering sonofabitch bastard."

Papa said, "Reva, we got his present yet?"

From the other end of the table, Mama said, "Unh-uh. We planned to fetch it tomorrow."

"Instead, why don't I take Bud and do the town after school?" Papa forced some cheer into his voice. "What do you say, Bud? You and me!"

I couldn't say anything so I just nodded. The radio program only gave me worse nightmares, and I went to school sleepy and voiceless. On the bus, my brothers played up the fight me and Ry supposedly had. One of the older boys said, "Man, I shoulda thought of that. No reciting in class, no answering when you're called on... Playing dumb, Bud—" he tapped the side of his head "—smart idea."

Chet balled his fists and said, "He ain't playing at it. He really is dumb."

"You know, mute-like," Jay added.

Cecilia held my hand with her cool, coarse fingers. Unlike Darlene, she worked in her father's fields. "Poor Bud," she said. "After you knocked out Buck, I figured you could take on anybody. I forgot you're still only seven."

Jay said, "He's eight today." At breakfast, he and Chet had given me eight pennies and two blood-red marbles. Darlene had given me a new, unsharpened pencil and an old storybook of hers about a Negro boy. She'd sounded out the title of *Little Black Sambo* for me, pointing at the letters while I moved my lips wordlessly, humoring her.

"Eight? You're catching up to me." Cecilia gave my hand a squeeze. "Be thinking about what kinda present you want. Tell me, soon as you get your voice back."

When Fleming and I reached class, Miss Wingate was busy at the chalkboard, showing a couple of boys how to add six and five. Eleven, I mouthed on the way past. Glancing my way, she nodded. Her eyes scanned my face: the stubborn bruises near my left eye, the birthmark surrounding my right. She pursed her mouth at me and held up her index finger, shushing me and leaving a faint line of chalk on her lipstick.

I'd tried and failed at humming or anything else that used my vocal chords, as if I forgot how to work them. I would've given anything to talk—even to stutter again, anything to avoid disappointing Miss Wingate by "playing dumb."

She sent the boys to their seats and dusted off her hands, which added to the faint white smudges on her dress. Glancing down at her fingers, she spread them like she was inspecting her nails. Never one to wear jewelry, she had on her left ring-finger a slim gold band with an icy-looking stone jutting out. She began the morning routines and then stopped in the middle of roll call, sparing me the embarrassment of not being able to speak at all, let alone stammer. She said, "I have an announcement, children. I'm engaged to be married to your principal, Mr. Gladney."

Many of the girls cheered and applauded. They whispered to one another with big smiles. The boys, including me, glowered.

I hadn't realized just how much I'd counted on her waiting for me to grow up. In another ten years, I'd have made a good husband: very nearly graduated from high school, since it only ran through grade eleven, tall and strong and handsome. From the left side anyway. I could've been hers; instead she was getting hitched to an old man; Mr. Gladney was thirty-five if he was a day.

A girl called out, "When's your wedding, ma'am?"

"We were thinking about mid-December."

"Hog-killing time," Fleming murmured behind me, echoing my thoughts.

I imagined a great emptiness yawning inside me as if I'd been hollowed out. I wanted to feel nothing at all, just like when Papa was beating me in the truck. I wanted to be detached like Mama, whenever he whipped me in front of her. Instead, I felt everything.

I felt my heartbeat; the warmth of blood in my face and ears and neck as I flushed; the dry, lifeless wood of the desk under my pressed-down palms; my bottom and back against denim and more dead wood; grit and the cold linoleum beneath my bare feet; the lump descending my throat like a ball inside a stocking. I tongued the twin gaps in my teeth where the new, adult me began to push through.

Miss Wingate said, "You're my favorite class, the best ever, and I wanted you to hear my news before anyone else at school. Now let's continue with the roll. Bud MacLeod?"

I looked at her and said, clear and loud, "I'm here."

I TRIED NOT TO THINK about talking. Tried not to jinx myself. Every time I had something to say, I imagined walking a tightrope. I did it again and again without fail, but I couldn't take it for "granite," as I was prone to say. Now I could blurt out, "Don't take it for granite," all morning long without a pause or a slip-up. Without a stutter. Like being able to snap my fingers when I was never able to do that before, now I couldn't imagine *not* being able to.

Of course, with my front teeth missing, I had a terrible lisp. But I was sure that would go away when the new ones came in. Miss Wingate asked me to stay inside a moment while everyone else went outdoors for dinner and playtime. She had me sit in the chair beside her desk and said, "Are you fighting with that older boy again?"

"No, ma'am. My papa beat me for being mouthy." I sprayed a little spittle with "mouthy."

"Your teeth. I hope he didn't..."

"No, ma'am. They was—were—loose anyway."

She sighed. "Well, you've been very outgoing today, putting up your hand to answer all the questions. You didn't trip over your tongue once. I'm so proud of you."

I'd hoped she had noticed my newfound confidence. Already sitting up straight, I pushed my shoulders back and thanked her. I dug the buckeye from my pocket and put it on the desk near the ring on her left hand. "This is for your wedding, ma'am. It brings good luck."

She smiled and held it between thumb and forefinger, turning the buckeye around in the light the way I imagined that she did with her engagement ring. "I can't keep your lucky piece, Bud. Little boys need them much more than grown women." She took my hand and closed my fingers around the nut, her ring glittering above my fist.

"I won't be little forever, ma'am."

"That's right. One day you'll be sitting in your favorite place with your best girl, holding her hand, and sliding a ring onto her finger." She gave my fist a squeeze and let go. "It'll be the happiest day of your life, but don't be so eager to grow up fast. When you're older you'll miss being a kid. Sure, you might get beatings and there are always bullies at school, but these are magical years too. Make sure you pay attention to everything that's good and fun. Isn't that right, Lucy?"

"Yes, ma'am." Her maid had entered bearing the cloth-covered tray with Miss Wingate's dinner. "When you get old like me, 'good and fun' is a scarce commodity, mm-hmm."

Miss Wingate set the tray aside after Lucy exited. I said, "I'm eight today. In nine years, I'll be seventeen,"

"Always looking ahead." She shook her head, her lips a gentle crimson bow. "Eight plus nine, that's right. A senior in high school. Then what?"

"A train engineer. And a cowboy. And a soldier."

"You can do it all. I know you can. Go on outside and join your friends." I retrieved my dinner sack and was headed for the door when she called, "Bud." I stopped, and she said, "Happy birthday."

"Happy engagement-day, Miss Wingate."

On the ride home, I sat between Cecilia and Chet, who were in the same class. She leaned forward so she could talk past me on the noisy bus. "Hey, Chet, could you help me with a math problem?"

Chet squirmed and looked at his hands. "Which one?"

"That multiplying one in the book, eleven times eleven."

"121, it's easy."

"Not for me. Could you show me how?"

"Figure it out." He leaned back, sweat dotting his upper lip.

On Chet's other side, Jay tapped our brother's shoulder with his fist and murmured, "Head full of stump water."

Chet dragged a sleeve across his mouth and stared at his lap. Cecilia continued to lean forward and look at him. I caught her eye and said, "I know what I want. For my birthday, I mean."

"Hey, you're talking! What happened?"

I shrugged. "It's like I always could." I didn't tell her that heartbreak seemed to have done the trick.

"Well you're doing a bang-up job. I can't give you as good a present as that."

"Yeah, you could. You could sit up with me when I'm fifteen." Beside me, Chet started to choke and Jay pounded on his back.

She whispered, "Law, Bud. You're asking to court me in seven years' time?" The light in her green eyes danced.

"That's right."

"I'll be sixteen and already setting up housekeeping with a fella by then."

I shut my eyes so she couldn't see how wet they'd become. "I reckon everybody'll be hitched before I catch up."

"You're looking in the wrong direction." She took my arm and turned me so I faced out the window. I hated that my birthmark was so close to her. She pointed at the farms and woods and untamed fields, her arm wavering in the wind. With a soft voice, her breath warming my ear, she said, "Somewhere's a little girl just three or four right now that's gonna be your wife, and she's playing in the sand and thinking, 'Oh, I hope Bud waits for me.' Honest and true." She bussed my temple, a light peck right on the port-wine stain, and said, "Happy birthday, Bud. You're sweet."

On our walk home from Hardscrabble Road, Chet said, "Come on, what'd she say? We all heard you talking. You can't play dumb no more."

Darlene had told my brothers that Cecilia kissed me after whispering in my ear. I had half-a-mind to give her back the *Sambo* book and the pencil I'd already started chewing.

Chet swept my legs out from under me and I sat down hard in the dirt, aggravating the aches that lingered. He said, "You better talk. That Ry gave me a bunch more ways to beat you up."

Jay said, "Save it. We're going after ol Ry for cleaning Bud's plow."

"He didn't touch me," I said, pushing to my feet. "Papa done it. But there's more." All three promised to keep the secret, so I told them about Papa almost shooting Uncle Stan and then Uncle Stan turning the tables. The story took a while to tell; the only thing I cut out was Ry becoming Rienzi.

Chet scratched his head. "Sounds like Wanda shoulda been a-warning Bud to stay clear of Papa."

"Naw," Jay said. "Then Uncle Stan would be dead and maybe Aunt Arzula too, and Papa would be in jail or off and gone."

Darlene said, "Maybe Mama has Wanda's second-sight. She'd told me something could happen to Papa and leave this big hole in our lives."

Papa seemed fine when we arrived home. He stood on the porch with our dogs at his feet. His white Stetson shadowed his face. He hollered, "School bus late?"

"Yes, sir," Jay lied. "Flat tire."

"Me and Bud are going to town for his birthday, so hurry it up."

I ran past him and dropped my used paper sack on the kitchen table for Mama to fill again on Tuesday. She sat there, shelling peas. "Don't forget to wear your shoes," she said. "I don't want folks to think you was raised in a barn."

"Yes'm."

"Oh my stars, you decided to talk again. Well, don't sass your papa. Maybe we can have a night without squabbles."

Papa kept rushing me, so I didn't have time to shine my shoes from the drippings bowl. Once inside the truck and rolling down the driveway, he said, "Jay told me you're talking again."

"Yes, sir."

"Just remember, no talking 'bout the other night."

"No, sir. I promised not to."

As we neared Uncle Stan's house, Papa jiggled the grip of the Colt in his waistband the way he sometimes adjusted his crotch. Stan knelt over the gunshot floorboards, prizing them off with a claw hammer, leaving a larger, cleaner hole in his porch. Scrap lumber leaned against the wall, ready for nailing. He kept his head down as we drove past.

Papa said, "All right then. I thought we'd get a bite to eat and see a picture show."

He didn't ask for my approval, so I settled against the seat and swayed and bounced as we rattled toward the highway. When we reached Bainbridge, I judged from the sun that we were still a couple of hours early for supper.

I said, "Papa, can we see the bikes at Western Auto, please?" With Christmas only two months away, my brothers and I had begun sharing our yearly fantasy of getting a Western Flyer.

Papa drove halfway around the courthouse square and swung into a diagonal space facing the gazebo, benches, and mown grass. We were only a block down from the Western Auto store and the Roxie Theater. "Sure, sure. I'll only be a minute. Stay in the truck." He switched off the engine and left me there. Checking for traffic, he crossed the narrow street and went inside the Cottontail Café.

The afternoon sun reflected off the glass fronting the diner, showing me a distant image of myself: the right side of my face, the port-wine stain. Before I glanced away, I thought I saw Papa and a redheaded waitress go through a door in the back. I looked again, focusing through my reflection, and didn't see him anymore.

I got out and climbed into the flatbed, hunkering down behind the tailgate so I could get a better view. No customers sat at the long counter and the tables were empty. With the waitress gone too, only the manager stood behind the counter, wiping it down. He wore a paper hat folded with a point in the front and the back, and had an apron with greasy, streaked handprints across the chest. He kept glancing at the backroom door and wiping the same spot.

The door in back opened. Papa stood there, his head bare, sorting a handful of change while a boy looked up at him. The boy was a year older than me, with Chet's brown hair and wiry frame. He dressed like other town dudes, in a long-sleeved shirt and tan trousers. With the money given to him, the boy bought a red Popsicle from the manager and came outside. He sat on the curb and nibbled the end of his treat, his pale lips turning cherry. Inside, the backroom door had closed again.

I'd once split a Popsicle with my brothers, each of us taking turns, and now I recalled the smooth and icy sweetness, and how sticky the Popsicle made my fingers. I pulled off my shoes and leaned my elbows on the tailgate, watching the boy. He wore chocolate-brown socks and penny loafers. A pink trickle of melted ice dripped off his fist and plopped onto his trousers.

He glanced across the street, peering at the little park and then at me. "Hey," he shouted, "what're you doing in Daddy's truck?"

I kneeled in the flatbed and yelled back, "This ain't yours. It's my papa's. We drove here."

"Liar!" The boy pointed at me with his half-eaten Popsicle. "You get outta there before I tell."

"Tell all you want. I'm staying put." I crossed my arms and sat back on my heels.

The boy looked from me to his Popsicle and sucked hard at the remaining red ice, eyebrows pressed together. He gnawed off the last bit and threw the wood stick into the street. The manager had come out from behind the counter and stood near the door, watching us. After an old Chevy trundled by, the kid ran across to me. His mouth looked bloody from the Popsicle stains. Shaking his cherry-stained fist, he said, "Get down from there, peewee! I'll put a whupping on you. Don't think I won't."

"You're nuts. I'm waiting for Papa to come back."

"He'll skin you when he catches you in his truck."

I said, "I'm in it all the time, dummy."

"You can't be. Daddy's on the road most every day—he ain't here regular."

"We live up the highway," I said. "What're you, touched in the head?"

"You've had it!" The boy clambered up the tailgate, rising to eye-level with me.

I punched his nose before he could get inside. I didn't want to believe what we both knew. If I could shut him up, it wouldn't be true. He swayed, fingers still clamped on the tailgate. I hit him again and he let go.

The boy sat down on the pavement, head bowed, hands in his lap. He cried hard, his shoulders shaking. Vibrations ran down his legs and caused his shoes to quiver. I'd never made anyone bawl before; I climbed down and crouched in front of him. His eyes squeezed shut during his crying jag, but soon he was blinking and hiccupping with sobs. When he raised his face, I looked into gray eyes identical to Chet's. Same as Papa's.

I offered him the wadded up rag from my back pocket, but he wiped a white sleeve across the snot and tears on his face. The sleeve also soaked up a long streak of cherry Popsicle from his mouth. I asked his name.

"Tommy." He snorted, turned his head to the side, and spit.

"What's your last name?"

"Same as Mommy and Daddy's."

"Goddammit, Bud," Papa shouted from the café doorway. "I told you not to get outta the truck."

I pulled Tommy to his feet, struggling to lift him since he was taller than me and didn't try to help. I said, "Tommy what?"

"Rush." He looked at the diner and then back at me. "It's your truck too?"

"'Fraid so."

Papa pushed his Stetson low over his eyes and marched across the street. Behind him, the man in the paper hat shouted from the doorway, "Hey, Mance, the least you could do is buy a damn burger or something." Papa waved the back of his hand, like he was batting a fly from his ear.

Tommy worked his jaw back and forth, same as I'd seen Papa do a thousand times. He whispered, "I ain't gonna say nuthin."

"Me neither."

Papa dropped his hand on the boy's shoulder and glared at me. "Tommy, get on home."

"Yes, sir." He glanced at me. "Daddy, you gonna stay in town tonight?"

"Can't. Gotta drop this one off with his folks and get back on the road." He turned Tommy around and guided him to the café, saying, "But I'll be back real soon. You know I'm gonna miss you awful, kid." Papa's shirttail hung over the back of his trousers.

"Me too. I love you, Daddy." He said it loud, as if he meant for me to hear.

"Me too." Papa prodded him past the man and pushed the door shut.

As he started back toward me, I levered my belly over the tailgate, snatched my shoes, and retreated inside the truck cab. He slammed the driver door and said, "That Tommy, dropped on his head one too many times. Poor kid treats me like his daddy. His mama and me went to high school together; I've helped her out ever since her old man skipped town."

The knuckles on my right hand had swollen; I covered them with my left and rubbed slowly, saying, "He was nice."

"Nice but real slow, know what I mean? We got another secret, you and me." He stared at me until I nodded. He ran a hand across his chest and over his shoulder a few times in a curious loop. His revolver pressed against the shirt covering his flat stomach, but the shirttail rode high, pinned between his back and the seat, and exposed a sliver of taut, pale skin. His fingers trembled a little on the steering wheel as he said, "Let's eat your mama's cooking. I'm a little sleepy—maybe got some epizootic coming on. We'll do town another time."

He didn't ask for my approval, so I settled against the seat and thought about my new brother. As we drove toward the highway, I wondered if he was the only other one.

# CHAPTER 14

Zipping along US 27, I recalled the last time Papa and I headed north together, with blood in my mouth but two front teeth still in my head. I gripped the door handle and remembered my urge to jump out. If I had, I'd never have known about Tommy. Thinking about that hidden part of my father's life put me in mind of the only secret I intended to keep: Ry was a girl named Rienzi. She was smart, maybe even smarter than Jay; I wanted to share secrets with her.

"Papa, please can you drop me at the Shepherds' place?" I said. "Where that girl Rienzi is staying?"

"I told you I ain't feeling good."

"I'll walk home, sir."

"I don't know how to get there."

"It's the next left turn, sir."

He braked hard, squealing the tires. A horn blared from behind and a large truck swerved around us. Papa said, "Seeing as how you remember, go on and git."

His short, hard jab against my mouth was still vivid, so I hopped out. Two cars honked and went around on the left, the second one nearly colliding head-on with a southbound driver. Papa yelled out the open passenger window, "Hey, ain't you stuttering no more?" When I replied no, he said, "Goddamn, I must've knocked it outta you. Happy birthday, B-B-Bud!" He peeled away before another truck overtook him.

I made sure both lanes had cleared and ran across the highway. An hour of good light remained. Maybe Rienzi could walk me home since she didn't mind the dark. I had to backtrack twice, not as certain as I'd been that I could find the Shepherd place. Finally, with the sun dropping past the tree line, I found the long dirt driveway that led to the white picket fence and gleaming house.

Rienzi's grandfather, a bald man with a big, hard-looking gut, answered my knock. I said, "I'm Rienzi's friend, sir. Is she around?"

"Went home, matter of fact. I took her and her trunk of books to the Columbus bus depot today."

"Home, sir?"

"San An-tone, where my son—her father—lives."

"Texas."

"'At's right. He telephoned that he's back from researching his doc-to-rate and gallivanting all over the wide world." I kept staring at him, and he said, "If you don't mind now, the flies are coming in and my supper's getting cold." With a nod, he closed the door.

I shuffled off the porch and walked toward home, watching as the last of the color faded from the twilight sky. By the time I reached the highway, darkness had fallen. More traffic sailed by than earlier. It was hard to judge speeds at night; one car had to brake hard to keep from hitting me as I ran across the road. The driver pulled over to the shoulder, pinning me with his headlights.

His door opened but I couldn't see him in the glare. Over the roar of passing traffic, a Negro man said, "I done flattened plenty of possums, but I ain't hit a white boy yet. You fixing to get killed, sonny."

"Sorry," I hollered. "Everybody's going lots faster than I think."

He laughed. "Ain't that the truth. Where you headed?"

"You know the MacLeod place, offa Hardscrabble Road?"

"Near Nat Blanchard's?"

"He's a friend of mine."

"You said the magic words—hop in."

I came around to the passenger side. The car was so dark that it blended with the night. If it wasn't for the chrome highlights, I'd have had trouble finding the handle. The driver ducked inside and closed his door, and I climbed in beside him.

After I introduced myself, he said, "Name's Bryson. Robert Bryson." He lifted a bottle to his lips and made gulping sounds. With a sigh, he tipped his head forward and said, "Ain't nuthin fancy—jest water. Seems like I can't hardly get enough." He pressed a stopper into the bottle and nestled it between his thighs. "There's some Co-colas in the backseat if you want." He checked for traffic and roared onto the highway, tires spinning.

I leaned over my seat and fished around in the dark until my hand found the rattling bottles in a wooden crate. I helped myself to one and accepted a bottle opener from Mr. Bryson. Pitching the cap out the window, I thanked him. "Wanda Washburn rides with you?"

"I show up at her place every morning. Imagine you knowing such a thing."

I chugged the warm cola, enjoying the peppery fizz that tickled my nose and lingered in my throat. After a loud bullfrog burp, I said, "Nat done told me."

He drummed the steering wheel with a half-dozen rapid taps and said, "And did Nat tell you about my Pierce-Arrow straight-eight?" My body pressed back into the cloth seat as he accelerated smooth and fast. The engine hummed louder, sending a faint tremor up through my feet. "Wooo!" he cried. "Pushing that foot-feed's like slipping on my favorite shoe." Oncoming traffic flashed past as he chuckled. "Man oh man, seven years old and still running slick as a whistle."

"I just turned eight, Mr. Bryson."

"Do tell." He eased off the gas pedal, ungluing me from the seat. "How you running?"

"Fair to middling." It was the answer I'd heard adults give for years; I'd always thought they were lying too. I finished my drink and returned the bottle to its crate so he could get back his deposit.

Mr. Bryon braked hard and turned us onto Hardscrabble Road. "That's the way to be. Don't get too high, don't get too low. You know how to shake off the blues, don't you?"

"No, sir."

"Sit in a fast car, sonny, something with lots of horses. What'chu don't wanna do is walk everywhere, what they call 'taking shank's mare.'" He tapped his lower leg and said, "Know what I mean? Too much time to study on your problems. Only folk that take shank's mare get the blues."

"What if walking's all I got, Mr. Bryson?"

"Then move like the devil's fixing to snatch your backside."

Later that night, with our parents gone to bed, I swore my brothers to secrecy again. I hustled Jay and Chet into the woods like Satan was indeed behind me. Even with the screen of trees and the loud chatter of crickets to hide us, I whispered my story about Tommy and the Cottontail Café.

Chet said, "He was a lot like me, huh?"

"He couldn't take a punch though."

"Well, that's something anyway."

Jay said, "So either our name oughta be Rush, or he gave Tommy a pretend name or Rush is the name of that boy's mama."

Chet said, "Or the Tommy kid was guying you."

"He knew Papa's truck right off," I said. "He aimed to throw me out of it."

Jay yawned, giving his voice a spooky depth while he said, "'Less he was nuts, like Papa told you." I asked if we should tell Mama, and he said, "Leave it. Their fights are bad enough as it is. Mama might kill 'im in his sleep."

Chet jabbed my shoulder, a surprise blow in the dark. "And if she doesn't kill 'im dead, he'll come for you. 'Member when you told us what folks was saying 'bout her and Uncle Roscoe? Nobody blabbed to Papa 'cause Mama woulda wrung our necks. Same thing here." He snapped a branch in his hands, loud as a gunshot. "What they don't know won't hurt them or us."

WHEN WE RETURNED FROM SCHOOL the following Monday, Papa's truck was gone. Damp laundry hung on a line strung between two trees in the side yard.

The cotton field lay picked over and unattended. Nat and Lonnie had hired out to other farms where they hoped to earn enough to get them through the winter. My siblings and I passed through the kitchen and dropped off our wrinkled lunch bags, which were so worn they felt like moth-eaten cotton. While Jay and Chet started the chores out back, Mama took me aside. She said, "They learning you numbers in school?"

I boasted that I could already count to fifty, but instead of complimenting me, she pulled me outside to the line of drip-drying clothes. Beside her beige foundation garments—with the amazing curves and pads and tucks that stymied my imagination about how women were shaped—Mama had hung my father's undershirts. Six of the sleeveless whites swayed from their clothes-pinned straps like prisoners dangling by shackled wrists. She told me to count them out loud and then said, "There's always seven. But in the week gone by there's just six."

I recalled seeing a pink triangle of Papa's flesh shortly after he steered Tommy back to the café on my birthday. He'd rubbed his hand across his chest, maybe unaccustomed to the texture of the shirt against his bare skin, maybe wondering why something didn't feel right. I couldn't tell her about Papa visiting my secret brother and the waitress, so I stretched up toward one of her drying underthings and grasped a heavily stitched, protruding cup almost twice the size of my hand. Water drizzled from the squishy fabric and trickled inside my sleeve. I asked, "What's this do?"

Mama slapped my hand away and said, "Never mind that. Tell me about your birthday." She crouched to my eye-level. In a softer voice, she said, "Won't you tell me? I know you got disappointed. No picture show. No supper even. That ain't right."

"Papa said he felt sleepy."

"Yeah, I know what comes before his best sleeping."

I said, "He was sick, some bug coming on."

"He got over it right quick. Did you stop anywhere?"

"On the way back. I wanted to see my friend."

"I gave 'im hell for putting you out halfway between home and Timbuktu. I mean, did you stop in town?"

"He, ah, I-I—"

"You're stuttering again. I ain't gonna hit you for telling the truth, Bud. What kind of mother do you think I am?"

"He took me to Western Auto. To look at the bikes." She let go, her mouth twitching. I rushed through the rest of my story. "Then he saw the prices and felt poorly and we left."

She stood, peering down at me. "That's near what he said. Nuthin more to it?"

"No'm." I decided to press my luck. "But I didn't get a proper birthday."

She glanced back at the dangling undershirts and said, "Get your chores done, and we'll set things right tonight."

Papa arrived home in time for supper, but Mama announced that he would get right back in his truck and take me and her to the picture show. "We owe the boy a proper birthday," she told him.

His glare slid from her to me, and I faced my plate so fast that my neck popped. He said, "I'll take 'im to the Ashers on Friday. He ain't gone in a while."

"That might be good enough for him, but it won't do for me. Here I cook your meals and keep house and work outdoors—and wash your clothes. The least you could do is take me to a damn picture once in a blue moon."

"You're spoiling this boy," he grumbled. "Outings two weeks in a row."

"You feeling all right tonight? Nuthin off-kilter inside?"

"Fair to middling." He speared an Irish potato through its eye.

Mama sat in the middle on the drive to Bainbridge that evening. She'd changed into her favorite muslin dress with the very low neckline. Her left hand rested on Papa's thigh, her wrist touching the grip of his Colt. She said, "You no-no-notice how Bud ain't stutterin no-no-no more?"

He chuckled and said, "His face clears up and he'll be all set."

I turned my back to them and rested the right side of my face against the cool metal door.

Mama murmured, "Now he can't help something that runs in the family."

"It don't run in mine."

"Maybe not, but other things do." She must've touched a sensitive place because he jerked, shaking the whole bench-seat.

He said, "From what I seen, he missed out on that."

"Well, he's small yet."

"That's what I'm saying."

They laughed, and Mama kept a playful tone in her voice as she asked him about what kind of vacation they might take together.

I stared up at the night sky, hoping to see the only constellation I knew, Orion's Belt. Not wanting to move my face from the door, I only saw a sliver of the heavens. I didn't recognize any of the bright dots that scrolled past. A street lamp glare soon erased my view of the stars and announced that we'd arrived in town.

Papa parked in a space near the Roxie Theater. When he got out, he adjusted himself in his trousers, which prompted a giggling comment from Mama. I missed her remark as I slammed my door shut. She exited on his side and said, "I'm good for more'n laundry, Mance. Speaking of which, you're missing a undershirt. I only washed six today."

"That right? Maybe one's under the bed." He stared at me and said, "Maybe one of the boys is playing a prank. You acting out, Bud?"

"No, sir." I walked fast to the theater door and waited for Papa to buy the tickets. He'd never gone inside with us before, so it was strange to see him under the bright lights of the lobby crowded with townies. The yellow glow made his hair look duller and emphasized the bent tips of his ears. He looked at the concession counter and all around, turning one way and then another as Mama kept walking toward the door that led to the seats.

I couldn't read the poster for the showing that night, other than "The" at the beginning. It looked like a story with lots of cooing and kissing. I knew all about that stuff; I'd gotten a buss from Cecilia after all. I studied the poster, looking for signs of gunplay or a fistfight, until Papa clamped a hand around my neck.

He said, "I told you to come on. You always got your head in the clouds." I had to trot to keep up as he marched me across the crowded lobby. In a low voice, he told me, "If you ratted me out, there's gonna be hell to pay—for you."

"I promised not to." I felt like a rube in my overalls and wrinkled shirt and bare feet thrust into battered shoes. Papa's hand on my neck caused the well-dressed town people to stare. The laughter I heard must've been directed at me.

Mama regarded my father alone, her smirking lips as red as Tommy's Popsicle. Points of electric light glittered in her dark eyes like the stars I couldn't name. Papa's hand stayed on my neck as he yanked me past her. She said, "We always sit in the first row."

He put me in a seat to his right. He'd originally sat me on his left, but switched me and Mama after noticing my birthmark and growling, "I can see that damn thing in the dark." It didn't matter, because a minute into the cartoon, he mumbled something to Mama and got up. He nearly crushed my toes before quick-stepping past the other people in the front row and disappearing up the aisle.

"Washroom," Mama whispered to me, leaning across the seat between us. "Go on and see that he comes back."

I couldn't turn my attention from Popeye's adventure, murmuring from the corner of my mouth, "If he catches me—"

Someone shushed us from the second row.

"Git!" She gave me a little shove.

I trotted in front of the audience and dashed up the aisle. The flickering pictures made the audience's upturned, laughing faces glow bluish-white. In the colored balcony, which led down to a side door where they had also bought their tickets, the Negroes looked darker than usual, as if the magical light couldn't reach them.

Papa was not in the whites-only washroom. I'd crept inside and kneeled to see under the stalls. Nothing but crushed cigarettes and crumpled paper. In the lobby, I described my father to the woman behind the concession counter. She said that he had left the theater a couple of minutes ago. I took my time strolling down the aisle as the newsreel played, upset that I'd missed the rest of Popeye and knowing that Mama would soon be angry too and ruin the rest of the picture show with her mumbled cussing.

She stared at me as I duck-walked in front of the other customers. I sat in Papa's seat, hoping it would be enough of a clue. Her sharp elbow jabbed me. "So?"

I whispered, "He left us here."

"I thought as much. Come on." She took hold of my arm and stood me up. As people shouted, "Down in front," she squared her shoulders and strode regally to the aisle. The music came on for the *Flash Gordon* serial, and she had to drag me out as I struggled to get a final glimpse of my birthday present.

On the sidewalk beside Papa's truck, she said, "Got 'im all spun up—now let's see where he unwinds." She pointed to the Western Auto across the street. "That where you went before?"

A row of Western Flyers in red, blue, black, green, and yellow beckoned from behind the plate glass window. I'd have gladly taken even one of the cheap American Flyer bicycles parked behind them if she offered. Instead, she said, "Bud! Look at me. Is that—"

Her face turned down the block, in the direction of the town square. She mimicked a Negro man's voice: "I sees your truck at da Cottontail Café lots a times." In a regular tone, she said, "You remember what that V8 Harris asked him? He never once took me to eat there. Told me the food was shit." Mama grabbed the shirtfront above my overall bib and raised the flat of her right hand. "I tried the sweet way earlier, child, but I'll slap you to next Sunday if you don't tell me the truth. Is that where your papa stopped on your birthday?" She jerked me onto my shoe tips and drew back her hand.

"Yes'm. He swore me to a secret."

"I'll give him some swearing." She slapped my left cheek once, a sharp blow like a hundred beestings. Letting go of me, she said, "That's for lying. Get in the truck."

I didn't want to wait for Papa to thrash me again, as he surely would. I shouted, "I can point her out, and Tommy Rush too."

"Who the hell's Tommy Rush?"

"The, um, the boy. Chet's age. I think..." I looked away after seeing her face: the parted lips and watery eyes. I realized that I'd returned her slap.

"Son-of-a-bitch," she said, giving each word equal weight. She crossed the street and marched toward the café. I hurried to catch up, wondering if she was talking about Tommy as well as Papa.

# CHAPTER 15

MAMA FLUNG THE CAFÉ DOOR OPEN SO HARD THAT THE HANDLE cracked a huge spider web in the glass storefront. Everyone in the packed diner turned to look as Roy Acuff sang about "The Great Speckled Bird" on the jukebox.

Papa faced us at a table near the back, with Tommy across from him. The redheaded, green-eyed waitress dropped a glass of cola, splashing her shoes and stockings and sending ice cubes skittering across the linoleum.

I didn't have to point her out to Mama, who took a few steps inside, brushed a golden wave of hair off her forehead, and announced, "Mance, I always knew you had a thing for blondes." She pointed a long, straight finger at the waitress. "Even Irish blondes."

A few men laughed but their wives shushed them as Papa pushed out of his chair, tipping it over. Tommy looked at me and then at Papa. He said, "Why's he here again, Daddy? Who's that lady?" Papa murmured something, and his son shuffled into the backroom. Before Tommy closed the door, he frowned at me like it was all my fault.

Papa said, "Mary, go in there with him."

She took a step, but the manager, in his paper hat and freshly stained apron, said, "Hey, Mance, I got a business to run here."

"My Florida freebies keep your business running, so shut up. Mary, git."

"'Mary, git,'" Mama pantomimed. "Is that how he gave you that kid, honey? 'Mary, spread 'em.'" She got a few more laughs, and Mary Rush sobbed and ran to the backroom.

As the door slammed shut, Papa said, "Reva, that's enough. The only wailing these folks wanna hear is from the jukebox." He looked around, maybe anticipating some laughs, but no one even smiled at him. Most turned to watch Mama again, and my birthmark got a few curious stares. I wished I'd stayed in the truck.

Hands on hips, she said, "You told me the food here stinks. Guess that's why you gotta keep your snout in that wild Irish rose." This earned her louder guffaws; even the less-reserved women joined in.

Papa stormed toward us, shouting, "Enough. Let's go."

I took another step behind Mama as she called, "Why the *rush*? First Mary Rush and now me. You give 'I'm in a rush,' a whole new meaning."

Papa silenced the customers' laughter with a slap across Mama's face. She nearly fell backward on top of me. Instead of responding with a slap of her own, she grabbed for the gun at his waist. Both of her hands clamped down on the grip of the revolver while he tried to pull it away. They rocked in a slow circle and cussed each other as shouting customers ducked under tables.

I froze, not wanting either of them to win. I wanted them to stay locked that way forever so nothing would change for the worse. As soon as somebody won, everybody would lose.

Papa let go with his right hand and punched her throat. It was the same short, quick jab that had bloodied my mouth. She staggered and coughed, her hands empty, her coloring as dark as my birthmark.

He drew his Colt and thrust it in her face, almost touching her gasping mouth. Thumbing back the hammer, he said, "Bye-bye, baby."

I sprang forward and wrenched his arm down as he fired. Mama screamed. She grabbed her bloody side and fell over. A table collapsed beneath her and chairs scattered. As I held Papa's forearm, his swelling muscles spread my fingers apart. He grabbed my hair, and several men jumped him from behind. We went down in a pile, all of them on top of me.

Papa fired again before someone yanked the gun away. As fast as they buried me, the men rolled off and regrouped. Papa tried to crawl away, but the customers grabbed his arms and legs. A burly man ran up and kicked Papa's ribs while Mama continued to cry out. A second kick dropped Papa onto his stomach. The man jammed his knee between my father's shoulder blades, which kept him down. Two customers ran out, shouting that they'd bring help.

I slid a few yards to where Mama lay. Her head rested in a woman's lap; her cheeks had turned the same dingy white as the linoleum and were wet with tears and sweat. Howling, Mama pressed the wound above her right hipbone with bloody hands.

Her eyes rolled wildly, looking past me, as if searching for somebody else. Anyone else. I wanted her to say my name, but all that came out was a long, terrible cry.

Papa still sprawled under the pile of men. His head was turned away from me. Then his back rose, swelling like an ocean wave, lifting the men who tried to pin him. Before they could force him back down, he faced me. With only the slightest strain in his voice, he said, "Happy now?"

I looked away from his flint-gray stare as Mama wailed. A lizard-thin doctor hurried into the café and asked some people to pull my mother's hands away from the bullet hole so he could look. The pitch of her screams rose like a saw blade biting into hardwood. I stared at Papa so I wouldn't see the gore; he was the lesser of two evils. I said, "Why, Papa?"

"'Cause she woulda done it to me." The burly man kneeling on Papa's back told him to shut up. Papa cussed him and got a rap in the mouth.

I blurted out, "What about Tommy?"

Through bloody lips, he told me, "Leave him alone. He's none of your business."

The manager unplugged the jukebox, silencing Roy Acuff. The police came in, two young men in blue short-sleeved shirts, with sweat stains as dark as their navy ties and trousers. Flat-topped blue hats perched on the backs of their heads with short visors pointing like beaks. One officer pulled Papa's arms behind him and snapped handcuffs over both wrists. The metal rings closed so tight that Papa's hands soon turned red.

A customer turned over Papa's Colt to the police. "The lady was hacking this fella about his love nest—got a kid and everything stashed here—when he up and shoots her."

"Horseshit," Papa shouted. "You're a Goddamn liar."

Both officers told him to shut up. No one else contradicted the customer. No one mentioned that Mama had grabbed for the gun first.

Everybody the police questioned pointed me out as the one who'd saved her life; they noted the splatter of Mama's blood on my overalls from the gunshot. I slumped in a chair beside the window she had cracked with the door handle. I didn't want to look at Papa's swelling hands, now turning purple, or the customers' pointing fingers or the blood that had spread behind Mama as the doctor worked to close one hole in front and another in back. Instead, I stared at the spider web of cracked glass and traced my fingertips over the raised, needle-sharp lines, leaving my own blood in the same place my parents had spilled theirs. I was the only one who bled on purpose. After all, the whole thing was my fault.

The officer who'd left his cuffs biting into Papa's wrists inspected two bullet holes in the linoleum, including one from the slug that had gone through Mama's side. He leaned over the doctor's shoulder and asked if she would live. "She won't live long," the doctor said, tossing aside another bloody pad, "if she keeps sassing-off at gunmen."

The policeman grunted and pulled a chair over to me. He spun it around so that he straddled the seat and leaned thick forearms across the back. His hands played with the braided leather handle of a sap, swinging it like the arm of a grandfather clock. The lead-weighted end was stained as dark as the palm of Papa's old baseball mitt. He said, "It's heavy, if you wanna play with it." I shrugged, and he said, "Most everybody thinks you swing it like a club, but really you just give it a wrist-flick." He demonstrated, snapping the bulbous tip toward me. With a smile, he said, "Puts a nigger on his ass in nuthin flat."

"Just them?"

"White folks too, I reckon. Even your daddy. Looks like you didn't need one though, to save your mama's life."

My fingers stayed on the razor-like spider web that kept me bleeding. I said, "No, sir."

"Your daddy tried to kill her, shoot her in the face, and you grabbed him. That right?"

"Yes, sir."

"You don't sound too pleased with yourself." While he talked, he unraveled and re-braided the sap handle, as swift as Mama fixing Darlene's hair.

"I promised not to tell about Papa's other family. But I did. I messed up everything."

"It's hard on a boy, knowing his daddy's two-timing, and has another kid and all. The way I see it, you kept everything from being a whole lot worse." He centered the hat brim on his forehead and parted the crowd of onlookers, heading for the backroom. Mary Rush let him inside.

The burly man who'd punched Papa and kept him down now helped the other officer pull him to his feet. "Sorry about having to sock you, Mance."

Blood had dried on Papa's mouth and chin. Somehow, his grime-smeared shirt shocked me more; I'd never seen him look dirty before. He said, "Save me a stool, Jerry. I won't be gone long." The officer shoved him out the door and a dozen customers followed; the other policeman soon joined the procession marching across the courthouse square.

Mama now lay on her left side, arm bent under her head for a pillow, facing me but with her eyes shut. She had quieted down, only whimpering as the doctor taped another bandage in place that stretched around to where the bullet had exited. He'd cut away some of her bloody dress and girdle, exposing flushed skin still wet from the alcohol he'd repeatedly splashed over the wounds.

Her eyes stayed closed as he asked how she was feeling: cold or hot, prickly or numb. "All that," she rasped. "And wide awake and sleepy. Everything and nothing. Son-of-a-bitch."

The doctor draped her exposed flesh with a pilled wool sweater donated by the woman who'd cradled Mama's head. He snapped his bag closed and said with a slight grin, "I hope that's not my mother you're disparaging."

"Everybody and nobody."

"You got someone to take you home?"

"I got nobody. There's just me."

The doctor glanced my way and winked. He said to Mama, "Your son is watching over you. He's a hero—saved your life."

"Just so I can cook his breakfast in the morning. Him and the others, eating me alive. A bullet woulda been faster. A kindness."

"I'll come out to your place tomorrow to check on you, Mrs. MacLeod."

Her eyes snapped open and stared into mine. She said, "Look for me in the kitchen."

I turned away, back to my web and the crimson streaks my fingers left on the window. The blood outlined every crack, seeping in, becoming a part of the place. Maybe the manager would leave the glass un-repaired and keep the slugs sunk deep in his floor: we'd always be a part of my secret brother's home. It only seemed fair, since he'd forever haunt us without even setting foot in our house.

The doctor came up behind me, translucent in the plate glass like a rail-thin haint. He tapped my shoulder and said, "Let's see those fingers." Tsk-tsking as I showed him the mess I'd made of them, he opened his bag again. Pads and white tape soon covered eight of my fingertips but didn't take away the hurt. He regarded me a moment. "I think you'll survive, young man. Might even heal faster than your mother." With a tap of my hand, he said, "Keep those clean for a few days, and give her some help in the kitchen, will you?"

After he departed, a few women leaned over Mama and asked how she was doing. "You should try it sometime," she said. Similar attempts to comfort her were met with other smart remarks. Finally, even the lady who'd cradled Mama's head in her lap left her alone on the floor, lying near darkened puddles of blood across which someone had laid napkins. She let Mama keep the sweater.

A few customers stuck around to gab with the manager and the soda jerk. Mary Rush stayed in the backroom with Tommy. The burly man who Papa had called Jerry now straddled the chair beside me just as the policeman had. A thicket of black curls atop his head and long eyelashes like a deer's softened his broad, ruddy face. One hairy forearm sported a blue-green tattoo of an anchor just like Popeye's. Introducing himself as Jerry Flynn, he said, "Sorry I had to peg yer old man. I don't take that guff offa nobody."

I shrugged. Not being able to touch the glass web anymore, I rubbed my bandaged fingertips together, aggravating the cuts so I could feel something.

"Well, I hope you don't hold it against me. What's yer name, son?"

I told him and asked if he was a sailor-man.

He smiled. "Not anymore. I been outta the Navy for a few years. Drive a bread truck now, delivering to stores." He said to Mama, "How 'bout I deliver y'all home?"

She muttered, "We got Mance's truck."

"You'll like riding in the van a whole lot better than a pickup, ma'am. Woman in yer condition oughtn't ride sitting up."

Mama took a few shallow breaths and said, "You fixing to carry me out like one of your bread loaves?"

"I figured we'd make a stretcher outta some cloth."

"This ain't a tablecloth kind of place." She tried a smile and said, "I usually get shot in the nicer joints."

I picked my way among the scattered chairs and tables to the backroom. My neck tingled from the stares of the manager and the others at the counter. I knocked twice. Mary Rush said, "I already told you fellas every—" She pulled open the door and stopped talking. Looking down at me, she moved to block my view of the tiny bedroom of faded yellow. What had once probably looked sunny now had the tinge of a flower long past its prime, in need of deadheading. Battered suitcases lay open on the bed with clothes piled inside and around them. Tommy knelt beside one heap and pressed down, hands deep in rumpled shirts and dresses like he was trying to pack himself too. She said, "What do you want?"

"A bed sheet. For my mother."

"I'm sorry about all this," she said. Her face flushed; she had rosy blotches around her eyes and nose from crying. "He shoulda come clean. Wait there." She closed the door and spoke softly to Tommy. After some bumping and more hushed talk, Mary edged open the door and handed me a rolled-up white sheet. I thanked her, and she said, "People warned me about a wife and family. Y'all get warned too?"

"No, ma'am. It took us by surprise."

"Life does that. We're going away from here—you'll get no more surprises from us."

"Can I say bye to Tommy?"

"No. Go on now." She shut the door.

I wrapped my arms around the sheet, hugging it to me as I returned to Mama and Jerry. She said, "Where'd you get that?"

"From Mary Rush."

"Good thinking, Bud. Now I get to lay on the same sheet Mance soiled with that hussy." The hard edge stayed in her voice, but her eyes had turned watery.

Jerry and I spread the bed sheet on the floor. We offered to help Mama slide onto it, but she said, "Don't anybody touch me!" She wriggled like a sidewinder, panting and cussing under her breath, until she stopped in the middle of it. Her tears slid onto the white linen as she gasped, "Christ, it smells like him."

Jerry recruited a strong-looking man to help. They each gathered two corners and lifted Mama a couple of feet off the floor. "Aye God," she moaned. "Hurry." I ran ahead of them, shoving open the café door. It swung wide and smashed through the cracked web, scattering blood-stained glass inside.

"Jumping Jesus," the café manager yelled. "What next?"

The large delivery van was parked across the street, taking up two spaces. Its side panel showed a beribboned girl chomping into a buttered slice of bread. Jerry told me to open the back. It hurt my fingers, but I shoved the heavy door above my head. The humid smell of baked bread washed over me.

Mama gritted her teeth. “Goddamn you, hurry!”

Jerry slid in and scooted backward, keeping the curve of her rump just above the floor until she was well inside. The other man didn’t stick around for any thanks. Just as well, because Mama wasn’t in a grateful mood.

# CHAPTER 16

Mama didn't even try to leave her bed for a week. She said it was the doctor's orders. Lonnie cooked for us and made sure we had dinners for school. Nat and his big-boned wife Leona took the evening shift, fixing our suppers and sitting up with us until bedtime. Whoever was in charge always made sure Mama was comfortable, but she mostly slept and sulked.

Jerry Flynn stopped by a few times to check on us in the late afternoons. He explained that he and Papa had often sat beside one another at the Cottontail and at a diner in Colquitt called Dora's. "Mind, we never talked much," he told me and my brothers on the porch one afternoon. "Yer daddy ain't one for spilling his guts."

"Just other folks' guts," Chet said.

Jerry nodded and opened his hands, as if what he wanted to tell us had escaped his grasp. He stood and said, "Who wants another ride in the bread truck?" Chet and I would slouch in the back with the sliding door pushed up. Jerry always had a loaf of "damaged" light-bread for us to snack on along the way and take home afterward. Jay sat up front and Jerry explained his delivery routes. On deserted stretches of road, he even let Jay stand beside him and steer the van.

Outside a country store, a clerk filled Jerry's gas tank from the gravity pump. Our new friend had set us up to RC Colas and "goober peas." We stood around Jerry, shaking salty, roasted peanuts into the narrow lip of our cold drinks. The hard part was trying to slurp all the foam that fizzed up. We had to drink the rest of the cola fast, before it went flat, which led to a lot of explosive burping.

"Y'all sound like a bunch of bullfrogs." Jerry got a laugh from the clerk and paid for the gas. "How are y'all planning to live, other than mooching offa the likes of me?"

I said, "Folks are still cooking for us."

Jay blew three notes across the lip of his empty RC bottle. "The fall crop's coming up," he said.

"But you still got bills. Are you renters?"

"Oh, yeah, the rent," Chet said, his mouth drooping.

"Y'all are gonna have to grow up fast. No more loafing on the porch with the dogs. But, I could use a hand with deliveries in the early morning—and I mean early, well before sunup. Job pays twenty cents a day and breakfast at Dora's when we're done. You can still walk to school before it starts. You up for it, Jay?"

My oldest brother said to Chet, "You can wake in time to get Bud up and do the chores?"

Chet said, "So you'll be the commandant and I'll be the general?" When Jay said yes, Chet grinned at me.

"What's my new rank?" I hoped to be a lieutenant like Nat. Or even a captain, a colonel—

Jay scratched his fingernail against the sleeve covering my shoulder, tracing three teepees, one over the other. "You're a sergeant now."

"Same as Lonnie?"

"Lonnie's a master sergeant," Chet said. "He still ranks above you."

I said, "I gotta outrank somebody."

"Darlene," Chet said. "And the dogs and cats and all."

Jerry asked, "What's your mama's rank?"

Jay said, "She's the cook, I guess."

"Cook's pretty important to a outfit. Oughta have a rank." Jerry collected our bottles for the deposit. When he returned, he said, "I'd make her a general alongside Chet anyway."

Chet looked Jerry over and leaned against the van, arms folded. "Why are you doing all this, Mr. Flynn?"

Jerry said, "I grew up without any folks at all, had to scrape all the way, so I know what y'all are up against. I figure when you're buried to your armpits, least I can do is give you a shovel." He placed his thick-fingered hand on my shoulder. "Also 'cause this new sergeant of yours did the bravest thing I ever saw anybody do, man or boy."

A WEEK AFTER THE SHOOTING, Mama called for me when I came home from school. She still lay in bed, her hair a regular rat's nest. Food stained the front of the housedress she'd worn for days. Near her pillow, a wan glow seeped through the old bullet hole Papa had shot through the wall. It looked like a blind eye. She said, "The county's lawyer came by, wanting me to testify. You too."

"In court and all?"

"Stop your shaking. I told 'im no. They can hang the sonofabitch without us. I won't sit there while they tell everybody about him two-timing me, about a whole 'nother family. Hell, maybe they found others he's got squirreled away...Anyway, we ain't gonna suffer one more humiliation for his pleasure."

"Is he really gonna get hanged?"

"Sorry, no he ain't. If he killed me like he wanted, then maybe." She rubbed her side while her jaw quivered. After a few hard swallows, she muttered, "I still can't believe he shot me. I thought we'd have it out like usual and he'd come home again, in a day or two anyway."

"What if you didn't grab his gun, Mama?"

She sat upright and put her small-boned feet on the floor. When she stood, she suddenly looked strong again. And angry. "Are you saying it's my fault? Is that what you're saying?"

"No, ma'am." I backed toward the door.

"That's why I don't want you to testify. You kept his secrets; you'd take his side against me. What else do you know? Why do you wanna hurt me?"

Tears burned my eyes as I blurted out, "I saved you."

"He wasn't gonna shoot. He only pulled the trigger 'cause you jerked his arm. You almost got me killed is what you did."

I rocked in place, hands over my ears to block out her ranting. I shut my eyes so I wouldn't see how her mouth twisted as she yelled at me. Mama shoved me against the wall and held me there.

"You've ruined us," she shouted. "Don't you understand that? How are we gonna survive on nuthin?"

I cried, shoulders pinned, proud of myself before but now so confused. "Jay's got him a job—"

"Twenty cents a day. Rent is five dollars a month, due in two weeks." She shook me. "I counted on Mance for everything."

"He woulda killed you."

"Then I'd be free of all this: your bottomless stomachs, the damn rent."

Darlene said from the doorway, "Mama, you'll hurt him. Let go!" After our mother had stepped back, Darlene continued, her voice getting shakier, "You said you had your eyes open. You said you had a plan."

"I'm not ready. All I got are prospects; I need time." Her face reddened and she began to cry as well. "Your father left me with zip; I don't know where his money is." Clutching her wounded side, she staggered back to the bed and sat on the edge. Mama's shoulders quivered as she sobbed, yelling at us, "Without more of your help, I can't afford a damned thing."

PAPA'S TRIAL ENDED BEFORE WE knew it had begun. Aunt Maxine and Uncle Jake had gone down to the courthouse in Bainbridge, "Just to make sure he really was going away," my uncle said on Thursday night, sharing supper at our kitchen table. Papa had waived his right to a jury trial, throwing himself on the mercy of Judge McCrory. The judge gave him five years at the upstate penitentiary. Uncle Jake reported that before the police led my father away, the judge said, "Hey, Mance, who's gonna deal with the Ashers until you're back?"

"Reva," Aunt Maxine said, "five years don't seem long enough."

"It's forever if you're broke."

Mama's sister glanced at me and my siblings before asking, "You gonna file papers?"

"Ha! If Mance thinks he's shed of me, he's got another thing coming. I'll get his money, every dime. Just you wait."

After our company left, we listened to Mama's plan for making enough money to survive. As she washed dishes, she said, "Nat can drive the truck. Two of you go down to Florida with him and get the usual haul." The police had given Mama the key to Papa's Ford as well as the gun that had almost killed her. Somehow, the money he usually carried had vanished; the police had said his pockets were empty. Rather than smashing the gun or at least selling it, Mama kept the snub-nosed Colt under her pillow.

Jay scratched his thumbnail along a splinter of wood, lifting it out of the table like raising the dead. "But Papa would pay them Ashers when he took delivery. They ain't gonna give their whiskey to us on credit."

"They'd sooner shoot us," Chet said.

She plunked the last plate in the water, swiped her hand around it, and set it in the wooden drain-rack. Wiping her hands on her apron, she said, "Maybe I should go. Throw myself on their mercy like your papa did in court."

"I don't know, Mama," Jay said. "They're real rough cobs. Better I should quit school to work for Mr. Flynn and get a day-job."

"You ready to be the man of the house?"

Jay shrugged, looking at the tabletop instead of Mama. I'd never seen him scared before.

Chet said, "Me and Bud could hire out after school."

"If it'll help," I added.

"'Course it will." Mama sat at her usual place. The head of the table remained Papa's, even in his absence. I wondered if I'd ever see her spot as the command post.

Darlene continued to stare at Jay, twisting her fingers. Finally, she said, "How can I help?"

* * *

Jay decided to make Friday his last day of school; he quit with a fourth-grade education. But first, well before dawn, he rolled out of bed and got dressed so he could walk to Hardscrabble Road and meet Jerry's bread truck. Chet didn't stir, but I came awake at the one yawn my oldest brother allowed himself as he headed out the front door.

Waking when Jay left caused me to fall into a stupor at school. I'd had trouble concentrating in class since my birthday-trip to Bainbridge; Mama's shooting had only made it harder to stay focused. Now, I couldn't shake off sleep. Miss Wingate—soon to be Mrs. Gladney—tried to keep me alert, calling on me often, but all I wanted to do was curl up on her long desk and turn the stacks of paper into a pillow.

Worse, I didn't even have a dinner: Mama had decided on Thursday night that we needed to hoard our food. She must've gone to see Mr. Gladney because he appeared before noon and announced, "Roger MacLeod has been added to the list for free dinners." He asked Miss Wingate to make sure I reported to the front office each day for my handout. The other kids stared at me. Even the ones dressed as shabbily as me had some kind of meal they'd brought from home. Many of them mouthed a single word: "Poor."

On the way to the office at dinnertime, Miss Wingate said, "I'll talk to my father about store credits for your family. Just until you get back on your feet." I thanked her, ears burning with shame, and she said, "You look like you could lay down right here and sleep for a hundred years."

I said, "Miss Wingate, you should see my brother Jay."

He leaned against a wall outside the front office, eyes closed. Of course, he and Chet and Darlene were also on the "pity list," as a classmate told me it was called. Darlene sat in the one available chair, staring straight ahead, as a half-dozen boys with dirty necks and torn, ragged clothes milled around. Chet had not come for the free food.

Miss Wingate didn't know my siblings. Jay came awake, and, while I made introductions, the front door was opened by a Negro man in a dark suit who glanced in and murmured in a surprised voice, "Miss Valerie."

"Hello, Brooks…morning, Lucy." The maid came through the door bearing a covered tray with my teacher's meal. Everyone watched her walk past and go down the hall, leaving a scent of warm roast beef that mingled with Miss Wingate's flowery perfume. Brooks closed the door, and Miss Wingate said, "I could stay."

I couldn't bear the embarrassment any longer, so I said, "No, ma'am. Thank you."

"Well, Bud, um, see you in class. Good to meet y'all." She waved to my brother and sister and left us.

In a moment, Brooks opened the front door again, this time for Mabel Boggs, a hatchet-faced spinster who ran the county charities. Papa had once pointed her out to me. Even adults called her Old Lady Boggs. She lugged a stained drawstring sack in one hand while the other hoisted a clipboard. The ragged boys made a half-circle before her, and she called their names, checking them off as she passed each one a tiny parcel wrapped in greasy brown paper. The boys clutched the handouts and bolted outside.

Old Lady Boggs stared at us and then glanced down at her clipboard. The school secretary came out of the front office and said, "The new ones, they're the children I telephoned you about this morning."

"I jotted 'em down here, but you said four."

The secretary looked us over and frowned. Her head bobbed as she counted me, Jay, and Darlene twice. Jay said, "Chet didn't come. We can take him something."

"The hell you can," Old Lady Boggs said. "If he's too shiftless to show up, he ain't hungry enough to eat." She slashed the pencil across her page and then summoned each of us in turn. I was last and accepted the slick package she thrust at me. Before she yanked the drawstring bundle closed, I saw Chet's meal, three small fritters, scattered in the bottom.

Each of us got the same thing: cornmeal mush fried into crispy disks. Darlene tasted one with her front teeth, and the secretary said, "Outside. This ain't a cafeteria."

So we followed Old Lady Boggs out of the school. While she crossed to a battered gray Plymouth sedan, we walked alongside the building, heading for the playground. The "doughboys" were days old and had no seasoning. Still, I finished mine in no time; Darlene had eaten hers even faster.

Jay said, "Jerry fed me good at Dora's. I'll see if General Blunt Stump wants these." He wandered the sandlot in search of Chet, and Darlene went to the other side of the hog-wire fence. She stood alone until Cecilia and one other girl joined her; all her other friends stayed away.

When we got home from school, Darlene wouldn't speak to Mama. She went to her room and stayed there until supper, which was one hardboiled egg apiece and doughboys. At least Mama seasoned hers. Instead of the regular cuss-fights and violent threats we used to endure, now we ate in silence. But nobody got hit.

After Mama finished eating, she told Jay, "I talked to the foreman at Ramsey Lumber outside of Colquitt. They could use a boy to sweep up and do odd jobs for fifteen cents an hour. You're to start on Monday."

"Should I tell Jerry I'm quitting the bread run?"

"Well, son, every little bit is gonna help. Besides, Jerry Flynn can drop you there. I'll come fetch you."

Jay stifled a yawn as he nodded.

Mama turned to Chet. "Come Monday, get off the bus at Mr. Blankenship's place and do what his foreman tells you. He'll pay you a quarter for four hours' work." Blankenship Farm was really a plantation; it always took first place for growing the most peanuts and sugar cane in South Georgia and ran a close second with other produce. Chet would have to walk an hour to get home unless he hitchhiked.

He said, "After school only?"

"For now you and your brothers are all working there on Saturdays if you're needed." Mama pointed to me and said, "You're going to Mr. Turner's after school."

I gave her a gap-toothed grin and lisped, "Cecilia's place?"

"Those teeth ain't come in yet? Aye God, they're as slow as Christmas. Now mind you don't remark on her father's hand."

Cecilia's father had been injured a few years before while grinding sugarcane. He'd slipped while jamming a thick stalk between the steel rollers and got drawn into the machinery. The rollers crushed his left hand before the gears could be reversed. Papa had hired us out to help at the mill, so we watched as workers hustled Mr. Turner into a jalopy and drove off. We also got to help clean the blood and gristle from the rollers and the trough beneath it that was slick with pink-tinged cane juice and crawled with yellow jackets.

After the accident, Mr. Turner qualified for government programs that allowed him to buy his own farm. Cecilia once told me that the hospital doctor gave her father the flattened hand as a keepsake. Mr. Turner had displayed his souvenir in a fruit jar of alcohol until somebody stole it.

I told Mama that I'd behave, while imagining the Turners' wide front porch, drinking lemonade and rocking in a swing with Cecilia. My birthmark tingled where she'd kissed it.

Darlene asked, "What can I do, Mama?"

"I'm starting a list of promising boys, honey. Your job is to do better than I did."

# CHAPTER 17

I MISSED A DAY OF WORK IN NOVEMBER. A CLASSMATE IN THE AISLE beside me had been coughing all week and had looked so pale and feverish that Miss Wingate had dismissed him early on Friday; she'd had her chauffeur Brooks, drive him home. By that afternoon I'd started coughing as well and skipped supper, complaining that my throat hurt. Actually, I had no appetite—the first time that had ever happened. Before sunup on Saturday morning, Chet kicked me awake, saying, "Jeez, Bud, you peed the bed!"

A bout of night sweats had soaked the sheets and mattress. Jay complained that my coughing had kept him awake. Chet went out to sleep on the back porch and my oldest brother made a pallet on the floor with a quilt I'd dampened. I had the bed to myself but my cough took on a loose, wet feel, like blunt knives scraping away my insides.

Mama felt my forehead in the morning. She shook her head and said, "I'll get your brothers to fill the big wash basin before they go off to Mr. Blankenship's. A cold soak might break that fever." She said that she'd make my excuses to the foreman before taking Darlene into Bainbridge to shop for courting clothes. After they'd all gone, I shivered in the galvanized basin with my hot forehead pressed against the goose bumps on my knees. For hours I sat there, doubled up and coughing into my submerged lap.

I lay on the mattress all afternoon, hot and then cold and burning once more. My shirt and overalls clung to me, and fever dreams plagued my sleep. I dreamed that Papa had my family all lay facedown on the porch. He said, "Bye-bye, baby," as he pointed his Colt. Instead of shooting, though, a ragged hole opened under each of us and we fell through. The rest of my family disappeared, but I landed beside the graveyard I'd made for my teeth. The wounded rabbit had dug them up and was eating the tiny bones like kernels of corn. When I reached out, the rabbit fur turned to piled stones. I was clutching the grave marker of Eliza Jean. Daylight came through the hole in the porch above, and Uncle Stan reached down to me. In his soft voice, he said, "Unh-uh. Let her sleep."

My brothers came in an hour before dusk. During my dreams, I'd kicked off the top sheet. I pulled it up to my chin as my teeth chattered. Jay said, "How's the patient?"

I hacked into my lumpy down pillow before replying, "Fair to middling."

"You cough any harder and feathers'll blow out the other side. Where's Mama?"

I didn't hear any sounds coming from the kitchen. "She ain't back yet?"

Chet said, "Truck's still gone. You up for some hunting?"

"I ain't hungry. I'll tell 'er where y'all went." I hadn't eaten anything all day, and I still couldn't imagine wanting food.

Jay peered at me and stepped away. "You reckon you got the consumption?"

A chill ripped through me like a whip cracking. I recalled the burned-up mattresses and bedding at the dump. Sometimes landlords evicted tenant families who'd taken sick; other houses were torched after TB had killed everybody. Because of me, my whole family could become homeless or dead.

I hoped they'd say something to cheer me, but my brothers backed onto the front porch. Chet said, "Think we might camp out tonight. We ain't done that in a coon's age."

Jay waved at me. "We'll bring you back something good, Bud. Maybe some red squirrel? See you tomorrow." He and Chet went all the way around the house and came into the kitchen to get the rifle and cooking gear.

Turning one way and tossing another, I couldn't complete one thought before my mind drifted onto something else. I rubbed the tip of my thumb against the underside of the buckeye, worrying at the dimple. Its contours, solid, smooth, and unchanging, gave me comfort. Finally, I slept again.

Mama and Darlene must've decided to stay for the late show—spending all the money we'd earned—because the sun had set for a number of hours before Sport and Dixie stirred on the front porch. I'd moved to the top end of the mattress after fits of sweating had swamped the lower half. I couldn't see the driveway from this new angle, but the dogs told me someone was approaching.

Our hounds didn't bark, but they sounded uneasy, pacing the porch and baying. I heard footsteps and panting: somebody ran toward the house. Whoever it was had the good manners to latch the gate after crossing into the yard. The deep breaths sounded like a man's. He vaulted the porch steps and stumbled into the dark house, bringing with him the rusty stench of blood.

I shouted, "Who's there?"

My voice made him cry out. He bumped into the bed and felt the mattress before he sat down hard. Lonnie said, "Oh Lord, Bud, I need help. I need a miracle." His silhouette rocked forward and back, hugging his chest.

"Are you hurt?"

"No, no, not me. Unh-uh." He couldn't seem to slow his breathing. The dogs looked through the front door, raised their heads, and howled.

I hushed them and said, "What can I do?"

"Where's your mama? I need her to take me away."

"I reckon she's still in town. Where do you need to go?"

"West of here. 'Bama."

"Why?"

"Don't ask me, Bud. Don't!" He sobbed into his hands. Another odor leaked out of his sweat: whiskey. "There was a fight. That's all I'll say."

I apologized and coughed against my sleeve. "You gotta go right now? My Uncle Stan's got a wagon and a mule."

"Too slow. I'll run there through the woods if I can't get a ride."

"Shank's mare," I said, thinking of Robert Bryson's advice. "Better run like the devil's after you."

"Oh, he is, boy. He's fixing to jab me good." Lonnie stood up. "I'm gone, Bud. You never saw me tonight."

"I know where a car will be come sunup." I started to tell him about Mr. Bryson offering a ride to Wanda Washburn every morning, but he knew all about it.

"Ain't your mama coming home? If I had my druthers, I'd pick her over that witch."

The hounds began to bark furiously. Soon, headlights swept the yard as a car came rolling up the drive.

"It ain't her," I said. "Them dogs know Papa's truck. Come on." I was woozy the moment I got to my feet, but managed to stay close to Lonnie as we dashed down the hall and out the back. We fled into the moonlit woods, following the same path where my brothers and I had run so often from Papa. Lonnie ran and ran and I tried to follow until I almost fainted. I must've sounded pitiful when I cried out to him, because he stopped on a dime. I leaned against a tree to catch my breath, coughing into my hands. The lightheadedness finally passed, and I said, "Who was that?"

"Deputy sheriff be my guess. You sure sound funny—you falling off?"

"I got me something. Jay says maybe TB."

"Lord, that's all I need. You oughtn't be stumbling around these-here woods with the consumption. Git on home." He crossed through a patch of moonlight and I saw blood on his right sleeve and all over the front of his shirt. It even stained his trousers. Blood speckled his face and neck and caked the back of his hands. He was awash in it.

I pointed and said, "Any of that yours?"

He pulled at his shirt, revealing a long gash that had split the breast pocket. "Maybe a little."

"I gotta make sure you're safe." Another coughing fit wracked me.

"I am—now git!"

I crossed my arms and said, "Nope. I lost my way. If you leave me here, I'll die."

Lonnie turned in a circle, fists in the air, ready to pound something. "Damn it to hell, if you ain't the most stubborn child. No wonder your daddy whupped you so much." He stomped around and cussed and said, "Lord help me. OK, let's go. But I might throw you to a gator if you make any more noise. Folk can hear you hacking over in Decatur County."

He led me through the forest lit with blue-white splashes of moonlight. Setting a fast-walking pace, he allowed me to keep up as long as I trotted. Over his shoulder, in a calmer voice, he said, "Never thought I'd come this way again."

"You had dealings with Wanda?"

"Just oncet. Trying to court her daughter."

"Was she pretty?"

"Tol'able. But they said she knew a thing or two...Um, she could cast this kind of spell over a fella. Make him feel good for a month of Sundays."

"Did she like you?"

"She did, but ol Wanda said I was trouble."

"I reckon she was right." I stopped to cough into my hands, almost passing out as my head throbbed.

"Thank you much, Bud. You's what they call 'cold comfort.' Lookee here." He pointed to a wagon trail with very short stumps around and between two tracks of dirt and chewed up leaves. He pointed first to the north and said, "That leads to the highway. This-a-way takes us to Miz Wanda's."

We followed the wagon trail for a quarter mile as it zigzagged around trees as broad as Lonnie was long. I asked who cut down all the timbers and Lonnie said, "The fella you promised would give me a ride. Bobby Bryson wanted to be durn sure he could get to Miz Wanda's doorstep with his slick auto-mobile. Only way to do it was with a axe and big ol crosscut saw." We emerged into a wide, moonlit clearing with a small wood cottage surrounded by gardens. Bunches of roots, withered leaves, and dried flowers hung upside down like bats from the porch rafters. He said, "I helped him do it—thought I was getting in good with Wanda that way."

"Did it help at all?"

"All she said was—"

"Lonnie Nugent," Wanda called from behind us, making me yelp, "you mighty handy cutting things. That's what I said." She propped her unlit flambeau against her shoulder like a club. "What'chu doing strolloping around these woods with a sick child?"

I said, "He's hurt, Miz Washburn."

"He killed a man tonight. Isn't that right, Lonnie? You done stuck a knife in Randy Stokes' neck and got hosed with blood. It came to me clear as day."

Lonnie looked at his spattered buckle-shoes and murmured, "He cut me first, ma'am."

"Randy was even drunker than you, wasn't he? You coulda knocked 'im cold with a matchbook."

"Didn't seem like it at the time, ma'am."

I recalled the policeman at the café with his leather sap, afraid of what could happen if she sent him away and he got caught. Fear drained away what little stamina I had left. I collapsed at Lonnie's feet.

They carried me into her parlor where she lit a lantern. Lonnie mentioned TB and Wanda muttered to herself, walking outside again. Lonnie pressed a cold, wet rag to my forehead and cheeks. In no time, I fell asleep.

A CAR HORN WOKE ME in the morning. I lay on a pallet made from an old quilt that smelled of cedar shavings. My clothes felt stiff from all the perspiring I had done the day before, but the night-sweats hadn't come upon me at Wanda's. Also, I was mighty hungry.

Lonnie stood in the doorway, waving to the driver. Threadbare overalls covered his strong, bare chest, and a white strip of cloth nestled tight around his ribs. He'd cleaned his coffee-dark skin until it glowed. His waving hand suddenly snatched something buzzing beside his ear, shook it hard, and discarded the pest on the porch floor. As he listened to Wanda talking to Robert Bryson, I thought about how much I'd miss my friend.

I sat up, coughed a little, and said, "Can I please have one more roof-slide?"

He laughed through his nose and shook his head. "Ain't much pitch on this-here roof. It'd be faster to crawl down." He faced me, slurping from a steaming tin cup. "You 'member drinking down all that nasty-smelling stuff Miz Wanda cooked up last night?"

"Unh-uh." I'd thought the tingling in my throat and chest had come from almost hacking my lungs out.

"Let's see how that fever of yours is faring." He walked over to me and crouched like a catcher. His warm, dry hand covered my head, palm pressing my brow and fingers going all the way to the back like a helmet. I felt like I could go back to sleep that way. He said, "I think we got it on the run."

Mr. Bryson tooted his horn again and hollered, "Last call for the Fugitive Express."

"Lord, I ain't never gonna be able to come back." He shook his head.

"Never?"

"Unh-uh," he said. "We'll give you a ride back home."

"Won't it be dangerous? Somebody might see you."

"I 'spect I'm gonna ride in Bobby's trunk."

I took his tin cup and drank from it. As the hot, bitter coffee sizzled down my throat, I imagined how mortified my parents would be: drinking after a Negro. I gulped some more.

Lonnie reclaimed the cup and toasted me, saying, "Sergeant." He looked into my eyes, long and steady. Despite the danger—drinking after a TB case—he drained it.

# CHAPTER 18

At the end of November, as I washed up for supper on the back porch, Mama took a slit-open envelope from her apron pocket. She said, "Bud's been keeping a secret. It says so in your first-ever letter."

I cleared my throat, a remnant of my minor TB infection, and asked, "Is it from Lonnie?" I'd insisted on going with him and Mr. Bryson all the way across the Alabama border. We'd released Lonnie from the Pierce-Arrow trunk behind a Negro diner in Dothan. Mindful of my ailing lungs and his wounded chest, he'd given me a last, gentle hug that I could still feel across my shoulder blades. Like he'd given me wings.

She shook her head. "I ain't even sure he can write."

"How about from Papa?"

"Oh my stars, no! Why would he—" She frowned at me and said, "Is there some other secret that man asked you to hide?"

"No, ma'am. I made a bad guess is all."

She stared a little longer. "I don't believe you, but I'm too tired to beat the truth out." Fanning her cheek with the envelope, her voice became playful again: "I'm talking about your secret girlfriend."

"Cecilia?"

"Do you have a crush on Bill Turner's girl?" She giggled. "Since I sent you there to work?"

"No! Unh-uh! I ain't guessing right."

"Bud and Cecilia sitting in a tree, k-i-s-s...You sure take after me, falling in love as easily as you can fall out of a boat. Go on, guess again."

I wanted to ask if Miss Wingate had written to me—she knew I could read a little. Rather than get Mama stirred up even more, though, I said, "I don't know nobody else."

"Rienzi? Rienzi Shepherd?" She withdrew the letter from the envelope, unfolded it, and indicated a name at the bottom printed in lettering much better than my own.

"She ain't my girlfriend."

Mama pointed at the page. "Here she says, 'I know you're keeping my secret. I know I can trust you.' And down at the bottom: 'I hope my present is giving you good luck.' Now, Bud. Presents? Secrets? Hopes and wishes? How on earth did you make a girlfriend in Texas?"

Jay's head popped around the doorway. He'd snuck through the house. "Bud's got a girlfriend in Texas?"

"Stop it!" I stamped my foot.

Chet appeared beside the porch, having crept around from the front. "Ry Shepherd's a boy. He taught me judo. Don't you know the difference between boys and girls, Bud?"

Mama laughed and said, "Rienzi sure sounds like a girl's name."

"Can't be a girl," Chet said. "That Japanese kid threw me all over the place. He saw me naked."

"I'm a girl and I've—" Then she paused and a scowl burned all the humor from her face. "Aye God, she's a Oriental. Where's your head at, Bud? This little girl ain't even white."

I said, "Quit it, everybody. Ry's a boy, I swear! A half-white boy!"

Mama shook her head and said, "Orientals are yellow niggers, Bud. Don't you know that?" She rattled the letter in my face and said, "C'mon, out with it now. What's the story?"

I snatched the page from her and tore it one way and the other and again and again, shredding until my fingers weren't strong enough to rip it into even smaller bits. The tinier I made the pieces, the more shame I felt at betraying my friend. The low growl I heard came from my own throat. I threw a fistful of scraps at her feet.

Mama slapped my face, twice. She shouted, "You're too old to be throwing tantrums."

Darlene stood in the doorway with Jay and said, "What's got into him?"

Mama crumpled the envelope and threw it at my feet. "I got no idea. But guess what? This Oriental boy-girl's coming back here to see you. I ain't saying when—that's my secret."

HALF THE PIECES OF RIENZI'S letter had blown away before I cleaned off the porch. I'd wanted to try to put back together what I could after supper but Mama wouldn't let me burn the kerosene needed to see. In the morning, the bits of paper I'd left on the kitchen table were gone. At least I saved Rienzi's envelope; she'd printed her address on the back.

During class, Miss Wingate told us to write ten sentences practicing the words she'd taught us. I began to compose a letter to Rienzi. My tongue edged out one corner of my mouth as I focused on making each shape perfect, nearly snapping the pencil in my tight grip. My writing slanted upward on the unlined page as I wrote, "I AM SORRY RIENZI. I AM A BAD FREND COS I LET YOU DOWN. MY MAMA GOT YOUR LETTER."

Miss Wingate stopped beside Fleming as she made her way up my aisle. She murmured, "Dayl Rdin?"

"Dale Arden, ma'am. *Flash Gordon.*"

She recited the letters of her name and said, "Do some sentences with the other characters. Poor Dale will be tuckered out before you reach ten. Have Ming—M-I-N-G—chop wood and feed the hogs. It'll do him good."

After checking another classmate's work, she touched my back and whispered, "This is so sad. Why is everything always your fault?"

"'Cause it is, Miss…ma'am." With just a few weeks before her wedding day, I was training myself not to call her by name so I wouldn't mess up when she became Mrs. Gladney.

She sighed and told me how to fix my misspellings. "What will your next sentence be?"

I printed *SHE RED EVRY THING*. I squeezed in letters as she made corrections. Slapping my pencil down, I said, "It's baby talk. If I was older, I could spell better words."

"If you were older you wouldn't be in my class." She patted my shoulder and said, "Let's enjoy our time together while we have it, OK?"

After she walked farther up the row, I sniffed her perfume. Then I silently repeated her married name five times before returning to my apology.

Miss Wingate accompanied me to the front office during the dinner break so she could go over my ten-sentence letter. She led me outside, where we stood alone to wait for Old Lady Boggs. Her eyes moistened as she scanned the paper a final time before handing it to me. "Please don't send this, Bud. It's too pitiful."

"Rienzi said she won't ever talk to me again if I tell her secret. And I did."

"Talk to her about it when she comes knocking. She'll give you another chance." My teacher pointed at the bottom of the letter. "This makes it sound like you're the one who never wants to see her again: 'I am sorry I can not be your friend.' That's a heartbreaker."

The Wingates' sleek black Cadillac turned a corner and cruised toward us. She said, "Written words aren't good enough sometimes. Face-to-face talking is better, especially when you want to explain and apologize." I must've looked doubtful, because she added, "You have nothing to be ashamed of."

"What if she stays mad at me?"

"You're such a sweet boy—who could stay angry with you?" She returned Brooks' greeting as he opened Lucy's door and held her tray as she got out. Before Miss Wingate went inside, she said, "If I was Rienzi, I'd let you make it up to me."

I tore up my letter with practiced motions.

* * *

On the Turners' porch that afternoon, I lived part of my daydream: drinking the sweet lemonade Mrs. Turner had poured for me while I sat on their whisper-quiet, freshly painted porch swing. Cecilia came out to sit beside me, which completed my fantasy. A mischievous smile dimpled her cheeks. She whispered, "I bet you're good at keeping secrets."

I was good at lying anyway, because I said, "Sure am." I wanted to see what would happen. She pinched my sleeve and led me off the porch like that, gripping the ragged cuff between her thumb and fingers. We circled around back to a rickety shed that housed what must've been Mr. Turner's old, busted tools from before he prospered. Blunt plowshares, mattocks, grubbing hoes, and pitted ax heads littered the wormy floorboards, and brittle-looking leather tack lay twisted in the cobwebs like dried snake skins.

Cecilia maintained a low tone, her breath warm on my face. "You like ooky things, dead critters in the woods and such, right?" The hinges of the door screeched as she opened it farther.

I was getting scared but I loved her attention. Not trusting my voice, I nodded. She took me inside the shed and squealed and shivered at the lacework of webs that seemed to breathe all around us. We used sticks to knock them aside as she told me to head toward the far left corner. I went first, destroying the webs that could touch Cecilia's face.

A patch of sunlight illuminated junk in the corner: busted kerosene lamps, tin cans, and moldering flour sacks and burlap pokes. She pointed her stick at a bag that stood on end. She said, "Careful, it might bite," and raced her fingers across my neck.

I jabbed at the bag and it made a dull clunk. A glance at Cecilia gave me the courage I needed to lift it up. Dust from the sack glittered in the sunlight as the specks drifted down over a small pyramid of canned peaches, pickles, green beans, and the like. I took a deep, musty breath and said, "What could bite me here?"

She gave me a big smile. "Fooled you! This is my secret though—all my favorite foods. Just in case."

"What could happen?"

"You never know when bad times'll come again. What's your favorite food there?"

"Peaches." I sat cross-legged and hefted the top jar, smooth glass and densely packed orange-yellow fruit and syrup. Next I looked at the beans and then pickled green tomatoes, inspecting each one and putting it aside.

I lifted a jar from the back and quickly blew a brown spider off my knuckle. This bottle wasn't packed full like the others. Inside was a gray tuber with mottled brown streaks; the vegetable skin was split all around and splayed like it had been run over. Jagged white insides poked out like splinters. The dusty sunlight flashed on the glass and I counted roots like five fingers. Mr. Turner's hand.

Cecilia's arms went around me and she grabbed the jar before I could fling it away. Screaming, I backed against her while she laughed in my ear. My legs thrashed and knocked over canned goods but nothing broke. I pressed my birthmark against her soft chest; her heart raced as fast as mine.

She set aside the fruit jar containing her father's mashed hand and rocked me as my breath slowed. "Daddy don't know where I hid that awful thing. You'll keep my secret, right?" I nodded against her bodice and she released me.

The whole right side of my face felt hot; blood pulsed in my ear. I said, "That was mean."

"I never had a little brother to joke with. Don't be cross."

"I love you." I covered my mouth, but the words had flown out like three carrier pigeons.

Her laughter shot them down. She said, "And I love you, little brother. Let's go before I get a spider in my hair." Before leaving the shed, Cecilia asked, "You wanna take home them peaches or anything?"

My feelings about Cecilia ran hot and then cold as I walked up our driveway. Every time I decided that she was terrible, though, I'd feel her arms around me and hear her steady heartbeat and, "I love you, little brother." I knew that she'd never tell my secret. The best way to keep one, after all, was to forget it.

Mama stood on the front porch, hands in her apron pockets. Darlene sat with the old porch swing rocked back; her toes were planted against the flooring. She couldn't push back any farther and she wouldn't let herself go forward. The tightness on her face matched Mama's. A fist squeezed my heart when I noticed that the dogs weren't around.

I called, "Where's Sport and Dixie?"

Mama said, "At Uncle Jake's. He might could use 'em."

"What about us here?"

"There ain't no 'here' anymore. Ain't no 'us' neither." She walked inside.

I asked Darlene what had happened, and she replied, "Mama says that Mr. Meriwether raised our rent."

"He's kicking us out?"

"Looks that way. We're going to stay at Grandma's."

"For how long?"

"She didn't say." She lifted her feet and swayed. The chains creaked like a tree limb that hosted a lynching. I asked her if Mama had given away our cats too, but Darlene said, "Mama says to leave 'em. 'They're wild things' she says 'and won't notice we're gone.'" She cradled her arms for a moment, as if cuddling a soft, wriggling feline.

The truck bed was loaded with farm tools, a couple of suitcases, and one scarred steamer trunk that Papa had always called the "hope chest." My clothes and my brothers' lay on the single-shot rifle, fishing gear, skillets and other kitchen doodads, including Papa's miracle corn-sheller. Army ants crawled over half-used flour, sugar, and cornmeal sacks that took up still more space. Mama had also added her broken Kodak camera, some letters tied with ribbon, and the Philco radio with its hoop antenna now bent like a saddle from being torn off its perch in a nearby tree. We could ride atop the pile if Mama kept her speed down. I noticed that she hadn't taken the brooms: it was bad luck to bring a used broom to a new home.

At supper, Mama told us that she'd driven around all day trying to find buyers for our livestock. Mr. Turner had bought Papa's horse, Dan. No wonder Cecilia's parents had been extra-nice to me.

"We got almost thirty dollars," Mama said. "The furniture is Mr. Meriwether's so it stays."

Chet asked, "What's the new rent?"

"Too much," she said to her plate. "More'n I'm willing to part with."

"But with thirty dollars plus what we're bringing home, we're almost rich."

"We got no way to work the fields and no milk and no eggs."

Jay said, "We could buy grocer—"

"And there goes the money." She snapped her fingers. "Gone. Y'all ain't making enough to keep a roof over us and put food in our stomachs."

Chet stared at his fingers, counting. "Mama, we're bringing in twelve dollars a week."

"He's asking too much—now drop it! We'll find someplace else soon enough. Make sure you don't leave anything behind."

While she washed, dried, and packed the supper dishes and utensils, my brothers and I added our slingshots and the cigar boxes of treasures. I envisioned Grandma's house and wondered if my brothers and I would share the parlor or bed down on the sleeping porch.

We left the front door open as usual before we bounded down the porch stairs into the moonlight. I looked back and expected to see Sport and Dixie, but of course they weren't there. Gone. I snapped my fingers. Gone. Mama started the engine and called to me, while Jay and Chet tested out places to sit. I remembered my tiny graveyard of teeth and wanted to crawl under the house to fetch them, but Mama leaned on the horn until I'd climbed in the truck bed. The blaring echo bounced across the fields and the woods and thundered back at us. How long would it ricochet inside the house and in what room would it die?

As we rode down the driveway and the connecting dirt road, items in the truck bed kept shifting; I had to find new handholds again and again. Mama braked hard in front of Uncle Stan's place, nearly pitching me overboard. She leaned out the window and yelled, "Bud, get your stuff. This is your stop."

My heart slammed around inside my ribs like a possum snatched up in a Croker sack. I said, "I thought we were going to Grandma's."

"Me and Darlene are. I told you before, there ain't no 'us' anymore."

My brothers looked at me as if I'd fallen over dead, which is what I wanted to do. Then they glanced at each other and realized they had the same disease. Jay called, "Why are we splitting up?"

"There's too many of you. Nobody's able to take us all in." When we yelled more questions, she shut off the rumbling truck engine. Lonely sounds of an empty night came to us: crickets and katydids, owls and whippoorwills. She got out, cussing to herself, and fixed her gaze somewhere above our heads as she explained that three of her sisters had each picked one of us. Jay was going to live with Aunt Maxine and Uncle Jake. Aunt Lizzie had chosen Chet.

"So Aunt Arzula picked me?" Ever the good soldier, I reluctantly climbed down and accepted my things from Jay. He mouthed that it would be OK, but he looked relieved at his fate.

"More or less," Mama said. Her gaze drifted to my aunt's darkened home. The last time I stood like this, placing the truck between myself and the ramshackle house, Papa was putting his Colt to Uncle Stan's head and Ry was fixing to become Rienzi.

Chet said, "How long are we gonna live apart?"

"Only until I can set up housekeeping again. You still got your jobs. I'll see you every other Sunday at your Grandma's."

Uncle Stan said from his front porch, "What's going on, Reva?"

"We lost the house, so Bud's coming to live with y'all. Didn't Arzula tell you?"

"No, she didn't, and no, he isn't. No offense, Roger."

Mama climbed back inside the truck and slammed the door. Through the open window, she yelled, "Don't make this tougher than it already is, Buddy."

She'd never called me that before; I felt as if I'd lost my name along with my home and family. I choked on exhaust and dust as she roared away. My brothers stared at me while they groped for handholds so they wouldn't fall overboard. Meanwhile, I was adrift.

Balancing my sole possessions—the Blue Cloud cigar box and cypress slingshot balanced atop my town shoes and clothes—I shuffled to Uncle Stan's porch. He sucked in his lips as he looked down at me. In his usual quiet voice, he said, "Guess that settles that, huh? I ain't faring too good against your family, Roger." He rubbed the crooked bridge of his nose and the cartilage made a popping sound. "Well, come on in. We'll figure out what to do with you."

Aunt Arzula lit the kerosene lamp in their parlor. Rubbing the bald spot on the side of her head, she said, "Bud, what's that you're carrying?"

Stan dropped into a chair. "Reva says you agreed to take him in. Somehow, she lost their house already."

I set my things near the lamp on the table. "Mr. Meriwether raised our rent."

Stan said, "He ain't raised ours in years."

"It's too much now. More'n she's willing to part with, is what she said."

"Ahhh." Stan shook his head. "Damn, what a world. So your mama went around today giving away her children?"

"And our dogs, and selling the livestock." I explained where my siblings were going to live and told Aunt Arzula, "Mama said that you picked me."

My aunt tugged at the high neckline of her innermost dress. She said, "I sure think I'd recall doing a fool-thing like that. We got no money to raise up a youngun."

Stan watched the dark rafters for a long time. Finally, he said to the ceiling, "Reva must be splitting a gut about this, dropping Roger here after all I've been through with the MacLeods." To me, he said, "Hope you don't mind sleeping where you did before, a pallet in the corner. We only got the three rooms."

Aunt Arzula snapped, "If you're living under our roof, you're gonna work. Same as we do." I told them about my job with the

Turners, and she said, "That'll help pay for your keeping, but I expect you to do chores too. I gotta spend time caring for Eliza Jean, after all."

Stan waved away any question I was about to ask regarding their long-dead daughter.

# CHAPTER 19

I NEVER MINDED STAYING BUSY, AND IT KEPT ME FROM THINKING about missing Jay and Chet. Every other Sunday, I figured, my heartsickness would be cured in the morning when I got to Grandma's and return twice as hurtful in the evening when we got split up all over again.

Aunt Arzula made me turn over every penny of the twenty cents I earned each weekday at the Turners'. She took half for my upkeep and saved the other dime for Mama. In addition to doing fieldwork and gardening for Cecilia's family, I was put in charge of Papa's stallion.

Cecilia joined me in the stable to brush the huge black horse's flanks and coo to him while I shoveled his dung. Dan grunted and sniffed her but didn't try to break her foot or crush her against the stall. Her soap-and-gingerbread smell mingled with the aromas of sweet hay and Dan's massive heaps of manure. She apologized for scaring me the other day. "If I'd known about you losing your home, I wouldn't have done it. Are your aunt and uncle nice?"

"He's real quiet, hardly says a word," I said. "I can't feature what he's thinking. He'll look over at me kinda funny while we're eating or doing chores." I listed all the things Aunt Arzula had me do. "Come next Monday, I'm to help her with the wash before I catch the bus."

"They're gonna work you to death. Put down that shovel and take a breather." She led me out of the stall and squeezed my bicep. "You could knock out two Buck Bradleys now."

I flexed to make the muscle a little bit bigger and grinned as her eyes widened. Quick as a rabbit, I kissed her smooth, warm cheek.

Cecilia pushed me away, saying, "Silly. Looks like you're all rested up." She returned to the stall and kept Dan between us, but she stayed until I finished my clean-up.

On Saturday, I had to help Uncle Stan hoe around the last of the pea and bean vines and the thick leaves of collard, mustard, and turnip greens. A cool, steady wind blew dust devils across the field, coating us with sand. The whole day, he rubbed a dusty hand over his mouth time and again, as if wiping away words that wanted to get out.

The sunset looked crimson in the gritty air. After washing his face and neck on the back porch, Uncle Stan didn't join me and my aunt for supper. Instead, he changed into a clean white shirt and black trousers held up by suspenders. His town clothes suited him much better than the overalls and frayed work shirt. Polished black shoes struck the floorboards in a confident rhythm as he strode out the front door, a big black X across his back. Aunt Arzula watched him go and then plucked a wad from her biscuit, rolled it into a ball, and tossed it under the table.

Her stove hadn't drawn well because of the dusty wind, leaving the bread and greens undercooked and sandy. Dirt blew into the parlor where we ate, so I closed the door and held it shut by looping bailing wire over a rusted nail. Aunt Arzula said, "Mind you open that before Stan gets home. It ain't fitting to be locked out of your own house."

"Does he go out every Saturday night, ma'am?"

"Come hell or high water." She chucked another biscuit ball under the table.

I wanted to ask if he always came home drunk, but I was only a guest and couldn't risk getting on her bad side. Besides throwing food under the table, she kept the corners and the space behind each door supplied with dough. She also tossed bread under their bed, where they kept their shoes and a small wooden box that I'd resisted opening. We endured a lot of cockroaches and flies. I wanted to ask why she tossed bread around and how come she wore three dresses, and what was her reason for forty-leven other strange habits. But I knew better.

Instead, I helped her crawl across the floor and lay baking sheets, linoleum remnants, and other flat things, making walkways through the house. In this case, she did explain: "Stan's gonna bring poisons in on his shoes. Can't have Eliza Jean crawling across that stuff."

She took their only kerosene lamp from the parlor to the kitchen to rinse the dishes, leaving me in the near dark. I shuttered the windows against the dusty wind and secured them using the same wire-and-nail fixtures that the door had. With the windows closed, the room turned black. I crossed through the bedroom and stood in the kitchen, where Aunt Arzula dunked each dish three times in her basin as she hummed tunelessly.

The wind wailed through the open kitchen window. Grit sprayed my face and coated the floor. I shouted, "Aunt Arzula! You want me—"

She screamed and dropped a plate into the water, splashing herself. Bending double, she shielded her face with multi-sleeved forearms, palms covering her head. The same way I'd defended myself from Buck Bradley's punches.

"It's me! Bud!" I ran to the window, squeezing my eyes shut against a blast of sandy air, and grabbed the shutters. With the window closed, her screaming nearly overwhelmed the hail-like racket of blowing dirt. I secured the shutters on the opposite side of the room and waited for her to calm down. "It's just me," I murmured, over and over.

She peeked between her arms. Grabbing up the dish from the water, she said, "Oughta be ashamed, scaring a body like that. Go on before I take a spoon to you."

I left the only lit room and traipsed to my pallet in the parlor. Sand covered my nightshirt and all the bedding so I carried everything to the opposite corner, stumbling over the walkways we'd laid. I shook out the grit and punched my pillow, holding it up like I'd grasped a bully by the hair.

Drifting dust made me sneeze as I shuffled back to my corner. I checked to make sure my aunt wasn't watching, and changed into my nightshirt. Before getting onto the quilt, I wiped off the soles of my feet. At last I was ready for bed. I missed Jay and Chet's feet bracketing my head, their legs keeping me safe from the haints and booger-men who could be lurking on either side. I'd never had so much elbow room in a bed, and I'd never been so sorrowful. Still, I was dog-tired from working; not even self-pity could keep me awake.

A crash bolted me upright a few hours later. The front door had been forced open and the wind blew dirt inside. A vague white form staggered in the doorway. Uncle Stan cussed his wife for locking him out. He took a step and kicked aside a baking sheet. I thought I was safe in the dark, but his rumpled silhouette pivoted until he faced my corner. In two long strides he was over me.

The white shirt glowed, seeming to float in the air above his black trousers. His shoes landed hard beside my legs as he straddled my pallet. Then he dropped to his knees, imprisoning me, and he leaned down. As the wind howled through the door, his gritty, callused hands clawed over my chest and found my neck.

"I know what you're playin at. I know why you're back." His voice slurred as he throttled me. Dirt from his hair and clothes sifted onto my face, and I felt like I was being buried alive. He squeezed harder.

His thighs immobilized my arms; my legs couldn't do anything but thrash and kick the air. I gulped through my mouth as his fingers tightened. In another moment he'd crush my throat.

"Won't you MacLeods let me be? Reva, then Mance, and now you! Jesus Christ, when will y'all stop?"

Aunt Arzula yelled from the bedroom door, "Baby! You're killing the baby again!"

Stan released me and sat upright, keeping me pinned beneath him. "Shut up! He ain't your baby." His hand slammed against my chest as he pushed himself up. Stepping over me, his shoe clipped my birthmark. Finally tears came to my eyes and I sobbed.

"Eliza Jean!" my aunt screamed. "No!" His sharp backhand knocked her to the bedroom floor. He stomped after her.

I ran out the front door. Though my aim was to hide in the barn, the wind pushed me along the road. I couldn't feel my legs or my arms or the swelling from his kick. Only the squeeze of steel around my throat, closing now, tighter, tighter. Ready to pop my head off. I let the wind blow me all the way home.

Once inside the house, I slammed the front door and looped our own wire in place over a bent nail. I raced across sand-strewn floors from one window to the next, shuttering them. Scraping our old bed across the floor, I blocked the front entry. The kitchen table required more effort, but I soon barricaded the back door. If Uncle Stan got through, I'd jump out a shuttered window and run to Nat's place. Maybe I should've gone there to begin with.

Standing in the dark kitchen, back home but all alone, I realized that I'd peed on myself while he was strangling me. I stripped off the sopping nightshirt, trying to keep the vinegary-smelling cloth from touching my face. With everything closed to the outside and as secure as I could make it, I sat shivering in the hallway, my naked back to the wall, and cried.

I'd left Aunt Arzula behind. She saved me and I didn't give a thought to helping her. My uncle kept his shotgun against the bedroom wall—if I could've gotten to it before him...then what? Would I have really killed him? Could I have avoided shooting my aunt as well?

Aunt Arzula had yelled, "You're killing the baby again!" Again. Poor Eliza Jean. No wonder he wasn't allowed at the old home place.

What would I find there in the morning? There was a part of me demanding that I go back. I needed to see what happened to her because of my cowardice. There was nowhere else I was wanted.

# CHAPTER 20

Aunt Arzula called to me from the kitchen, "Keep outta Stan's way. He's peeved that you didn't do your chores."

I'd seen my uncle out in the garden in his ill-fitting work clothes, shaking off sand that had buried the plants, re-staking poles knocked over by the wind. The air sparkled in the sunlight, as if the wind had left a million crystal flecks suspended, waiting to be pushed to a distant land. The haze made me squint just like I had when the gale was howling.

Uncle Stan had seen me come down the road. All he said was, "You get homesick?" His soft question had none of the slurring rage of the night before. He sounded cross but seemed to expect me to disappoint him. He turned his back and resumed toiling.

My aunt had a black eye and a swollen spot beneath her jaw. If she hid a thousand bruises under her outfits, she didn't let on that she hurt.

I walked through the swept and straightened house. The twin-barreled shotgun leaned against the wall where I remembered. What if I'd used it?

In the kitchen, I said, "I'm sorry."

"Don't apologize to me. Stan's the one slaving away in the garden."

"About last night I mean. I could've helped you but I ran away."

She stared past me until I wondered if she had any more recollection of it than my uncle. "I used to love to run," she said. "I ran everywhere. But now I keep them brogans on my feet so I won't step on Eliza Jean. You remind me so much of her: that sweet dreaminess." She shrugged within the three dresses, snapping a few stitches. "I can't say for sure why, but it hurts to look at you, like something getting in my eye. Almost makes me mad."

Her gaze swept over me and returned to a spot in the corner. "Ain't that strange?"

FOR SOME REASON I COUNTED on being able to go to our old house—to flee there or just wander from room to room and absorb the familiar smells—whenever I took a notion. Nat caught me on Monday as I came from the Turners'. He stepped off his porch and said, "A new family moved into your place."

"They bought it?" I tottered back a few steps.

"Renting, like y'all done. I told Mr. John Greer 'bout working there afore. He said I can keep sharecropping and my boy Ennis and his family can live in Lonnie's old home come spring. Seem like nice folk."

"At least you'll still be around. Seems like everything else is changed."

He gently pushed my collar aside and peered at my neck. "How you getting along with your uncle?" I told him about a plan I made to flee with Aunt Arzula on Saturday nights, and he said, "Bring her down here. Me and Leona would love y'all's company."

"OK, but you can't let on that you're taking pity on us; we're just visiting is all."

"I know the rules, Bud, Lord knows I do." The stern tone left his voice and he smiled at me. "Only fuss we'll make is keeping your water glass full."

The next Saturday evening, when Uncle Stan set off in his clean shirt and trousers and shined shoes, I told Aunt Arzula, "We oughta look in on Nat and Leona Blanchard down the road. They're not what you'd call neighbors," I said, "but I feel bad about not seeing 'em more. Before Mama got shot, we visited with 'em lots. You know, to make sure they was hanging on."

She nodded and said, "Colored folks gotta hard row to hoe. Maybe I oughta bring them some canned green beans, you reckon?"

We took green beans, pickles, and a round of cornbread. I tried to hurry my aunt along in her too-big brogans, but she kept fretting about not bringing enough charity. Twice I had to talk her out of going back for more.

As we approached, Leona was sitting on her porch with a shawl around her massive shoulders to ward off the chill. She stared toward the woods across the road and hummed "Old Ark's A-Moverin," a gospel tune that Nat liked to sing in the fields: "Old ark she reel. The old ark she rock. Old ark she landed on the mountaintop." She stood when she saw us and shouted, "Great day, I was praying for some comp'ny. It gets so lonely out here. Good evening, Miz Arzula. How you, Bud?"

She and Nat sat us in their tiny parlor, fell all over themselves giving thanks for the food, and acted like royalty had come to visit. They laid it on pretty thick, but Aunt Arzula seemed to enjoy being the center of attention. She only tossed one ball of dough under her chair.

We'd kept the front door closed—"It's getting right nippy don't you think, Miz Arzula?"—but I thought I'd heard Uncle Stan muttering as he headed home. I imagined him staggering along the dirt road, dirtying his shoes, and then bursting into the house to find no one. Would he bust a chair or fire his shotgun through the roof, something to satisfy his rage? Or would he collapse on the bed and cuss himself to sleep?

To draw out our stay, Leona put the kerosene lamp in the bedroom and stretched a white sheet across the doorway, securing it on a pair of nails. Backlit, with her silhouette on the screen, she performed a shadow play while Nat strummed a six-string guitar that he appeared to have cobbled together from three or more instruments. "My Lord, what a mornin," Leona sang. "My Lord, what a mornin. My Lord, what a mornin, when stars begin to fall." Ten fingers wiggled as her arms descended. "This is a love story," she intoned, "about a boy and a girl who meet on that great day when the heavens came down to earth..."

Later, Aunt Arzula shuffled home beside me, humming and swaying in the moonlight. Over and over, she pantomimed stars wavering downward. "I swannee, Bud, that sure beat a night at home. Too bad Stan couldn't have saw it."

I said, "Maybe we should do it again next week. Nat and Leona could use the company."

UNCLE STAN HAD DONE NOTHING to wreck the house the previous night, though my pallet seemed to have been kicked once. I'd made sure he was sleeping hard before I lay down.

The nights had become much colder, but even the days failed to warm up; the sun had gone behind a quilt of gray clouds. On Sunday, Uncle Stan loaned me a thin wool jacket of red and black checks and took me hunting with him. He toted his shotgun and walked along with hardly a sound. I had to trot to keep up, probably scaring away most game.

Some bushes rustled up ahead and I expected my uncle to take aim, but he stood still. A gray, bristly razorback—one of his, judging by the leanness of the hog—emerged with a long stick in its mouth. It snorted at us, proceeded up the path, and then took a quick left turn.

As its sinewy flank disappeared, Uncle Stan said in his soft voice, "He's not long for this world. Hogs carry around sticks when a frost is coming." First-frost meant hog-killing time.

We trailed the razorback deeper into the woods. My uncle pointed out its tracks to me in the brittle leaves and told me to stay quiet. He led me to a clearing almost entirely covered by a gigantic pile of sticks and hay and pine straw. The stack loomed six feet high and a dozen feet across and had the sweet stink of a hog pen.

What most impressed me was the warmth. It reminded me of standing close to the radiator in my classroom. Instead of a pinging sound, though, I heard a hundred whispered breaths and a low rumble, like snoring or thunder. Uncle Stan murmured, "Watch this," and fired one barrel at the sky.

The giant haystack exploded with hogs. Razorbacks poured out as if vomited from the earth. All of them shrieked and squealed as they surged away from the pile. I leaped onto the closest tree and shimmied up, just in time as a tusk slashed at my foot. Straw and sticks rained down on my yellow-pine perch while hogs swarmed beneath me.

Then laughter rose above their cries and grunts. The boyish, gleeful hooting came from a nearby cedar. Six feet above the ground, Uncle Stan wrapped his arms around the tree, one hand clutching his shotgun like a bouquet. He held the trunk tight, the way I'd always wanted to be hugged. His cheek pressed against the bark as he cackled.

It took several minutes of coaxing before he got me out of my tree. "God, that was something, wasn't it?" he said, wiping his eyes. "Like every hog in creation came out of there." Sticks, straw, and hay hung in the tree limbs and blanketed the forest floor.

I picked up a large stick and imagined smacking him with it. Instead, I tossed it into the middle of the clearing and laughed.

The frost came on Thursday, which turned my mood around about the approaching weekend. Though I didn't like the slaughtering, I'd have all the meat I could eat for days. The thought of boiled chitlins and hog feet and fried brains with scrambled eggs turned my thoughts from the necessary bloodletting, another Saturday night escape from Uncle Stan, and Miss Wingate's wedding day.

I DIDN'T GET A CHANCE to offer final best-wishes to my teacher before the weekend; my aunt and uncle kept me out of school on Friday to help prepare for the hog-killing. Aunt Arzula went to the old home place to clean out washtubs, scour the sausage mill, and sharpen the knives. Because Uncle Stan was banned from there, he always threw in with the Turners and their neighbors along Hardscrabble Road. On Friday morning, Uncle Stan enlisted me to help drive his three least-skinny hogs toward Mr. Turner's holding pen. We used the pointed ends of broken broom handles to keep the razorbacks trotting along the road. Normally

I'd look at an animal's face to see its expression and make up a personality for it. Now all I saw was breakfast, dinner, and supper for the last two weeks of the year and most of 1939.

I waved to Mr. Clemmons as he passed in his mostly empty school bus. He called, "Save me a pork chop, Bud." I wondered if he made a request for a different part of the hog from every child he saw that morning. Town dudes would own the school for a day; come the weekend, though, the country kids would tuck-in to a trough of plenty.

Once the hogs were settled in the pen, Uncle Stan volunteered to prepare the scalding-drum. Mr. Turner said to dig in a spot ten yards from the gate of the holding pen and gave us the shovels he cradled with his bad left arm. The stump below his elbow was shiny and dark red, like the color of the meat we'd hang up for smoking come Saturday.

My uncle dug into the sand and started a pile on his right. I stood opposite him and began my own mound. Our purpose was to dig a pit big enough to hold a 55-gallon drum. The barrel would lean at a forty-five degree slant. We'd fill it from the well and, in the morning, build a big fire at its base. Each freshly killed hog would get dunked in the boiling water, scalding its skin so the hairs could be scraped off.

Despite the cold weather, we soon broke a sweat. My uncle always seemed to relax once he'd dampened his skin. His upper-body rose and fell like a piston, and he began to speak. "How you liking it, Roger?"

"It's easy work, sir." Ankle-deep, I tossed aside another load of sand.

"I mean staying with me and your aunt."

I gave him a shy smile and said, "It's easy work, sir."

"Well, you don't complain, I'll give you that. You don't say much of anything, matter of fact. You're always watching though."

Uncle Jake had said the same thing, and both men were right. Knowing that I didn't understand half of what I saw didn't stop me from taking it all in. I was more afraid *not* to look. To head off a scolding, though, I said, "I ain't trying to spy, sir."

"Nuthin wrong with taking a good look around." He shoveled the deeper end and had to heave the sand up high, like a gravedigger. "Let me tell you what you see." Holding my gaze, he said, "You're seeing a unlucky man."

"Sir?"

He paused, forearms leaning on his shovel. "Most folks get a bunch of chances in life. I got one, and I backed out. Never got another." He wiped a sleeve across his face and said, "Me and my best friend went down to the Army recruiter soon as we got outta high school. Seventeen years old, strong as oxes, ready to take on the world." With a sigh, he resumed digging. "The Great War was over and no fighting in sight. Pulling a hitch in the Army woulda been easy as pie. We passed their tests, and my pal signed the enlistment form and handed the fountain pen to me. Guess what happened."

"Was it out of ink?"

He snorted and returned to his work. "No, I was. I lost my nerve; the sap just plumb ran out of me. I told him, 'So long,' and hightailed it out of there." His shovel bit into the bottomless floor of sand. "I been sharecropping ever since."

I began scooping out the incline that led down to him. "You didn't go back?"

"No, I signed a marriage certificate instead. The justice of the peace was me and Arzula Elrod's 'recruitment officer.' It's been boot camp ever since, with no furlough." He smoothed the sand at his feet with swipes of his work shoes. "'Course, if I'd joined the service, I wouldn't be standing in this fine hole and you wouldn't be here either. See if you can roll that barrel into place."

On our walk home, as the sun slunk behind the treetops, Uncle Stan said, "Did you see that?" He pointed at the trench that bordered our dirt lane. A straw hat bobbed through the tall ditchweeds and then ducked.

I crept closer and saw Rienzi Shepherd offer a carrot sliver to the rabbit I'd hunted. Her free hand drifted up very slowly, showing me her palm. I peered down at the rabbit's scarred, pink flesh, where its tawny hair wouldn't grow. Rienzi whispered, "Don't be afraid, don't be afraid," until the rabbit leaned forward and took the offering. It nibbled all the way to her fingertips.

Working its fuzzy mouth, the rabbit looked up at me and then past my shoulder. It flattened its ears.

Uncle Stan said, "Hey, what's this?"

When I looked into the ditch again, the little troublemaker had fled.

Rienzi said, "You should've written that you'd moved." She wore her usual tomboy outfit, her long braid coiled beneath her hat. I introduced her as "Ry Shepherd" to Uncle Stan. She glanced over my uncle; I knew she was recalling the night she stood up to Papa and his gun a short distance away.

He said, "That's a neat trick. I bet you catch a lot of supper that way."

"No, sir. It trusted me not to."

"Wait 'til you're hungry, Ry." He rubbed his hand across his mouth. "You won't believe what folks'll do when they're hungry." I could tell that his Saturday thirst had started a day early; I wondered if talking about himself had triggered it.

I said, "Ry, I got lots to tell you."

"Y'all talk," my uncle said. "Remember, Arzula's at her ma's tonight, so there's not much supper. I'm gonna go out for a while. See you later." He said goodbye to Rienzi and walked fast toward home.

I whispered after him, "No you won't either." To Rienzi, I said, "I hunted that rabbit for a long time. It kept chewing up Mama's garden."

"It has to eat too, Bud. What your uncle said about hungry people is true for everything."

Soon, Uncle Stan set off for his favorite whiskey-joint, his black suspenders making the usual big X across the back of his white shirt. I murmured, "You recall how drunk he was, shooting the floor and falling on his face?"

"Of course." Rienzi sat beside me with her legs dangling in the ditch. "That's what happened to his nose, right?"

"Yep. He gets that drunk every Saturday. For some reason he's starting early this week."

"What happened to your stutter?"

I told her about everything that had gone on since she went back to Texas. By the time I finished my stories, I was close to tears as we sat in the cold, blue twilight.

Rienzi said, "It's amazing you're still here."

"I keep your buckeye close." Within my pocket, I rubbed the depression on the underside of the nut. As usual, it soothed me; the shell was turning black from so much handling.

"What I meant was, why haven't you run away?"

I said, "Where would I go? Everybody I know is here."

"Everybody except your friend in Texas—why didn't you write to me?"

"I wrote a letter, I did. But my teacher said I oughta talk to you instead about…something."

Her mouth began to form a question, but no sound came out. She narrowed her eyes into harsh slashes and said, "You told about me."

"My mama opened your letter."

"I didn't spell anything out."

I said, "You wrote about me keeping your secret!"

"You couldn't make up something?"

"She said your name sounded like a girl's. She guessed it and my brothers heard. Darlene too."

"They all know?" She shook her head and asked what Jay had said.

"Nuthin much. Chet wouldn't believe it."

"Because no girl could beat him, right? I don't understand why you told everyone."

"I didn't! Mama…Forget it. Never mind." I pushed to my feet and brushed the sand off my overalls. "You staying long?"

She walked along the edge of the ditch, saying, "A few days only. I'm celebrating Christmas early with my grandparents."

I noticed that the anger had left her voice. "You still mad at me?"

"Disappointed. I guess it's not really your fault. Your family's not around to tease me, so maybe it's all right."

"I don't wanna be here when my uncle gets back. You hungry?"

"Not enough to eat that poor rabbit."

"Maybe we can get a squirrel." I ducked inside long enough to grab a couple of biscuits, my slingshot, and some rocks I'd collected along the railroad track. It was too hard to find ammunition in the woods at night.

She examined my slingshot and said, "Couldn't we go fishing?"

"They're not biting—it's too cold."

We entered the woods, following a narrow path. With the moon not yet risen, I couldn't see well. I had to rely on the sounds of scrabbling claws and the sudden shaking of tree limbs to find a target. Amazingly, Rienzi could stay quiet for long periods of time.

The stretch of forest we were in didn't pan out, so I veered toward the route Lonnie had used. As the temperature dropped more, I began to shiver. I imagined that Uncle Stan had staggered home by that time. Now I needed to stay out an hour or so more, until he'd fallen into a drunken, deathlike sleep. He'd barely breathe until daybreak; I sometimes wondered if he tried to will himself to stop altogether.

Rienzi spotted the wagon trail I was looking for. I said, "We can take this to Wanda's place."

"You think she'll have something to eat?"

"I hope so. That biscuit didn't do me." I led her south. The dirt and leaves chilled my feet as I walked along a rut made by Robert Bryson's tires. Rienzi chose the other track; when we stretched out our arms, like crossing a tightrope, they weren't quite long enough for our fingertips to touch.

I watched the path in front of me; my night vision improved to an amazing degree with each passing moment. The crickets had ceased their chirping, so my hearing got better too, even detecting a low-pitched hum. Rienzi halted, but I walked on a few steps, noticing more and more details of tree trunks and the forest floor. The humming got louder. Then I saw my shadow in front of me.

"What is that, Bud?"

The fear in her voice made me turn.

A ball of light at least six feet in diameter hovered behind her. Thrumming vibrations jabbed deep inside my ears, and the light pulsed from the soft yellow of churned butter to an angry blaze. I shouted, "It's the Dutchman. Run to Wanda's!"

I snatched her hand as she stood mesmerized, pulling her until she ran alongside me. The Dutchman surged forward, our path brightening as it gained on us. The thrum became a roar that seemed to ripple my skin. Soon Rienzi had pulled away. She yelled for me to hurry.

Wanda's gardens and porch appeared up ahead as if in the light of midday. The Dutchman drew near and my shadow shrank away, becoming shorter and squatter until I appeared to outrun my silhouette. Hairs on the back of my head stood on end—the haint was reaching out to touch me.

I dodged to the left and sprang onto a young tree. Shouting for Rienzi to climb, I scrambled up the slender pine. Brittle bark fell away as I shimmied toward the top. The haint hadn't followed me upward; he was chasing Rienzi.

She ran toward Wanda's porch, but the Dutchman was overtaking her. I climbed until I could bend the top of the pine under my meager weight. As the tree creaked, dipping me lower, I shouted, "Hey, you haint. Come and get me!"

The Dutchman paused and reversed course as I dropped in an arc toward the ball of light. It waited for me at the spot where I'd land, as if to swallow me up.

Rienzi yelled, "Over here," and straddled a cypress so thick that her feet couldn't touch on the other side. Still, she managed to climb while I sank closer to the pulsing globe that deafened me with its growl. When I saw that she was safe, I tried to climb back down the pine trunk as it cracked and limbs fell away. Too late.

The tree snapped about ten feet from the top. The huge log of wood crashed right through the haint, which didn't even flicker as it repositioned itself—as if to grab me when the rest of the pine gave way. With a tremendous bang, the trunk broke near its base and then I fell fast, grasping the tree.

The top end of the shattered trunk caught in hefty oak limbs while the base dug into the forest floor, and I stopped. The impact almost shook me from my hold; coarse pine bark scraped my hands and cheek. My tree balanced at the same slant as the scalding-barrel we'd positioned at the Turners. The Dutchman waited a dozen feet below me, ready to gobble me like a piglet.

The haint circled the nearly fallen pine as Rienzi yelled over to make sure I was all right. Every part of my front felt like it had been kicked by hobnail boots, from my face to my crotch. My voice sounded as squeaky as hers as I called back, "Hunky dory."

After another few revolutions, the Dutchman circled Rienzi's sturdy, upright tree and looped between ours for a while, making a figure-eight. Then it surged into the woods. Its glow gradually disappeared.

When the crickets resumed their chatter, Rienzi said, "You think it's safe?"

"I think I'll stay here 'til morning."

"What was that, Bud?"

"A haint. Like we told you before."

"But ghosts aren't real."

I shouted, "So why are you up in a tree?"

"Calm down. I don't pretend to know everything."

"Yes, you do. Uh-oh." A low rumble jarred the night. Two lights, side-by-side, swept toward us. "Stay there—he brought a friend!"

"It's a car, you goof."

Robert Bryson's black Pierce-Arrow bumped along the path toward Wanda's. He had to stop because of the treetop lying across his path. As Mr. Bryson dragged the timber out of the way, Wanda looped beneath me and Rienzi, just as the Dutchman had done. She shouted at us, "What do you think you're up to?"

I said, "About a dozen feet, ma'am."

# CHAPTER 21

Mr. Bryson drove us back home, dropping me off first, warm and well-fed. Wanda had reheated a pot of leftover stew and sent us away with a warning not to "snoop around places you don't belong." She'd called the haint a "spirit light" when Rienzi asked. During the drive, Rienzi talked to herself about what the Dutchman really was. It would've been funny to listen to except that her obvious fear added to my own.

I had to walk into Uncle Stan's bedroom before I could hear his shallow breaths. The dying glow in his fireplace painted him in shadowy orange. Pungent whiskey seeped from his pores. I knew I should've been as scared of him as the Dutchman. At that moment, though, he seemed—and smelled—more like a rotting corpse than a monster. I was still so frightened that I dragged my pallet into his warmer bedroom and curled up beside the hearth. Light from embers looked a lot like the haint's, and sleep didn't come for a long time.

As hard as he slept, Uncle Stan woke up before dawn to get to work. He nudged my shoulder, jolting me upright. "Not much to eat now," he said, pressing one of my aunt's stale biscuits into my trembling hand, "but there'll be plenty more later on." His breath smelled foul, and his dusty overalls and a sweat-stained work shirt didn't mask the sour odor that still oozed from his skin.

Running for my life the night before had left me exhausted and jumpy. I followed my uncle outside, scuffing along as I rubbed sleep from my eyes. My toes curved upward to avoid the cold flooring.

When we got to the Turner farm, Cecilia's father had started a fire beneath the big scalding-drum filled with water. Some other kids and I stood over the pit to warm ourselves while the adults got the knives and axe in place and made sure a .22 rifle was loaded. The water began to steam. Big clouds of vapor rose from the pit and expanded overhead until a cold breeze shredded them.

I went over to the pen to help Uncle Stan feed the hogs. Buckets of slops and corn poured into the trough lured the razorbacks from their huddle in one corner. They stretched and shook themselves like dogs and made their way to us.

A husky farmer named TJ Rawlins hefted his axe. He climbed into the pen with his wife Mazy, who was armed with a long knife and dressed in a smock covered in rust-brown stains. Uncle Stan and a farmer named Smalls followed them. As the hogs ate, I told the boy leaning against the pen beside me, "Hey, Martin, bet'cha Mr. Rawlins'll go for the biggest one." At the old home place, Uncle Davy did the choosing; he always picked the fattest one first since it would be the heaviest work.

"Unh-uh," Martin said. "He always picks the one with the most fight in 'im."

Sure enough, TJ turned a muscular, tough-looking razorback from the trough. The hog snorted and thrust its small, curved tusks at him. TJ chopped the axe down one-handed, striking the razorback between its red-rimmed eyes.

The hog's legs splayed like an overloaded table and it collapsed. The blow only stunned the thick-skulled creature, so Mazy plunged her knife into its throat. Blood sprayed across her smock and hand and steamed in the cold air. The hog died with a long sigh. As it bled out, the other hogs glanced around, but continued to eat. Others that hadn't fed shouldered their way to the trough.

Uncle Stan grabbed one hind leg, Mr. Smalls took the other, and they dragged the dead hog out of the pen. Blood trailed them like glue pouring out of a bucket. Martin slammed the gate shut and looped a wire over the adjacent fencepost. "See," he said to me, "told ya. Let's race."

He beat me to the scalding-drum, where the men dunked the hog headfirst into the boiling water. They counted the seconds aloud and pulled the hog out when they all called, "Ten!" Pungent steam rose from its loosened skin and now the boiling water looked pink in the dawn light. By afternoon, even with more water added, the scalding-drum would appear to be full of bubbling blood.

Uncle Stan and Mr. Smalls turned the hog around, cussing as they singed their hands. They each gripped a foreleg and shoved its back-end into the water for a ten-count. When they pulled it out again, they dragged it to a mat of burlap sacks. "Let 'er go, boys," Uncle Stan said. Martin and I took up pieces of burlap with some other boys. We rubbed from the stinking beast's rump to its head, going against the grain. Wet, stiff hair eventually clung to our fingers and arms and even our faces. I had to keep spitting bristles out of my mouth.

Uncle Stan strung wires through the hog's tendons where its rear legs joined the hooves. He and some other men dragged the hog to the scaffolding. On a count of three, the men lifted the hog. They staggered under its dead weight as the tallest farmer tied the wires to the crosspiece. The men let go, all giving the same long sigh that the razorback had. Its forelegs reaching for earth, the hog hung upside down. Wives, sisters, and daughters moved in for the gutting while the men returned to the pen for another kill.

The women had set up a butcher station beside the scaffolding: a broad table with knives, cleavers, and the sausage grinder clamped to one end. Washtubs lay nearby, some empty and some brimming with well-water, and a huge kettle boiled. When we boys weren't scraping hog-hair, we had to keep the various fires going.

Rienzi had accepted my invitation, arriving as I carried a flaming stick of heart-pine to the Turners' two-story smokehouse. "Come on," I called to her, "this is the fun part." I almost said her name; despite the tomboy outfit, I couldn't help seeing her as a girl.

She managed to fool the others though. Cecilia had dashed over from the butcher table, her hands pink and wet from washing them in cold water. "Hey, Bud," she said, "who's that boy?"

I told Cecilia about "Ry" Shepherd, who had stopped a dozen yards away and opened a lumpy burlap sack as she studied something on the ground.

"What's he doing stooped over there?"

"Probably looking at a bug. He likes to do what he calls 'examining' on bugs and leaves." I yawned so wide I almost drew in the fire from the end of my stick.

"You boys are strange."

"You're the one showing off your daddy's smushed hand."

She put her cold, damp fingers on my mouth. "That's our secret, remember?" As Rienzi approached, Cecilia said, "Hey, Ry Shepherd," and introduced herself. She studied my Texas friend's features the way Rienzi looked at nature.

I said, "I have to make a fire in the smokehouse."

"I haven't missed the hog innards, have I?" Rienzi said. She withdrew a large balance and a notebook from her sack. "I wanted to weigh everything on this butcher scale Granny bought for me."

Cecilia wrinkled her nose. "We'll be killing hogs all day." The .22 rifle fired in the hog pen. After TJ had clobbered the first few with his axe, the razorbacks wouldn't let him get close enough to strike again. Fortunately, the small-caliber bullet couldn't pierce a hog's skull and ruin its brains.

I herded them to the smokehouse and shut the door behind us. There were no windows. My heart-pine torch provided the only light.

Above our heads, a lattice of rafters spanned the building, with meat hooks every few feet. The dirt floor was covered with long Spanish-bayonet leaves I'd cut the previous afternoon with Martin and some other boys. I kicked some aside and pointed out greasy orange pools in the dirt. "This here's from past years' smoking, Ry. The blood and all drips down and carries off some of the salt while the meat's curing. Grandma says that during the War Between the States, she and her folks got salt by putting greasy dirt from their smokehouse into boiling water."

Rienzi nodded but Cecilia said, "Ugh. Did they cook it to eat?"

I said, "The dirt fell to the bottom, but the salt mixed with the water."

"It was diluted," Ry said. "Like sugar in tea."

"I reckon. So they saved that water and boiled it all away. Somehow, the salt was left." Before Rienzi could speak again, I blurted, "Anyway, that's how they got salt during the war."

Cecilia said, "From hog-bloodied dirt? Eeeeww, I won't ever salt my watermelon again."

The girls helped me clear a firebreak all around a pile of long green leaves. Flames raced across the heart-pine stick when I laid it down. Soon, a smoky fire began perfuming the air.

As we went back outside, I explained to Rienzi that insects wouldn't fly into a dark, smoke-filled place, so we wouldn't lose any meat to wasps and blowflies and such while we were hanging it. I'd light other leaf piles as the day went on until the smoke sweetened every breath and cured the meat that dangled above. I pictured the salted hams, sides, shoulders, and chops, and six-foot lengths of sausage. Dripping flour sacks would be filled with boiled, seasoned remnants from the hogs' heads and even their tails; souse was so rich-tasting that I had never eaten more than a small slice in one sitting. After choking down Old Lady Boggs' fritters every week, though, I planned to take a big bite.

After Rienzi dug through washtubs of kidneys, livers, and lungs, weighing and recording in her notebook, she helped me, Cecilia, and other kids clean the intestines. We stripped out the obvious waste, turned the yards of slick, pinkish gray coils inside out, and washed them in cold water. Rienzi drew stares, and Martin whispered, "What is he anyway?"

"Ry? His father's from Miller County. His mother's from Japan."

"Is that somewheres up north?"

"East or west, one. A long ways." I set aside a wide, clean intestine to be filled with ground sausage, and put a thinner specimen in the chitlin pile. Cecilia's gorgeous sister Geneva and two other girls were plaiting lengths of slender intestines together like braiding their friends' hair, twining three at a time to give the boiled chitlins more bulk and make them look less like pig guts.

I reached for another bloody rope just pulled from a fresh kill, no longer bothered by the overheated-skillet stink of blood and organs or the greasy steam from the nearby tub where Mrs. Turner rendered lard from fatty trimmings. As dinner approached, all I saw was plenty to eat for the first time since last year's slaughter.

Mrs. Turner served up plates of boiled chitlins, scrambled eggs with brains, boiled hogs' feet, and cracklins left over from rendering the lard. I sat on the sandy yard between Cecilia and Rienzi and ate my cracklins first. Still warm, they tasted like fatty pieces of bacon rescued before the cook could burn them crisp.

Geneva sat nearby. Soon, Martin and every other boy crowded near the Turner girls, balancing their own plates of hog meat. I gulped down eggs that were scrambled with tender brains so slick with lard that much of it slipped down my throat before I could taste it. I took my hog's foot and looked around for a quieter place to eat it.

Rienzi said, "Let's go back to the smokehouse. I'll scoop up some dirt and show you how to get out the salt." As we walked that way across a grassy field, she said, "You really like her."

"Who?"

She sighed. "Cecilia. Her sister's pretty too."

I took a large bite of the boiled foot so I wouldn't have to answer her. When I finished chewing, she hadn't said anything more, so I shrugged. "They're all right."

"You keep looking at her. The whole time you were telling about your grandmother, you stared at her."

I said, "I look at you too."

"I don't care if you do or not. I was talking about your crush on Cecilia."

"She don't mean nuthin to me." I raced her to the smokehouse, but stopped short when I heard a man laugh behind the building. It was just a short bark, but I recalled Uncle Stan in the woods after he made the hogs burst out of their haystack.

Rienzi won the race, tapping the door half-heartedly. I shushed her before she could ask why I'd quit.

A voice sounding like Mr. Turner's said, "At least you don't have a daughter who hid your pickled hand somewhere." He giggled a little drunkenly.

Uncle Stan's tone chilled me more than the fresh breeze on my sweaty neck: "I don't got a daughter."

"Hey, Stan, simmer down. Bless your heart, you get fuzzed up faster'n—"

"I won't drink with a man that runs down my family."

"I didn't say anything about 'em." After a pause, Mr. Turner said, "We better get back."

"Checkin your watch like a damn city slicker. Can't even look at the sky like normal folks. It's quarter to one; gimme five minutes on both sides and I'll bet your flask it is."

"Thirteen 'til."

"Ha! See what happens when you buy them fancy things? You stop noticing. Down the hatch!" In a few seconds, he sighed. A thump and dragging sound followed, as if he'd leaned hard against the building and slid onto his rump. "Only thing I'm good for, Walter. Tellin time without a watch."

"That ain't true, Stan. C'mon, let's go."

"Couldn't even do that, I reckon, if I'd gone in the service. Chickened out."

"Lots of married guys enlist. Why didn't—"

"Arzula. Said she'd take rat poison if I ever left her, even for a night."

"Jeez. We better go." There were shuffling sounds, and Mr. Turner said, "No, no, you won it fair and square."

"I did leave her one time, Walter. Just for a Saturday night, a little escape." Footsteps rounded the back of the building and walked along the side. Both men dragged their feet a little.

I pulled Rienzi inside the smokehouse and closed the door. Small, contained fires glowed in orange pools; otherwise, the building was absolutely dark. The smell of curing meat and sweet smoke calmed my fear. I tried to think of sausages and ham instead of haints and rat poison.

Mr. Turner said, "And see how women make a big deal and then nuthin happens? You left and she didn't kill herself."

Voice cracking, my uncle said, "Arzula poisoned Eliza Jean."

"What're you talkin about?"

"She killed my baby girl." He sobbed and banged his fist against the wall.

I almost cried out. Inhaling hard, I began to choke on the smoke.

Uncle Stan continued, "Oh Christ, Walter, she had Eliza propped up in a chair, facin the door for me to find on Sunday mornin. Blue in the face, her little hands too. A teaspoon by her on the chair."

"Shit, Stan, really? Where was Arzula?"

"In bed, curled up with the rat poison bottle. It'd tipped, spilled all over her and the mattress. So help me God, I wanted her to be dead. But she was fast asleep."

I sank to my knees as the tickle in my throat became a harsh scratching, like some creature tried to climb up into my mouth. Breathing slowly through my nose didn't help. My TB-weakened lungs heaved as I covered my lips with both hands. The longer I held in the cough, the louder it would be.

Mr. Turner said, "What did you do?"

"Buried my baby. Along with the spoon and that rat poison. I buried Eliza's clothes and anything else she'd touched. Almost erased her." He snapped his fingers. "Gone. When Arzula woke up, she yelled at me for spillin poison on her and the sheets and went to look for our girl."

Tears streamed from my eyes. I let out small, nasal coughs but it wasn't enough. Rienzi asked in a whisper if I was all right. My throat burned. I longed to lie down and hack like the consumption had returned.

Stan replied to a question I'd missed, telling Mr. Turner, "She said I did it: poisoned Eliza, tried to kill her too." He pounded the wall again. "She began to wear lots of clothes, like she was dressin more'n one wacko. Startin throwin food on the floor 'cause she thought our baby was still crawlin around somewhere." Another sobbing fit overtook him as he said, "Ten years I been livin with—"

I coughed hard and that led to louder and longer coughs. I fell on my side, giving into it, trying to shove out every wisp of smoke from my chest and head. The door swung open.

Sunlight cut through the haze of smoke. A man stood there in silhouette; his left arm ended in a stump. Mr. Turner said, "Bud, what're you doin in here?"

As I writhed and gurked, Rienzi said, "I'm sorry, sir. Um, we were getting a snack."

"What are you, buzzards? Let the meat cure for God's sake." He dragged me outside and laid me on the dirt.

Uncle Stan leaned against the corner of the building, pointing at me. "You get all that, Roger? Think you know everything now? You don't know shit." Mr. Turner shielded me until my uncle shambled away, heading toward home.

# CHAPTER 22

We slaughtered twenty-two hogs that day. By evening I could wring blood from my clothes. My fingers ached from stripping intestines and repeated dunks in chilly water. For many reasons, I couldn't stop shivering.

Cecilia helped me and Rienzi overturn and rinse out the huge galvanized washtubs of bloody water. The thirsty sand swallowed every drop, though wherever the water touched the ground, rosy patches remained like port-wine stains on the earth.

Mrs. Turner had gone inside to heat water for her family's baths. I judged that I could get home and wash with a wet rag before Uncle Stan returned from even more drinking. If there were signs that he'd stayed home, I could always jump in Spring Creek and dry off beside a campfire. I tucked my filthy hands in my overalls, careful not to touch the buckeye, and told Cecilia, "I gotta clean off. I'll come back with my uncle tomorrow to get our share of the kidneys, livers, and all."

Rienzi pointed at one of the remaining washtubs covered with a towel. Flies scrambled over the thin cotton that protected a pile of hog organs. "I can help you carry it. Sometimes you treat me like a girl."

Cecilia laughed and said, "At least you'll grow up big and strong. Boys got it made. You just try being a girl sometime."

"No thanks!" Rienzi wiped a bloody sleeve across her cheek. Red streaked her skin like war paint. "Let's hurry. Granny says she's fit to be tied about me always staying out so late."

Slowly, we made our way off the farm and down Hardscrabble Road. The sun had set, leaving a pink haze to the west. On the wind, smells of chimney smoke and roasting meat darted around us. We made less and less progress as our arms needed longer periods of rest.

For the first time, I talked about overhearing Uncle Stan and Mr. Turner. "When my uncle was strangling me that one time, Aunt Arzula hollered 'You're killing the baby again.' I thought he'd wrung Eliza Jean's neck."

"Maybe he did and he told Mr. Turner a lie."

"Why bother? Why not keep his mouth shut about it?"

"I've never been around drunks—I don't understand them." Rienzi put down her end and we switched sides. "The way he looked at you scared me worse than getting chased by the spirit li—I mean, that luminescent phenomenon."

I didn't even try to puzzle that one out. A car trundled down the road, kicking up cold dust. The headlights swept over Rienzi, and I remembered how she had looked when she took off her hat and uncoiled her braid for Papa. I said, "Cecilia thinks you're cute. Will you tell her your secret?"

"No need, she won't see me for a while. This is my last day; my daddy came home to Texas and wants me back in San Antonio. Will you write to me this time?"

"I will, I triple-promise."

We had to drag the washtub the final twenty yards to the porch steps. I told her I needed to rest before hauling the tub into the kitchen. My arms trembled and I couldn't flex my frigid fingers without pain.

Uncle Stan had left the house open. Before he went, though, he'd built a fire in the bedroom hearth that still cast a bright glow. I saw from the blaze that it hadn't burned very long—we'd have some time to warm up before he returned.

Putting my freezing hands and feet near the flames was like dunking them in boiling water; they felt scalded, not singed. I closed my eyes, enjoying the heat on my face. Soon, I was aware of how much colder my back felt than my front. When I turned around to warm my shoulders and spine, I saw Rienzi leaning against the bedstead with an open box in her lap.

"Hey!" I said. "Put that back under the bed. You can't snoop through other folks' stuff."

"Take a look at these photographs." She fanned out a number of sepia images like she was going to ask me to pick one. "You won't believe it."

I took the seven snapshots from her. In the first one, my younger-looking aunt and uncle stared back at me. She wore only one dress and kept her hair under a bonnet. Uncle Stan touched her hand but didn't hold it; even then, his face showed resignation, like the last of the hogs about to be butchered.

Grandma Elrod was in the next photograph holding a baby whose face was too small and blurry to see. I glanced at the back of the picture. Someone had written "Ma and Eliza Jean."

My aunt and uncle posed at the old home place in the next shot. Aunt Arzula held the baby this time, but again her daughter's face was too hard to make out. The fourth photograph showed them with Eliza Jean and an older couple in front of an unpainted house. A tree must've been blocking the sun because a portion of the older man's face was in shadows. On the back, the same faint brown handwriting: "Arzula, Buddy, Eliza Jean, and Mister and Missus Borden."

I explained that Uncle Stan's surname was Borden, and Rienzi said, "I thought his first name was Stan."

"Maybe it's a nickname my aunt had for him. He told me there was lots of Buds out there; that's why he likes Roger better."

"Who gave you your nickname?"

"Mama. Why?"

"Keep going."

Two more stills showed Stan, Arzula, and Eliza with his parents, once on the porch and once by a pond. I said, "I can't ever make out Mr. Borden's face. The same side is always dark, no matter where the sun's at."

She touched my right temple with fingers like firebrands. "Have you ever seen a picture of yourself?"

Instead of answering, I quickly revealed the last photograph. It was a group shot in front of the old home place: Arzula, her many sisters, a few husbands including Stan but not Papa, some young children, Grandma holding Eliza Jean, and Grandpa Elrod, who'd died before I was born.

The handwriting on the back identified everyone. Mama's name was missing. I flipped over to the picture. She wasn't there. Then I looked at the careful school-girl printing again and recognized it from letters I'd seen written to far-off cousins and old friends. It was hers. I said, "Mama took all these snaps and wrote on the backs."

"Would she have called your uncle 'Buddy'?"

"Maybe so." I told her that when Mama abandoned me at Uncle Stan's door, she'd used that name. I'd thought she was talking to me.

Rienzi went into the kitchen, and I yelled, "Hurry, we have to go!" She rummaged among the cupboards and brought back a thick-bottomed jar and a brown-tinted bottle. She pointed at the bottle label and said, "Rat poison. They have six more." Setting the poison aside, she said, "Let me show you a neat trick." She took the pictures from me and held one of the shots of the Bordens beneath the jar. I looked down into the glass: the photographed faces appeared wider and a little larger. My uncle's father had a port-wine stain.

She said, "I heard that it can skip a generation sometimes." She held the snapshot of Grandma and Eliza Jean behind the crude magnifier. I saw it in the yellow firelight: Eliza Jean had a birthmark that marred her cheek and jaw and all of her neck that showed above the blanket.

I said, "Uncle Stan passed it on to his baby girl?"

"That's right, and Buddy passed it on to his baby boy."

I held my head and moaned, "So my aunt and uncle are my real parents?" Even as I said it, I knew the truth was worse.

Rienzi didn't spare me. "No, Roger. Your mother and Stan."

I covered my ears, rocking on my haunches, but still I heard her say, "When we hid behind the truck, he said he doesn't talk to her anymore. He said that he was banned from your granny's home about eight years ago. How old are you now?"

"Stop it!" Every harsh thought I'd ever had about Mama screamed for attention. Papa had called me a sonofabitch bastard. He was right on all counts.

I bolted out the backdoor, slamming it behind me. A brutal gust of wind chilled the sweat that had sprung out on my face and neck. I spun around, wondering where to go. Run to the old home place and ask Mama if it was true? Should I go see Jay or Chet?

From the front yard, Uncle Stan bellowed, "Git outta there!" I heard a scratching like claws on tin as I ran to the barn. "Blasted coons! Roger, damn it all—you left the meat out here."

I'd just closed the barn door behind me when his mule Viola snorted from her pen. The sudden noise almost drove me outside again. I found a rickety ladder and climbed to the loft. Burrowing into the scratchy hay, I thought of gopher holes. Papa knew I wasn't his, even if he didn't know for sure who to blame. Other than Mama.

Now that I knew, I wish he'd really found me in the woods. I'd rather have been an orphan than a bastard. And I'd rather have had a mysterious daddy than either Papa or Stan—an unknown father would've been far better than an unknowable one.

Rienzi dashed in and eased the door closed. She whispered, "Bud, I saw you come in here. Where are you hiding?" She walked around the barn. From the muffled footsteps and bumping of tools, it sounded like she checked every square foot, maybe the way a scientist would. She mounted the ladder and was soon kicking through the hay.

Not wanting a toe in my eye, I murmured from my den, "Here. Near the back."

She sat beside the straw hideout I'd made. "I'm sorry I upset you. Sometimes I forget that finding out new things can hurt."

A long, wailing shout came from the house. I hunkered deeper into the hay while Uncle Stan called my name and cussed me. He'd found the open box.

Rienzi said, "It's empty. I have the pictures here."

"He knows...that I know everything now. I wish I didn't. I wish you'd left things alone."

"It's always better to learn than be ignorant, even if it makes you sad."

"That so? I thought I was a orphan for a long time. Then I was sure where I belonged." Uncle Stan continued to rage inside the house; I kept talking so I couldn't listen to him. "Now Jay and Chet are only half-brothers. Darlene's just a half-sister. I was born because Mama cheated—I'd thought she was a little better than Papa. Now I wish I could be that orphan again."

"But then you wouldn't know your true father."

I said, "Anybody could be him. A nice uncle, a perfect stranger. I could pretend where I belonged."

"That's all make-believe, like living in a storybook. At least you can talk to your mother and father. I never knew Mommy."

A thump outside preceded a crash of wood on the back porch. Uncle Stan must've tripped while trying to bring in more fuel for the bedroom fireplace. He cussed, but in a sobbing, self-pitying voice. I said, "Listen out there. You think I can talk to that?"

"You can when he's not drinking."

Outside, Uncle Stan shouted, "Arzula—dammit, gimme a hand with this wood."

My aunt said, "Just look at the mess you made."

I brushed hay off my blood-encrusted clothes. "She came back at a bad time; he's gonna pop her. If I can lead 'im away with the snapshots, you get her in here." I took the photographs from her and went to the ladder. Pressing the sides with hands and feet, I slid down without touching the rungs and scampered outside.

Aunt Arzula's kerosene lamp cast a dim yellow light on the porch. Uncle Stan crawled on the floorboards, pushing the scattered wood into a pile. I hollered, "I'll help you. Aunt Arzula, could you please check in the barn, ma'am? Viola's acting up."

Uncle Stan pointed a stick of kindling at me. "Thanks to you, we got half-chewed livers and lights all over the yard."

I pictured the torn-up hog lungs and other organs coated with sand, like they'd been battered and were ready for the fryer. My aunt said, "You two are impossible. Can't you do anything right?"

Instead of going into the barn, she shuffled in her brogans around the side of the house. Soon she called to us about how ruined each piece was.

"Git over here, son." Uncle Stan held on to a porch post. "Guess I can call you that now."

I dragged my feet as if I wore my aunt's oversized shoes. Before me, I held the photographs. "I'm sorry I snooped. I won't tell."

"Tell? Shit, I reckon everybody in the family knows but you and Mance."

"I won't tell him, sir. I promise."

"It don't matter." He rested the side of his face against the post and said, "God, I'm so sick of it all, Roger. So tired. You ever feel like you wanna sleep forever?"

"Yes, sir." I offered him the snapshots, and he took them. For the briefest moment, his finger brushed mine.

He glanced down at the pictures fanned out in the starlight. "I wish I had one of your mama. Reva won't let herself get trapped in a snapshot or anywhere else. Go to her, Roger."

"I live here now."

My father pawed at the tears in his eyes. "'Member what you told me she said? There ain't no here anymore, son. There ain't no us." He turned away, snapshots in hand, and staggered to the back door. "Your friend's waitin behind you. Go to your mama. Hide from me one last time."

Rienzi took my arm and led me past the barn and a fallow field. I stopped on the dirt road and looked back. In the front yard, Aunt Arzula tossed a sand-coated remnant into the washtub and dusted off her skirt. She turned in a small circle, kerosene lamp held high, as if looking for more. Except that she kept up her slow spin, like Mama searching her walls and ceiling for danger during a thunderstorm.

I said, "We should go back. He won't try to hurt me tonight."

"I have to leave. Come with me as far as the highway."

We walked under a sky that seemed so close you could pluck out a star. Rienzi didn't try to talk; she gave me the gift of quiet.

As we neared US 27, I asked her when she aimed to come back. She said, "My daddy will be home for a while. We usually take a springtime trip together, so I might be back next summer. Write to me."

"I'm warning you, I don't write too good."

"My daddy says we learn by doing. You have to write to me in order to improve."

"It's OK with you that I'm a bas…that my father isn't my brothers' daddy?"

She said, "If it's OK with you that I never knew my mother."

"So long as it's OK with you about my birthmark."

"And that I'm only half-white."

"And that I'm—" I laughed and said, "I can't think of anything else wrong with me."

Rienzi patted my back and said, "I can't either."

She wished me a merry Christmas, told me again to write to her, and set off for home along the highway shoulder, lit briefly by passing cars. I made my way back, wondering just what time it was. Above the eastern treetops, the sky glowed with the promise of a sunrise.

The waxing moon above didn't show any sign of retreat. Almost full, the Man in the Moon—with his huge sunken eyes and gaping mouth—hollered from the heavens. Mama had always told me he was singing. Darlene had reckoned that he was having a good cry, while Papa said, "Goddammit, there ain't no man up there." But my brothers and I could almost hear his screams.

Smoke tickled my nose before I guessed there was a house fire. I ran back to my father's place. Flames shot through the roof; the center room was ablaze. Orange light flickered from a big hole in the side wall and colored the rising billows of smoke. On the road, someone had stacked my few possessions: the scuffed town shoes, folded clothes, and my slingshot all held down the lid of the Blue Cloud cigar box.

I eased toward the house and, in short order, went from shivering to sweating. Fierce heat and waves of smoke made me crouch low on the front porch. The parlor had not caught fire yet, so I slid inside and crawled on my belly toward the bedroom.

Burning logs fanned out from the fireplace and flames raced up the walls and through the rafters. My aunt sat upright on her side of the smoldering bed, a soaked nightgown clinging to her. In her arm, she cradled the brown rat-poison bottle; a spoon lay across her open palm. Her head tilted back with eyes bugged and mouth agape. A silent scream worthy of the moon.

My father had propped himself beside her, like they were a happy couple enjoying their fireplace. He too was doused with something that darkened his clothes and glistened on his skin. Even with the heavy smoke I could smell it: kerosene.

The box where he'd kept the photographs sat on his lap. Above the lid, his hands still gripped the twin barrels of his shotgun. He'd hooked his naked toe through the trigger guard. The blast had made the hole I saw from the outside—it had utterly destroyed his head.

Fire scurried across the ceiling and dropped hot embers onto my head and back while I puked. The floor had become so hot that my vomit sizzled. In the bedroom, rafters began to tumble down. The whole house twisted: the walls were about to fall in. I scrambled out the front door.

The air was shockingly cold outside, as I sat beside the things that my father must've set out for me. His Christmas present. Soon, I could feel the heat while flames ate up the parlor and went to work on the porch. Plumes of orange and yellow danced across the planks. I recalled the hole my father shot in the porch before Papa almost put a bullet in his head.

Fiery wood fell into the breezeway as the floors gave way. The house groaned as it seemed to swallow itself. Burning rafters pulled in the walls. The tin roof warped and crumpled. Everything settled around the foundations, those pillars of stones stacked like grave markers. I lay on my side and pressed my birthmark against the dirt and watched it all burn. At some point, the heat comforted me. I fell asleep, facing the pyre.

* * *

THE SELF-CONTAINED BLAZE KEPT ME warm through the night. When I awoke in the blue predawn light, the collapsed house still burned beneath its splayed and twisted roof. The metal rippled with the ongoing fire it covered; tin that hadn't burned away bore a hellish rainbow of heat rings, black and blue on the outside falling into orange and glowing red.

Blackened rafters jutted out like spears that had brought down an elephant. At the center of the fire, where the heat and light still radiated, heart-pine floors would burn among the foundation stones until the wood turned to ash. Flames would devour everything.

Curiosity-seekers had not yet arrived. With the cold night, the smell of wood smoke was expected, and typical early bedtimes meant that no one would've noticed the midnight sunrise. However, I did wake to see many pairs of eyes watching from the fields surrounding the house. Owls and hawks circled overhead as their prey paused to warm their fur in the open.

While I walked out the stiffness from sleeping on the cold ground, I spotted the scarred rabbit near Aunt Arzula's ruined garden. It had salvaged a clutch of heat-withered mustard greens, chewing them as it stared at me. The pink wound on its back made an easy target for the hunters above.

I saw how calm the rabbit appeared in the face of certain death. When Rienzi had fed it, she'd whispered, "Don't be afraid," and it wasn't. Muscular confidence rippled its tawny fur, defying the awful scar. A cruel life had not bowed the creature I'd hunted.

One of the hawks wheeled and plunged, swooping down like an arrow. I screamed at the rabbit. I ran at it, waving my arms; it discarded the scavenged food but held its ground. Waiting. Watching. The hawk surged below the treetops with talons poised. At the last instant, the rabbit raced for the undergrowth and safety. It got away.

In those moments, I saw the courage to stand firm and the wisdom to flee. I saw what I had to do.

# BOOK THREE

# CHAPTER 23

THANKS TO MY TRUE FATHER, MAMA SET UP HOUSEKEEPING again. He'd stuffed crumpled one-dollar bills, a few fives, and piles of coins in my Blue Cloud cigar box. A little over sixty-seven bucks: he had probably given me every cent he'd ever put by. Still, I was disappointed that he didn't include a single picture of himself. My father had erased his face in every possible way.

We lived in a number of rentals through 1939 and into the war years. Mama eventually moved us back into the home of my early childhood, with Papa's bullet hole still in her bedroom wall. Fretting more and more about her looks and "wasted life" as she aged deeper into her thirties, she returned us to the place where everything had begun to go wrong. Apparently she'd agreed this time to whatever price the landlord demanded.

No matter how much Mama spent on herself and Darlene, we always seemed to come up with another job and a bit more money. To make sure we never got split up again, Chet followed Jay's lead, quitting school to work full-time at the sawmill. Try as they might, though, time separated us like cotton in a gin.

Darlene was the first to go, married at fourteen. Then she divorced but immediately married again at fifteen. By the time Jay enlisted on his seventeenth birthday in 1944, she'd moved to Atlanta with husband number four. On the morning of that June wedding, I overheard Mama hissing at her, "Aye God, I never said you had to get hitched to each and every one of 'em."

Instead of dropping out of school, I doubled-up, going to classes in the summer and wrangling any advanced tutoring I could manage. I still earned money, taking over Jay's bread run with Jerry Flynn and helping Cecilia's parents, but I profited from books much more. It wasn't merely my love of learning that kept me away from home; Mama had become more open about her "no-hitch" rule of courting. Whenever a stranger's car hunkered in our yard, I'd choose to camp out with coursework instead of going indoors.

The extra schooling leapfrogged me from a year behind students my own age to a year ahead, bounding me across the street to Colquitt High before my former first-grade teacher took a job there. Now Mrs. Gladney taught English and other courses in the upper grades, while her husband took over as high school principal. When I saw her in the hallway at the start of my sophomore year, she held my shoulders—we were now the same height—and sized me up. "Bud, your wish came true. You're growing up fast."

"Ma'am, would you call me Roger now, please?"

"Of course." We moved from the busy hall into an unoccupied classroom that smelled of floor wax and window cleaner. Mrs. Gladney had given up her sweet perfume. She continued, "I remember outgrowing my nickname, giving away my toys."

I touched my birthmark, which had kept pace with my growth and, if anything, was darker than before. "Some things'll always be a part of me. I use to daydream I was a snake; anything I didn't like about myself I'd shed away."

"Do you still think about that?"

"No, ma'am. Not for a long time."

"I'm glad, Roger. Better to think of yourself as a tool that gets used for a lifetime. An axe, for example." She explained, "You can keep your head sharp for years and years, but your body will show the scars and stains. Eventually, even the blade will become dull." With a glance at her wedding band of white gold, she said, "At the end, all of us are worn out, but if we just stayed in a dark shed all our lives, we'd be useless from the start. Anyway, it's better than being a reptile, don't you think?"

I lingered as long as I could with her, still giddy in her presence. She told me about her two children, one toddler and one baby, and I asked as many questions as I could. When Mrs. Gladney said she needed to get to homeroom, I told her, "After I do a hitch in the military, ma'am, I want to go to college for a teaching degree."

"How wonderful! You like school that much?"

"I like you that much—you showed me what I could be." That earned me another precious minute with her. Finally, though, I had to let her go.

No matter how much I learned from my teachers, Rienzi stayed ahead of me. She had an advantage. Barricaded for safety in her father's San Antonio home after the Japanese attacked Pearl Harbor, she had all the time in the world for studies. In her letters, she called herself a "prisoner of war." I knew something about that, because the Third Reich had invaded South Georgia.

Jerry and I watched the Army build the prisoner-of-war camp outside of Colquitt, long barracks and small, sturdy houses. A ten-foot-high chain-link fence topped with inward-slanted barbed wire surrounded the compound. Jerry pointed at pipes lying beside an enormous pit. "Know what's going in there? A big ol latrine. Like a outhouse for dozens of guys, except it'll have showers and sinks along with toilets. Indoor plumbing."

"We don't have any of that and we're winning the war."

"If you were a GI or swabbie you'd have that stuff and more."

Jay wrote to say that the Army had forced him to grow up very fast. He described the drills and constant marching and often sent stories clipped from *Stars and Stripes*. In his September 1944 letter informing us that he was shipping out to the Far East—the censors wouldn't let him tell us where—he included a blurry copy of a commendation he received for improving the bayonet mounting on the M-1 Garand rifle that most infantrymen used. He wrote, "The Krauts skedaddled from Paris and we got the Japs (sorry, Ry) on the run too. Too bad my invention won't get made before the war's over, maybe by Christmas!" For days after that, I had sweaty nightmares of him stabbing at a shadowy enemy with a bayonet that kept falling off.

A few weeks before my fourteenth birthday, a convoy of trucks delivered hundreds of POWs: captives from the Afrika Korps. The German officers stayed in the camp, but the enlisted men were hired out by farmers, who'd lost most of their local laborers to the war effort. Most of the Germans wore broad-billed caps that peaked in the front and bore a silver-gray patch of an eagle perched above a swastika. The caps were the same color as their light-olive cotton twill uniforms. On their left shirt-cuffs they wore a patch that declared "Afrika" with flanking silver-gray palm trees. Some of the prisoners opted for looser-fitting uniforms made from surplus CCC denim, with a giant "PW" painted in white across their backs.

At the entrance to the camp, a huge sign proclaimed "Visiting Prohibited," but the military police let me and Fleming and other boys trade at the opened gate with German prisoners. They'd give us a penny for each English word we taught them. Many of the words they'd pay for multiple times; we wore our shabbiest clothes to encourage their charity.

Prisoners of war received rations from the Red Cross that we couldn't buy in town, so Mama would send me to the camp with homemade biscuits to trade for cans of evaporated milk. Fleming discovered a real talent for haggling. Whenever one of the Germans wanted a Hershey chocolate bar but balked at his asking price—which could include two cakes of soap, a roll of bandages, and a button or a patch off their uniform—Fleming would cry, "Hey, you think Hershey's easy to come by? Don't you know there's a war on?"

Mr. Turner hired ten Germans to help with the peanut harvest. School closed for the annual community activity, so I worked alongside the POWs and a dozen white and black laborers who were either too young or too old for the draft.

The prisoners arrived by truck after sunup. The Army didn't post a guard, though an unarmed soldier always came back with dinner at noon and took a quick headcount. Before nightfall, the POWs would mount the returning truck to have their supper at the camp.

My favorite German was named Hermann Lohbeck. I'd learned his name while bartering at the prison gate. Tall and strapping, with my blond hair and Mama's dark brown eyes, he looked like my idea of a soldier in his desert uniform, even if he was only eighteen and my country's enemy. Hermann spoke English with deliberate precision, trying hard to hide his accent. We worked the same row, shaking sand from peanuts and the long, tangled vines and draping them to dry out over knee-high slats. Smaller boys hurried to stay ahead of us as they nailed the slats into poles, like crosses planted upside down.

Hermann said, "Roger, please, what are the first names of Mr. Turner and his wife?"

"I don't know. Why?"

"The information is for my diary. I want to get all the details correct. Do they have children?"

"Two daughters, Geneva and Cecilia."

"'Geneva' like the city?"

"Right. She's married and lives in Athens. Georgia, not Greece." We piled up the vines until they stretched five feet across and towered several feet above Hermann's head. He tossed a final bunch over the top, and we worked the next thirty yards on the row, cloaking another upside-down cross.

He said, "And the younger one's name again, please?"

"Cecilia. She's fifteen." I spelled her name for him, closed my eyes, and vigorously dislodged sand from more peanuts and roots. I was coated with grit.

"Oh, you do not like her?" He made a face while he throttled some vines; I realized he was mimicking me.

"No, I like her a lot. I was just knocking off the sand."

"Ah, you like her a lot. She is pretty, yes?"

"She's beautiful."

He said, "She is. I saw her when we arrived here."

Cecilia walked along the rows lugging two water buckets with gourd skimmers so we could all refresh ourselves under the warm morning sun. Where auburn hair touched her damp neck, it turned the color of black cherry cola. She'd tucked most of it under a wide straw hat like the one Rienzi used to wear as part of her disguise. In her floral-print dress, however, Cecilia made no attempt to hide that she'd become a young woman.

Hermann and I filled up the adjacent peanut pole while she made her way to us. After a quick smile, she said, "Water?"

I sipped from a skimmer and let the cold water trickle down my dusty throat. Afraid of appearing undignified, I didn't take off my hat and dump water over my hot scalp. Hermann had no such qualms. He whisked off his Afrika field cap and doused his head, flattening the short blond hairs. The water clung to his long eyelashes and closely shaved chin and washed dirt from his face in long, slender columns.

Before I introduced him to Cecilia, he patted his face with a sand-colored kerchief. His desert-tan made his teeth look very white. "You are lucky, Cecilia, to be friends with Roger, a fine young man."

"He tries to look out for me." She raked a few sweaty strands under her hat. "More like a big brother than a younger one," she said, still bitter about a lecture I'd given her about not getting too serious too quickly about boys. I didn't want to see her with husband number five before she turned twenty. Besides, I still planned to court her in a year.

"That is a good thing," Hermann said. "I have lived...nightmares, Cecilia, seen friends die. The world is a scary place. Here you are, surrounded by brutal men: Field Marshal Rommel's elite Afrika Korps."

She tilted back her head and gave his face thorough study. "Should I be afraid of you?"

"Didn't your father warn you to stay away from us?"

"He doesn't know I'm out here."

Hermann glanced toward the distant back porch. "You might get in trouble, except that you have a strong American boy to protect you." He slung his arm around my shoulders and squeezed. I felt surrounded by muscle like leather and bones of steel.

Her brave smile turned shy as she glanced at me. For one moment, a girl's blush replaced the flirty, cynical mask she sported lately. She said, "How'd you learn such good English?"

"In school, before I was drafted and sent to the deserts of North Africa." He let me go. "Roger also teaches me new words. I pay him a penny apiece, but I will run out of money long before I learn everything he knows."

"Yeah, Roger's a smart one, always watching." She looked past us and said, "The others are waiting."

He took a final drink. "Don't keep your true friend waiting, dear Cecilia. He might not be there when you decide to call for him."

Now it was my turn to blush. She said, "Pleased to meet you, Hermann. 'Bye, Roger." She set off toward the next group of laborers while we resumed working. Less than five minutes later, Cecilia's mother summoned her with a shout and the crack of a bullwhip. I wasn't sure if the lash was a warning to her or for us.

I watched Cecilia abandon her water buckets and go inside with her mother close behind, coiling the whip. "Why'd you lay it on so thick?"

"What does that mean?" He topped another pole, and we moved farther down the row.

"Building me up like that: 'strong American boy,' her 'true friend.'"

"I spoke only facts. She likes you, but you make her afraid somehow."

"I know things about her. I've seen her with older boys. One time, I caught her with whiskey on her breath."

He again pantomimed me, rattling peanut vines furiously. "She wants to do that to you for what you saw?"

"No, but she tries to avoid me."

"Ah, then we will do what your Patton and the Briton Montgomery did to my Field Marshal: be everywhere at once."

Hermann had all kinds of "stratagems"—I repaid him a penny for that one—to put me in Cecilia's presence: searching out Mrs.

Turner to offer help, since she was keeping Cecilia close; delivering a tin of crackers, courtesy of the Red Cross, as a gift from the POWs grateful for the chance to work and earn money; and, his best idea, asking her parents' permission for Cecilia to bring around water under my supervision. By the last day of peanut stacking, I was spending most of my time with her and still earning money.

I refilled the buckets at the well and carried one for her. When we approached a group of laborers, regardless of whether they were white, black, or POWs, I let her precede me and chat with the men as they slurped from the skimmers and poured water over sunburned necks and overheated scalps. Everyone behaved toward her with excessive politeness.

At the edge of the field, we took a break. She said, "You don't need to be my chaperone. Everybody knows their place."

"If I don't stay with you, you'll get called inside."

"God, these Germans have more freedom than me. My parents are armed guards and they've handcuffed me to you. Any of these prisoners can bolt for the woods with nobody to stop them."

"I know what that's like," I said, "wanting to escape."

"So how does it feel now to be a jailer? Huh?" She walked to the house.

I carted a bucket to Hermann and took a drink from the ladle. He dipped his kerchief in the water and tied the sopping bandana around his neck. "Your friend Hermann knows, yes?" He splashed his face and wiped dirt from his eye sockets.

"Oh yeah, she's putty in my hands." I earned a penny explaining it to him.

Mr. Turner continued to purchase POW labor after the peanut harvest; I got Hermann steady work this way. Soon, Cecilia's father requested the Germans by name. When Christmas approached, he invited Hermann and several other prisoners for a Christmas Eve meal with his family. Cecilia invited me to join them, maybe a sign that my new friend's stratagem had worked.

The first time I heard Hermann speak German was when he led the singing of "Stille Nacht" and "O Tannenbaum" in his clear tenor. We taught them a few carols learned in school, and they explained how Kris Kringle came from "Christkindl." In Germany, the Christ child delivered presents, not Santa Claus.

"In America," Mr. Turner said from the head of the table, "it's the parents that play St. Nick." He signaled to his wife, who brought out a box containing a wrapped present for each of us. I got a new bone-handled pocket knife, probably at Cecilia's suggestion; she'd made fun of the broken tip of my old whittling knife, calling it a screwdriver.

The Germans received clothing and snacks. Two of them cried aloud as they held up socks and crew-neck shirts. Hermann challenged me to a swordfight, his unwrapped Hershey bar against my knife. As we gently parried, he said, "Quartermaster Fleming will have to lower his price."

I shouted, in imitation of Fleming's falsetto, "Hey, don't you know there's a war on?"

"I do, and you have lost." He slipped past my knife and touched the chocolate bar to my breastbone. As Cecilia laughed, he told her, "Roger is not dead, merely sweeter."

"You're right," she said, gazing at me. "I can tell already."

RIENZI'S CHRISTMAS CARD FEATURED A country snow scene with the word "Peace" emblazoned across the sky. Inside, she wrote, "Roger, I hope 1945 will bring peace at last. The war news is promising, but my father says that my mother's countrymen are proud and stubborn. Remember, I'm an American and I root for the Allies without reservation. I don't know what my mother would do if she were alive. Probably, she would cry, which is what mothers have always done, the world over.

"Please send me the latest word about Jay. Is he safe and unhurt? Has Chet completely thrown aside fighting and judo (ha ha!) for work? Do you still battle over chores and other small things?

"Thank you for your latest photograph. I wouldn't recognize you without it, I'm sure. You look taller and more filled out. Think you're strong enough to flip me? Don't worry, I'll still be easy to recognize, even if you're hosting Japanese POWs alongside the Germans.

"After armistice ("penny" word #1) and the subsequent peace treaty, people's feelings should calm down enough for me to travel safely. With the tides of battle turning so decisively against the Axis, my father and I haven't been subject to the hatred we encountered in previous years. Someone even left a commiseration (#2) of sorts on our doorstep: a drawing of a slant-eyed, tearful man with spectacles and buck teeth and the words 'Too Bad—So Sad.' If the artist and his friends thought this was funny, maybe it's the first step toward healing.

"I appreciate your punctual (#3?), thoughtful letters. Please keep writing to me, my faithful friend. Your words bring light as bright as the Dutchman's into my woeful cell and edge open my prison door a little more each time. Sincerely, Rienzi."

On a Saturday in February, Chet and I collected firewood on sleds and pulled them down Hardscrabble Road toward home. My teeth chattered so much that I could barely hear him. He was telling me his plan to hobo around the country until he turned seventeen the following year. I needed to warm up by working harder, so I interrupted him. "My turn to pull the heavy load."

"I'm still the general and I'm still hauling it. You can pull all you want after today."

"You better let me or else."

"Or else what?"

Chet let me throw the first jab. He probably felt sorry for me and wanted me to think I had a chance. Ten punches later, I pulled myself out of a ditch.

As we trudged onward, my thoughts bounced between finishing high school and whether I should live a hobo's life until I could enlist. Then I wondered what to write in my next letter to Rienzi and considered asking Cecilia to sit up with me before I hopped a freight train. Then the '42 Chrysler Royal Sedan raced past us.

When Chet told me, "Papa's back," I recalled the rabbit watching the hawk streak toward it. I could think of nothing else during the rest of our journey home.

Chet was true to his word. On Sunday, he insulated his jacket and overalls with slender, money-filled Prince Albert tobacco cans and put his spare clothes into a rucksack. I sat on the mattress we used to share and watched him, trying to memorize his strong, bony face, the casual way he'd wrenched open each rusty can to double-check the amount—the sum always matched his penciled figure on the lid—and the grace of his movements, so sure and spare.

He settled the rucksack straps over his shoulders. "I'm ready," he said.

"I'll walk you as far as Hardscrabble Road."

"No. I wanna step off that porch alone. Once I leave the house, I gotta feel like I'm on my own."

"I wish I could go with you."

He glanced up the hallway; Mama was hard at work in the kitchen. "Tell her goodbye for me."

"She doesn't know?"

"I knew I'd say something you'd have to pay for. She won't miss me—she hasn't missed my wages for a long time. Her boyfriends buy her anything she needs."

I eased off the bed, trying to hold in my grief, to present the same stony expression he did. "You'll write to me?"

"Fifty-two times a year. I promise." Chet shook my hand and then he left.

# CHAPTER 24

We celebrated the victory in Europe that May. Even the POWs seemed relieved; Hermann hugged my neck and cried for a long time. By the time Japan surrendered in September, though, shifting moods made the prisoners unpredictable. Hermann and others were happy, looking forward to returning home, while we did fieldwork in the morning. By dinnertime, some of them were scared about what they'd find at home and others cried about family members who might've died. When the truck picked them up before sunset, many of the Germans talked with eagerness about rebuilding their country, while others—especially Hermann—stared at their surroundings with a different kind of longing.

A week after my fifteenth birthday, Hermann sat with me beneath a sprawling live oak at the edge of the Turner property. He ate his dinner of chicken and peas while I enjoyed a final ham steak, the last of the sweetly smoked meat before the next hog-killing. He said, "Roger, it breaks my heart to know that the Army will send us home soon."

"Don't you miss Bavaria? You're always telling stories about hiking and skiing."

"I have lived and fought in deserts for years." He scuffed his heel against the ground. "The sand and heat here are different, but now even more familiar. I cannot go back to a land of rock and cold. I cannot rebuild a place I do not love." On his peaked field cap, he'd plucked away the swastika threads. The silver-gray eagle now clutched at nothing.

"Will you escape from the camp?"

"Some tried to tunnel out, but they hit a lot of water."

"I could teach you to dowse so you could avoid—"

"The sand always fills in their holes regardless. I need to make my own plan."

"How can I help?"

He snorted. "You are not afraid of an enemy prisoner running loose in America?"

"I want you to stay here—you've always been my friend."

He waved to Cecilia at the other end of the long field of peanut plants almost ready for drying. She strolled toward us with her notebook; Hermann was teaching her more German Christmas carols and songs. He said to me, "And she is still your friend?"

"Thanks to you."

"Anything more than that?"

"I'm afraid to…I think some boys messed with her before you came here. Got her drunk and maybe hurt her."

"Ah, you are still protecting her. Do you plan to keep her for yourself?"

It was my turn to snort as Cecilia drew near. "She won't be kept. Anyway, I'm not the keeping sort."

She said, "What are you keeping? Hermann, if you want your secrets kept, Roger's your man." I looked away, realizing that I'd just told a secret about her.

When I got home that evening, Mama said, "Jay sent a letter. He's stationed in Japan, but says he likes the people now that they're not shooting at him. The women are very graceful and refined, he says. Oh my stars, imagine if he ends up with a Oriental girlfriend too."

"Mama, I told you that Rienzi isn't—"

"She wrote you." She handed me the envelope from her apron. "You always look to see if I slit it open. I swannee, I did it the one time. How many letters have you got since then?"

"A bunch, I reckon." I rubbed the envelope between my fingers, anxious to go outside. "Chet would know the exact number."

"Aye God, don't bring up the little coward, that ingrate who wouldn't even say goodbye to his poor mother."

He posted his letters every Saturday. They arrived from Atlanta, Chattanooga, Bristol, and across Virginia. Mama tossed every letter in the oven, but she repeated his news to me over supper, as if she'd memorized them word for word.

She said, "Left with my heart under his shoe, just like his father."

The comparison riled me. My uncles reported seeing Papa in Colquitt and Bainbridge, but he hadn't tried to contact us. The hawk circled, waiting, watching. Did he see us as the enemy, responsible for his years in the penitentiary? The more I thought about Chet getting lumped in with Papa, the angrier I grew.

I tucked Rienzi's note in my back pocket. I knew better than to mention Stan but I did it anyway, like touching a smoking skillet to confirm that it's hot. I planted my feet, prepared to take what came, and said, "Why did you step out with Stan Borden, my father?"

Mama raised her hand to slap me but then looked me over. Maybe she saw something different than she expected. Instead of bashing my cheek, she raked her hair, as if that's what she'd intended. A look of relief softened her expression: now she didn't have to pretend anymore. She asked if he'd told me.

"No, ma'am. I saw the snapshots and pieced it together."

"Jesus, he kept those? Poor Buddy. He never knew what he wanted, but he could never say no to what came his way." She dropped into a chair and pointed a finger at me. "Don't you dare judge either of us, him married to my crazy sister, and me…You can't know how Mance was with me. How puny he made me feel—and that was even before he tried to shoot my face off. Don't think for a second that you understand what I been through."

I joined her at the table, feeling braver by the moment. "Was Stan good to you?"

"He did his best, bless his heart. That's why you're here; I loved him that much."

"What do you mean?"

"I didn't need to have you, you know. But I wanted to keep a part of him. It like to have killed me, telling him he was banned from Ma's. Banned from me too. The instant that Ma saw you, she knew."

I rubbed my temples as I tried to take it in. "What do you mean you didn't need to have me?"

"There're old granny-women that can take care of it, cheap. Some doctors too, but they charge a arm and a leg. Don't you know about such things?"

"No'm."

"You never wondered why you stayed the youngest all these years? It's 'cause I didn't want to keep any of the others. You came from the last time I was in love."

As I SAT IN THE hayloft, my mind was addled from imagining a dozen younger brothers and sisters, maybe a few of them bastards like me. Maybe all of them. Did some of the money we'd given her over the later years go to granny-women and doctors?

The envelope in my back pocket crinkled as I shifted in place. Barely enough daylight remained for me to see; fortunately Rienzi didn't write much this time. I had to read her note twice before the words broke through my shellshock: she was coming to visit in a week.

I rolled back and shouted, arms and legs in the air. My sudden excitement surprised me. I must've thought we would trade letters forever. Here was the perfect antidote to Mama's latest bombshell. Rienzi would say again that it was always better to know—now I could debate with her in person.

She'd written as a postscript, "My grandparents insist that they throw me a belated 'sweet-sixteen' party next Sunday evening at 6. It'll be just the four of us, if you can come. If you can't dress up, they'll understand."

I clambered down the ladder and uncovered the trapdoor I'd installed. I crouched near the stable where we kept Dan; Mr. Turner had returned Papa's old horse when we moved back in. Dan whinnied at me and watched with those huge brown eyes, now gentled with age. I dug up my tobacco cans and squinted in the near-dark as I counted out ten dollars and change. I carried a fresh dollar-fifty in wages from Mr. Turner. All told, I could afford a dress-up outfit.

"Roger!" Mama called from the house. "You got a pretty visitor."

It couldn't be Rienzi. From the date of her letter; she definitely meant to arrive the following week. Then I smiled to myself, admitting that I found her pretty in my memory. Somehow, the fact that I never touched her beautiful braid made me envision the softest silk flowing between my fingers. Was imagination preferable to the truth? If I never found out what her hair felt like, I'd always have the best texture in my mind. I'd never be disappointed. Of course, that would mean that I never touched her hair: knowledge would be better than daydreams.

"Roger! Where are you at?"

I put the money away and trotted into the barn lot. Cecilia waved at me from the back porch. She said, "Thank you, Miz MacLeod," and waited for me while Mama walked inside. The sky at dusk had turned to swaths of peach and strawberry. Red sky at night, Jerry had told me: sailor's delight.

Cecilia wore makeup that outlined her eyes and shaded her lids. Her cheeks bore a powdered blush. She'd dressed in a simple white blouse, topped by a fake pearl necklace, and a calf-length skirt of aquamarine with matching high-heels. A pale sweater dangled from her index finger, disappearing behind one shoulder; her jutting elbow looked as round and smooth as the goddess statues in my history book.

I joined her on the porch. "Your parents are letting you out now?"

"My father dropped me off here. You should've seen how pleased he looked when I said we had a date."

"A date?"

"You'd bragged about how well you can drive—take me for a spin."

Mama said from the lamp-lit kitchen, "Spin nuthin. Take her to supper, Roger—you got paid today. Don't she look nice?"

My complexion turned the same shade as Cecilia's rouge. She cocked her hip at me and posed, and I stared hard at my feet. "Yes'm. She won't want to be seen with me." I wriggled my bare, filthy toes on the floor and rubbed a moist palm over my threadbare overalls.

Mama said, "Nonsense. Change clothes, put a shine on your shoes, and do town. You'll forget all about your letter-writer."

We'd traded Papa's old Model B Ford pickup for a newer marmalade-orange Chevy truck. As I shifted it into drive, I apologized to Cecilia for taking so long to get ready. I also asked her to excuse the dusty leather seat, and I told her yet again, "I could just take you home if you want."

"Roger, if you say that one more time, I'll jump out."

"OK, sorry. You want to go into Colquitt?"

"Let's go to Bainbridge and make it a proper date."

"I feel like a field hand taking out the boss' daughter. Heck, that's just what I am." I tried to shoot the wilted cuff of my only dress shirt, but it slid back over the knob of my bony wrist. Cotton twill slacks bunched at my groin and under my rump. Not for the first time around Cecilia I was very aware of my body's response to her—thank goodness for the dark.

As I turned onto Hardscrabble Road, heading toward the highway, she said, "If you're done feeling sorry for yourself, can I ask a question? Who's 'your letter-writer'?"

"Just somebody I met a long time ago."

"Why does your mother want you to forget her?"

I pressed the brake too hard, making us lurch forward in the seat. "How do you know it's a 'her'?"

"Am I supposed to make you forget about a boy? Are you being funny? Or are you, you know, funny…that way?"

Chet once told me about a town dude who touched another boy while they were swimming; he gave me all the warning signs of what he'd called a "queer." I deepened my voice and said, "What way?"

"Roger, who is she?"

"Just somebody I met a long time ago."

Taking the conversation in circles didn't deter her. She said, "Is she pretty?"

"I haven't seen her since we were little kids."

She touched my sleeve and said, "But she makes your mother afraid."

"Hey, what is this?"

"I want to know who my competition is."

This time, I skidded to a halt on the dirt road. "Stop teasing me."

"Teasing is for girls who stop short. Surely you've heard that I don't tease." Headlights shined through the back window, illuminating her face. She held my gaze with such frankness that I looked away.

A horn bleated and a rattletrap truck pulled around us. The driver shouted through the passenger window, "Hey, kids, get off the damn road if you're gonna neck."

As the truck sped away, Cecilia laughed. She said, "Sounds good to me. There's a little trail on the right. Park us there." When we'd stopped again, she told me to kill the engine. I shut off the headlights too. Her voice dropped to a whisper. "I hope you don't mind the dark." She kicked off the high-heels and shifted around in the seat, as if tucking both feet under her bottom. "It's so dark that now you can't watch me."

"Watch you do what?" I had to swallow hard before I said it; my throat had gone dry.

"You never just look at anybody. You watch. Like a part of you is separate from what's going on. Detached, removed." Her cool fingers touched my mouth and then slid over my cheek. Her hand was the perfect shape to cup my face. Pads on the fingers and across her palm fit just right, enfolding me from my birthmark to my jaw.

The springs in the seat creaked as she slid closer. Her breath warmed my lips. "Don't watch us together, be here with me. Don't touch my skin—feel me."

I gripped my thighs. If I leaned forward even a skoash I'd be kissing her. I mumbled, "This girl, the letter-writer…"

"Is she sweet and innocent like you? I know things, Roger. I'm not proud of it, but if I show you, maybe that'll become ours." Her free hand traced a widening spiral on my chest. "Take away those bad memories for me. You're a good boy. You'll do that, won't you?" She leaned into me.

I turned my face into her cupped hand, and her kiss bumped my cheek. "I'm sorry," I said. "I can't."

She balled the placket of my shirt within her fist. I thought she would try to rip my heart out. I expected her to slap me or spit in my face, but she continued to hold me instead. She grasped the cloth, not to tear it but to hang on. Tears dripped from her voice as she whispered, "You're sure?"

"The one who writes me—I think I need to try with her."

"Why not me?"

"It would be you, if I didn't know her. Maybe if she wasn't coming next week, if I knew she'd stay away forever...No, sorry, even if it was—"

"Forever? You'd wait that long for her?"

"I...I reckon so. I didn't know that until today. Now, I can't stop thinking about her."

She patted my cheek and released me. Her crying became louder as she hunkered by my side. I was afraid I'd broken her heart. She said, "Oh God, you could've made it so easy for me. Now I have to be brave."

I gave her my kerchief and asked what she'd meant. She said, "Hermann told me he'll wait forever for me. That's right, the singing POW. He told me today he'll escape and hide out forever in the woods until I was ready."

"I thought he tried to pair me up with you."

"He did. He said he knew his love for me was impossible and thought you and I could be happy together. I'd tried to ignore my own feelings. Today, we told each other everything."

I took her tear-dampened hand. "So why'd you want to be with me, here in the dark?"

"Because I could be happy with you. You'd treat me gently, tenderly. I decided that if we became a couple tonight, I could bury my feelings for him."

"So if I kissed you and you showed me the things you know, you'd stay with me but dream about him." I let go of her and crossed my arms.

"I think so. Are you mad?"

"You're darn right I am. Even if I love someone else, I hate it that I came in second place with you."

She gave my shoulder a light punch. "OK, Romeo, do you want me or not?"

"I want you...to be happy. It's all I ever wanted for you. So that means breaking Hermann out of the prison camp."

FOLLOWING SCHOOL ON MONDAY AFTERNOON, I told Mr. Turner I had stomach flu and needed to go home. He said, "We've gotta get the fields ready for the winter crops, Roger. Can you work half-speed? Hit the outhouse whenever you want, but I need every man out there."

I returned to the row where Hermann weeded, and picked up the gooseneck hoe that had belonged to Jay. "You sure they're shipping y'all home this week?"

He said, "That is the rumor."

"That's been the rumor every week since VJ Day."

Hermann patted his face with his sand-colored kerchief. "If it is true this week, then I will miss you."

"You'll miss Cecilia too. She told me on Saturday." We started hoeing again, talking to the ground we shaped.

"You are not angry that I have stolen your girl?"

"She wasn't mine to steal. She loves you—it's you she picked."

He said, "Every night I dream that I am locked in a box and shipped across the Atlantic and then overland to Bavaria. Only then, when all is lost, am I released."

"I can get rid of that nightmare; me and Cecilia made a plan on Saturday." Hermann edged closer, still working the soil. I explained that I would bring a horse for his escape with Cecilia, but, while I was gone, she'd have to pretend to be me in case her father looked out and did a headcount.

He argued with me in whispers, but finally said, "Roger, you could go to jail for this."

"In a way, would that make me a prisoner of war?"

An hour before the Army transport would arrive, I watched Cecilia hurry to the outhouse on schedule. I waited a precious minute before clutching my abdomen in feigned panic and running for the two-holer. My knock on the door made Cecilia gasp. She said, "Don't!"

"It's me." I pantomimed frustration, stomping in a small, angry circle outside the door, and then dashed into the woods behind the privy.

Cecilia soon joined me, her hair now pinned up so she could conceal it under my hat. I led her deeper into the woods and kicked aside pine straw from Jay's overalls and work shirt, which I'd hidden on Sunday. She said, "Now I'm not sure about this. A girl can't get by as—"

"Believe me, I've seen it done. Anyway, you'll need a disguise until you're far away from here."

"Are you sure you don't want me? I'm scared."

"It'll work, I promise. You better hurry." I posted myself as guard while she changed clothes.

"Roger, I need your help." Like a model in Sears and Roebuck, she wore only white cotton panties and a conical brassiere. She turned her back and unclasped the cups over her breasts. "Bind me," she said. "Use the stockings."

"What? There's no time for this."

"I just thought of it. My chest ruins the disguise." Without waiting for my response, she stooped to pick up her nylons. The profile of her full, pale breast nodded below her arm. She held the toe of her stocking against her left breast and passed the nylon over her right. "Come on, now, help me flatten myself."

Trembling with excitement and shame, as well as the knowledge of time running out, I pulled the sheer nylon taut under her arm, drew it across her back, and passed it back to her. We used both stockings, and I tried hard not to steal another peek at her bosom.

She covered herself within Jay's shirt. Working to fasten it, she made slow progress. "The buttons are on the wrong side," she said. "I'm used to them on the left."

I shifted from foot to foot, saying, "Come on, come on." I pushed her hands away and secured the bottommost buttons, my quivering fingers mere inches from her panties.

"You don't need to protect me anymore." She stepped into the overalls and worked on tightening the straps. The overall bib covered her like a breastplate.

"I'll come back with Dan. See you at the shed." I pushed my hat onto her head. "Go, before I'm missed."

Trotting out to the field, Cecilia kept her head bowed, face hidden under the wide straw brim. I bundled her clothes, circled through the woods to the shed, and left them atop a small wicker suitcase she'd readied. Glancing at the sun every few minutes, I ran home.

For the first time and probably the last, I was happy to see a stranger's car parked beside our truck. In the field, Nat and his son Ennis waved as they worked on preparing land for winter vegetables. I hurried alongside the house, hearing Mama's laugh from behind the bedroom shutters. A man said, "I'd better be going," in a familiar voice, which propelled me faster toward the barn.

Dan snuffled when I entered. On Sunday, I'd practiced settling his saddle and other gear, working with him over and over, so he was patient as I went through the motions again. I hung a bag of feed and two filled canteens from the pommel, and led Dan out of the barn.

Footsteps and voices echoed from the house. I jammed my foot into a stirrup and swung atop Dan. He broke into a canter that soon became a gallop as we roared down the dirt drive. When I glanced behind me, I saw the door of the man's green Studebaker Champion swing shut like a wing closing. I screamed at Dan to hurry. The last thing I wanted was for one of Mama's lovers to stop me for a chat.

Dan carried me onto Hardscrabble Road. When I glanced back again, the Studebaker had turned in the opposite direction, but closing on me was the Army two-and-a-half-ton truck, come to take away the POWs, maybe for the last time.

I passed the Turner's driveway and spurred Dan to a cow-track farther up the road, which would lead to their old shed. I heard grinding gear-changes as the soldier made his turn. Dan balked at taking me down the overgrown path, but my time was running out. In my best Papa-imitation, I said, "Dan, giddup." Dan glanced back at me, but his legs had already obeyed.

Cecilia waited for me outside the shed with her traveling case. Beside the door, her father's awful, smashed hand bobbed in its fruit jar: a paperweight holding down her good-bye note. I secured Dan's reins to a tree, and we listened as the truck rolled back down the drive.

She took my hand when brakes squealed at the intersection with Hardscrabble Road. "It didn't work, I know it didn't. He's gone."

A distant voice was followed by a whole chorus of louder exclamations, and she began to cry. I whispered, "Don't be afraid… it's all right. We can try again tomorrow."

She threw her arms around me, weeping against my shoulder. I murmured, "Don't worry. It could be anything."

"It's singing, Roger." Her sobs now mingled with laughter. "The Germans are singing."

As the truck roared away from us, I understood the voices briefly before the sounds faded away. They sang in English, "I need no shackles to remind me, I'm just a prisoner of love!"

Careful footsteps in dry leaves announced Hermann before we saw him. He scanned the woods and ran to us, heedless of the noise. Cecilia wiped her eyes and gave him a long, hard hug.

When they continued to rock in each other's arms, crying and murmuring, I told Hermann that he'd better get changed. I ushered him into the dim shed where Cecilia had left a pair of her father's overalls and a work shirt that she'd swiped. Soon, he brought out his uniform, neatly folded. I said, "How does freedom feel?"

"I'm just a prisoner of love, my friend. I give you a lifetime of thanks." We embraced.

I held Dan's reins while Cecilia mounted the saddle, and cupped my hands for Hermann so he could push up behind her. I handed him the wicker traveling case.

She pointed Dan toward the cow-track, working the bridle with one-handed confidence. On the verge of tears again, she said, "Your letter-writer's a lucky girl."

"She doesn't know it yet. Good luck."

Her free hand swept down and touched my face. She said, "I love you too." A firm nudge from her heels sent Dan back down the path.

# CHAPTER 25

I burned Hermann's uniform that evening and buried the buckles and other remains. On Tuesday afternoon, Mr. Turner waved a letter at me and asked if Cecilia had said anything at all about eloping with a boy from school. "Hell," he said, "I hoped it was you, if it had to be anybody."

"Thanks, sir. Cecilia's special—I'm glad I could sometimes hold the reins for her."

While school was in session, some officers had visited with the Turners and questioned the locals who'd worked alongside Hermann. Cecilia's parents did ask me later in the week if she had become friendly with the missing POW. I said, "She liked the Christmas carols he sang. Honestly, though, I was sure that she and I would start courting. She broke my heart too."

The Army patrolled US 27 and the dirt roads, looking for Hermann, as did the High Sheriff and his deputies. I noted a Jeep on Hardscrabble Road and a radio car on the highway as I drove to Rienzi's party on Sunday.

Rienzi had deceived me. She never told me she had an older sister, who I observed on the porch sipping a Coca-Cola as I arrived.

I waved and parked beside the house before I realized that the young woman in the knee-length skirt and short-sleeved silk blouse was the birthday girl. Rienzi had cut her hair in a pageboy style that swooped in to touch her cheeks. Her face remained a place of gently curving features framing dark, almond-shaped eyes. Her bust and hips had filled out, but echoed the same geometry of peaks and slopes.

Only her voice retained a girlish quality. Her hello didn't squeak as before but it remained in an upper register, like a bell.

My blue cotton tie flapped in the breeze. I pressed it against my starched dress shirt, hand over my heart. Unsure of how to greet her beyond hello, I raised my arms to hug her, dropped them, and repeated the spastic motions while she laughed musically. She leaned in and kissed my cheek before stepping away.

Ginger and cinnamon-sugar aromas coupled with the tingle on my cheek to make me lightheaded. I took a swallow from her cola to lubricate my mouth and throat. "Did you have problems getting here?"

"I memorized the bus schedules, remember?"

"I mean trouble with people. Why do you always play this game?"

"Because you never speak precisely," she said, smiling. Though I couldn't see any makeup on her face, her mouth looked redder than before. I wondered if she'd taste like cherries. "It's fun to tease you. You always puff up like a globefish."

"It's dumb, as you used to say." I glanced away from her face, afraid that she'd think I was staring, and looked instead at her lovely legs and small feet turned inward. Every part of her seduced me. I licked my lips and said, "So, no one bothered you?"

"I got a few looks and the bus driver told a Negro lady she could sit beside 'Tokyo Rose,' but that was all. It'll keep getting better."

I handed her a small, gift-wrapped package from my pocket and said, "Happy sweet-sixteen. You fit that description."

"Thank you." She poked a slender index finger against my chest. "But don't start treating me like a debutante."

Her grandmother opened the door then, to find me skewered on the end of Rienzi's close-cropped fingernail. She invited us in for supper and birthday cake.

We ate and caught up on things we hadn't bothered to write about. I recited what I recalled from Chet's latest letter, posted from Richmond. Meanwhile, Jay had toured Nagasaki and described it as a preview of the end of the world. Rienzi told us about going back to regular high school and finding that she had gotten so far ahead while self-studying with her father's college textbooks that she planned to get an early diploma and move on to the University of Texas. I bragged about my own advanced schoolwork, but whenever I named a course, she'd finished that one and the follow-up subject too. Every time she buffaloed me, I got a little madder. As soon as I simmered down, though, I discovered that she appealed to me even more.

Her grandmother took a two-layer chocolate cake from the sideboard and set it in front of Rienzi. Sixteen wax columns jutted from it like closely grouped arrows. Her grandfather lit every wick until Rienzi's face glowed. She said, "Roger, help me blow these out."

I'd never had a birthday cake, let alone candles, so she had to tell me the order of things. I made my own silent wish with my cheek next to hers, feeling the heat of the candles on my face and her warmth beside me. Soft black hair, more like satin than silk, brushed my skin. She inhaled loudly as a prompt for me to do likewise. We blew at opposite ends and worked toward the middle, finally puffing at the same flames. The intimacy ended with our pursed lips not quite touching and acrid gray smoke curling before us.

She opened my present first. I'd bought it with the leftover from my clothing purchases. Inside a slim box, she uncovered a pocket knife with an embedded compass on one side and a thermometer on the other. The wood handle was as dark as the buckeye in my pocket. She announced the temperature and oriented herself toward true north, which happened to be in my direction. With a smile, she threw out her arms and hugged me tight. If I had seen her looking the way she did now and knew how soft and supple she'd feel against me, I would've mistakenly bought her something feminine.

Her grandparents had done exactly that. They presented her with a pile of boxes that yielded dresses and jewelry. She thanked them, finding something unique to compliment about each one. All the while, though, she used my gift to slit open the wrappings.

After eating the chocolate-frosted cake, I thanked everyone for having me. Then I took a measured, hopeful breath and said to Rienzi, "Would you like to go for a ride?" She gave me an icing-tinged grin.

Inside the truck, she said, "Look at you, all dressed up, driving a truck as orange as a forest fire. You don't look at all like your pictures." She kicked off her shoes and crossed her legs, nudging me with her toe. "You've really filled out."

As with Cecilia, I felt grateful for the cloaking darkness. "So have...So have you got, uh, anyplace you'd like to go?"

"Just drive us around." She dipped her face into the air blowing through her open window and said, "I can't believe I'm back again after so long."

"Nothing around here changes."

"People say that about home, but everything changes. My grandparents told me about the German POW camp and an escape that has everyone excited. Men and women are returning from the service; what they've seen and done will change everything even more."

I'd made a few turns to get to the highway and cruised toward Hardscrabble Road. Pulling onto the dirt track, I said, "Are we the same? You and me?"

"I hope so. You aren't angry with my kidding, are you?"

"No. But you, ah, want to stay friends?"

"Of course. That's why I wrote so much. You'd be surprised about how few people I know. You're the only friend I have."

I said, "Do you ever want more than that?"

Stubborn and obtuse as usual, she replied, "More than one friend? I guess I'll make some when I go to college."

No geezer in a rattletrap truck needed to tell me it was time to go parking. I pulled onto the same path where Cecilia had directed me. What had she done, in what exact order, to seduce me? I switched off the engine and killed the lights. "I hope you don't mind the dark."

"San Antonio is so bright at night, you can hardly see the stars. Look, there's Cassiopeia and the Little Dipper and Pegasus—"

I touched Rienzi's face as she peered up through the windshield. "I saved myself for you. On this very spot. You remember Cecilia Turner? The hog-killing?" Not the romantic images I intended to conjure. I tried again. "She's very beautiful now, like a movie star." I wanted to make her feel that way, to show her. My hand trailed down her neck like soft rain, flowed over her collar bone, and covered her firm, round breast.

She took my hand in both of hers. Her voice became a breathy burlesque, "Golly Moses, so you're saying you could've poked her on this very spot? On this very seat? Gracious!"

"Don't make fun. Not now." I tried to pull my hand away, but she wouldn't let go. "I'm saying you're so special to me that I saved myself. I want to be with you. I want us to be a couple." I tried to rescue my trapped hand by prying it free, but in an instant she held them both. Rather than entwining my fingers romantically, she clamped down over them and dragged me closer.

From less than a foot away, she seethed, "Do I owe you? I mean, seeing as how you passed up on a movie star. The least I could do is hike up my skirt, right?"

"That isn't what I want."

"What then? Tell me."

"I want us to…to have a romance." Her grasp was hurting me; I heard my knuckles begin to pop.

"I'd say this is a bad start, Roger."

I tried a new tack, if only to free myself. "It's my birthmark, isn't it? I disgust you."

"Don't be stupid. Am I supposed to say 'Oh, my dearest, I've hurt your tender feelings,' and give in to you?"

"There's nothing to give in to. At least let me go. Please."

She laughed and another knuckle popped. "But where will your hands go next?"

"Stop!"

"I still like you, Roger. But you have to be invited to grope me." She kissed me hard, a wet, lip-sucking, chocolate-tasting kiss that finished with her tongue licking my open mouth. I was even more surprised when she slid under me. She still gripped my hands as her knees rose into my chest. In one fluid motion, she rocked her arms and legs and heaved me out the passenger window.

With a grunt, I belly-flopped in the field. My entire front hit the ground at once: face, torso, and legs. Only my wrung-out hands were spared. I spit out dirt and gasped while the headlights flicked on and the engine cranked. Rienzi shouted, "Next time, learn some manners before you try to make love to me."

She stole my truck. High grass hissed beneath it like water on hot coals as she roared away. The taillights flickered, spent flames that vanished in the dark. Ribbons of exhaust wafted past me like candle-smoke. That was all that remained.

How could a smart boy be so stupid? Exhausted, I decided to go to Spring Creek to wash off and consider how I'd ruined everything. Maybe I'd drown myself. I set off and hiked through the dark, deep woods. I imagined sinking in the water and never rising again, becoming part of the earth and sea and food for the fish. I could be useful.

Before I had the chance, though, the Dutchman found me.

# CHAPTER 26

I didn't reckon on the Dutchman sneaking up from behind again. The trees before me slowly brightened until I could make out lichen on rotten logs and the hairy arms of poison ivy wrapped tight around slender trunks. My shadow overlapped them; dark bands extended from my shoe tips and climbed up the pine bark. Parts of my silhouette disappeared in gaps between the trees, narrow strips of me lost forever in the woods.

When I turned, the Dutchman hovered about a dozen feet behind me, a perfect sphere. Its buttery yellow glow touched my clothes and skin. Low-pitched vibrations drilled deep into my brain. It wavered, backing away and then moving toward me and retreating once more. Trying to make up its mind when to attack.

I was terrified but I refused to run. The spirit light became the color of fire and it thrummed louder. How right that I should die alone in the woods on a moonless night—I should've remained afraid of the dark. I scrunched my toes, cursing my shoes. I wished I could feel the forest floor, clutch the dirt. Too late. The haint surged through me.

I forced myself to look. I wanted to see the Dutchman's face before I died. The glow felt like cool water on my skin and seemed to sluice through my hair. Its brightness didn't increase as the spirit light flowed into me. Nor did it have a solid core, no image of a vengeful man about to reach through my ribs, grab my beating heart, and snatch my life away. It touched me all over, but with a tenderness I'd only rarely felt. The haint seemed shy but curious. This was no monster. I recognized the quality of its embrace from the comforting fingertips of Mrs. Gladney, Cecilia's cupping of my face, and Rienzi's joyous hug. The Dutchman was a woman.

The light dimmed as it moved behind me. My shadow on the trees faded and became part of a dark cocoon. When I turned, the haint had disappeared. It didn't drift away as I'd seen it do before, still visible even from a long way off. It vanished. Finally dead, I thought, but then knew that I was wrong. Something deep inside said that the spirit had let go. It had released its tenuous hold, had found whatever it sought. It departed, never to be seen again.

Peacefulness settled over me for the first time in many days. My toes uncurled, and I bent down and felt the forest floor. Its damp coolness was just like the haint's touch. Perhaps the spirit and the earth were one.

I strode over the narrow paths, confident of my course, at last feeling a part of the woods and the night sky and the wind slipping among the trunks and sweeping down through the canopy to wash over me. Deeper into the forest, where the air stilled, I surged through the fog that stood as motionless as I had. I penetrated it just like the glow had passed through me. As I approached Wanda's place, I imagined I had become the haint.

By the flickering light of the flambeau she'd wedged into a nearby stump, Wanda hung bunches of twined herbs and roots from the ceiling of her porch. I was one with the tender stems, shrugging off the rich dirt that clung to my many arms. I became the spout of fire whirling over the end of her torch, spinning with hands waving above my head. My body stretched. It grew thinner and then pointed at the top and bulbous down below as a droplet of pine oil slipped from the flaming wood and I rolled into a ball as the oil let go and we fell through space and splattered onto the stump in all directions. I seeped down among the tree rings, found the roots, returned to the earth, and sprouted up through my feet. I stood before Wanda.

"Roger," she said, "you been witched." Her teeth gleamed yellow in the firelight as she bit a length of twine in two.

"I feel fine. Better than I have in a month of Sundays."

"There's good witching and bad. I know the look of both. What'chu been up to?"

"I was fixing to come see you about a judgment."

She yanked knots around her last couple of bundles and slung the drooping bows over some bent nails in the porch rafters. "You know I'm no judge, and there ain't enough of me to be a jury. Go to the white folk in town for that."

I sat on the porch with her and told her about the past few days, though I suspected she knew everything I'd done. I said, "Have I messed up everything? Would Cecilia and Hermann be safer if I'd minded my own business? Should I have just tried to be friends with Rienzi?"

"You freed them. Even the boy that's really a girl; you've opened a door for her by closing another one." She laughed through her teeth. "All you've ever wanted to do is escape from this place, but you're freeing everybody else first. And more'n just regular folk." From the porch floor, she lifted the cotton-picker's satchel stained with damp spots and leaf-green smears. "I was thinking of my mama just as you came creeping along. In my head, I was singing them songs she loved. She practiced all that good magic."

"That's how you knew I looked witched?"

"That's how I knew she touched you." Wanda pulled back my shirtsleeve and wiped her hand across my forearm. She held up her empty palm to me. "You's sparkling, boy. Mama done that and now she's finally at rest. I ain't gonna find her no more when I go a-wandering."

I expected flecks of gold or mica dusting my skin, but whatever she saw I couldn't. For a moment, though, I summoned the touch of light again: gentle ripples through my hair, mothering caresses that now clouded my head with sleep. My neck bent like a stem no longer able to support its heavy flower. My face dipped down and I stifled a yawn. I whispered, "Your mama had real soft fingers."

"That and her singing is what I remember most." She traced a swirling pattern with her fingertip over her empty palm, as if writing in the sparkles she'd lifted. With a sigh, she closed moist eyes and pressed her palm against one mahogany cheek and then the other. Her eyes had cleared when she looked at me. "You wanna sleep in my parlor again tonight?"

Sunshine tumbled through the uncovered windows when I awoke. The car horn that roused me sounded again with a mild, respectful peep: a question rather than a summons. I sat up and wiped drool from my face. The white quilt beneath me with its tiny, precise stitches held an oval stain like the center of a buckeye. Patterns from the quilt had left marks in my cheek, reminding me of the swirl Wanda had traced on her hand.

I walked to the open doorway. Robert Bryson sat behind the wheel of his shiny black Pierce-Arrow straight-eight. His sedan still looked good, though it was almost as old as me. Mr. Bryson, on the other hand, looked like a raisin—Wanda's long-ago water curse had left his face shriveled. He tipped back a long-necked brown bottle and gulped. His cheeks pulsed and his skin seemed to fill out. When he stopped drinking, the illusion faded and wrinkles creased his face again. He stepped from his car, came around front, and opened the passenger side. His dark, rumpled suit looked moth-eaten and his wire-framed glasses were bent. With pride, though, he shot his wilted shirt cuffs while straightening his spine. We helloed each other as Wanda rounded the corner of her home, wearing the same homemade dress as the night before.

She paused at the open car door and looked back at me. "Got a biscuit and a bream on the porch for you. Don't be nibbling on my herbs though. You a dear boy, but you ain't no deer, boy." Mr. Bryson laughed too much as she sat in his car. He pushed the door closed, soft as shutting a dresser drawer.

I said, "Am I still sparkling?"

She replied through the open window, "Gleaming like Spring Crik in the sunshine. Ain't he, Mr. Bryson."

He shaded his eyes and squinted as he peered at me, hamming it up. "He sho is, ma'am. Just like you says. A spitting image of Spring Crik yonder. Mm-hm."

Wanda stared at me, her mouth a grim line. Without a change in her expression, she winked.

From the height of the sun, I judged the time to be about nine. I'd missed Jerry's bread run, my advanced tutoring, and the start of school. The pan-fried bream Wanda left for me was so satisfying—I seemed to experience its memories of effortless swimming in a body built for speed and darting maneuvers—that I decided to play hooky and go fishing. After all the extra schoolwork, I'd earned my truancy. Later, I'd call on Rienzi and ask for another chance.

I never recalled a time when I felt so confident in my decisions. Suddenly I didn't care what anyone thought of my actions: they were mine, right or wrong. It was as if the spirit had taken away my fear. Then I remembered that I stopped feeling afraid when I sat in the darkened truck with Rienzi. My confidence had grown before the haint touched me, when I decided to face it. The courage to stand firm: that was a present I'd given to myself.

Still, the spirit did impart a gift: the intense connection I'd felt with everything the night before had not disappeared. As I went home to change clothes and get my fishing gear, I no longer watched my world. I felt it bone-deep. Details remained sharp: the crushed green velvet of moss; pale, overlapping lines a beaver had gnawed in a tree trunk; a tan snail shell lying among beige stones. With a bit of concentration, I felt myself slide through the curving walls of the moist shell interior, follow the paths of tree roots, and reach skyward with the tallest limbs. I laughed out loud.

I wondered if drunks could feel something akin to that magic. Maybe my father had felt that way after a belt or two, before those tender feelings collapsed within the angry fire of more liquor. Just as some men did anything for a taste of whiskey, I'd become addicted to that intimate connection with my world. What would it feel like to kiss Rienzi again?

* * *

Mama had a recurring visitor at home: the green Studebaker Champion again squatted on our dirt driveway. Circling around toward the backyard, I intended to fetch my pole and cooking gear. I stopped short.

Along the opposite side of the house, I noticed that Rienzi had returned the truck. Then I saw beneath Mama's shuttered bedroom window, Ennis' eight-year-old son Tom knelt with the right side of his face pressed against the bare planks. His left eye was closed and, for a moment, I thought he'd fallen asleep with the boards as his pillow. Then I remembered the decade-old bullet hole Papa had shot in the bedroom wall. Tom peered through with such concentration that he didn't hear me walk up. His left eye snapped open when I came within a few yards of him.

Tom fell onto his seat, crab-walked backward, and got his feet under him. Without a word, he dashed around the truck and off toward his home on the other side of the peanut field. He ran as if I'd drawn a bead on him and was about to fire.

Bracketing the bullet hole were well-worn grease marks that matched the curve of Tom's cheek and forehead and the side of his nose. His mother called, "Tom Willis! Where you at, boy?"

From behind the shuttered window, a man said, "I swear to God, every time I'm over here she's calling for that pickaninny." The same, familiar tone I'd heard while stealing Dan. Mr. Gladney's voice.

Mama said, "Willodean calls for that boy every day, believe you me."

I should've continued my walk to the barn, but I had to see his pitiful face. I knelt beside the house and spied through the hole.

Mr. Gladney sat with his back to me at the foot of the bed. He wore a sleeveless undershirt and boxers. Always a stout man, fat now lapped over the elastic band of his shorts and puckered the backs of his arms. Moles dotted the doughy skin of his neck and shoulders like leopard spots. His hands rested in his lap; he appeared to be showing Mama something.

She stood in the doorway wearing a new store-bought dress of royal blue, knee-length and short-sleeved. Her arms looked so pale compared to her raw, work-reddened hands. Blond hair, unpinned and wild, framed her face with curls like tusks. A nasty smirk pulled up one side of Mama's mouth as she stared at whatever he showed her. She drawled, "The least you could do is put a pillow on the floor for me."

He turned to get one from the top of the bed, his face splitting with a broad grin. His right hand stretched toward the bullet hole and me. In his left, Mr. Gladney gripped the base of the largest tallywhacker I'd ever seen. I gasped as Mama reached for it.

I fell backward and thumped my head on the dirt. For a moment, the impact knocked the pictures from my brain.

"What the hell?" The shutters flew open. With his thick chest and head framed in the window, Mr. Gladney stared back at me. His look of triumph—Mama's same nasty smirk—melted into shame as I refused to turn my face from him.

"What's wrong?" Mama's high-heeled shoes banged the floor, coming closer.

"Nothing." He reached through the window and grabbed the slats of the shutters, revealing sweaty thatches under his arms. Mr. Gladney looked away, giving in before I did. Pulling the shutters inward with a slam, he said, "Maybe it was a squirrel."

"Well it sure wilted you, Walt." Mama snickered and said, "Let's have that-there pillow."

I imitated Tom, crab-walking until I could get to my feet. Down the driveway and onto the dirt road, I strode. Maybe before last night I would've run crying with embarrassment and guilt and anger, but now I simply made up my mind. I'd had enough. Like Jay and Chet and even Darlene, I knew I had to move on.

My father's old place looked swept clean when I approached it, as if Stan and Arzula never existed. The outbuildings had been knocked down and harvested of all useable wood. I took a broken, mildewed board and paced off the yard, trying to remember the number of steps to the house and Eliza Jean's grave. I imagined reaching down through the sand and finding what my father had buried but could never escape: the small, curled skeleton; a few scraps of disintegrating cloth; and the brown, sand-choked poison bottle and tarnished spoon. Before I left—forever, I thought—I packed the earth tight like a tucked-in blanket and planted the board as her grave marker. I carved her name and the year of her birth with my knife. Thinking of my Greek studies, I pulled the last coin from my pocket. I pushed the nickel deep in the sand, hoping it would pay for her passage in case she hadn't yet made it across the Styx.

I KNEW THAT I COULD make up to Rienzi for my gross immaturity. However, she had left long before I reached her grandparents' place. Her grandmother said, "She told us this crazy story about tricking you into giving her the keys and then stealing your truck. Don't you young people beat all! Rienzi laughed about it one minute and then bawled her eyes out the next. This morning, she told her grandfather that she wanted to go back home, so he took her to the Trailways depot in Columbus."

"Please thank him for dropping off my family's truck. Did she say when she'll be back, ma'am?"

"No, but she said that if you stopped by, I should give you this." From her apron pocket, she took a tiny metal cup topped with glass. Rienzi had pried the compass out of my gift to her. "She told me to say that she knows you'll find your way someday."

Standing on the shoulder of the highway, turning north with the compass and then south, I decided that I had only one choice. With no money, I couldn't get to San Antonio to make amends with Rienzi; even hitchhikers and hobos needed to eat. There was no way I would go back to school either. Facing Mr. Gladney didn't upset me; we both knew I had something on him now. But I didn't want to see his wife lecturing from the front of the room every day. I didn't want to try to make small talk as she tutored me so I could graduate early. I didn't want to pretend that the man she had to lie with—the one who had given her children, the one who would reach for her in the night—wasn't going to bed with the smell of my mother still on him and the triumphant smirk on his face.

Skirting Colquitt, I tromped through barren fields and logged-out woods while I made my plans: I needed to get a full-time job until the military would take me. Since I never wanted to spend another night under Mama's roof, I had to find somewhere to live.

Ramsey Lumber Company was still the biggest employer in the county. Mr. Ramsey had died the previous year, but his widow still owned the mill and let the managers run it, putting to rest any fears that it would close and force scores of laborers out of work. The Seaboard Railroad main line ran right past the business, and I followed the tracks to their back gate.

The property consisted of long buildings in a U-shape that surrounded a huge lumber yard. Fifteen-foot-high towers of sawn boards cured in the outdoors like temples built to honor a sun god. The thud of wood being stacked in the yard provided a steady rhythm that punctuated the more distant screech of timber running through cutting and planing machines.

Near the front entrance, a young Negro on a tractor called over the rumbling diesel engine, "It's a sight, isn't it. You looking for work?" I told him I was, and he directed me to the left arm of the U. "The one with the furnace stacks and boilers."

Getting a job turned out to be as easy as giving my name. While I talked to a clerk who stared at my birthmark, another man walked over to the paper-strewn desk, crossed his big arms, and said, "You kin to Jay and Chet MacLeod?"

"Yes, sir. They're my brothers."

"What's Jay think of the Army?"

"He likes almost everything about it, now that we won the war."

The man smiled and shook my hand. "I'm Gus Clayton, the foreman here. If you're a relation of Jay and Chet's, you got a job any time you want it." As the clerk got busy, Mr. Clayton said, "You can start tomorrow in the yard. Eight in the morning, report to Calvin, the colored boy that rides around on the tractor."

"Could I work a half-day today?"

"Today you need to go into town and buy some work clothes and brogans. You don't wanna get turpentine on them fancy duds." When I told him I had no money, he took a five-dollar bill from his pocket. "Your pay's forty cents an hour. You'll be working off this loan on your first day."

I thanked him and slid the money into my trousers. Trusting my confidence, I said, "I don't want to wear out my welcome, sir, but is there somewhere in the mill where I could spend my nights?"

He considered a moment and then pointed to the far end of the building. "Yonder in the furnace room, beside the boilers. You can sack out in there where the fireman starts his nightly rounds. Show up at eight tonight. If you make any problems for him, though, you'll have to go."

Already in debt to my employer, I walked to Colquitt and bought used dungarees and coarse leather work shoes at the hardware store. It was noon, and I wandered around town with forty-one cents, a compass, and a buckeye in my pocket, and nothing in my stomach.

When images of Mama and Mr. Gladney intruded into my thoughts, I focused on the warm sunshine and smells carried on the light breeze. I followed the aromas of grease and strong coffee to Dora's, the Negro diner where Jerry Flynn treated me to breakfast each day. His bread truck was parked out front. Through the window, I saw Jerry's back and hunched shoulders as he leaned over his plate at the counter, flanked by colored men on both sides. Facing them, Dora's teenage daughter Trudy wiped crumbs and cigarette ashes from the countertop into her cupped hand.

A few of the customers glanced over their shoulders when I stepped inside. They all propped their elbows on the counter, arms pointed upward, cigarettes clamped between their fingers. Gray threads drifted from their smokestacks. Billie Holiday sang "Lover Man" from the jukebox and Trudy hummed along. She called to her mother who was flipping burgers, "Your pirate's done come back from the sea."

Jerry turned and lifted his half-eaten burger in salute; the crescent moon of browned bun and pink meat smiled at me while his jaws worked on chewing. I took a stool beside him and said to Dora, "Cheeseburger and a RC, please." I dropped my clothing purchases underfoot and put a quarter on the counter. Dora slapped down another pink disk of beef. As she cooked the sizzling meat, her backside swayed to the music.

Trudy rang up my order. With a two-tone bell, the cash register drawer sprang open and struck the hip she'd turned to meet it. She gave an exaggerated bump to slide the drawer closed, earning some customers' whistles. The whole world had gone into heat lately, myself included. After all, was I really any different from—

"Apple don't fall far from the tree," Jerry said. "I sat next to yer daddy in here once, a few weeks before that night in Bainbridge, and he done the same thing as you, staring off into space. 'MacLeod's on his own little cloud,' was what I thought. Me and him and you are the only white folks that ever come in here. The rest are missing a helluva meal and a good show to boot." He took a sip of coffee while Dora slapped the cap off a cold RC and thumped the bottle in front of me before dancing back to my burger on the fry table.

I apologized for missing work. Jerry shrugged and said, "You're missing school, too."

"I quit."

He took a bite of his sandwich. "You fixing to deliver bread for a living?"

"Naw, just to get to Ramsey's sawmill on Monday mornings. I got a job there today."

Dora put my sizzling sandwich in front of me. Yellow cheese dripped from the bun and mixed with the pink puddle of juice on the plate. The silky-voiced baritone of Billy Eckstein came on the jukebox with "Jelly, Jelly."

I said, "I was hoping that you could pick me up at the crossroads like usual and drop me at O'Neil Gowdy's store across from the mill." The smell of yeasty bread and charred meat and sharp cheese filled my nose and then the aromas joined the heat and flavors in my mouth. I chased it with a swallow of icy cola. Now, I seemed to taste things all the way down.

Jerry said, "You gonna walk home?"

"I quit there, too. I'll stay at the mill most nights and camp in the woods on weekends."

"Reckon you had a fight with yer mama."

"She's got plenty of company—she won't miss me."

Jerry finished his coffee and said, "Sure she'll miss you. Her company ain't got nuthin to do with you."

"No, not anymore."

THE NIGHT SHIFT FIREMAN'S VOICE had a deep, hollow sound, as if he stood inside one of the enormous boilers. "Mr. Clayton said he found some company for me."

"I hope you don't mind me sleeping here." In the furnace room, a pine table and chair nestled against one wall; on the floor, curly wood shavings and sawdust mounded, blown in from the planing mill during working hours by a pipe nearly as tall as me that thrust from a wall. The scraps were used to keep the furnace fired and maintain steam pressure in the boilers; warm hummocks of wood gave off a sweet aroma that smelled better than any bed I'd ever known.

He said, "I'll try not to wake you when I go on my rounds." He took a key from his pocket and unlocked a box on the wall above the table. From inside, he removed a bulky time-clock and a small black pistol, which he pocketed.

I nudged a pile of sawdust and shavings with the toe of my work shoe. "Are there snakes around here?"

"I've never seen one."

"Then why the gun?"

"Someone murdered the fella that worked here before me. Eased up and put a bullet in his head. The killer didn't take anything; he shot the poor bastard and left."

"And he was never caught?"

"Nope. Still out there."

I saw now that the chair had dark, uneven stains in the wood. The table too looked marred beneath a layer of sawdust. I said, "Uh, would you mind if I went with you on your rounds?"

He awoke me every hour with a kick on the sole of my brogans. I stumbled after him, panning his flashlight as he made a tour of the darkened mills and the moonlit lumber yard where the towers could hide any number of maniacs. In designated spots, he handed me the pistol while he "punched" his clock with a key, to record on a paper tape when he'd done his job. Throughout the night I spent one-quarter of every hour half-awake and sometimes armed.

A killer was still at large. I didn't think the job could get any worse than that.

# CHAPTER 27

WHEN THE STEAM WHISTLE BLEW TO START THE WORKDAY, men in the yard had already begun stacking rough-cut lumber in fifteen-foot-tall wooden shelters so the planks could dry. They also took freshly sawn wood to the kilns for curing and carted seasoned boards to the planing mill for a satin-smooth finish. Mostly, they bent over and straightened and then paused to stretch their sore muscles, splinter-embedded fingers spread against lower backs like whalebone trusses.

I liked the relative quiet of the lumber yard. A birdsong could sometimes be heard over the clatter of board-stacking, the roar of the giant circular saw cutting through felled trees under one roof, and the screech of the planer in the other building.

"How do?" a Negro man called to me, stepping down from his tractor. A tow-behind trailer was loaded with large rectangles of wood and a keg of nails. He wore his gray felt hat low like a gunslinger, and a big hammer slung in the loop in his overalls, dangling like a six-shooter. I told him I was reporting for work, and he introduced himself as Calvin Chambers. "You'll like working out here. The fall weather's fine and you can hear a mockingbird now and again."

I told him my name and we shook hands. He led me to a nearby trailer half-full of planks from the sawing operation. With a clarity that my teachers would've admired, he explained how to stack the rough-cut boards so they'd dry correctly within the fifteen-foot-tall forms he built. After I demonstrated that I'd understood, he drew his hammer and shot me down. "Pleased to meet you, Roger." Calvin blew off the imaginary gun smoke from the end of the handle.

I discovered that if I bent from my knees instead of the waist, my back didn't protest as much while I stacked the heavy lumber. Still, I had to take breaks to stretch and groan. Sometimes, I emulated the laborers who lay flat on the ground to rest their tortured spines.

Calvin often built his forms nearby, using a single hammer blow to drive in each nail, as precise as a machine. He told about his ideas for building devices to do all kinds of work, steam-powered nail-guns, board-stacking machines, and such. It was a little like having Jay back from service overseas.

When I asked him what we'd do for a living if machines took our work, he said, "You'd get to build the machines. Though I've read stories in *Astounding Science* about machines building other machines. Still, people would have to design all that."

"Before I quit high school, I was taking advanced classes," I said. "But I don't know near enough to do that. Sounds like you got a diploma and then some."

He set down his hammer. "You're wrong there. I only finished the seventh grade."

"You quit school too?"

"School quit me. There's no colored high school in these parts. Grade school was as far as I could go—and had to walk miles to get there, starting at age six. Still, the school board didn't pluck out my eyes after grammar school. I read everything I can get my hands on."

"I know how that feels," I said, "having some magazine or book you haven't opened yet: like pulling a treasure chest out of the sand and waiting a moment before you see what's inside."

"Savoring it, right. I'll bring in some things that I think you'll like."

Though I was always dog-tired by sundown, the watchman often found me on my pile of warm sawdust and wood curls reading Calvin's books and magazines by lamplight. On Fridays I walked home after work. I'd slip into the barn, put the wages I'd saved into my tobacco cans, and grab a fishing rod and some cooking gear I'd stashed for a weekend on Spring Creek. Sometimes a car was parked near the house when I arrived—Mama seemed to have two rotating Friday-night visitors, neither of them Mr. Gladney—and sometimes the truck was gone. Wanda let me camp out in her parlor on rainy weekends, but mostly I sat alone and fished.

I also wrote to Jay at his last posting, telling him not to reply to me because Mama would read any mail sent to the house. I asked him to get word to Chet, since I didn't have his latest address. While sparing Jay from the details about why I left home and quit school, I did apologize: his and Chet's sacrifices to keep me going until graduation had been wasted.

Writing a letter to Rienzi proved harder. My newfound confidence sounded arrogant on paper. I'd gnaw on the fleshy pink of my pencil eraser and gaze at the living woods and the soft swells of Spring Creek, wanting to tell her how mannerly and respectful I would be with her. Soon, though, I decided that the power of words had their limits. Instead, I'd have to show her. I hoped that she would wait that long.

ON THE FIRST OF MARCH, a teenager appeared at the lumber yard in the afternoon. I remembered him from school, a senior who I'd seen briefly before I quit. A town dude, Joe Don Murphy, dressed in nice trousers and a clean, starched shirt like Papa used to wear.

I made him wait as I stacked more boards, just to show him I was doing important work. I wanted to tell him: "I ain't slumming here like some no-count truant. I'm doing a man's job." Even if it cripples me, I'd never add. Finally, I wiped my hands across my gunny-sack apron and offered to shake.

His mouth twitched as he squinted at my fingers sticky with turpentine. "Mrs. Gladney wants to see you at the school," he said, stuffing his hands into his pockets.

My hand stuck out between us as I blinked a few times. "When does she want me to be there?"

Joe Don flinched as the buzz saw in the nearby building sheared off bark from a gigantic log. "Half-past five today. She said she's expecting you."

"Tell her I'll be there."

"She knows you will. She said so." He looked me over, head to toe, and walked toward the front gate.

I knew she planned to make the case for me to finish school. I wouldn't explain why I quit; I'd lie if she pressed me. Though the trip would be a waste of her time and mine, I looked forward to saying a proper good-bye.

The school floors smelled of wax and ammonia and gleamed beneath the silver dome-lights mounted in the ceiling. My soles squeaked as I walked the empty hallways, doors closed and rooms dark on either side of me. In my stained clothes, with my hands still a little sticky from turpentine and my back throbbing like a regular working man's, I could imagine that I hadn't set foot in a school for years. Those days were long behind me.

Mrs. Gladney's door stood open at the end of the hall. Sunshine and electric light spilled out onto the clean linoleum. I softened my footsteps and eased up the corridor, wanting to hear her at work.

Her scratching pencil made a flourish, perhaps underlining a term-paper grade. She said, "Roger, I hope you're not planning to scare me."

"No, ma'am." I stepped around the corner and used my best classroom English. "Joe Don said that you wanted to see me."

Mrs. Gladney pushed away from her desk and faced me. She wore a demure jade-green skirt with matching shoes and a long-sleeved white blouse topped with a gold necklace. Since I'd seen her in October, a new tightness creased the corners of her eyes and pinched her mouth. She looked older than her thirty years. For the first time, I noticed not a beautiful woman, but a person—someone with troubles—and I merely wanted to help. I still admired my favorite teacher, but no longer did I covet her. It felt like a little death inside me.

I murmured, "Is everything all right, ma'am?"

"I planned to ask you the same thing." She gestured to the chair beside her desk, the top of which was covered in stacks of paper and theme books. I sat and adjusted my posture to ease the now-constant ache in my back. She said, "You're hurting. I can see it in your eyes." Before I could protest or tell her the same, she continued, "Schoolboys shouldn't look so pained."

"I'm not in school anymore, ma'am."

She pointed at me with the blunted tip of her Ticonderoga pencil. "And you dropped out before you wrote a composition for me. I want it now."

"You sent Joe Don to fetch me, ma'am...so I could write a paper for you?"

"In part." She passed over a few blank pages and the pencil she'd used. Small teeth marks marred the orange-painted wood that was still warm from her grip. She said, "Give me one hundred words on whether it is ever acceptable to lie."

As I tried to form a question, the lines deepened around her mouth; she barely contained whatever was gnawing on her. She said, "That's right, Roger. Is it ever acceptable to lie? Write that at the top of the first page. You have a half-hour to complete the assignment." She took out another pencil from a collection that rattled in her drawer and opened a student's composition book. I stared at her while she flipped through pages to the most recent essay. Without looking up, she said, "You better get busy."

Eraser tapping my lower lip, I considered past reasons for lying and the falsehoods I'd planned to tell her today. There was no doubt in my mind that some lies were good: if we always told the truth about what we did and thought and felt, there'd be no living with each other.

Scratching out as much as I wrote, I ended up with the following: "It is acceptable to tell a lie when you might do much more harm with the truth than with a story that will spare a person's feelings or protect someone's secrets. Revealing some secrets can be so cruel that it is better to keep them safe than to tell people what they do not really need to know. A lie is all right when it can do some good without hurting anyone." I counted the words and had about thirty to go. Rereading the piece, I nibbled Mrs. Gladney's pencil, enjoying the compression of the soft wood against my teeth until I thought about her mouth doing the same thing. My bite marks overlapped hers.

She wrote a B at the top of a page and closed the last of the theme books. With a smile, she said, "I've watched my students chew their pencils in nervousness or boredom for years and never thought I'd do it. Like smoking—you consider it repulsive and then one day you're puffing away like everyone else." She looked at the pencils in her desk drawer. "All of these have my teeth marks on them and I've only been addicted since…well, right after you dropped out."

"I have thirty more words to go."

"The number you use isn't nearly as important as your ideas." She took the paper and read my work, holding the page in both hands. A faint tremor in her fingers made my essay quiver. Her glance slid back to me a few times before she set the paper down. "Say you've stolen a loaf of bread. The baker asks you if you did it. What do you tell him?"

"I say no. But as soon as I can, I leave money to pay for what I stole."

"You may have heard about the German prisoner who escaped. Say you liked him and helped him to steal away. This is a person, not something you can pay for later. Would you lie to the police? The United States Army? President Truman?"

After a moment of hesitation, I said, "If I helped him, it would be because I liked him, because he wasn't a Nazi, just born in the wrong country at the wrong time—I'm just supposing now—and deserved a chance to become an American and live free. So, yes, I'd probably lie to protect him."

"And yourself, don't forget. In both cases, you'd lie to keep from being punished. So, is it always OK to lie?" I shrugged, and she said, "What do you think of liars?"

"It depends on why they lied, ma'am."

"Would you like them if they lied to protect a friend?"

"Maybe."

"To do some good without hurting anyone? To right an old wrong?"

"I reckon so, ma'am." I began to squirm until a jabbing back spasm stilled me.

Her voice rose as she leaned closer. "Would you lie to keep a secret from a friend?"

"So I can protect another friend, ma'am?" I flinched when I saw her eyes, small and glassy, like Papa's when he'd beaten me.

I drew back, but she grabbed my wrists in a grip tighter than Rienzi's and said, "So you can protect someone you hate!"

Turning my face away from her, I cried, "No, ma'am."

"But what about sparing your friend's feelings, like you wrote?" She held on while I tried to pull away. "Tell me! Would you rather hurt me with the truth or with a lie?"

"I'd never hurt you. Please let me go."

"What do you know about Mr. Gladney?"

"Nothing."

"Tell me what he's been up to."

"I don't know anything."

"Liar! When did you last see my husband?"

"I-I-I..." Tears tumbled out of my eyes. She released me, crying as well.

"I'm sorry, Roger. It's all right." She offered a wrinkled kerchief from her purse. Rosy patches of blush and dark streaks that matched her eye makeup already marred the white linen.

I declined it, pulling a faded rag from my back pocket. Red ovals on my wrists outlined the impressions left by her fingers. With a sniff, I said, "It's harder to be sure in real life than on paper. I reckon I deserve a failing grade."

"No, you don't deserve to fail." She dabbed at her tears and sighed. "I checked your records. You only needed two more credits to get a certificate of completion. Not as good as a high school diploma, but handy to get into college. You could teach next door to me someday."

"I can't come back to finish up, ma'am. Just like I can't live at home again. I think you know why."

She dropped her gaze and sat still a moment. Hopefully I'd given her what she needed to know. Her fingers plucked at another stack of papers—out of nervousness, I thought—until she withdrew a folder with "MacLeod, Roger" typed on it.

When she looked at me again, the old gentleness had returned to her eyes. She said, "You had very high marks in all your coursework. I was looking forward to teaching you more of Bookkeeping and Senior Composition too." With her bite-marked pencil, she swirled a C at the top of my paper. "It's not your best work, but you did write something that I hope you won't recant: 'A lie is all right when it can do some good without hurting anyone.'"

"I meant what I said, ma'am, about never hurting you."

"And I'll always remember you for that." She touched my hand, soft this time instead of insistent. "I gave you that particular theme for a reason. I hope that you'll understand and forgive me for something I've done."

"You'd never do anything to hurt me, either."

"I pray that I haven't. Now, look at this." She opened my folder. On top of a few dozen sheets of paper lay a typed letter stating that Mrs. Valerie Gladney had tutored me in Senior Composition and Bookkeeping and administered the appropriate tests, all of which I had passed. She recommended me for a high school certificate. Beneath her flowing signature and the words "Approved By," her husband Walton Gladney had scrawled his name and the current date.

I swiped away more stinging tears and said, "Why would you risk your job by lying for me, ma'am?"

"I feel somehow responsible for what happened. A wife always blames herself, I suppose."

"How did you get Mr. Gladney to sign it?"

The tightness returned and set her mouth into a hard line. "Even a wife who blames herself can be very persuasive—it also helps to have long, sharp knives in the house." When I blinked at her, she blushed and said, "At our wedding, my mother advised us to 'never let the sun go down on an argument.' Mr. Gladney should listen to his mother-in-law. My additional advice to you, as you're out in the world and planning someday to take a wife, is to never close your eyes at night when you've made your lover mad enough to hurt you."

I rubbed the bruises on my wrists as I pictured what Rienzi was capable of doing to me. "It's not my place to ask, ma'am, but will you stay with…will everything stay the same for you?"

Her shoulders slumped. She said, "Remember first grade? Early in the term I wrote on the board: 'I OBEY THE RULES.' I was raised to honor marriage, Roger. My family doesn't believe in divorce."

I gestured to the letter she and the principal had signed. "You don't obey all the rules, ma'am."

"I know. Once I had the idea, I convinced myself that it wouldn't hurt anyone. Mr. Gladney's belief that I would—that I will—harm him proved sufficient to…motivate him." She twisted the band of white gold on her finger, moving it up past one knuckle and then the other. Before the ring cleared her fingertip, she slid it back in place and said, "Knowing that I could do no harm and a lot of good allowed me to see it through. A divorce, though…a divorce would hurt everyone but me."

"It's none of my business. I'm sorry for—"

"I'd love to have you teaching in the next classroom. At least come back and see me some day. Please?"

I stood and thanked her, my eyes wet again. "I won't ever forget you."

"Do better than I did. Be smarter." She pushed out of her chair and hugged me. "As long as I've known you, you've been stumbling along after the grownups. I did this because you deserve a chance to catch up. I did this because I couldn't give you what you deserve most of all."

"What's that, ma'am?"

She touched my damp cheek and said, "A decent childhood."

THE NEXT DAY, MR. CLAYTON passed along word that Ramsey Lumber had a new owner. Before week's end, a number of trucks surrounded an area at the edge of the lumber yard, the farthest point from the noise of the mills. I climbed high atop a tower of lumber and watched crews of workmen frame and roof a large office. They eventually carried in paneling and furniture and painted the exterior a blinding white. As a final step, they hung a lacquered oak door that had frosted glass in the top third of it.

On Monday morning, I returned to the top of one of the fifteen-foot stacks to see why Mr. Clayton had sprinted past. By the time I'd reached the top, the office door had closed. A half-dozen other mill hands stood on the lumber piles, all watching, waiting for some sign about what the new owner was like and what plans he might have for our livelihoods.

Mr. Clayton emerged first, backing out the door. He laughed and chatted with the man, who stepped over the threshold and closed the door behind him. The owner followed the foreman's pointing finger, perhaps getting an overview of the operation that could make him even richer or that he would now run into the ground. Despite the extra weight around his middle and an expensive suit, I recognized the white Stetson on his head and the shadowed face.

I muttered, "Papa's back."

# CHAPTER 28

THE WIDOW MRS. BONNY RAMSEY HAD MARRIED AND SIGNED OVER the sawmill to her new husband, Mance MacLeod.

I couldn't avoid him forever. I didn't know if Papa had read a roster of his workers or merely stumbled upon me, but a day after he'd taken a tour around the sawmill, he caught me in the lumber yard taking a short break. I'd lain on the ground to rest my back. To ease the spasms, I imagined spreading across the dirt like a puddle. My contours took on the shape of the earth.

Calvin rapped hard at his form, joining the edges together with too many hammer blows. I sat up. Papa marched so close that his shadow covered me.

The new white Stetson shaded his eyes and pressed down the tops of his ears. He wore a cream-colored linen suit that should've wrinkled like the devil, but stayed smooth over his heavy frame. Instead of a revolver, he now wore a massive ring of keys at his waist. His mouth twisted downward into a familiar scowl as he said, "What the blue blazes are you doing?"

"Stretching out my back, sir." Upon standing, I realized that I was now taller than him. Still, I moved out of striking distance.

"I was afraid you fell sleep. Now don't be setting a bad example to the others. Being my son don't mean you can loaf." Papa leaned forward and lowered his voice. "You and me, together, gotta learn these folks how to put in a good day's work."

Maybe I didn't hear him right over Calvin's hammering. When I imagined our reunion, I thought he'd acknowledge me but nothing more. I didn't expect much, and I certainly didn't think he'd couple us together like boxcars. For some reason he'd put Mr. Hyde away and presented himself as good Dr. Jekyll. He softened his gaze, but I expected him to lash out any minute. I said, "I'll set a good example, sir."

"Thank you." Papa turned his back and walked to the planing mill where the machine squared-up another board with a prolonged scream.

Calvin wiped his face on a sleeve and said, "Your daddy's a hard one to figure out."

"I'm glad you heard him. I thought I was dreaming."

"You told lots of bad stories on him, and then he shows up with smiles and thank yous."

"I didn't think he knew how. Be honest now: he did give me a scolding."

"As rough as a pinch on the arm. And you only got it because you two—together—need to set a good example for the rest of us." He whacked the edges of a new form together, a big grin on his face.

When I next saw Papa, I still expected Mr. Hyde to emerge, snarling. Wrong again. He stopped a group of us outside O'Neil Gowdy's store before we began to eat dinner. "Gentlemen," he said, removing his hat. His chin dropped into a roll of fat at his neck, and he intoned, "Let's bow our heads and thank the Lord for His nourishment of our bodies and our everlasting souls."

A MONTH LATER, PAPA SENT an assistant to summon me to the office. On the frosted glass of the door, a painter had printed, "Mance MacLeod, Owner." I reminded myself that he didn't own me, that I wasn't even kin to him. I rapped on the lacquered oak and said, "It's Roger, sir."

He reclined in a red leather chair behind his mahogany desk, which was lit by a brass lamp with a green glass shade. Oak paneling walled his office, and fresh-cut heart-pine—maybe the last in South Georgia—spanned the floor. A leather desk blotter as big as a heifer, with maple triangles at its corners, sprawled across the table.

"Look how well your papa's done," he said. "All thanks to my salvation." Beside his fat black telephone sat a clothbound Bible with a purple satin ribbon marking a page halfway through it. I'd never seen him read any book before, let alone Scripture.

His high-speed ceiling fan chilled the room; the constant rush of cold air on my sweaty head almost hurt. There were no chairs on my side of the desk, so I continued to stand. Harsh sunlight blazed through the frosted glass; on the floor, oblong letters spelled out, "Mance MacLeod, Owner." The shadows almost touched me.

He steepled his fingers and said, "I'm glad you're using the proper name I gave you. It's about time you got shed of that pet name from Reva. Maybe you can get totally free of that sinful woman's influence."

"I don't live at home anymore, sir."

"Praised be. You're coming to supper at my house tonight. You haven't met your stepmother and her son yet."

"Did Mama ever divorce you, sir?"

"Reva don't know it, but Judge McCrory took care of it for me." His smile displayed many capped teeth. "C'mon, let's go. It's the biggest house in the county, so we have lots of space for you. Imagine that, Roger, a room of your own."

I ground my molars. A new family, a new home, a luxurious life with him at the head of the table again. "I've had that for a while. After you shot Mama, everything went to hell—"

"Don't blaspheme, boy. I know all about what happened."

"Jay had to quit school to support us all—"

"I said I know."

"Chet—"

He smacked his blotter with an open palm. "God…bless it, I know. You blame me for everything. God forgives, Roger. I took His love into my heart and He washed my soul clean."

"What about my soul?"

"You can get saved as easy as me. Holding onto the past is bad for you. Jesus will untwist you and work out the knots, until you forgive and are ready to be forgiven." He began to thumb through his Bible.

I stared at the top of his head and the ears that folded down as if he wore his halo too low. "And, just that easy, you're blameless for everything you've done."

He traced his middle finger down a page of Scripture, not looking up from the words. "I did hard time in the Big House. I paid my debt, son."

"And what about your other debts? For keeping a family on the side?" My eyes burned but I kept the tears in check. "For beating us bloody over nuthin?"

"You need to turn the other cheek before anger eats you up. When I accepted Christ into my life, I let go of my anger. I was reborn. You need to put yourself in His hands, Roger. Now listen to this-here—"

"No, you listen! You can't run us over and say it didn't matter. You can't pretend all those awful years didn't mean a thing."

"We had some rough times, sure. I reckon it hurt to see your mama get shot."

A cool blue flame swept through me, burning away any lingering fear of him. Not caring about consequences made me feel powerful. "I saved her when you tried to blow her head off, you bastard."

"You watch your language. It's all water under the bridge."

"Bastard—just like me. You're no more my father than Bonny Ramsey is my mother."

A vein throbbed in his reddening forehead. "You're going too far, son."

"Son? I guess you never figured out what happened between Mama and Stan Borden."

Papa swiped his arm like a scythe across the tabletop. His green-shaded desk lamp tumbled over, jerked out of its wall socket, and crashed on the floor. "I knew it! That shit-heel is roasting in hell this very minute."

Plenty of sunshine still poured into the room, but his shadowed name on the floor had lengthened, creeping up my body. Papa's clenched hands opened slowly, as if letting go and reaching for the light. His brow, pale again, reabsorbed the pulsing vein. He said, "It doesn't matter. I've always loved you like my own flesh and blood."

"What you did to me you call love?"

He said, "You were always in your little dream-world—"

"Trying to escape from you."

"Is this what you wanted? To call me names? To insult me and try to get my goat? Does this make you feel better?"

"I just want to set things right!"

He stood and thrust out his jaw. "Do you wanna hit me? Twice? Three times? How many blows before you'd be satisfied?"

"How many times was it for you, Papa?"

"My conscience is clear. Washed clean in the blood of the Lamb." He folded his arms and grinned.

I snatched the brass lamp from the floor and wrenched out the cord. The green shade had shattered, so I wielded the base like a club. "Tell me you're sorry for all you've done."

"I've asked for God's forgiveness and received it."

"Apologize to me."

"Are you setting yourself above our Lord? He's not only forgiven my sins, Roger, but He's rewarded me. Come home and see what I can give you."

"Give me back my childhood, you sonofabitch." I whirled and threw the lamp through his frosted window, destroying the backward letters, wiping the shadow of "Mance MacLeod, Owner" from me, and bathing me in sunshine.

I ground the glass beneath my feet as I stalked to the front gate.

# CHAPTER 29

I met Jerry Flynn at the crossroads before sunup, overall pockets weighted down with my savings of sixty-three dollars and ninety-eight cents that I'd dug up from the barn on Sunday night. Instead of climbing onto the seat beside him, I walked around the front of the bread truck. I offered a handshake through his open window.

"What's this?"

"It's good-bye—I won't need a ride any more. I had it out with Papa and quit the mill."

"Quitting another thing already? Every boy fights with his old man. It's part of becoming one yerself. Report for duty and you'll get yer job back for sure."

"It was damn final, the way we parted."

"What'chu gonna do?" He snorted. "Sharecrop?"

"A long time ago, I learned when it's wise to run. I'll knock around like Chet did 'til I reach seventeen."

Jerry touched the blue-green anchor on his hairy forearm. "Who said I joined at seventeen?"

"You mean I have to wait even longer?" I felt lightheaded, gripping the window frame.

"I mean you don't gotta wait one day more."

"So I could've joined when I turned fifteen?"

"You looked like a kid then. That sawmill's burned off all the peach fuzz." He turned off the truck engine. Cicadas clicked and buzzed, filling the silence. "What'chu do is take a old Bible and make a family tree inside the front cover. Fake up anything you don't know and, by yer name, put down a birth date that'll make you seventeen. Uh—" He traced the air, working the subtraction. "—1929. You tell that Navy recruiter in Albany you was born at home in the country with no doctor to make out one of them birth certificates."

"Then what?"

"Then get ready for your anchor tattoo, Roger." He started the truck and pumped the gas pedal a couple of times. He said over the roaring engine, "You need dropping anywhere?"

"I have a Bible at home. I'll fake it up and hitchhike to the recruiting office." I offered my hand again. "Thanks for everything, Mr. Flynn."

Instead of shaking it, Jerry raised his hand edge-on to his eyebrow and snapped off a sharp salute. I imitated him and, by his nod, knew I'd done it right.

ROOSTERS HAD BEGUN TO CROW by the time I stepped onto Mama's porch. If Jerry's scheme worked, maybe I could sign up for duty on the Texas coastline and see Rienzi during a furlough. If it didn't, I wasn't sure what to do. I wouldn't move back in with Mama.

She hadn't stirred, so I eased through the parlor and slipped into the room across from hers. From under the bed, I took out a stained, moldering Bible from among the books I'd scavenged over the years. I also removed the town-clothes I'd bought for Rienzi's birthday party and my Blue Cloud cigar box.

I changed clothes and transferred the money to my trousers. No one had weeded or swept the front yard in a long time. I carried my gear over to Lonnie's former home, now Ennis and Willodean's place. The field was empty; he and Nat must've taken a rare holiday to go fishing on Spring Creek. I heard Willodean out back, getting onto their two boys about not helping with the wash: "Lord help me, children, y'all's gonna put your mama in a early grave."

I walked through the front door of the two-room shack. In the parlor, a couple of quilt pallets lay side by side and the air smelled of children who'd spent every day outdoors. I crouched and set my Blue Cloud cigar box between the beds. The Indian chief on the cover looked sadder than I'd noticed before. Inside, her boys would find blood-red marbles, arrowheads, a worthless train-flattened nickel, and the loose change I added from my pocket. I saluted Chief Blue Cloud and walked out with my Bible.

At Nat and Leona's, I went around back and hugged her neck while she labored over her own washing. Before we said goodbye, I wrote a note for her to give to my longtime friend. He didn't have much schooling, so I kept it simple: "Nat, Thanks for holding my hand until I got used to the dark. I'm sorry I have to let go now. Love, Roger."

I sat on their front porch and invented my family tree on the inside cover of the Bible. My inventions got bolder as I went along, with Jay and Chet both on the wrong side of twenty and Darlene edging toward thirty. I assigned her a fictional husband and three adoring children and hoped she would be happy.

I varied my writing, even switching hands a few times, so the chart appeared to have been completed over many years by different people. In a few places, I put down only a month and year for a birth. I liked the look of it, a record that simple folks might've scribbled down to record who came from whom and if they'd gone to their reward, bless their hearts. For me, I put down February 1929. It seemed fitting that Mama and Papa would leave something off, distracted by a cuss fight or simply neglectful.

With dress shoes slung over my shoulder, I hitchhiked east along Hardscrabble Road. Warm sand pushed from under my bare feet as I tried to imagine life on a ship, with nothing but rolling, pitching steel underfoot, nothing to dig my toes into, no such thing as a natural foothold. I felt conflicted, what with Jay and Chet in the Army, but Jerry's Bible trick had worked with the Navy, so I kept walking the forty miles to Albany, left thumb sticking out as my arms swung.

Around mid-morning, I caught a lift on the highway from a farmer who took me as far as Newton, and a shoe salesman got me the remaining twenty miles to Albany. He dropped me curbside, across the street from the storefront Navy recruiting station. My shirt and trousers stuck to my skin as I sweated in the noonday sun. The buzz-cut Navy man gave me a small nod through the plate-glass window of his office. As I slipped on my shoes, I said a prayer that I would pull off this trick.

When I opened his office door, the recruiter said, "Took a while to gird your loins?"

"Yes, sir, it's an important decision, but I'm ready." I introduced myself.

The lieutenant junior grade shook my hand and said, "You from around here?"

"No, sir. I hitchhiked from Colquitt."

"That's quite a ways. You're seventeen?"

I showed him the inside cover of my Bible and gave him the story Jerry had suggested. He returned it and offered me a chair beside his desk. "You need to pass an aptitude test before you can enlist," he said.

The officer presented me with a page of questions and a pencil. He gave me a half-hour to complete the English comprehension and math problems, but I only needed ten minutes. I could tell he'd read my answers upside down. "Perfect," he said. He put my score at the top of the page, signed it, and asked me when I wanted to leave.

Just like that, I thought, I was enlisting in the Navy. I told him, "Right now."

He laughed and said, "I'll pick you up on the courthouse square in Colquitt tomorrow at oh-nine-hundred. That means nine in the morning. I'll get you on a train that'll leave for San Diego, California, in the afternoon, fifteen-hundred hours. What time is that?"

I thought for a moment. "Three o'clock?" He nodded like a proud parent, and I asked, "Do I bring anything?"

He pointed at the Bible. "You'll want to bring something to read. It's a long ride to San Diego. Can I give you a lift back home?"

"I don't want to put you out, sir."

"It's no bother. I need to pick up a friend over there." He posted a note on the door, locked his office, and showed me to his car, parked in a diagonal slot at the curb. He owned a low-slung two-door Ford Deluxe Coupe in cherry red. I ran my fingers along the sleek fender, and he said, "Stay away from liquor and women, Roger, and you'll be able to afford some nice things, even on an ensign's pay."

My white-lies about school and family mounted as he drove me to Colquitt. Entering town, he said, "Roger, let's run by the high school." I glanced over and he was looking at me. He parked diagonally at the curb near a hardware store. "I need to take a look at your school record. Is there a problem?"

I held up my hands. "Sorry, I didn't graduate with my class. I earned a certificate, not a diploma."

"It's not that, Roger. You scored perfect on that test, so I don't care if you never finished the ninth grade. It's just that your folks didn't fill out your birth date in their Bible."

"I was born on the…sixteenth. Can't I just write a sixteen in the Bible?"

"It'll only take a minute to peek in your records. You sound scared. What'll I find there?"

I laid my hand on the Bible between us, sweat popping out on my forehead. "The family tree's a fake. I'm not seventeen until next October." I glanced at the Navy recruiter. "Sorry I wasted your time."

"You didn't waste a thing. I expect to see you at my office door next year."

"You don't really have a friend around here to pick up, do you?"

He said, "That was my lie. I just wanted to get to know you. Be patient, Roger. I'll see you next year." Before he drove off, I saluted him, but he just waved. "Nice form, but we don't salute civilians, son. I'll be proud to return it soon, though. Until then, remember: no booze, no broads."

I waved him around the corner and took the pencil from my pocket. After correcting my birth date in the Bible, I caught a ride south to Bainbridge where I'd often passed an Army recruiting office near the Cottontail Café. If the Army didn't work out, I'd try the Marines or hitchhike to Florida with some vacationing Yankees or stow aboard the Seaboard Railroad and hobo for a time. I was going to exhaust every means of escape.

THE SOLDIER ON DUTY AT the Army recruitment center waved me in when I knocked on his door. I introduced myself to the sergeant and said, "I'd like to enlist, sir."

"I need a proof that you're seventeen, MacLeod. You bring your birth certificate?"

"Just this, sir." I handed him the Bible and gave him the story.

"Good enough." He hardly glanced at the inside cover before asking me to sit beside the corner of his desk.

I expected his exam to be identical to the one I'd aced, but all the English and math questions were different, some harder and others easier. I got one wrong. Still, he complimented me on my score, signed his name at the top, and said, "When do you want to leave?"

"Right now."

He glanced at his watch. "You might just make the bus. Hold on a minute." He rolled a form into his typewriter and, using just his index fingers, clacked out my travel orders. With a yank that made the platen zip like a motor, he pulled out the paper and said, "Let's go."

I followed him at a trot down the street to the bus station, going in the opposite direction from the Cottontail Café, the orders nestled inside the cover of my Bible. My stomach trembled with a thousand butterflies. I tried to take in everything around me, memorize the smells of car exhaust and suppers cooking and hot tar, the feel of the late-day sun, the scenes playing out of townie men in their suits and fedoras, the women spruced up in skirts, tight blouses, and pearls.

A Trailways bus idled by the loading curb. The slot above its broad front window bore a sign reading "Columbus."

The sergeant purchased a ticket to Fort Benning for me. He shouted for the driver to hold the door and pressed the paper stub into my hand. "You all right, MacLeod? You look like you're about to faint."

"I just can't believe it's happening."

"Nothing's gonna happen if you miss your bus." He gave me a small shove toward the bus door.

I took a seat in a middle row, the Bible on my lap. With a screech, the bus door swung closed. Vibrations from the engine carried up through my shoes and made my legs tremble even more.

My travel orders said to proceed to Fort Benning in Columbus for additional examinations and enlistment in the Army if I passed every test. I traced my fingers over the black ink and then touched the other side of the form, feeling the letters stamped hard into the paper, as permanent as an engraving.

The sergeant tapped on the glass beside my shoulder as the driver put the bus in gear. I lowered my window, smiling down at him. After a loud rumble and a moment of hesitation, the bus pulled away from the curb. The sergeant called, "Good luck, MacLeod. Send me a postcard when you turn seventeen."

I COULD BARELY EAT BREAKFAST the day after I'd completed the Army examinations and prolonged health inspections at Fort Benning. Just one step away from my escape into the service. After chow hall, a sergeant left us on the drill field where a lieutenant waited. I held my shoulders back and head high and crossed my fingers, hoping to repeat the oath of enlistment. Just as the officer was about to begin, a private trotted out with a clipboard from which a single sheet of paper dangled. The lieutenant glanced at the page and called, "Who's MacLeod?"

My chin dropped to my chest. I lifted my hand upward with the fatalism of the rabbit watching a swooping hawk. The Army had discovered my real age. If they'd discovered my lie, would they shoot me or throw me in jail?

The lieutenant told me to stand beside him. "You won't be taking the oath," he said. "I'll talk to you in a minute." I made my feet move as everyone stared, and I hung my head while the other recruits swore their oath of enlistment and became U.S. Army soldiers. They filed out.

"You've got to go back to the medics," the lieutenant told me. "Something came back on one of your tests."

A private escorted me to the base hospital. He presented me and the clipboard to a medical sergeant, who glanced at the page and said, "You failed your chest X-ray. We need to take another one."

In the X-ray room, I took off my shirt and the technician pushed the icy metal plate against my chest. I thought I could feel the invisible beams jabbing through my skin and organs and pitting my ribcage. The X-rays also sparked a thought: maybe the Army would tell me I was dying before they sent me home to do it.

The medical sergeant took my X-ray plate and led me to an office where a major, dressed in a white lab coat and uniform, filled out paperwork. Not even glancing at me, the major tapped the film plate and said, "Those white spots on the lungs come from childhood TB. Lots of country folks have them. Nothing to worry about." He made a note on the clipboard page and signed it, finally looking up at me.

I tried to keep from grinning at him but failed—I wanted to kiss his feet. The major rolled his eyes, returning to his paperwork.

I was taken back to the lieutenant's desk in the recruiting office. The officer checked the revised paperwork, nodding. He stood and told me to repeat after him: "I…state your name, MacLeod… do solemnly swear that I will support the Constitution of the United States…and I solemnly swear to bear true allegiance to the United States of America…and to serve them honestly and faithfully, against all their enemies or opposers whatsoever…and to observe and obey the orders of the President of the United States of America…and the orders of the officers appointed over me."

I nearly stuttered for the first time in years as I completed the oath of enlistment.

The lieutenant welcomed me to military service. "Maybe not the Army, though." He lifted another page. "While they were shooting your X-ray again, I took a second to review your exam. You made the top score, more than good enough to get into the Air Corps—sorry, the 'Air Force' they're calling it now. You can go to Fort Jackson in South Carolina, with the Army, or I can send you to Lackland Air Force Base in Texas. San Antonio."

If Rienzi rejected my love, then the unexpected luck of getting to San Antonio would turn to heartbreak. On the other hand, Jay had gone through Fort Jackson and Chet planned to do so; maybe we could all end up together at the same base one day. I quickly told the lieutenant my decision. Then I had a lot of time to ponder the wisdom of my choice. A sergeant gave me a set of orders to carry, a train ticket, and meal vouchers to use along the way. He also gave me an authorization to spend that night in the Armed Forces YMCA in Columbus. The slips of paper shook in my hands like the rattle of rain on a tin roof.

My train was due to leave at oh-seven-hundred the next morning. I left the YMCA dormitory at oh-four-hundred, unable to sleep, and wandered the abandoned streets.

When I arrived at the depot, the Seaboard train waited there already: a dozen cars of shiny steel and dark windows behind a sleek diesel engine. A constant tickle ran from my stomach into my throat and back down. My fingertips tingled with a thousand pinpricks and sweat made my scalp itch. I paced the length of the locomotive and back, again and again, until my feet ached in the dress shoes. The ribbed steel of a passenger coach felt cool and slick beneath my fingertips. I had to keep touching it to show myself it was real.

A Negro man about Nat's size pushed a broom across the concrete platform, catching gum wrappers and cigarette butts. After the second time I passed him, he said, "Got a big trip ahead of you?"

"I just joined the military. I'm a little nervous."

"Be a piece of cake for a country boy like you."

"Even dressed up, I look like a rube, huh?"

He leaned on the broom handle and shrugged. “Don’t know ’bout that, but I seen the back of your neck twicet now. Fella don’t get that kinda sun strolloping around town.”

“You think it’ll be a walk in the park?”

“Relax, Country. You’re used to taking shank’s mare everywhere you go—marches are gonna be like going to grandma’s for you. Town dudes’ll be falling out all around and you’ll have to keep from whistling.”

I showed him the Bible in which I’d folded my orders and tickets. “I brought along something to read.”

“Can’t go wrong with the Good Book. You pick out your passage for the day?” He explained, “Every morning, I close my eyes, flip open to a page, and point. Sometimes, it gives me something to study on all day long and into the night.”

I followed his instructions, touching my finger to Psalm 78, verse 38. I read aloud, “Yet he was merciful; he forgave their iniquities and did not destroy them.”

“That’s powerful-good advice, Country. You can ponder that one your whole trip.”

I did, all the way to San Antonio.

# EPILOGUE

On New Year's Day 1947, Robert Bryson stopped his old sedan for me along US 27. I lowered my thumb and tucked my hand into the warm pocket of the Air Force greatcoat bundled around me, overjoyed to see him again. The ebony finish on his Pierce-Arrow straight-eight gleamed like his eyes behind their bent wire spectacles. He still waxed and polished his sixteen-year-old baby more often than the car-crazy San Antonio airmen fooled with their latest hot-rods.

I opened the door, saying, "Thank you, sir." My chilled breath jetted out in short smoke-signal puffs. "This is getting to be a habit with us."

He took a long pull on his bottle of water while I got settled beside him, placing my military cap over a knee. I put an olive-drab knapsack on the floorboard with barely a sound. Traveling light, I'd only packed spare clothes and my moldering Bible. I often pondered how it provided for my physical escape, while Papa used his trying to escape his sins. Apparently, they'd caught up with him.

Mr. Bryson said, "I heard from Nat that you were gone for good."

"I thought so too," I said, "but a part of me never left. I keep having these reminders, smelling or tasting something or hearing a voice that makes me think of home."

"For better and for worse. I know that feeling." Mr. Bryson checked for traffic and pulled onto the highway, driving fast. We talked about the Air Force, and he asked, "You gonna fly one of them, what-chu-call-em, fighters?"

"No, sir. My birthmark is too recognizable; pilots can't have distinguishing marks. Being grounded doesn't bother me, though—they let me fly a desk in an office."

The car interior was much warmer than the outside, where my buzz-cut scalp had suffered windburn, but the air carried a stale reek. I'd grown used to daily baths, tooth brushings, and indoor toilets, but I knew that I'd once exuded the very same odors.

Mr. Bryson gave a big sigh and murmured, "You back here on account of your daddy?"

"I got emergency leave. My brothers and sister are coming too." I watched for his reaction as I said, "Jay wrote that Papa had been shot to pieces."

He nodded, his glasses tilting catawampus on his nose. "Bless his heart, somebody murdered 'im at that sawmill of his. Graveyard dead."

"Maybe that killer who shot the night watchman came back. Any idea who did it?"

"I ain't got a clue."

"But what are folks saying?"

A parenthesis dented his cheek as he grimaced. He slowed the sedan at an intersection and turned onto Hardscrabble Road. With a glance at me, he said, "I don't listen to gossip. About your mama or anybody."

I held his brief gaze. "Thank you for that."

We were all gathering there, a reunion of sorts. Papa's revolver had lain under Mama's pillow for years. Did she bother to reload it? I wondered if, with my newfound sense of smell, I could tell whether it'd been fired recently: all six rounds. Surprisingly, I looked forward to asking Mama about it, matching wits with her.

Mr. Bryson stayed quiet after that, so I didn't push him for more hearsay. The sky darkened to gunmetal gray, and small white flakes curved down at us, looping as they hit the windshield like the flip on the ends of Rienzi's hair. I touched the breast pocket of my uniform, where I kept a picture of us taken in front of the Alamo. Maybe not the best of omens, but I'd stand arm-in-arm with her at the gateway to hell or anywhere else.

"Well I'll be," Mr. Bryson said. "Ain't seen snow in a month of Sundays."

We crested a low rise. Ahead of us, a small barefoot boy in overalls and a thin plaid jacket dragged a makeshift sled loaded with firewood, shoulders hunched against the cold. A dozen branches had fallen off the pile along the way, making a dotted-line path to him. The biting wind had turned his neck a florid pink below short, tawny hair.

I shrugged out of my greatcoat and wrapped it tight to hold in the warmth. As we coasted toward the boy, I pointed him out and said, "Let's give that little soldier a furlough."

# ACKNOWLEDGMENTS

Few books are written without the help of others and none are published without the resources and assistance of a team of supporters.

I benefited first and foremost from my late father-in-law, Vernon McDonald, who related countless anecdotes about growing up in Miller County in South Georgia in the 1930s and 1940s and contributed the front cover photograph. Keenly intelligent, witty, and open-minded, he was a great man as well as a sensational storyteller. While this novel is entirely fictitious, his tales provided the colors and textures of a time long past and a place that no longer exists as he knew it. If you felt like I transported you there—if you could see it, smell it, taste it—if you smarted as Papa's belt snapped and grinned as you sailed off the tin roof into Lonnie and Nat's waiting arms—then the credit goes to Mr. McDonald. He owned the time machine; I merely made use of it.

And, of course, I wouldn't have met him if I hadn't fallen in love with his winsome and lovely daughter, Kate. She was doubly blessed, having had an equally smart, funny, and kind mother, Betty, from whom she also inherited outer and inner beauty. Really, I was taken with her whole family, her brothers included: Steve and Ashley, good men both. I wouldn't be a writer today without Kate's encouragement and belief in me. In fact, I wouldn't be much of anything.

It's never easy to have your work critiqued, but I was fortunate to receive excellent advice and spot-on "wordsmithing" from many fine writers, including Michael Buchanan, Kathleen Boehmig, John Witkowski, Mark All, and Sid Versaci. I became friends with them many years ago through the Atlanta Writers Club (AWC), among other writing organizations. They and the

AWC continue to play an important part in my life, so I'd also like to acknowledge my other best friends in the club—Marty Aftewicz, Valerie Connors, Clay Ramsey, Adrian Drost, and Ron Aiken—and so many more members I have the honor and privilege to know. Best of luck to all 700+ of them: I hope you will enjoy their books soon if you haven't already. I wrote this novel a few years before my friends in the AWC Roswell Critique Group could help me improve it further, but I want to thank them as well for their support and encouragement during my ongoing journey as an author.

I certainly want to express my appreciation to SFK Press and Steve McCondichie for resurrecting this novel after I regained the rights to it. When you turn over your work to others, it's a leap of faith for you and for them. Thanks for jumping into the unknown with me, y'all!

To encourage you to share your reaction to *Hardscrabble Road* with fellow readers, I propose a trade: a short story featuring Bud, his family, Ry, and many of the other characters, in return for your public feedback about the novel. If you will post your review of *Hardscrabble Road* on Amazon.com or Goodreads.com and e-mail the URL (web link) of your review to me at GeorgeWeinstein@gmail.com, I will send you a PDF of this short story. Thank you in advance!

Finally, my deepest thanks to my readers. It's the ultimate leap of faith for you whenever you devote precious time and money to enter a world of someone else's devising, counting on being entertained at the very least, and maybe desiring a stronger emotional connection to the characters and the story. There are countless other ways you could've spent your resources, so my sincere hope is that you think Bud's adventure is worth your investment.

George Weinstein
Roswell, GA
2018

George Weinstein is an author of numerous novels and Officer Emeritus of the Atlanta Writers Club (AWC). His work has been published locally in the Atlanta press and in regional and national anthologies, including *A Cup of Comfort for Writers*. Since 2009, he has managed the Atlanta Writers Conference, a twice-yearly opportunity for writers to meet with agents and editors, advance their writing ambitions, and occasionally make their dreams come true.

You can contact George with book club invitations and speaking requests and read more about him and his written work at www.GeorgeWeinstein.com.

Made in the USA
Monee, IL
21 October 2021